# Not Yet Drown'd

# Not Yet Drown'd

A NOVEL

Peg Kingman

W. W. NORTON & COMPANY
NEW YORK LONDON

Printed in the United States of America
First Edition



Manufacturing by R.R. Donnelley, Bloomsburg Division
Book design by Brooke Koven
Production manager: Julia Druskin

Library of Congress Cataloging-in-Publication Data

Kingman, Peg.
Not yet drown'd : a novel / Peg Kingman.—1st ed.
p. cm.
ISBN 978-0-393-06546-6 (hardcover)
1. Scots—India—Fiction. 2. Voyages and travels—Fiction.
3. Bagpipe music—Fiction. 4. India—Fiction. I. Title.
PS3611.I62N67 2007
813'.6—dc22

2007015574

W. W. Norton & Company, Inc.
500 Fifth Avenue, New York, N.Y. 10110
www.wwnorton.com

W. W. Norton & Company Ltd.
Castle House, 75/76 Wells Street, W1T 3QT

1 2 3 4 5 6 7 8 9 0

*To DT*

*and to the memory of SR*

# *Contents*

SCOTLAND


1 *Introductions, Graces, Cadencies &c Transitions* 5
2 *a stranger wild & rude* 21
3 *worthy of Attention, as will afterwards appear* 31
4 *In Which there is Some Art & Practise requird* 43
5 *But this is all mistake* 55
6 *the most bungling Excecution* 76
7 *Runnings, Variations, Allegro* 94


AT SEA


8 *obvious to a Competent Judgement* 111
9 *A very agreeable Vicissitude or Variation* 130
10 *more cultivated Geniuses* 147
11 *the particular excellency of this Grace* 164
12 *an ackward Pitiful, Clownish Fellow* 189
13 *Such a Contemptible Notion* 205
14 *Deviation from the Proper & native Style* 221
15 *quite opposite to the Original Design* 239


INDIA


16 *something very Peculiar in the Taste* 262
17 *the most fertile Invention & nicest Judgement must be distress'd* 282

18 *Cut with Strength & prodigious Quickness* 297
19 *This is one of the True Species* 319
20 *very obvious to a knowing Ear* 335
21 *the whole Scope is perceivd* 346
22 *the most despicable Idoea* 360
23 *a Sett of Men approaching an Enemy* 378
24 *To play amidst Rocks, Hills, Valleys, & Coves where Ecchoes rebounded* 392
25 *a gracefull Conclusion to the whole* 406

*Author's Afterword* 427

# *Acknowledgments*

I am very grateful to my son, Joseph Turner, who drew the boats and propellers; to M. J. Wilson and Doris Eraldi, who read early and often; to Chris Caswell, who gave me the Great Music and license to play it; and to David Smith, David Christianson, David Brown, Dr. Rajesh Sachdeva, Prof. Udaya Narayana Singh, Imran Ali, Dharmendra Tiwari, Anup Kumar Saha, Ranesh Roy, Harsh Vardhan Rathore, and Alasdair Caimbeul, who so patiently answered questions.

To the degree that this novel has some authentic feel of Scotland and India in the 1820s, I am profoundly indebted to the people on the spot who recorded what they saw, said, felt, and thought. The eighteenth- and nineteenth-century observers whose writings I have absorbed include Elizabeth Grant of Rothiemurchus, James Nasmyth, Reginald Heber, Fanny Parks, and, of course, Joseph and Patrick MacDonald—among many others. I have gratefully made use of their observations, their anecdotes, and even their very turns of phrase.

I am indebted also to Andrew Schelling, A. J. Alston, and especially Shama Futehally for their translations of the exquisite devotional songs of the sixteenth-century saint Meera.

To Gail Hochman, for her unflagging energy, articulate good sense, and kindness, I am deeply grateful; and to my editor, Starling Lawrence, who could drive a four-in-hand with silk thread for reins.

From the bottom of my heart I thank my husband, David Turner, for his staunch encouragement and support.

*Namaste.*

# Not Yet Drown'd

Published by Henry Fisher, Caxton, London, 1825.

# I

## *Introductions, Graces, Cadencies &c Transitions*

Catherine MacDonald loathed boats; and as usual, she was shivering with cold. Why had she let herself be talked into this pleasure outing? And how many hours of misery stretched ahead before she could hope to get ashore? To get dry and warm?

"There he is!" cried her brother Hector.

"Where?" demanded the captain, gripping the gunwale and peering into the nearly opaque curtain of rain blowing across the Firth of Forth in a northwest gale.

"There. There! Do you see?"

Catherine ventured out from her seat in the warm lee of the iron boiler to look for herself. The chilly rain pelted her, plastering the dripping ostrich plumes of her bonnet against her pale cheek. Her cloak was drenched and heavy; underneath, the muslin gown must be soaked, for rivulets of icy North Sea raindrops ran new channels down her thin back and her sides as she moved, and into her shoes. "Where?" she said, joining her elder brother and the captain at the rail of the steam launch *Dram Shell*.

"Just . . . just there," said Hector. "For a moment when the mist thinned, I had a good look. I am sure it was he. Keep watching."

Catherine peered into the rain. She might as well have been peering into a bucket of milk.

As the black stinking plume of smoke from *Dram Shell*'s coal-fired boiler eddied about them, Catherine could see cinders on Hector's ruddy face and hair, and a smut on his good linen stock. His nose and cheeks were bright red. Her own nose felt cold, and her hands, gripping the rail for balance, were curiously mottled with blue behind the freckles. All about them on the heaving gray swell rode ferries, wherries, fishing smacks, yachts, barges, and prams, all of them carrying drenched Edinbourgeois dressed in their best, come out to welcome their king on this historic occasion.

Some considerable distance out, she could make out two more streaming black plumes of coal smoke; these, Catherine knew, must mark the positions of the two steam paddle wheelers *James Watt* and *Comet*, which were supposed to have in tow what all had come to see: the king's yacht, *Royal George*, carrying King George IV, cruising up to Edinburgh to visit his North British subjects on the occasion of his sixtieth birthday.

The birthday had been two days ago, on August 12, 1822. But even in August, Scottish weather could be relied upon to thwart the best-laid plans of kings and men.

For a moment the scrim of rain thinned, and Catherine could clearly see the two steamships plowing heavily upwind like straining cart horses. And there, in their wake, was the royal yacht flying the Royal Standard. The yacht was sleek and elegant, certainly; but Catherine thought that under tow, with her sails furled, she appeared just a little effete.

"Aha! There, upon the afterdeck!" said Captain Keith, and passed his glass to Catherine.

She looked through it, but the lens was streaming with raindrops and she could see only a silvery blur. She wiped the lens and tried again, but their little *Dram Shell* was heaving ponderously on the sickening gray swell, and it was difficult to fix on anything at such a distance. Better to squint into the rain.

There were at least half a dozen portly and dignified naval officers on deck. But among them stood a particularly large and corpulent figure which drew her eye; exquisitely turned out, she could see, in a splendid admiralty uniform. Could it be himself? Catherine was shivering hard. For a moment her view was blocked when a heavily listing ferryboat crossed in front of them. Then a cheer went up from a bunting-festooned launch which had drawn quite near to the royal yacht; and the heavy figure acknowledged it with a languid but cordial hand to his cocked hat.

So perhaps it really *was* His Majesty.

Or perhaps it was only an admiral.

Catherine's dark green ostrich plumes dried rapidly, a little too close to the fire in the nearly-warm drawing room of Hector and Mary's Edinburgh house. The maid had brought up the tea, but Catherine had not yet poured; she was waiting for Mary, her busy sister-in-law. A vast piece of canvaswork lay across Catherine's lap, and she was threading her needle yet again (canary yellow this time) when she smelled burning feathers. Throwing down her work, she snatched up the plumes, shook them, and blew on them. Three of them fluffed up satisfactorily, but the tip of the fourth was shriveled and scorched. Catherine tossed it into the fire; it flamed up and instantly turned to writhing ash, filling the room with a horrible smell. She felt as bedraggled as her feathers—drenched, scorched, shaken, blown, and fluffed—and was quite unwilling to venture out again that night. She felt fragile, as though her bones were made of quills.

"You mustn't wait tea for me, Catherine, my dear," said Mary, darting in the doorway for a moment like a little black bird. "Pour for yourself. I must just go upstairs and look in once more before I can sit down with you. . . . What is that vile stench? Not the tea! That man has cheated me for the last time; he promised me it was best souchong. Oh, no, I see—your poor plumes! Never mind, I will lend you mine for this evening."

"Ah, no, Mary," protested Catherine. "I wish you would go to Mr Clerk's ball with Hector instead of me. I do not mind in the least staying in with the children, and I am sure Hector would much rather dance with his wife than with his sister."

"I cannot go, my dear, for I have given the nursery maid leave to go out tonight to see the bonfires. And my father is coming in to sit with me for an hour or two. But the truth is, you know, I do not feel quite comfortable with Mr Clerk, though he is so amusing, and so clever. I hate to be made to blush, and I believe he does it apurpose. You do not mind him, I know, and you need not dance if you do not like it, for they know that you are only just out of mourning. And I will look after poor Grace for you, as well as I can."

Mr Clerk's ballroom was like the inside of a headache. The fiddlers contorted themselves on a platform at the far end of the room, their elbows pumping like steam pistons; and a fine hectic state of abandonment had been achieved by the flushed and panting dancers. Catherine—having danced with her brother, eaten a slice of ham, drunk a glass of brandy punch, and spoken with her host, Mr Clerk, and his sister, Miss Bessie—now sat near an open window. The rain was blowing away and the misty sky was oddly tarnished by the glow of an epic bonfire on the high round brow of Arthur's Seat, to the south of the city. The fire appeared to hang in midair. Presently Catherine saw Hector making his way toward her, skirting the dancers. Hope arose; perhaps he was ready to go home? But no: "Come upstairs; Mr Clerk promises to delight us," Hector shouted into her ear.

"Have I not had delights enough for one day?" she said, but she followed him out to the hall, where the notable advocate and collector John Clerk awaited them.

"Did you ever see such a swirrrrling flurrrrry of tarrrrtan, Mrs MacDonald?" drawled their elderly host as he hitched himself up the broad stairs, leaning heavily on his cane. He wore plain evening dress, more seemly on a man with an imperfect leg. "Tell me, you two young Highlanders, how do you like my authentic genuine traditional Highland ball?"

"Your fiddlers are true musicians, sir," said Hector. "Their playing has force, spirit, and fine expression, particularly in the quick measures. Do I recognise two of Neil Gow's sons?"

"So they claim, and if you vouch for them, I suppose I must believe it. I have been told that you play quite a pretty fiddle yourself. A musician as well as a natural philosopher. And yourself, Mrs MacDonald—well! It was a pleasure to see you dance. What do *you* make of my Highland ball?"

"I never saw any genuine Highland assembly so splendidly turned out as this, Mr Clerk," said Catherine. "But the dancing is nothing to boast of. Such slapdash reels! The sets so slipshod! I daresay that no one in Edinburgh has danced a reel these twenty years. Why do you not give us a nice modern quadrille, familiar to everyone? So much safer for satin slippers, and for the toes inside of them."

"That is just what my sister said," replied Mr Clerk. " 'Reels and flings, John!' says she, very scornful. 'How quaint. Can you not keep your curiosities and antiquities out of my dinners and balls?' But you see, I was quite right to insist. 'Tis the spirit of the moment, after all—flinging and reeling hither and thither. And everyone so well behaved—thus far. I do hope the king actually comes ashore before we all forget our manners. How long before your wild hielandmen pitch into one of their bonny little wars here in Edinburgh? You are all so spendidly armed: knives, swords, precious little jeweled dirks and pistols. I had not realised there were so many ill-set gems in the kingdom."

"Yet not so many Highlanders, in truth, under the tartan," said Hector. "I spoke a few words in the supper room just now, to one of your guests in full Highland dress. I thought he had a look of the Grants, and he wore a badge of pine, you see. So I just asked him—in Gaelic, you know—whether he'd had to venture far to find a fresh sprig of pine in this city. And the oddest look spread over his face, and he said, very loud and clear and with a most appalling accent, '*Je n'ai pas eu le plaisir de faire votre connaissance, monsieur*.' "

"Ha ha ha! Tall man, dark, quite decorative, and a better crop of hair than any man needs?" asked Mr Clerk. "Ha! That is my Mr Coates, Glasgow-born and -bred, not a word of the Gaelic, to be sure. A coal family, all of them much given to litigation. Very good clients they have been. He is exceedingly vain of his legs, I believe, and delights in any opportunity to don his Highland costume, the better to show them off."

"His legs?" asked Hector. "I did not notice anything remarkable about his legs."

"No, no, he is only a pretty fraud. I collect them, you know: frauds. Sometimes by mistake, alas. But I am growing wiser in my old age, I hope," said Mr Clerk, as he unlocked the door of his private museum and stood aside to let them pass. Inside, the high fiddle tones from below were muted, though the deeper rhythm of stamping feet seemed amplified. A dark bronze figure of the many-breasted Ephesian Artemis stood vibrating on a pedestal, tapping in time.

"The entire house is shaking," said Catherine.

"Timber is not what it used to be—nor stonework either—in these new houses," observed Mr Clerk as he lit a pair of lamps on a large round table in the center of the room, then adjusted their shades. Artlessly he set one lamp on a low stand, where it illuminated from below a set of four small pictures, exquisitely drawn and brilliantly coloured. The second he carried across to a large glass case, and folded back the hinged glass panels enclosing its front and top. Inside were three gleaming brass devices, each trig, tiny, and complete, fit to enchant any natural philosopher of mechanical bent. "My models, Mr MacDonald. They move. Look," he said.

Hector looked; Catherine too.

"Here is a condensing steam engine of the beam and parallel motion construction, all complete but with this side cut away for viewing," said Mr Clerk. "I move the flywheel 'round by hand, thus. There are the steam valves and air pump. Watch the piston move in the cylinder. And the slide valve. There are the steam passages, you see, all in exact due position and scale and relative movement."

"A thing of beauty! Such an elegant execution! Again," said Hector, transfixed.

Mr Clerk rotated the flywheel again, slowly.

"Superb!" cried Hector.

"Now this one," said Mr Clerk. "A direct-acting machine, you see—no beam or parallel motion. It operates this tiny lathe and rotary saw blade, and this belt. Look how sharp; the blade cuts through this bit of pasteboard in an instant."

"Charming! Such neat castings, and all rendered to the nicest tolerances! May I operate it? As smooth as—as . . ."

"I knew you would appreciate them. But I have saved the best, Mr MacDonald, and the newest, for last. See, here is a model of your own marine steam engine. Complete, you see, with the rotary propelling device of your own design at the bow."

"Oh, sir! Catriona, do you see! And complete with bearings, and packing—is it felted wool? That has always been one of the difficulties, after I solved the problem of gearing, of course. For this rotating shaft is so long and subject to such stresses that there must necessarily be some degree of flexibility. This, Catherine, my dear, is a perfect model of my steam engine with the rotary oar, the one that is in *Dram Shell*, you know. We were out with Captain Keith aboard her today, sir, and I may say she performed flawlessly. Now this, you see, is the very pattern which I am to take out to Calcutta for Crawford and Fleming. So much superior to side-wheel and stern-wheel designs. More efficient by far, you understand—and so much narrower overall, unaffected by rolling or wind, yet allowing free use of the sails. And, sir, such a pretty piece of work! The sweet curve of the blade! Who made the model for you?"

"I am sitting just now for my portrait to a local man—rather gifted, an engineer as well, I believe. In any case, he is an admirer of your design—calls it a 'spiral oar.' And he has a talented son with a taste for machines and metals. I commissioned this model from the son."

"Let me hazard a guess: Nasmyth, father and son? Of course! Oh, yes, I meet them often at the lectures at the Mechanics Institute."

"Mr Nasmyth promises to finish my portrait soon. If ever it is completed, it will have to go here in this dark corner, next to my father and my grandfather."

"So that is your famous father. A stylish piece of painting, too. Sir Henry Raeburn's work?"

"Yes; a good eye in your head. There on the old man's dining table you see the notorious bits of cork representing ships of the line. Salt spilled here to represent this; walnut shells there to represent that. We never did break him of the habit. Look, here I have his *Essay on Naval Tactics*, all three volumes. And his original manuscript. I wonder what the old man would have made of steam navigation. Your new technology will sweep away his entire premise. We will be independent of wind."

"That I doubt. Yet I found myself quite puffed with pride today to see the king's yacht coming in under steam power. My thoughts were perhaps even a little disrespectful: There *Royal George* lies helpless but for *James Watt*."

"Ha ha! A Radical notion!"

"You will not quote me, sir. Yet, you know, despite all the advantages that steam can offer the navy, it is the merchants who are showing them the way."

"Profits have a way of illuminating matters," said Mr Clerk. "I wish you the best of luck in this undertaking of yours for Crawford and

Fleming. For the country trade between China and Calcutta, I believe? Aye. And the sooner, the better, for I am sure my sister spends far too much on our congou and our pekoe. Did you know that Mr Fleming has invited me to invest in this venture? A sixteenth share. Just between us, I am quite seriously tempted. Now, here, Mr MacDonald, is another thing which may interest you as a musician. You play the best modern Italians, no doubt, but perhaps you used to play the old Gaelic tunes as well?"

"Oh, aye, long ago."

"In your youth? Not so terribly long ago then. And a bit of a piper, too, I believe?"

"A wee bit, then."

"And that is more than plenty, if you ask some people. So tell me, do you know what this is?" Mr Clerk picked up a neat little black book and held it out to Hector.

Turning it over, Hector examined it and opened it to a page at random. Looking over his shoulder, Catherine saw that it was a bound manuscript of perhaps fifty or sixty pages, measuring no more than seven inches by nine. The handwriting was old-fashioned and meticulous, and the ink had faded to brown. Scattered through the text were many odd-looking musical notations.

Hector read aloud from the page where he had alighted: " 'Introductions, Graces, Cadencies and Transitions,' " he read. " 'The small compass of this instrument allows not scope enough for such graces as are peculiar to other instruments, but the abundant variety of cuttings invented for the pipe are the principal graces of it when well executed.' " He turned back to the first page and read the title: "*A Compleat Theory of the Scots Highland Bagpipe* . . . mmm, mmm, Skye and Mull, aye! By J. MacDonald. Oh, sir, what a fine thing! This is MacDonald's original manuscript!"

"Canny lad! Do you know it, then?" asked Mr Clerk. "And I had expected to confound you. Even copies are rare, for only one small edition was ever printed, and that some years ago."

"I do know it. I recognise it because my brother—our brother—was awarded a copy when he won the piping prize. The most improved, you know, not the chief prize. In—what was it, Catherine?—it must have been about the year 'fifteen, just about seven years ago. Aye, because Sandy was just fifteen at the time. He was already a fine piper, better than I could ever have hoped to be. But I used to borrow his prize copy from time to time and try to make it out. Even then it was considered an oddity. It is not at all the way the music is played nowadays, the Great Music. Nor the way it is written—quite old-fashioned. Making this so much the more valuable, I suppose. A very curious thing. How did you come across it?"

"It belonged to a client of mine for whom I waged an epic campaign through the Court of Session. We prevailed at last, at the Inner House, but my fees had rather mounted up by that time, and my client had grown fonder of his hard-won money than of this little manuscript—so it became mine. I believe he had it of the fellow who'd brought it back from India. But the author, this Mr J. MacDonald—I don't suppose he was any kinsman of yours?"

"No, Joseph MacDonald was a Strathnaver man," said Hector, "with plenty of kin of his own. It was his brother who posthumously published the two volumes of music we are fortunate enough to have from him. First was a collection of vocal airs—some genuine old specimens, as sung in the Highlands and the islands. Much later, the brother published this curious treatise you have here: *A Compleat Theory*, all description, instruction, and technique, how the pipes ought to be played—in MacDonald's opinion. But he gives only a little of the music itself, just a few phrases by way of illustration here and there. Alas, the greatest treasure of all has been lost, it seems. That would have been his collection of the *ceol mhor* tunes themselves—the ancient Great Music of the pipes, you know—which MacDonald was supposed to have been compiling during his voyage and in India. Unless your client knew something about that?"

"He mentioned nothing of the sort to me. But other collections of that old music must exist, surely," said Mr Clerk.

"Surprisingly little, sir; perhaps a scant two dozen tunes have ever been set down at all, and those not scientifically noted. How much is lost and forgotten already, buried with the old pipers who learned that Great Music by ear? Alas, that Joseph MacDonald was so untimely cut off!"

"A casualty of what, do you know?" asked Mr Clerk.

"Oh, that Bengal climate, I daresay—some malignant fever or

other. That was back in the 'sixties; I have been reassuring my wife that India is considered much healthier nowadays."

"I sincerely hope for your sake and hers that it is," said Mr Clerk. "But I fear we are boring your sister. Mrs MacDonald, I beg your pardon!"

Catherine had been moving quietly about the gallery from one picture to the next. Here was a gruesome Saint Sebastian; here a bare pink Magdalene; and there a heavily forested Germanic hunting scene in which the anuses of the dogs and horses were most lovingly and attentively rendered. "Tell me, what do you think of my Indian miniatures?" asked Mr Clerk waspishly, returning to the four exquisite little paintings under which he had set a lamp.

The Indian miniatures would have made Mary blush, but Catherine resolved not to shy from them. One showed a lady standing at the edge of a garden pavilion playing a stringed instrument while storm clouds boiled up over distant hills. Her tunic was transparent and her figure as ripe and tempting as the fruit on the trees. In the next, a man with an elegantly curled mustache pushed the same lady, or one who looked like her, on a swing while in the foreground fish and ducks disported themselves among the lotuses in a tiled garden pool. In the third, the lady had been divested of her tunic and was being caressed by the man; shyness apparently made her look away from him. The two of them were entwined on a low daybed scattered with magnificent pillows and bolsters, while an ensemble of musicians played in another pavilion in the distance. The fourth picture showed servants bringing pitchers, goblets, platters of sweetmeats, and a hookah. The lady played her lute and sang while her lover gazed at her as he lounged against a large jeweled bolster.

"Do you think they are a suite?" said Catherine. "It seems to me the faces and clothing in these two do not match the others. And though these have a similar look, the colouring of this fourth one is quite different—another artist?"

"You are observant. At least two different artists, I agree, working in a well-known genre—probably *ragamala*—with traditional subject matter."

"Ah . . . I wonder why these Hindustani painters depict the principal figures in profile, while the others, the servants and musicians, are seen full- or three-quarter face."

"A class distinction, just so. It is an old tradition in eastern portraiture; the profile depiction is the most respectful. Perhaps it has to do with the indiscretion of gazing into the face of the mighty. We moderns do something similar, you know: Our coins depict our kings in profile and, oddly enough, in Roman dress."

"Ah! Quite true, come to think of it. These are very prettily coloured. I do admire them." And though Catherine was not blushing, she found herself moved by the paintings, by the bliss of the lovers. She could remember feeling that.

"It is a pleasure to show them to someone who really looks, and really sees," said Mr Clerk.

They returned downstairs, Mr Clerk negotiating the steps with some difficulty and leaning heavily on Hector's arm, so that Catherine went ahead. She waited for them halfway down, but they had stopped, on the landing above. So she reentered the ballroom alone, with a feeling that they were talking about her.

Hector came and found Catherine at last, and the two of them walked home. It was after midnight, but the pavements were far from empty. People were roaming about the city in high spirits, singing and talking, their voices ringing through the long streets. The bonfire atop Arthur's Seat was burning higher than ever. Catherine linked her arm through Hector's and fell into step with him, but he was not talkative; probably he was pondering a technical problem.

"What occupied you and Mr Clerk all that time on the stairs?" she ventured after a few minutes.

"What? Oh," said Hector. "Oh, various matters."

"I daresay you were talking about me."

"Very self-important, my dear! Do you imagine that all your acquaintance have nothing more fascinating to discuss?"

"I can feel it, you know."

Hector said nothing; they stepped aside as a couple of well-turned-out carriages passed, probably homeward-bound from the theater.

"What did he want to know?" said Catherine, holding Hector by the arm, though he would have set off once more.

"He asked about Sandy."

"And you said . . . ?"

"I said, 'Our brother Alexander died in India last year, sir, when a dam burst during the monsoon flooding.' And he said he was very sorry to hear it."

"Mmm. What else?"

"Well . . . that I am eldest by four years. That you and Sandy are—were—twenty-two years old, and twins. About James's wreck with that horse; and that you are left with the little daughter of his first marriage."

"Hmm! No wonder I was feeling it. What else did he want to know?"

"Why your name was still MacDonald even though you had been married."

"Ah! These lowlanders cannot quite understand just how thick upon the ground we are, the MacDonalds of Skye, can they?"

"I explained it to him."

"Aye. And why these personal inquiries about us, do you suppose?"

"I daresay he is assessing the risks of that sixteenth share which Crawford and Fleming have offered him."

When Hector knocked at his own door, no one came. After a few moments he dug in his pockets for his key, and they let themselves in and went upstairs. At first it seemed that the drawing room was empty. "Have they gone to bed and left these lamps burning?" said Hector.

But a snort issued from the deep chair drawn up before the embers of the fire, and suddenly, too loud, a man's familiar voice said, "Splendid! Indeed! Oh, Hector! Where is Mary?" Mr Hay, Mary's father, habitually scoffed at any suggestion that he was subject to post-prandial drowsiness. "Aye, the children. One of them, oh, teething, Mary said. She was here just a moment ago."

Hector built up the fire, and Mary came in. "Your Grace is just an angel," she said to Catherine. "She has been up and down the stairs all the evening, fetching and carrying for me. The baby is so fretful; it must be that tooth. He is asleep at last, and Grace is with him. What did Miss Bessie give you for a supper? I want to hear of every dish."

"Ham—a real ham all pink and iridescent, not a mutton ham," said Catherine, well prepared for this question. "A gigot of lamb. A saddle of venison with juniper berries. Prawn paste made with butter and parsley. Asparagus. A vast dish of little potatoes, much peppered and parsleyed. Poached salmon with a lemon sauce. A Dundee cake, generously spiced and anointed with rum. To drink, a brandy punch, and a large jug of Athole brose, I believe, for the gentlemen."

"My mouth waters to hear of it. Hector never notices, so he is never able to tell me in any detail. But we had a good little supper of our own, had we not, Dad? Some nice slices of turkey breast with bread sauce and dripping. Oh, will that child never sleep? Now what?"

"I will go," said Catherine, taking a candlestick to light her way, but the wailing stopped as she climbed the stairs. She went instead to the room which she and Grace shared, and laid her heavy cloak across the bed. A faint unfamiliar scent hung in the chilly room—not flowery but spicy, mossy, peppery. The flickering candlelight showed a parcel on the small table under the dark uncurtained window.

The parcel, about ten or twelve inches long and wide, was expertly wrapped in layers of oiled silk. It was tied with hemp twine, the knots and ends sealed down with wax, and the wax was stamped with a familiar signet. Written in ink across the top was her name in English, and below it in Gaelic: *Catriona NicDhonaill.* The handwriting was that of her twin brother, Sandy, who had been dead for more than a year.

The waxy knots would not yield to her fingernails, and her scissors were downstairs in the drawing room with her canvaswork. She could hear the voices of the others as she came down the stairs: ". . . and he has offered all of us a prime place on his front steps—Picardy Place, you know—for the king's entry tomorrow morning," Hector was saying to Mr Hay as Catherine entered. She was bearing the parcel as though it were the Honours of Scotland. Something in her face or manner made them fall silent and look at her.

"How did this come here?" she said.

No one knew. The house had been in an uproar all evening. The servants, granted a night out, came and went with their friends, suitors and acquaintances. "I have been up and down the stairs twenty times this evening," said Mary, "and I answered the door twice—no, three times. Once it was two boys looking for their friend; wrong house.

Once it was a messenger with a letter for you, Hector. I put it on the worktable in your study. Once when I finally got to the door—I thought the kitchen maid would go, but apparently she had gone out already—no one was there. I shall have to ask the girls in the morning."

Catherine cut the twine and unwrapped the parcel, which emitted the same faint peppery scent she had first noticed in her room. The soft folds of a Kashmiri shawl fell open, revealing a sheaf of papers, rolled and tied; and a small box made of burnished ivory or bone and bound in silver.

Sandy, my dear! she thought. But how surprisingly painful, this joy—like blood coming back into frostbitten fingertips. Catherine put a hand to her heart, and buried her face in the gossamer shawl to hide her emotion.

The shawl was as light, soft, and downy as ostrich plumes, and smelled of cloves. The dizzy convoluted swirls, pieced and embroidered, were in every shade of red, green, azure and gold, swimming on a black ground.

"Oh, splendid!" Mary's father was saying. "Very fine indeed. I have seldom seen better. That would fetch a pretty price. May I see?" He owned mills in Paisley, near Glasgow. His weavers had been busy for the last six months producing acres of tartan in anticipation of the royal visit, but they were now free again to resume copying Kashmiri shawls for the enthusiastic home market. Here was a handsome new authentic design to copy. Delicately, respectfully, he felt the fine fringe between knowing fingers.

Catherine untied the thick sheaf of papers, more than a hundred pages, and spread them flat. There was no letter; it was a musical manuscript in Sandy's handwriting. Titles in Gaelic headed most of the pages; a few had English subtitles as well. Hector looked over her shoulder. "Why, it is *piobaireachd*," he said. "Pipe music. I know this tune, 'The Fairy Tune'; Mr MacKay used to play it." Hector sang the first line of it using the strange onomatopoeic syllables peculiar to pipers. "*Hohiodro chehoche hee he Ihe I* . . . That phrase along there is different from what I remember, though," and he sang it again in his plain, true voice. Then, paging through the manuscript, he read off the archaic titles: " 'The Piper's Warning.' 'A Bhoilich,' that's 'The Vaunting,' yes. 'Is Fhada Mar So Tha Sinn'; I do not know that one. 'Weighing From

Land.' Sandy used to play that—a fascinating tune if you are the piper, but rather tedious otherwise. I was just saying to Mr Clerk what a pity that so few of these old tunes had ever been set down. What is this? 'Fhathast Gun a Bhith Bàthte,' 'Not Yet Drown'd,' " and he sang the melody aloud as he read it from the page. His voice trailed off to silence.

Catherine and Hector looked at each other. "But that is 'Sandy's Tune,' " she said.

"What do you mean, 'Sandy's Tune?' " asked Mary.

"Sandy made it himself when he was fifteen, the summer he won the piping competition," explained Catherine. "He never played it for anyone but us. It had no name then; we called it just 'Sandy's Tune.' 'Port Alasdair.' "

"Curious," said Hector. The page exactly resembled all the other pages of the manuscript, where it occupied an unobtrusive middle place. "Most curious, indeed."

Not yet drown'd? wondered Catherine.

"Do open this, Catherine," said Mary, examining the little silver-bound ivory-inlaid box. "It looks like a little treasure chest with this domed lid. What could it be? The latch is the neatest thing I ever saw; look, the hasp is engraved with this swirling design, and the pin is a splint of ivory."

Catherine drew out the ivory pin and opened the lid. The little chest was filled to the brim with a fragrant mass of dried curled leaves, dark brown with golden tips. She stirred them with her finger, then brought them to her nose and inhaled deeply of the malty scent. "It is tea," Catherine said. "Tea of some kind. Very fragrant, sweet. Do smell it. What type is that?" she asked Mary.

Mary could not identify it, though she knew every kind of tea that every Edinburgh purveyor had ever claimed to offer for sale: Keemun, souchong, Yunnan, congou, Pouchong, gong fu, pekoe, Wuyi, and more. It was none of these.

There was no letter, not even the briefest note. There was nothing to date the parcel. Sandy's name did not appear in it or on it.

"He must have sent it before the monsoon, early last summer," said Hector.

"How could it have taken so long to arrive?" asked Mary. "More than a year. And why is there no letter? Why so mysterious?"

"Perhaps his friends packed up his personal effects after . . . after the flooding, and sent them home to you," Mr Hay proposed. "Curious that they omitted to enclose a letter of explanation, however."

"According to the officers of the East India Company, all of his personal effects were lost when the wall of the tank burst," said Hector. "His entire villa was engulfed instantly, along with everything and everyone in it."

"Well, not quite everything, apparently," said Mary.

"That is Sandy's handwriting on the outer cover," said Catherine. This was indisputable. "And his seal."

"It was he who sent it, then, sometime before July of last year," said Hector. "Parcels and messages often do go astray. It may have taken a very circuitous route. Must have. There is no other explanation."

Catherine thought about other explanations, each of which posed other puzzles.

"Mrs MacDonald, may I beg you to lend me this shawl long enough to have it copied?" said Mr Hay. "Ten days at the most. It is such a fine thing of its kind. . . . I am obliged, most obliged."

Except for the shawl borrowed by Mary's father, Catherine secreted the inexplicable parcel and its silk wrappings on a shelf in the back of the wardrobe in her bedroom. She placed them there by feel in the dark. Eight-year-old Grace was already in the bed the two of them shared. Careful not to disturb her, Catherine slid carefully between the cold heavy linen sheets. Grace was not asleep, however. As Catherine settled herself, Grace quietly commenced to speak, as she did every night. Her light young voice was nicely calibrated to the intimacy of a small bed, in a small room, in a tall dark sleeping house.

# 2

## *a stranger wild & rude*

To Catherine, the tea sent by Sandy tasted like nothing. It made a dark red-amber liquor that was only hot and wet. Once brewed, the spent leaves were the colour of copper. She tried to really taste it, to truly notice its qualities, as if it could tell her how Sandy had sent it and what he meant by it. But although food and drink were no longer mere ashes in her mouth (as they had been for the first months of her widowhood, when she had become so painfully thin), it was just like everything she managed to swallow now; it generated no sensation at all. It was up to Mary to notice and enjoy the sweet malty fragrance, the brilliant garnet tones, the substantial body and velvety feel in the mouth, the astringent finish like chestnuts.

"But it's not quite like any tea I've ever had before," said Mary. "I wonder if my tea merchant could put a name to it. . . . Do you know, Catherine, I asked each of the girls about your parcel, and not one of them had any notion how it arrived here. It is mysterious."

"Everything about it is mysterious," agreed Catherine, and setting down her needlework, she took up the little silver-bound ivory coffer and turned it over, examining the decorations engraved on the silver. Some of the designs were like the complicated infinite-knot designs found on old-fashioned Celtic brooches, bracelets, knives, and the like. She had seen them all her life, and had never given them a moment's thought; they were just primitive old-fashioned decorations. Now she wondered for the first time what they meant—not only to the smiths whose work she had always known but to the maker of this particular box, from so distant and different a place. It had other, unfamiliar decorations, too. The most intriguing was a pattern of sinuous, swirling irregular forms over a darker stippled background. What could that be? She sighed and, taking up her canvaswork again, found her place: a long, straplike leaf of indeterminate species. It was a large piece of work, for it was intended someday to be a sofa cover.

"Where could Hector be all this time?" said Mary. "I had expected him back before now. He and my father were going to watch the king's entry, of course, at Picardy Place, and then he was just to go down to the ship with Mr Fleming to make sure that both his engines had got safely carried aboard and properly stowed. But I suppose I shall have to make a fresh pot of tea anyway when he comes in, so we might as well finish this."

Mary refilled their cups and, sighing, took up her sewing again. "How I hate to think of his being gone away from me for so long, and the voyage so filled with dangers, and the climate in India so unhealthful. When he first began talking of this journey, I scarce believed that the time would ever arrive. But here it is upon us. We have finished all his shirts but this, and filled his trunks, and his two precious steam engines are actually on the ship. Everything is ready except for me. I have not yet schooled my spirit. I have not found out how I shall bear it."

"Yes, learning to bear the unbearable is . . . slow," said Catherine. "A lesson one learns anew each day."

"My dear! My complaint must seem trivial to you."

"Far from it," said Catherine with a smile. "I have been admiring your spirit. You have been so cheerful, so whole-hearted, so courageous."

"Oh, not courageous."

"You are, though, and so is Hector. Of staunch and willing heart is what I mean."

"Well, my staunch heart is aching already," said Mary. "I could wait a long, long time if only I could be certain there would be an end to it. Only there is no such certainty, is there? No assurance at all."

"No, and there never has been any, not even when he is here, not even though he has succeeded thus far in always getting safely home to you each night."

They both pondered this for a while. Then Mary said, "But you will stay with me, I hope, Catherine. You know you may make your home here as long as you please. And poor Grace, too."

"Thank you, my dear. Your kindness has done me so much good already. Soon I shall have to take up my own life again, but not quite yet."

They both stitched in silence for a time, then Mary said, "It does gladden my heart, of course, to see Hector so happy. He quite means to make his fortune."

"And so he may. It is a great thing to have designed an important new style of engine, and to have it taken up by so forward-thinking a firm as Crawford and Fleming. People say that steam power will transform the country trade between India and China. And as the firm is paying for Hector's passage, and his expenses in India, and even allotting cargo space for him to trade on his own account—why, it is quite as good as a partnership—or better, in being without risk of expenses; it is no wonder that Hector is so confident of success. You won't mind, Mary, when he comes home a rich nabob!"

"Riches from the East; aye, so he promises me. And yet we're quite well enough as we are, quite comfortable, and I am my father's only child, after all. But it's different for men, I suppose. So many things are different for men." Mary shifted, and put down the shirt she was hemming. "Catherine, do you think it is possible, actually possible, for a man—a youthful, healthy man—vigorous, of an ardent nature, to, to remain faithful to an absent wife? For so very extended a period of time? My dear, he will be gone two years! Perhaps more. That's what I cannot bear, the thought . . . And yet how can I expect . . . If I had a truly generous spirit . . . but how could any wife reconcile her heart to . . . ?"

"Ah, never fear, Mary; you are the center of his universe. You are his roof and his pillow, the comfort of his house, the fire on his hearth. You are his lodestone. No matter where he goes, you are that place in the north where the needle of his compass always will point."

"It is just that ever-ready needle of his compass which worries me!" cried Mary, and they both fell back laughing.

"Miss Johnstone to see Mrs MacDonald," said the maid rather loudly, for they had not heard her at the door.

"Oh, a Miss Johnstone? Who is Miss Johnstone?" said Mary, reaching up to smooth her always-smooth hair.

"I beg your pardon, ma'am. For Mistress Catherine MacDonald, if you please," said the maid. "She said she was expected, so I put her in the master's study."

Catherine was expecting no Miss Johnstones. Curious, she went downstairs and found a carefully dressed woman, perhaps twelve or fifteen years older than herself, wearing a brilliantly embroidered Spanish silk shawl and standing erect before Hector's desk. "You are Miss Johnstone?" said Catherine. "How may I be of service to you?"

"I guess you're pretty surprised to see me," drawled the unknown lady in an American accent. "It looks like nobody opened this letter I sent along last night saying I'd call here today. Maybe you'd better read it now. I guess that would be the quickest way of explaining all this business." She pointed to a letter lying on Hector's desk. It was indeed addressed to herself, Catherine saw, taking it up. But the handwriting was so decorative as to have been misread. The letter had been lying neglected all day in the excitement of the royal entry.

"How unfortunate!" said Catherine. "I beg your pardon. Won't you be seated?" she added courteously as she opened the letter. There was a brief note wrapped around a more substantial inner letter. The note, in the same decorative hand, read:

*Miss Arabella Johnstone will be much oblidged by Mrs MacDonald recieveing her on Thursday at five o'clock. With a view to arrangeing about the enclosed from Judge Grant of Grantsboro Plantation, Virginia. Trusting the named time will suit, unless Mrs MacDonald likes to fix another appointment by return.*

This was the inner letter:

*Grantsboro Plantation, Virginia*
*June. 20th. 1822.*

*Madam,*

*The sad news which prompts this letter has only just reached me from my Glasgow agents, and I immediately take pen in hand to offer my sincere, though belated, condolences upon your bereavement. Although I was not personally acquainted with Mr James MacDonald, his reputation was well known to me, and while my poor sister lived as his first wife I knew her to be a happy woman.*

*Please accept also my grateful thanks for your care and custody of their poor orphan, my niece, to whom there now remains no living relation but myself. My wife joins me in desiring to receive the child at Grantsboro Plantation as soon as possible, here to be brought up among our own seven children, who are her cousins. Whereas Grantsboro, by the excellency of its tobacco, supports in excess of two hundred souls, both white and black; and whereas I furthermore have the honor and duty of presiding as chief magistrate in this county, you may rest assured that my niece's prospects among us here will be all that is comfortable and desirable.*

*The bearer of this letter is Miss Arabella Johnstone, my wife's sister. I do hereby authorize Miss Johnstone as my deputy to assume custody of the child, relieving you directly of all further responsibility, and to return with her to Virginia as soon as may be convenient.*

*The enclosed draft on my Glasgow agents will reimburse you for the costs of the child's maintenance since her father's death.*

*I have the honor to be,*
*your obedt. Humble servt.*
*A. Grant*

Catherine needed a long moment to find her voice, and some polite words. "Forgive me," she said at last, "but this is very sudden, and quite unexpected. I fear that we are not in the least prepared for such . . . for such a turn of events, and I find myself unable to respond without reflection. Perhaps you would be so good as to call again at this time tomorrow. By then I shall find an opportunity to . . . to consult with . . . with my advisors."

But Miss Johnstone objected: Tomorrow would not be convenient, because she had another engagement. It was best to settle these things promptly. And there was no time to be lost, because she suspected that her maidservant, a foolish black girl she had brought from Virginia, might take it into her head to run away. So, she proposed, it would be best that the child be introduced to her now, this minute. Then they would choose a time, two or three days hence, to accomplish the actual transfer.

"Oh, but I am afraid that is quite impossible," Catherine started to say when the door opened and Grace burst in, then drew up short, apparently surprised to find anyone there. What unfortunate timing! For an instant Catherine thought of pretending that this was some other child, but then she thought better of it. "Well," she said, "I am forestalled after all. Miss Johnstone, this is my stepdaughter, Grace MacDonald. Grace, this is Miss Johnstone. She is, ah . . . your uncle's sister-in-law. She has come from America to . . . to see you."

Grace sketched a curtsy, but she did not utter a word.

"Not only to see you, dear, but to bring you home to your own people, your own kinfolk," said Miss Johnstone in a cloying tone especially suitable for addressing good little children. "Did you know that you have seven dear, good cousins awaiting for you, and a dear, good aunt, and a dear, good uncle?"

Grace made no reply, so Miss Johnstone went on. "And a nice big new house, in such a nice warm climate—much warmer than here. And a music master, and a dancing master, and drawing lessons. You'll have new dresses as pretty as you please. You'll even have a little pickaninny of your very own to wait on you and play with you. Won't you like that?"

Grace made no reply.

"And as you must learn to be an American girl now, I have brought you a little book as a present. You must study this little *Life of Washington*, for every good American child makes a solemn resolve to emulate the greatness and goodness of our brave General Washington. His was a true nobility, you understand, for it derived from his character and his command of his passions, not from crowns and sceptres. Hmm! You must especially study the incident of the cherry tree, for a good child must never let a lie cross her lips, let the consequences be what they may. I am sure you're a good girl, aren't you? You don't tell lies, do you?"

Grace remained silent.

"Can't she hear me?" Miss Johnstone asked Catherine in a low voice.

"Aye, she can hear you. But our Grace does not speak."

"Is she mute?"

"No, she is able to speak; but she does not, except sometimes to me. Perhaps it may cheer you to know that she never does tell a lie."

"Well! How unaccountable! I suppose that the child . . . that her understanding . . . Has she the usual powers of understanding? Has she been taught to read and write?"

"Our wee Grace was able to read and write very well by the time she was four," said Catherine. "However, she too was in the carriage with her father when it overturned. Aye, a runaway horse over the cliff. There was some injury to her head, but she came to herself, more or less, within a day or two. Since then, however, the ability to read has been lost—for the time being, we suppose."

"Shocking!" said Miss Johnstone.

"And since then, Grace does not speak, nor eat, in the presence of anyone but myself," added Catherine.

"Well! I call that naughty! But I guess some good management will soon put a stop to that. My sister and I are quite wonderful at managing children. No nonsense is tolerated in our household, I guess! What a strange complexion, though," remarked Miss Johnstone thoughtfully, as though Grace were indeed deaf. "That unfortunate hair, and those freckles. Was it her father who had that bright coppery hair?"

Catherine's own hair was a similar colour, but she took no notice of the insult in this question. She only said, rather mildly—surprising even herself, "My husband was quite bald by the time I met him." Bald indeed! Where had that come from? James's hair had been thick until the day he died.

Grace raised an amused eyebrow at Catherine's lie.

"What a pity," said Miss Johnstone. "Particularly as wigs have gone so entirely out. Fortunately Judge Grant has kept all his hair. Well, *her* hair can't be helped, I guess, and my duty is clear. Only, what my sister will say about a red-haired child, I don't know."

"Perhaps you would like to reconsider, or write to your brother-in-law for further instructions under the circumstances," suggested

Catherine. It seemed that the American woman was on the brink of changing her mind altogether about this disappointing Scottish orphan.

"Oh, no! Writing would take much too long. And there's my Annie, you know; I have to return as quick as I can, before she takes it into her silly black head to run away. She hasn't got any notion of natural feeling or loyalty. My duty is clear. No matter how . . . we can't always have things our own way, can we? No, I'll call for the child on Saturday, Mrs MacDonald. Any messages in the meantime will find me at my hotel; here's the address on this card. And don't bother with clothes or that kind of thing. Judge Grant has sent along some money so I can buy her everything she'll need. He was very generous . . . though I'm sure none of us expected . . . Small for her age, isn't she? Well! There is satisfaction to be had in doing one's duty. Good-bye, then, Mrs MacDonald, and little miss—until Saturday."

As she saw Miss Johnstone out, Catherine said only, "I shall be sure to communicate with you before Saturday." Then Catherine and Grace turned to look at each other in wonderment. "But you must not come bursting into rooms, Grace!" Catherine said severely after a moment. "I would have given a great deal for that woman never to have set eyes upon you."

"I was only looking for string, Catriona," said Grace. "I did not know anyone was here."

"You are too young to call me Catriona," Catherine said. "Here is the string; now do go upstairs, my dear."

Where was Hector? Catherine urgently wished to consult him.

When Hector did come home a short time later, he was not alone. Mr Hay was with him, and so was Mr Fleming, who was part-owner of the trading firm Crawford & Fleming, which had invested in Hector's new marine steam engine design. There was also another man whom Catherine did not know, a gentleman whose seamed brown face and upright bearing would have marked him anywhere as a sea captain—as indeed he proved to be. "May I present Captain Mainwaring," said Hector. "My sister, Mrs MacDonald. Captain Mainwaring commands the ship *Increase*, my passage to Calcutta, you know. He has got my two engines stowed in the hold in the neatest manner possible, and I have seen my cabin as well. Nothing could be more commodious, and every need provided for."

Talking all at once, they noisily made their way upstairs to Mary's drawing room. Mary gave them fresh tea, and had the maid bring up cardamom-scented shortbread from the kitchen. Hector was in a fine flow of spirits, and Captain Mainwaring's conversation proved lively and agreeable. Mr Hay was jovial; Mr Fleming seemed courteous but reserved. To judge by his high forehead and his receding black hair, Catherine guessed him to be a few years older than Hector. But his green eyes under thick black brows were lively, and his mouth was mobile and expressive. When Mr Fleming had the grace to laugh at a moderately clever remark of Catherine's, which no one else understood, she concluded that Hector was justified in liking and respecting him.

But all the while Catherine was aching for them to leave, so she could tell Hector about the appalling Americans who meant to have Grace.

ꕥ ꕥ ꕥ

"WHAT IS A PICKANINNY?" demanded Grace as Catherine slipped into bed beside her in their darkened room.

"Still awake? A little black slave child," said Catherine.

"She said I should have one of my very own."

"Aye."

After a while Grace said, "That is an evil woman. I will never go with her, you may be sure. Never."

"Of course not," said Catherine. "I should never let you go." But she had consulted her brother at last, after the people had gone; and Hector thought they had better get legal advice.

"Well," said Grace, "will I give us a tale?"

"Do, pray," replied Catherine, as she always did. And Grace, collapsing back down under the covers, launched into her story in Gaelic, her earliest language. Most of Grace's stories featured the ancient heroes, maidens, and musical turns of speech that would have been familiar to old nursemaids. But other people and events also figured in

Grace's stories; she freely made warp and weft of the people and places she encountered from one day to the next. Tonight's story seemed to be based loosely upon the tale of Dar-Thula.

Catherine had begun to share a bed with her orphaned stepdaughter in the first weeks of their bereavement. At first, Catherine had told stories to Grace, but Grace soon took over. Catherine had welcomed the sound of the light young voice rambling on through the darkness in the soft lovely language they both knew from the cradle. It was like being carried off to sleep by a faraway lullaby.

Tonight, Catherine could hear faint music welling up from a lower floor of the house. Hector was playing his violin in his study, as he often did at night. He tuned, carefully, played a favorite little phrase from Corelli, then tuned again. There followed an unknown Italian tune; he did a bit of scrupulous work on a difficult passage, repeating it slowly several times, then played the passage a tempo again, perfectly, and continued to the end of the piece.

The tone of Grace's voice had changed; she was speaking now of a wicked old *cailleach* who walled up little children in dark caves to starve them. The *cailleach*'s name was Clach nan Iain, which, in English, Catherine realised with some amusement, would be Johnstone.

Downstairs, Hector played an old MacDonald air, slowly, with feeling. He always understood the emotion in a piece of music, and his skill was sufficient to express it. Catherine was drifting close to the edge of sleep when she heard the fiddle's small voice begin a familiar tune, followed by a variation in traditional piper style. Although the fiddle's pure timbre and single voice could sketch only an outline—it had neither the power nor the background of drones which distinguished pipe music—it was still an interesting tune, and much more interesting now that she did not think of it as just "Sandy's Tune."

# 3

## *worthy of Attention, as will afterwards appear*

"One shilling," said the woman seated at her high desk, seated so firmly and broadly that she overflowed her stool.

The tall, neatly dressed, shining black girl standing before her silently handed over the coin, which she had borrowed from the barmaid at her inn. The employment broker deftly stowed it out of sight. "Now," she said, "what sort of place? Laundress? Scullery? Dairy or poultry yard? Rough sewing? What sort of work can you do?"

The girl drew herself up to her quite considerable height. "Ladies' maid," she said proudly. "I wait on ladies. I dress them and take care of their clothes. I dress their hair, too. Fancy sewing, not rough. I do the fine mending and starching, the bleaching and the ironing, and I press their pleats and frills all nice and neat."

"And have you a good character from your last mistress?" asked the proprietress.

"I . . . No, ma'am. I did not ask her for a character."

"Mmm?" But this faint encouragement did not elicit any explanation. "Without a character, most ladies will be loathe to take any chances on you." She tapped a fingernail pensively on her desktop. "How old are you?"

"Eighteen, ma'am."

"H'm. I daresay you'll go anywhere? Not particular about town or country?"

"No, ma'am, not particular. I always live in the country before."

"And you're not in trouble, I suppose?" The broker pointed an inquiring eyebrow toward the girl's flat belly.

"Oh, no, ma'am!"

"Mmm. Well, you may sit down. It is possible that one of my ladies may take you upon trial, even without a character." With that the broker turned to the next applicant, and the tall black girl looked about for a place to sit. Backless benches were ranged about the walls of the low, dark room, and there was an air of obsolete gloom. The employment brokerage occupied part of the ground floor in one of the old town's old houses, in one of its dark, noisome medieval wynds in the shadow of High Street. Everyone in the room was looking at her. There were dark-shadowed eyes in lean sallow faces, pale bulging eyes in broad freckled faces, red-rimmed rheumy eyes. All were blank, flat, and unreadable, and all were trained on her. The black girl found a place where she could lean on the wall and think.

Every time the door opened, an icy northern draft blew over her, and the door opened often. Couriers came and went, bearing messages. A steady stream of women and a few men sought places of all kinds. Four ladies came to interview candidates; they were seeking a plain cook; a nursemaid; a footman; a girl of all work. Interviews took place in an adjoining room, and two of the ladies, finding themselves suited, engaged their new servants on the spot. Among the candidates on the benches ran a quiet but constant murmur of talk. As time passed, they began to rustle through the parcels they had brought, and furtively ate sausages, onions, bread, cheese, smoked fish. The black girl realised that the dark-haired woman next to her was holding out food, offering to share. It smelled delicious, richly spiced; and she accepted a share of it thankfully. "What sort of place are you seeking, miss?" asked the stranger politely. She had an odd singsong accent, difficult to understand, so the black girl explained carefully and clearly.

"I also am a ladies' maid," said the stranger. "We call it 'ayah.' I am seeking a place with a family sailing to India."

"India! Is that a warm place?"

"Ah! Butter melts! So warm, not like here. I have never been so cold, so dreadfully cold in my life as here," said the stranger.

"Yes, my toes, they been frozen ever since I set foot here. Is it very far away, India?"

"Very far. The voyage to come here took eight months, eight so-long months! Many storms. And my poor lady and her baby both died during this so-long voyage, so I am arriving in this strange, cold land with no place, no lady to serve, and just a very little money, very little. The ship captain, he is a kind man. It was he who told me to come to this office and seek a place with a family who will go to India, very soon I hope, so I shall be having my passage home again."

"Lots of folks leaves Scotland and goes to India?"

"Oh, yes, very many, even ladies. I shall be finding soon a place, no doubt."

"So you come and sit here every day?"

"Oh, yes, why not? I have paid my shilling, and so I have paid the right to come here every day."

"And I can come here again, even if I have to go away now?"

"Oh, yes, certainly. You can be coming here often as you please. The woman, she will remember you." Thus reassured, the black girl left, to hasten back to the inn where she was staying, for very little of her time was at her own disposal.

❧ ❧ ❧

IF EVER SCOTTISH law were brought to bear upon the matter, there was some risk that Grace might be compelled to go to America in the custody of her only living relatives: such was Mr Clerk's opinion. But any legal proceedings, he pointed out, would be exceedingly protracted and expensive, for the matter had its ambiguities. And under the circumstances, as they had been explained to him, a distinctly more plausible plan suggested itself. If Mrs MacDonald was adamantly resolved not to be parted from her red-haired stepchild, they must simply make themselves scarce until the brief period of time Miss Johnstone had apparently allotted for the task of collecting the child should expire.

"In short," said Hector, who was reporting this advice to his sister, "you need only take to the heather. But Catherine, my dear," he continued, preparing himself for what he knew would be the difficult part of the argument, "Mr Clerk also expressed a view which has some weight with me, and which I am not sure you have duly considered."

"I know what you are going to say. Pray spare yourself, and me."

"Nay, but Catherine, I must. These people, her people, can give Grace every opportunity, the best prospects in life. Will you so hastily renounce on her behalf all that she has a right to claim, all her birthright? And this renunciation is based simply on your dislike of this woman, this appalling woman who is after all only a messenger? It is a most consequential decision, not to be made without sober and disinterested consideration. And then, you know, they *are* her people, her only people, and we are not. Catriona, my dear, by what right can you presume to separate her from her only living kinfolk?"

Catherine would not meet his eyes; she frowned instead at the canvaswork on her lap, fiercely punching her needle through it, stitch after stitch.

But Hector went on to ruin the effect of his argument by saying, "And there is no need for you to make such a sacrifice of yourself. You are young still, and by the grace of providence may have a long and happy life ahead of you. Here is an opportunity to be honourably quit of a responsibility which is not even rightfully yours."

"Honourably quit! She *is* rightfully mine, Hector! I am the only mother she can remember, and she is the only daughter I am likely ever to have."

"Of course if some promise has been made, a last promise to her father—"

"Oh, Hector, don't be officious. I am not bound by promises but by conscience. And by feeling. No wonder you don't understand."

"Oh, conscience," retorted Hector, "and feeling. Well, of course I have no business with those, have I? Pistons and gears are more in my line? You have Mr Clerk's advice, and my own. No doubt you will do as you please. When did you ever do otherwise?"

Not fair, not fair. When had she ever been able to do as she pleased? Always there had been duties and responsibilities. The foremost duty, when attempting to discern a proper course, was to set aside one's own desires and inclinations—to set their magnetism well aside where they could not influence the compass—while yet steering clear of the fallacy of supposing that the most unpleasant and difficult route was necessarily the right one.

And then it so often appeared that all courses had their pains and difficulties, that Scyllas and Charybdises lay on every hand.

True, her own heart faltered at the thought of parting with Grace. Could this be selfishness? Yet how could there be virtue in sending her to live in the bosom of that Grantsboro family in America? Catherine's spirit curdled at the thought.

But supposing the Grants had been superior, good, kind people who would love and foster Grace. And supposing Grace knew and loved them, and dearly wished to go to them. Supposing all that, what, then, would lie before Catherine in her own life now? She was twenty-two years old, with money enough to live a quiet, independent life: a moderate sufficiency. But sufficient to enjoy what? If there were no child passenger in her barque, what course would she steer? This question had been lying before her for some time. She had averted her notice of it for the past year while becoming accustomed to widowhood; yet there it remained. Was it possible that she clung to Grace to avoid her decision?

Coming to the end of her thread, she secured it, then spread her needlework on the floor at her feet. Usually she saw only the few square inches she was working on: a flower, a leaf, a bird, a scroll, a swirl. The larger design was generally indiscernible in the two and a half yards of coarsely woven canvas bundled across her lap or draping awkwardly onto the floor. With it spread out, she could see the whole.

The future sofa cover was far from finished. The camel-back sofa shape was already old-fashioned, and the sofa for which the cover had originally been designed stood she knew not where. She had found this piece of work already begun by some other hand, a couple of years ago in her husband's house. Who had begun it? Who had designed it? Who had painstakingly stitched the young, handsome man, the pretty woman within the cartouche at the center? The woman was seated on a grayish-brown lump—surely a mossy rock—and playing a lute. The man had a spaniel at his heel. The faces and figures were well done, the tiny parallel diagonal stitches all neatly laid up against one another, completely covering the coarse weave of the canvas backing. Then there were trees, flowering bushes, rabbits, birds, a brook with fish in it. Some of the patterns were already stitched; some were only faintly sketched on the canvas. A great deal of it was entirely blank, not yet designed at all.

Upon first coming across it, in the attic, she had wondered whether

James's first wife—Grace's mother—had begun it. Feeling daring, she had brought it down and resumed work on it. Such a difficult blend of tactful delicacy and brusque practicality was required of second wives! James had said nothing about it; but when did men ever notice women's needlework? Of course it might have been his mother's work; or perhaps some unknown aunt or cousin had started it. But Catherine decided eventually that it was certainly her own work now.

Writing the letter to Miss Johnstone proved difficult. Catherine tore up her first attempt, and thought about asking Mr Clerk to do the job instead. But she tried again, and eventually succeeded:

*East Thistle Street, No. 12, Edinb.*
*August 16, Friday, '22*

*Madam,*

*I am very sorry you should have had the trouble and expense of a voyage from America, for I find upon due consideration, and consultation with my advisor upon the points of law, that it will be impossible to send my stepdaughter away to America with you. Enclosed you will find Judge Grant's bill upon his Glasgow agents, which is to be returned to him with my thanks for his unlooked-for liberality. It is not in my power however to accept any compensation for my own stepdaughter's maintenance and expenses, as my late husband, her father, in solemnly entrusting her to me, has left means sufficient to provide for her. Neither she nor I has any past, present or future claim upon Judge Grant's benevolence.*

*With best wishes for your*
*favourable return passage,*
*Believe me to be,*
*Your obliged servant,*
*Catherine MacDonald*

She sent it off before evening to the inn whose address Miss Johnstone had left, and then told Mary what she had done. "If the woman has any sense," said Catherine, "she will not send for Grace tomorrow. But I believe she may be . . . well, not to say pigheaded. Let us say, of tenacious character; so it is possible that there may be an unpleasant scene. All the servants must know that I am not at home to her or to her servants, nor is Grace."

"Oh, I daresay she will not send for Grace at all, having received your letter," said Mary. "It is hard to imagine that she would try to insist. But I will do as you wish; I will see that all the people of the household are warned and prepared."

ഌ ഌ ഌ

SATURDAY WAS THE DAY of the King's Levee, to be held at Holyrood House Palace. By eleven o'clock in the morning, every one of the streets leading to the palace was choked by queues of carriages; virtually every carriage in Scotland was at a standstill, facing east toward Holyrood. In each carriage was a gentleman, or perhaps two or three of them, each as splendidly got up as he could possibly manage, in court dress, military uniform, or Highland dress, depending on what he considered himself entitled to.

The streets and pavements were crowded with people on foot, too—not grandees come out to go to the Levee, but the less grand, come out to have a good look at the grandees. What a pleasant thing to walk about and peer into their carrages at them, and talk about their faces and their clothes! Agreeable to have a bite to eat as one walked about, and something to drink; agreeable to meet one's friends and go about with them awhile, then meet up with another group of friends and saunter about some more.

A tall black girl made her way among carriages across the broad, crowded High Street and down South Bridge, then down into the damp foul wynd and into the front room of the employment agency. The woman behind the high desk did remember her but said there had been no inquiries for ladies' maids today.

The black girl turned and scanned the faces of the people sitting on the backless benches. The brown-skinned black-haired ayah greeted her with a nod of acknowledgment and a warm smile, her straight white teeth luminous in the dim room, so the girl went to sit with her. "No ladies bound to India yet?" she asked the ayah.

"Oh, not yet, not just yet. But I am confident. A mistress will appear, in time. The door will open and my mistress will come in seeking me, seeking just precisely such an ayah as I am. A mistress will come for you, too, through that very door. Now, how shall you know her, your mistress, when she comes in?"

"What do you mean, 'know her'?"

"What I mean is this: When she comes, by what will you recognise her? Mine, for example, will be very sad. And very pale."

"All these Scottish ladies are pale, pale as corpses," said the black girl. "I bet they glows in the dark."

"Ha ha! Like ghosts; and such terrible red noses they are having! But this one I think will be pale of her sorrow. Yet I think she is a courageous and intelligent lady. Now, as for yourself—excuse me, miss, I do not know your good name. You have a great desire, I see, a burning desire; it is a determination. I think you shall have your desire, miss. You shall have it, and it shall have you. What is your good name, please?"

"Annie."

"Annie. I am called Sharada. So, Annie: the mistress you have now, the one you are wishing to leave, what sort of mistress is she? Is she lying abed late in the mornings? Is she careless with her dresses, dragging her frills in the dirt and tearing them?"

"Oh no, she never lie abed, nor permit anyone else a minute's ease neither. She say her prayers on her knees oh so often—dozen times a day. And I'm obliged to kneel down on my own poor knees and bow my head, too, at prayers every morning and every night. She say that's my duty. But I kneel down behind her, not in her sight, so she can't know if I do bow my head and close my eyes or if I don't!"

"O-ho! I think you don't, then," said Sharada.

"She pray on and on, all about duty and resolve. I guess she do plenty of duty alright, and stubborn as a mule, too. That's the 'resolve' she always going on about. She come all the way here to Scotland to fetch a poor orphan and take it back to America. But now that orphan won't go! The orphan know better than that, I guess."

"Have you served this mistress for a long time, then?"

"All my life, far back as I can remember," said Annie.

"And why have you never yet left her?"

"But they never allows me, in Virginia. I belong to them. If I ever dare run away, they only fetches me right back again. I'm only free here. The barmaid at the inn told me I'm free long as I stay in Scotland, and the porter, he swore it. He say he glad to marry me his own self, except he's married already. But here I'm free, so here I stay. Nothing in all the world can make me go back to Virginia. But I have no money, not a penny, so I come here to get a place."

"Your mistress has gone out this morning, I think? So you can be sitting here for a little time?"

"She gone to the house where that orphan live, to fetch her away. She gone with the porter, and his wheelbarrow, and her prayer book, to tell that orphan's folks they're obliged to give her over."

"The orphan has fond relatives, then? This is not a usual sort of orphan, I am thinking."

"It's mighty peculiar. Those folks won't let her go, not even for money. I know 'cause I saw the letter. My missus, she leave her letters lying about; she don't know I can read."

"Your mistress is trying to buy the orphan, then? For money?"

"She set on getting that orphan one way or t'other. See, it was just after her mean little old dog gone and died, and she was mighty torn up about that—and just then, the master, he mention about this one orphan way up here in Scotland. There's plenty of orphans in America she can have for nothing, but no—those ones won't do. Somehow she got herself set on having this particular Scotland orphan, and she pester the master night and day, day and night—all about the 'obligation,' she call it, 'til he just give in one day and let her go and fetch it, just to have some peace in the house at last! He's the biggest judge at the courthouse, but the man who can rule that woman ain't been born yet. So then she gone and sailed all this long way to Scotland, and now she go back and forth to East Thistle Street just dead-set on getting ahold of that orphan no matter what. She call it her duty."

"East Thistle Street? I have seen East Thistle Street. It is a very short street."

"I never have seen it. The letter say, East Thistle Street, number twelve—the letter from the orphan's lady."

"Indeed? So very interesting. Do you remember the lady's name?"

" 'Course I do, I remember everything. The orphan's lady, her name is Missus Catherine MacDonald—a Scottish name, I guess, but it sound just like a American name, too."

"So very interesting. And your mistress is in East Thistle Street now, at this moment, to see this Mrs Catherine MacDonald?"

"See her, and make her give up that orphan."

"So very, deeply interesting. And if she cannot succeed?"

"Oh, but she always do get her way; that's what she is fondest of in all the world. That's why she never has brung herself to get married yet."

~ ~ ~

"NO, NEVER INDEED, we certainly are not at home, none of us, to Miss Johnstone," repeated Catherine to the maid, who had come up to make sure. The maid went back downstairs to tell Miss Johnstone, who had been left standing outside on the doorstep. Catherine and Mary crept out to the stair landing to listen. They could not see the street door, which opened into the entry hall below, but they could hear the maid's polite murmur.

Miss Johnstone's reply, however, carried remarkably: "Then I'll just stand and wait here on the doorstep until they *do* get home," they heard her declare in a terrible tone.

"As you please, ma'am," said the maid, and shut the door and locked it.

Five minutes passed, or more. At last Catherine stole a darting glance from the little window above the stair that overlooked the street, and saw that the American woman remained on the doorstep. Her porter with his wheelbarrow waited on the pavement below.

"Will she just stand there, do you think?" whispered Catherine.

"So pigheaded! I think she will!" whispered Mary.

When another ten minutes had passed, they looked again, and saw that she still stood on the doorstep just as before.

"Won't she go? I do wish Hector were here," Mary whispered.

"I think you have got your wish," whispered Catherine. "Don't I hear him now?"

They listened; someone had joined Miss Johnstone on the doorstep. "May I be of some service, ma'am?" Hector's polite voice was saying, and Mary rolled her eyes. "Are you unable to find an address on our little street?" he said.

"Oh, and I did warn him!" Mary whispered, "but he is so absent-minded, especially when he has been dining out at certain places, and that is just where he has been, I fear."

"Oh, no, I've got the address aright, but the people inside say they're not at home!" exclaimed the loud American voice. "Not at home! Well, they'd better not want to come home, then! Or leave home, either, I guess!"

"Ma'am, you are agitated," they heard Hector say disarmingly. "Perhaps there has been some mistake. Won't you come in while you compose yourself?"

Catherine and Mary heard the door unlocked, and Miss Johnstone ushered in. "Pray, ma'am, am I to understand that your business is with someone here in my house?" said Hector now, in the hall below. Catherine heard the little chair in the hall creak; the woman must have seated herself.

"I guess you'd be Mr MacDonald? Aha. Well, I am Miss Arabella Johnstone of Grantsboro Plantation, in Virginia, and I'm here to fetch away my brother-in-law's own niece and her things. And what do I find but locked doors and lying servants and people peeking out from the curtains. I never was so badly treated in all my life!"

"Surely, ma'am," said Hector, still courteous, "you received Mrs MacDonald's letter informing you that she would be unable to part with her stepdaughter, and that there was no occasion for you to come here this morning?"

Mary and Catherine exchanged a significant look; Hector had remembered, at last, who this woman was. And here was Grace, suddenly, creeping under Catherine's arm to rest her chin upon the stair railing. Catherine would have sent her away if she could, but now she did not dare even to whisper. They all held their breath to listen.

"Well, some rude message of that kind was sent to me," they heard Miss Johnstone say. "Of course I didn't pay it any mind. I know my duty, and if Mrs MacDonald doesn't know hers, she'll have to learn it. I didn't come all this long way just to be trifled with by someone who's not even related to the child. No, no; that girl goes with me, and I'm not moving until I get her."

Grace nuzzled Catherine's arm, and Catherine laid her hand upon the sleek bright head.

"I fear that is impossible, ma'am," said Hector. "My sister certainly will never part with her stepdaughter, who was entrusted to her by her late husband. I fear you must resign yourself to a disappointment. Perhaps it may be some consolation to know that the child is among those who cherish her and are well able to look after her."

"High and mighty! Fine airs from such a low sort!" cried Miss Johnstone.

"Good morning, madam," said Hector in quite a different tone. "My man will see you out. Robin!" he called. After a plausible interval of time, Catherine heard the footman emerge from the kitchen door at the top of the kitchen stairs. "Robin, you will see Miss Johnstone out," said Hector.

There was a crash. Had Miss Johnstone knocked over her chair? Was she tossing the furniture about? "I know what you are!" she cried. "I asked around—of course I did! I'm no fool, let me tell you. You're nothing but a mechanic yourself, a common workman; and your womenfolk are liars and cheats!" Did Miss Johnstone sense an audience? It seemed to Catherine that she pitched her voice to the galleries: "I may be a poor lone female in a strange land," she cried, "but I guess I know my way around judges and lawyers, and some other kinds, too, don't I! I know how to fix all that! Don't touch me, dirty man! I won't be handled! I can see the door for myself." Miss Johnstone took herself out the door and down the steps to where the porter and his wheelbarrow still awaited her in the street.

# 4

## *In Which there is Some Art & Practise requird*

That was Saturday. On Saturday night, Grace's Gaelic bedtime tale featured hosts of "car-borne chiefs" driving about Edinburgh in all their martial glory, in the best Ossianic style; and by their combined efforts driving the wicked *cailleach* Clach nan Iain from the field in ignominious defeat. For purposes of this story, Grace had promoted her uncle Hector to the chief of car-borne chiefs.

On Sunday, the newspapers carried long accounts of the King's Levee, including a description of his attire: full Highland dress! Most impressive, but wasn't his kilt perhaps somewhat shorter than was usually worn? The king did not appear in public on Sunday, not even to go to church.

By Monday morning, a *bon mot* regarding the king's kilt was being repeated everywhere: "As he is to be among us for such a short time," a lady was reported to have said, "the more we see of him, the better." This was thought to be very good indeed. On Monday, the king appeared in a field marshal's uniform.

And on Monday evening, Mr Clerk called upon the MacDonalds unexpectedly, and met privately with Hector and Catherine. A rumour had reached him that an American spinster had retained a solicitor to assist in securing custody of a certain orphan. The solicitor in question was clever and wily, perhaps unscrupulous; in short, a writ might already be in preparation. If Mrs MacDonald remained determined not to be parted from her stepdaughter, then Edinburgh was an unlucky place for the two of them just now. Catherine assured him that she would certainly never give up Grace, and agreed to begin her preparations for departure instantly.

"No, no," said Mr Clerk, "you mustn't tell me where you're going. Far better for me not to know. What a pity you'll miss the king's Drawing Room. Were you to have been presented?"

But Catherine had harboured no ambitions of being presented to the king in any case.

"I was thinking of home," said Catherine to Hector and Mary after Mr Clerk had gone. "The old house."

"So was I," said Hector. The old stone house where they had grown up, Hector, Catherine and Alexander, was on the Isle of Skye. It stood on a promontory above a sea loch, behind an ancient ruin crumbling on a rock just offshore; its face to the sun, shoulder to the wind, and its back to a sublime prospect of the Cuillin. No one had lived in the house for some years, but it still belonged to Hector. "Andrew Dubh and his wife are still there at the croft, I know," said Hector. "She is a pretty fair cook, and she has some girls who can do the rough work, and that niece of hers is still nearby. You wouldn't be utterly cast away."

"It's too far," said Mary. "Surely there must be someplace less remote. You could go to my father's house, in Paisley. Miss Johnstone could not know about that."

But her solicitor might. Hector and Catherine were certain that Paisley was not sufficiently safe.

"And how are you to get there?" said Mary. "Hector, there is not time enough for you to take them all the way out to Skye and still return here again before your ship sails."

"We can go without Hector," said Catherine stoutly. "It is not so difficult. From here to Fort William by coach, then the overland journey through the glen to Arisaig. And from there to Skye it is just a brisk short crossing in someone's boat."

"Oh, my dear, it will be difficult. And what about a maid? You cannot possibly go anywhere without a maid, Catherine. You know you simply cannot." Even Catherine had to concede that an attendant could not be dispensed with.

"You must engage a maid, then, directly," said Mary. "There is an employment broker near the Grassmarket; I will take you there tomorrow morning, my dear. And we will engage your places in the Fort William coach, too. Now let us begin packing your things. How I grieve to part with you just now! I had counted on your companionship a good while longer, and now I must do without all of you at once. Grace! Where is Grace? Tell her she must collect her things instantly."

Catherine's trunk, the one she had brought when she had arrived at her brother's house some months ago, had been wrestled down from the attics at the top of the house, wrestled by the footman down around the tight landings and narrow, steep stairs. It stood open now in the room she and Grace shared. It was half full again but still giving off its own peculiar scent of desolation and sorrow. For the moment, Catherine was alone; Mary had gone to see about some missing linen, and Grace to amuse the baby in his nursery upstairs. Catherine reached up to the highest shelf of the closet, and her hand touched the silk-wrapped parcel from Sandy. She brought it down and set it on the little table. She put her nose to it and inhaled deeply, for it still smelled of sweet spices and foreign sunshine. *Catriona*. Her gaze dwelt upon the loved handwriting, the childhood name. She missed Sandy so much. Tricky, clever, slippery Sandy. What would Sandy have done if afflicted by a Miss Johnstone?

> She remembered the time, when they were eleven years old, slipping out in the twilight of a July midnight to go and rob a rich cache of bird nests. The nests were almost always undisturbed, and therefore sure to be full of eggs or even downy hatchlings, because they were perched on the rim of an ancient ruin, a hundred feet above black rocks and white surf below. It could be reached only by a precarious causeway, and only at low tide; and to go there was strictly forbidden. Sandy and Catherine set off through the half dark, but were followed by Catherine's burly, determined little dog, Luath, who was always eager for an adventure and trailed Catherine everywhere. They tried to send him back, scolding him in harsh whispers. He

understand perfectly well what they were saying, but he refused to obey. Their reproaches shamed him, sunk him to the ground, but he remained defiant and would follow.

When they ventured out onto the causeway, however, he was unable to cross it himself, and it was too perilous for Catherine to carry him, heavy and squirming. He stood instead barking shrilly after them as they picked their way intently over the black slippery rocks, over the mussels and green seaweed, the coral and winkles. They called to him to come; he would not. They threw rocks at him to make him hush; he would not. They feared that his commotion would raise the household; and indeed, they saw a light struck in one of the back windows of the kitchen. This dog would be the betrayal of them; they were forced to retreat. His joy as they returned across the black rocks to him made him wriggle and whimper. Catherine protected him from Sandy's wrath; it wasn't his fault. They sneaked back into the house undetected.

The next night they tried again, timing their attempt according to their intimate knowledge of the daily rotation of tide and moonset. With a joyful Luath trotting behind, they went first to the byre at the farm at the bottom of the hill. There Sandy pulled out a rough hessian sack he had brought and, by means of a bit of dried herring, succeeded in seizing one of the thin suspicious cats who lived there, and tying it inside the sack.

With this squirming parcel slung over his shoulder, they set off toward an upland patch of wooded ground crowning the hill, the only trees within half a mile. Luath was beside himself with passion about the sack just out of reach. At a nicely-judged distance below the patch of woodland, Sandy stopped and, teasing Luath for a moment, made Catherine hold him while he released the furious cat. The cat got its bearings in an instant, took into account the plunging, barely restrained dog, and streaked for the cover of the trees, its body extended in a most beautiful curve, its utmost sprinting speed. Catherine tried to hold on, but Luath, though short legged, was strong, and his nails were raking her. He leapt from her arms and plunged after the cat; and after listening for a moment, Sandy and Catherine ran down the hill to the causeway. They heard nothing as they crossed; then, as they gained the offshore rock, they could hear distantly the near-hysterical barking of a dog that has treed its quarry. They picked their way among the ruins—for there was rumored to be a yawning well somewhere about—and out to the seaward, windward side of the ancient fortifications. The seabirds rose off their nests, flapping and mewing. The nests themselves were everything they had imagined and more—a treasury of spotted mottled eggs and downy nestlings. The children tucked the fragile treasures into the bosoms of their jackets, then picked their way back across the causeway again, noting the chuckling black water lapping a little higher; and a light in the shepherd's hut; and a lantern bobbling crazily high up on the hill, coming down from the patch of trees at its crown. Again they slipped into the house undetected. But they did overhear, next afternoon, the shepherd's disparaging remark about the silly tyke who had raised such an alarm about a cat in a tree, and never again would he break his rest on the alarm of so foolish a dog as that one, a shame to call it Luath. *His* dogs knew better.

Tricky Sandy—master of decoy, even then. They had eaten the birds' eggs raw, and succeeded in slipping a pair of nestlings under two broody hens in the poultry house, hoping to raise a tern or a gannet as a fantastic tame pet. But these fosterlings did not survive; Sandy showed a desiccated little carcass to Catherine a few days later. They placed it in a cranny they knew about outside their window, and secretly monitored its dwindling to a mere scrap of parchment and quills, light as a dry leaf.

❧ ❧ ❧

"AND THEN I grind the gingerroot and the garlic to make a paste," Sharada had been telling Annie, when the door slammed open against the wall in a vicious gust of east wind. "A thick paste, you understand, and mixing it with just a little fresh yogurt, and perhaps some lemon juice if I have it, and quite a lot of ground black peppercorns, and rubbing it well into the flesh of the fowl, which I have slashed, you see, to let in the flavors . . . " Her voice failed as they saw the ladies who entered, carrying parcels: first the rosy-cheeked, black-eyed one who seized the wayward door; then the pale thin russet-haired one.

"Yes, certainly, ma'am," the owner of the brokerage was saying to the ladies. "I have several nice quiet women, experienced ladies' attendants. If you will describe your establishment and the duties of the position, I shall be most happy . . . ," she murmured deferentially as she ushered the two ladies into the inner room. The red-haired lady was replying in a low voice; and then the door was shut behind them.

Annie smoothed her hair, checked her fingernails, and took a few deep breaths. When the proprietress emerged and gave a brisk nod, Annie was perfectly ready. She made her way among the benches to the inner room, and shut the door behind her.

ꕥ ꕥ ꕥ

SO TALL! So black and shining! Catherine and Mary gazed at her for a long moment, and the girl gazed back, her hands clasped in front of her. Her fingernails were opalescent ovals at the tips of her long fingers, noticed Catherine; the fingers very black on top, with pink just showing underneath. That is a bold girl, Catherine thought, and felt pleased by this. "What is your name?" asked Catherine. "And your age?"

"Annie, if you please, ma'am, and I am eighteen years old." The girl's accent was surely American, and she looked very young for eighteen.

"Eighteen, are you?" said Catherine.

"Today is my birthday," said the girl stoutly.

"Well, then, Annie, I am seeking a ladies' maid. My establishment is a very small one, for I am a widow with an eight-year-old daughter. Your duties would include waiting on me and my daughter, and serving at table. I intend to set off for a journey away from this city quite soon, and may remain away for some time. If I were to engage you, could you come to me directly, and are you willing to make a journey?"

"Yes, ma'am, I can come directly, this very day if you please. And I know all about setting off for a journey, even a ocean journey. I know how to pack and unpack so quick and neat, and how to keep things sweet and dry, never musty. I keep all your nice things in perfect order, ma'am, and I always lay my hand on just the very thing you want."

"What was your previous place?"

"In America, ma'am, a place called Virginia."

"Oh!" said Catherine, and was struck silent, for she suddenly knew who this grave dignified girl was. A minute ago she'd had no idea; now she simply knew. It was like the moment when the churning cream suddenly congeals at last; now, irreversibly, it is butter.

Catherine considered. The temptation to engage the girl was powerful. It would be such a neat and complete retaliation for Miss Johnstone's impertinence—not only to fly away with the disputed Grace but to rescue the slave girl as well. It appealed to Catherine's sense of chivalry. But so risky, so unwise! What had she just said to this girl about her plans? Only that she intended to set off for a journey quite soon with her daughter. What if this girl should deliberately or inadvertently pass along this information to Miss Johnstone? And what if Miss Johnstone's pride should be all the more inflamed by this insult, so inflamed as to pursue them implacably? Catherine wished she had said nothing about a journey. All this reflection took only a moment, no more than a slight hesitation. Catherine said, "I must consider . . ."

"I do the prettiest needlework too, ma'am," said the black girl. "And if there's no laundress nearby, I can do all the washing and starching and ironing ever so nice, pleats and frills neat as anything, and never a scorch or a smut. And as for hairdressing, my lady always boast to her friends what a hand I have for dressing a head. She always lend me out to do all their heads whenever there's a ball. I'm always clean and punctual, and very careful and quiet to wait at table, too. And ever so discreet, ma'am, I never carry tales about anything I hear."

"Discreet, are you?" asked Catherine. So valuable a quality, discretion! "Hmm. No, I shall have to consider . . . until tomorrow, perhaps. Will you be here again tomorrow?"

"I can't say for certain, ma'am, for my time . . . I have certain other duties. But that lady out there, she know how to send for me."

On impulse, Catherine said, "Well, and here is a birthday present for you," and held out the smallest and prettiest of her several neatly tied parcels. The girl froze, not moving to take it, until Catherine reached forward and placed it into her hand.

"What a dreadful crush!" said Mary when she and Catherine had emerged once again into the crowded street. All the streets of the town were clogged once again by carriages, for it was the afternoon of the king's Drawing Room—his reception for the best ladies of Scotland. The carriages were full of these ostrich-plumed best ladies in their most splendid finery, and the crowds were, if possible, even greater than they had been on Saturday; for while gentlemen could take themselves to the palace and home again, the ladies required escorts and chaperones.

"How she stared when you gave her your new gloves!" said Mary as they threaded their way among carriages stopped on the bridge. "But Catherine, my dear, why do you not take her? She would be the very thing for you and Grace. Is it because she is so very black? Do you not know that my father's own man is a black African? He has been with him for ever so many years; they have quite grown old together. And no one could be kinder, or cleverer, or more perfectly honest. You would soon grow accustomed to it, I assure you."

Catherine laughed. "Oh, my dear Mary, that is not it at all! Have you no notion who the girl is? Whose servant she has been?"

"Why, no. You did not ask her the family's name, did you?"

"No need to ask. I know. That is Miss Johnstone's slave girl, bent upon running away while she has the chance."

"Never!"

"Aye. I am certain sure of it."

"Oh!" said Mary as they made their way up to the booking agent for the coach at the saddler and harness maker in the High Street. "Are you sure? Oh, Catherine, it makes my heart flutter to think of that poor creature held in slavery! And her birthday! I wish I had given her something, too. Are you not tempted to engage her just to save her from so monstrous an unjustice?"

"Very strongly tempted. It would be the most complete coup, wouldn't it? But prudence bids me to think hard before taking so provocative a step."

"Aye, Grace's safety must be your first consideration. How clever you are; I would never have had any notion of her being Miss Johnstone's servant. And if I did tumble to it, I would have been quite carried away by indignation. Well, if you don't engage her, Catherine, I must try to find a good place for her among my friends."

"Mary, you have the kindest heart in the world. . . . We must part here, I think: I shall inquire about the coach, then stop at the mercer's for some green worsted. But my dear, as the milliner is on your way, may I trouble you to step in there once more and buy me yet another pair of new gloves, just the same as before? I don't know what possessed me to give them away. I shall see you at home in East Thistle Street."

The saddler, when Catherine entered his shop, was displaying a nice selection of brass and nickel harness ornaments to a couple of well-dressed lowland gentlemen. Catherine went to the back of the shop, where there was an office for booking seats in any of the regular coaches whose routes originated here. Lying open upon the counter was a large ledger; and Catherine saw, reading it upside down, that it must be the register of bookings.

She looked around, catching the saddler's eye. He apologised and promised to wait upon her as soon as possible, and she assured him that she was in no haste. Then, when he had turned away again to his gentlemen, she quietly paged back through the ledger. The names and destinations of each day's passengers—to Glasgow, to Fort William, to Inverness, and to all other points near and far—were neatly listed, all in the same legible handwriting. Here was the record of who had been traveling; and when; and where they had gone—as anyone might find out, who cared to look.

She settled herself to wait until the saddler should be at liberty to sell her two places, and to write her name and Grace's neatly into his register, too, on the page for the Glasgow coach for the following morning. This would serve as well as any cat in a hessian sack.

MARY HASTENED HOME with another new pair of gloves for Catherine, and with a pretty little ivory needle book as a parting gift, and with sufficient almonds, sultanas, currants, candied orange peel and glacé cherries to make Grace's favorite Dundee cake, which would travel well and keep for a long time if wrapped in cheesecloth and stored in a tight tin. Going straight to the basement kitchen, she had the cook warm the dried fruits and grind the almonds while she herself creamed the butter and beat in the sugar. While stirring vigorously and chatting amiably with the cook, she kept one ear cocked, listening for Catherine's return. Instead she heard the nursemaid bring in the children from their afternoon romp at the laundry-drying greens across Queen Street. By the time she had beaten in all the flour and leavening—working up a sweat and an aching arm—she was beginning to feel uneasy; what could be taking Catherine so long? She mixed in the big spoonful of rum for its fine aroma, and all the chopped fruits and ground almonds, then turned the fragrant batter into the baking tin, which the cook had lined with greased paper. The cook opened the oven door for her, and Mary slid the heavy tin onto the rack in the center of the oven for its long bake. Then, at last, she went upstairs to investigate.

No Catherine, but Catherine's big trunk stood in her room, closed and apparently ready to be moved. At the top of the house, in the nursery, Mary kissed her children and smiled at Grace, and inquired of the nursemaid, who confirmed that the other Mrs MacDonald had not come in. And do look, the dear baby has produced his new tooth at last! And indeed he had, the drooling, red-faced darling, chewing wetly on his coral with the silver bells mounted on the ends.

Mary tried to sew, then tried to balance her account book, but she found she was too restless to sit down. She stirred the fire; she went to the window a dozen times; she went up to the nursery to look in on the children again; she went to Catherine's room with the parcel of gloves and the little present of the needle book. The trunk was closed but unlocked; she opened it and put the parcels inside. Among articles of clothing and paper-wrapped books was nestled the posthumous package from poor Sandy, dead in India. She shut the trunk again and went down to the kitchen to check her cake. She heard the hall door open and close overhead, and footsteps. After hastily setting the cake to cool, she went running upstairs.

Hector had come in at last from his friends at the Mechanics Institute. It was a comfort to share her alarm, but when he heard that they had encountered Miss Johnstone's maid, he became worried, too, though he tried to pretend that he was not.

"Surely she had a great many last-minute errands to attend to," he said, "and the streets are still clogged with carriages, everyone trying to get home again after the king's Drawing Room today. Such a day for ostrich plumes! I wonder if there remain any birds in Africa yet unplucked? As they are wearing so many feathers, one might suppose that all the ladies could get themselves home again just by taking to the air."

"I had supposed that ostriches were flightless," observed Mary.

"I stand corrected, my literal-minded dear. You are quite right; they are terrestrial birds, and so are the ladies."

To the cook's great annoyance, they waited dinner for half an hour, while the soup congealed. Finally they sat down and ate without appetite, listening more than tasting. Afterward the little children and silent Grace were brought in for their usual quarter hour of infant conversation and a sweet treat, and Hector and Mary played with them for longer than usual as a distraction. But eventually the children were taken away again and put to bed while the August sky was still quite light.

By half past nine, the blue sky was finally fading, and shadows were deepening in the corners of the drawing room, where Hector and Mary sat together over the dregs of their tea. There came a knock at the street door; they heard the footman open to someone who was not Catherine; for there was the timbre of an unfamiliar voice in the hall downstairs.

"The person below says she has a message for your sister, sir, for Mrs MacDonald, of the most extreme urgency and importance," said the footman. "I have told her that Mrs MacDonald is not at home, and she begs to speak with you instead, sir. She appears to be in a state of considerable anxiety."

Hector clattered hastily down the stairs, too anxious for dignity. There in the hall stood a slender foreign-looking woman with a plain shawl over her plaited long black hair. She was as dark eyed as a gypsy. She looked agitated and exhausted, and was breathing hard, as though she had been running.

"You are Mr Hector MacDonald, brother of . . . of Mrs Catherine MacDonald, who is living here in your house?" asked the foreign woman. "Oh, sir, I am coming here with warning for your sister. Oh, yes, sir, her plan for going away to Glasgow tomorrow morning is known to the American woman. That woman has been hiring some men to be stopping her and the child at the coach in the High Street in the morning."

"To Glasgow! You astonish me! May I know who you are, and how you know this? And why you have interested yourself in my sister's affairs to such an extent?"

"Oh, I am not coming here to speak of myself, sir, no thank you."

"No?"

"But where is Mrs MacDonald, please, sir?" asked the foreign woman.

"She is—she is not here."

"So much I was knowing already!" she cried. "But is she safe? And the little red-haired girl? Was Mrs MacDonald knowing already of this danger?"

"I do not know where she is. She never yet came home this evening. I am filled with anxiety about her, and what you have just told me makes me fear for her safety. Pray, let me know who you are, and the sources of your information."

They heard someone coming up the stone stairs from the street. Hector swung the door wide; it was Catherine, thin and wan.

# 5

## *But this is all mistake*

"How do you know?" demanded Catherine of the foreign woman.

"A boy came running to the inn, bringing to the American lady Johnstone a message. He came downstairs then for something to eat, and in the kitchen he was boasting as he ate, boasting of his great exploit, running all across the town from the coach office, seeking first of all a solicit man."

"A solicitor, do you mean?" prompted Hector. "A lawyer?"

"Yes, yes. And this solicitor sent him on, still running, to the American lady Johnstone. And now he was to run back again to the solicitor, carrying the lady's reply. He went away full of cheese and ale, so very proud of all this running. Then the lady Johnstone sent for my friend Annie, who is her maid."

"Your friend Annie—is she a black girl from America?" asked Catherine.

"Yes, ma'am, yes, precisely, the girl you were meeting today at the broker's office, yes. Then Annie was returning to me in the kitchen and telling me farewell, for her mistress had bidden her be packing the trunk and receiving the child early in the morning, then departing from the city, and indeed from Scotland."

"All this she confided to you?"

"Oh, yes, ma'am. She is my friend."

"Were you there at the broker's office today, yourself?" demanded Catherine; and the hairs at the nape of her neck were abristle.

"Yes, ma'am. Today, every day, I am there. I am seeking a place with a lady bound for India."

"I did not see you," said Catherine.

"No, ma'am, but certainly I was seeing you."

Catherine scowled, doubting—and fearing. This foreigner—this stranger who had been observing her, unsuspected—how was she to be trusted? At last Catherine said, "How does it happen that you were in the kitchen of that inn?"

"I was bringing a special festive dish for my friend Annie, as today is the festival of her birth, her sixteenth year."

"Sixteen? She told me she was eighteen."

"Indeed, did she, ma'am? But she is sixteen, I think."

"I do not understand why you have given yourself so much trouble on my behalf."

The slight foreigner looked down. Then she said, "It is not so very much trouble. You were kind to my friend. You presented her a gift on her birthday festival, gloves! And . . . that is all."

"May I know your name at least?" asked Catherine more politely.

"Oh, excuse me, ma'am, my name is of no importance. But you may be sure that I am wishing well to you, Mrs MacDonald, you and all your relations, too. Good night, then." The Indian woman bowed slightly to them, with her palms pressed together under her chin, then went out into the dark street. Catherine looked after her, watched her sleek head outlined by the modest shawl drawn close over her hair as she passed under the new gaslight at the corner, then disappeared. The faint foreign spice scent of her still lingered in the hall.

Catherine did not let herself contemplate how terrifying: this nocturnal visitation by an angel, this warning to flee the city. To save a child.

"Oh, never to Glasgow! Certainly not," she declared to Hector, and to Mary, who had come down to the entry hall. "I had never the slightest intention of getting on the Glasgow coach tomorrow morning. I had intended only to lay them a false trail—only to give them a red herring to follow. But my little scheme is ruined already, because they have found it too soon. I had supposed that tomorrow would do, but now I think that Grace and I had better do our flitting right now, tonight. I must get my trunk all the way to Leith. Shall we borrow the footman's handcart tonight, or hire a wagon tomorrow to bring it, think you? By then they may have set a watch on the house."

"And have you been down at Leith all this time? We have been so anxious about you."

"To Leith and back, on foot, to my sorrow; and a blister to prove it. But thanks to your amiable Captain Mainwaring, I have comfortable rooms at the inn there. He gave up his own rooms to me, as there are none to be found in the entire city just now, you know. He will go and sleep on his ship. He insists he will be more comfortable there, quite at home. And he has very kindly and discreetly engaged two berths for Grace and me on a little merchantman bound for Inverness, due to sail within a day, or two at the most. He promises to say not a word to anyone—I believe he supposes it is a matter of a debt! But he has been very kind, most generous with his help, and I think his discretion may be relied upon. And all for your sake, I am sure, Hector, as he is most taken with you and your rotary propelling machine."

Grace was roused; the footman and his handtruck summoned. Shawls and wraps were found; kisses and promises exchanged. "Yes, my dear, I shall be sure to engage a maid in Inverness, never fear. A nice wholesome country lass," Catherine assured Mary.

"Oh, wait!" cried Mary as the trunk was eased down the stone steps. And she ran to fetch the Dundee bannock, cooled now and well shrouded in cheesecloth, inside a good tight tin so it would keep for a long time.

Despite her fatigue, Catherine lay awake, while Grace slept beside her. The inn was not quiet; the streets of Leith were not quiet; and her mind was least quiet of all. The laying of false trails had come easily to Sandy, but not to her. Any feint of Sandy's devising would certainly have proven far more successful than this feeble effort of hers had been. She liked plain speaking and plain dealing. It seemed to her that the real shape of her thoughts and intentions must betray themselves—

angular, unconvincing shapes under the deceitful bedclothes draped artfully over them.

She was troubled by the remarkable persistence of that American woman. How was it to be accounted for? It seemed to Catherine that the woman prided herself upon her tenacity; perhaps she believed that tenacity was itself a virtue, a badge of dutiful resolve.

In her pride, how long might Miss Johnstone carry on her search? How great were the resources at her command? What measures, fair or foul, might she resort to?

No one could scour every nook and cranny and bolt-hole and croft in all the islands and all the Highlands, Catherine assured herself. Not even the English army had ever succeeded at that. Surely she and Grace would be safe on Skye until Mary could let them know that Miss Johnstone was defeated and gone; then they might come and go as they pleased.

Meanwhile, Catherine would keep Grace constantly under her own eye. Within arm's reach.

To Skye, then; but not by the overland route she had first intended. Instead, they would go to Inverness by sea; then by boat down Loch Ness to Invermoriston; then hire horses and an escort for the short overland journey through the glen to Dornie. From there it was only a dash by boat over the sea to Skye, and to the old house.

Over the sea to Skye. She had small faith in boats; they seemed such fragile little cockleshells. It was a handicap for an islander, not to believe in boats. Over the sea to India! That was unimaginably distant and strange and dangerous. Sandy had gone; and now Hector. So many people perished there, or on the long dangerous passage—people one knew and loved.

Not yet drown'd. Not *yet* drown'd. Not yet *drown'd.*

Catherine had once seen a drowned fisherman tangled in his own nets: dreadful. Not to be thought of when lying awake at night. She pushed away that image and summoned a pleasant one in its place: Sandy playing his pipes, that summer when they were both fifteen. Composing that tune of his. He would go up on the hill, way up behind the big house, up to where someone in old times, ancient times, had set up a circle of vast stones—upright sentinels, or monuments. No one knew what they were, but there they still stood—except where two had fallen—in a rough circle crowning the hill. Sandy would stand up close to one of them, one particular broad, lichen-studded stone that loomed twice his height. He would face it and play his pipes. Why stand there, right under it? It was so he could hear himself, he said. The stone flung his sound back to him, like a wave breaking against a cliff and falling back onto itself. Otherwise the sound only dissipated into the universe. He liked to feel the sound of his pipes crashing back down onto himself.

"Sandy's Tune." He had worked out his tune that summer. Catherine could hear him from far away, from down on the shore, working out its variations. He would play that tune, among the many he knew. So many of them were laments! Sometimes he would play a certain old heart-wrenching tune just to tease her: "Cumha Catriona," "Catherine's Lament." It had rolled off her, then, when she was fifteen. But now she knew what it was to lament; to suffer losses, bereavements.

Oh, the loneliness! Oh, James . . .

Grace turned over beside her and nestled deeper into her pillow, sighing.

And Sandy, gone; and now Hector was going too. India.

That dark gypsy-like stranger was from India. How mysterious, her sudden apparition, bringing a warning in the night, like a fierce dark angel.

Angels! Yet more preposterous than boats.

Below, the tireless fiddler in the inn's public room launched into a jaunty jig. Judging by the sounds coming up the staircase, few people remained below; but those few survivors were the loudest and the merriest, those whose capacity for drink was greatest.

By daylight, Catherine was better able to govern her doubts and calm the discursiveness of her mind. The pair of rooms given up to them by Captain Mainwaring were good. Their sitting room had two windows overlooking the street, and the tiny room adjoining contained the bed, draped in a fashionable cotton chintz cover of brilliant mustard and turkey red, and a narrow stand for candle and basin.

There was a little bustle in the hall outside the door of their sitting room, and then the maidservant brought in their breakfast. She was a brisk, tidy girl with straw-coloured hair neatly combed, and the food was plentiful and well prepared. Catherine felt something like well-being return to her as she finished her ham, a well-cured ham nicely marbled with veins of pearly fat. A shaft of brilliant morning sunshine splashed across the table, which was set under the larger of the two windows. Just now, at this present moment, all was well enough. The oatcakes were fresh, and the butter had a country taste.

She made Grace understand that she must remain indoors—not venturing even so far as the common rooms of the inn—until Captain Buchanan, of the Inverness-bound coastal merchantman *Die Vernon*, should send for them to come aboard, perhaps tomorrow, perhaps even today.

If Catherine peered out at just the right angle, she could see down the street to the water, and a slice of the Leith pier, which was thick with people of all estates coming and going. Boats and barges and skiffs and yachts were tied up all along its length, casting off and drawing in. In the deep water were innumerable larger craft in all the stages of coming and going and staying, forests of masts, herds of hulls. Her narrow slice of view did not include any of the royal flotilla, nor *Die Vernon*, but she knew that Captain Buchanan would send for her and Grace as soon as his cargo was stowed and they could come aboard, as soon as wind, tide, and trade allowed.

People passed in the street below, and bits of their chat floated up through the open window. Catherine began to feel herself soften and relax. Grace was curled into the only easy chair, playing cat's cradle with a loop of grubby string and idly whistling a familiar old tune belonging to the MacDonalds.

"Grace, must you whistle?" said Catherine.

Grace stopped whistling.

"You could work on your sampler," suggested Catherine as a matter of form. Grace only smiled; she never worked on her sampler.

Safe enough for now.

That was Wednesday. The day passed fine and fair; Captain Buchanan did not send for them.

On Thursday morning, there was a message from Captain Buchanan. He now expected to sail on Saturday and would send for them and their trunks in ample time. The wind had backed during the night, and the morning was gray and drizzly. Catherine watched umbrellas passing and repassing on the street below, but opaque mists hid the water, boats and pier at the bottom of the street. As the day drew on, the rain grew heavier. Before dinnertime, it was coming in torrents, drumming in black bursts on the cold weeping windowpanes and seeping under the sill.

Catherine and Hector had agreed when parting on Tuesday night not to risk sending messengers who might be followed. She had not heard from Hector, nor did she expect to. But she felt isolated from him, and from the entire city and its doings. At dinnertime the little blond maid brought up a day-old newspaper, saying that someone had left it below and she thought the lady might like to have it. Catherine read with interest about the plans for the king's visit to Edinburgh Castle. This visit was scheduled for Thursday afternoon, for this very hour.

The rain continued, merciless.

That evening, just after the tea had been brought up, a dripping young midshipman from *Increase* came, bearing a damp letter from Captain Mainwaring. Enclosed in the captain's letter was a note from Hector. Captain Mainwaring begged that Mrs MacDonald would do him the honour of being among his guests tomorrow, when they would view the Royal Review of the Yeomanry on the Portobello Sands from the comfortable privacy of his barge, which would be just offshore. Then they would dine aboard *Increase*; Hector and Mary had already agreed to be his guests. He would send a closed chair to her inn, and all the arrangements would ensure the most complete discretion. Hector's enclosed note urged her to come; it would be a good opportunity for them all to say a real farewell.

Catherine would so very much have liked to go! Even a day on a boat must be pleasanter than another day inside this room. But it would mean leaving Grace alone and unguarded. Catherine thought of arranging for the little blond maid to look in frequently; but in the end she could not bring herself to it. She sent back the damp midshipman with a regretful note explaining that she was unable to leave Grace.

How very gratifying then, two hours later, to see the same midshipman back again, wetter still and carrying yet another note. This invitation included Grace as well. "Of course you'll come too," said Catherine when Grace scowled. "Your Aunt Mary will be there, and Uncle Hector, but no one will expect you to say a word. And I will arrange for you to eat by yourself if you like. We both of us need to get out of this wee room."

ᔕᔕ ᔕᔕ ᔕᔕ

FRIDAY DAWNED BRILLIANT, and the sun glancing off the wrinkled blue waters of the Forth broke into shards and darts of dazzling light. Leith was crowded already, but Catherine and Grace, both of them bonneted and veiled, were carried quickly down to the pier in the promised closed chair, and bundled discreetly aboard a little skiff belonging to *Increase* without attracting any notice. The sailors at the oars put a crisp precise snap at the end of each long hard stroke; and the town fell quickly away behind them at the end of their seething wake.

Catherine was surprised at how the little boat skimmed over the dark water. Amazingly soon the tall *Increase* loomed over them, and the skiff turned smartly against its high curved hull. A bosun's chair, like a sling on a scaffold, was rigged ready for the visitors, and Catherine and Grace found themselves hoisted aboard before they had time to feel apprehension. They were welcomed with great cordiality by Captain Mainwaring; and by Hector, Mary, Mr Fleming, Mr Clerk and his sister Miss Bessie Clerk, who had all come aboard earlier.

Catherine had never been aboard an East Indiaman. She marveled at the neatness of every arrangement; this vessel was quite unlike the slatternly coastal traders and noisome fishing boats she was accustomed to see. The deck shone pale as straw with scrubbing and sunbleaching; and the thick ropes deployed all about in bewildering multiplicity were arranged in cunning hanks, scrolls, and curlicues according to some arcane custom. The crew wore stiff canvas shirts and trousers of a dazzling white that rivaled Mary's best table linen. The men appeared well fed, cheerful (in spite of their undoubted sobriety), and respectful in the extreme.

While Grace went with her Aunt Mary to see the cargo in the deep dark hold, Hector took Catherine to see his own little cabin. They passed through the cuddy cabin, where Catherine admired the polished table, elegant chairs, and bright brass fittings. "So very handsome!" she exclaimed. "I dare not hope that Captain Buchanan's *Die Vernon* will be half so pleasant as this, whenever we may be allowed to go aboard. He expects now to sail tomorrow, and we are holding ourselves in readiness to depart upon an instant's notice. In the meantime, we do not show our faces outside our room."

"Prudent," said Hector, "although that American woman seems to believe that you are still at my house."

"Does she? How can you know?"

"Early on Wednesday morning, a bailiff came to the door with a packet of papers which I suspected of being a writ to be served upon you, my dear. I said you were not there, and of course he did not believe me; but he could do nothing but set a watcher in the street. Blackguardly looking fellows they are, too. One or another of them has been standing about ever since, not troubling to hide himself in the least. There was one when we left this morning, and there he stands now—for all I know—waiting for you to come out."

"I hope you were not followed, coming here."

"No, they do not follow me in my comings and goings. It is you they want. The sooner you two are away, the better."

"You could not be more eager for our departure than we are," she said; and wondered uneasily at the American woman's extraordinary persistence.

Hector ushered her into his own little cabin, which took up one corner of the stern. There was a writing table, a bookcase, a gimbled lamp, a tray-tabletop suspended from the beams low overhead, and a number of cleverly devised lockers for his private stores. "How neat it is!" Catherine cried, trying the mechanism by which the dressing table closed over a washing apparatus. "So ingenious! Every convenience! And then at night, I see, your bed is to be suspended here, to lull you to sleep by the ship's gentle movement." A large window with venetian blinds, now drawn up, let brilliant shimmering darts of sunlight reflecting off the water dance upon the varnished walls. "I never imagined such comfort could be found aboard ship. I am quite envious; what a pleasant time you shall have!"

"Every reasonable comfort, to be sure. As for pleasure, that must depend on the company. Mr Fleming has the cabin opposite mine—just there, you see—so I am sure of at least one congenial companion, and I have heard that several miscellaneous young gentlemen are going out to take up various appointments. But it is not settled who is to occupy this large cabin between Mr Fleming's and mine. A newly appointed judge and his family were to have had it, but he has just been struck down by an apoplexy. You see it is quite as well fitted out as mine, and rather roomier, with this very handsome window curving across the stern, and two neat sofa beds, and this closet with room enough for two more hammocks as well, for servants I suppose."

"Oh, I am seized with the fancy to take it myself, for Grace and me. How long is the passage? Four or five months? Four or five months of sea air, congenial company, novel sights, and no troubles to pursue us, no writs, no Miss Johnstones. Grace and I would be quite set up!"

"Yes, until you found yourselves disembarking at Calcutta, to encounter its heat and its fevers, its discomforts and dangers."

"It is mere fancy, dear Hector, only a charming conceit. You know how I feel about boats, even such solid reassuring ships as this one. I could never bring myself actually to embark on a long ocean voyage. But I have not heard you admit until now that Calcutta might pose any discomforts or dangers. In Mary's presence, it is all safety and sobriety, trade and profit, porcelain tea sets and coromandel screens."

"Oh, aye, porcelain tea sets. I have received some amazingly detailed instructions about porcelain tea sets. But what shall I bring back for you from the Indies, Catherine? You have not yet told me what your heart longs for."

"What my heart longs for! What a question."

"Oh, by way of tea sets or embroidered silks or ruby eardrops, I mean."

"There *is* something, Hector," Catherine said, fingering the venetian blinds. "Yes, there is something I want from India. From you." She turned and looked full in his face, waiting for him to read her meaning. "Sandy," she whispered at last.

"Oh, Catherine," he said sadly. "There is nothing anyone can do. Am I to raise him from the dead for you?"

"How can you feel so certain? Hector, when you are there, you must find out what really happened. Where he has gone."

"He has gone from the land of the living, my dear. Gone—lost to us forever."

They stared at each other. It may be so, thought Catherine; but perhaps not. One might hope and wish otherwise; one might succeed even in believing otherwise, from time to time. "But here is Mr Fleming," she said, mustering a suitable expression as Mr Fleming appeared at the doorway. "Good morning, sir. I am admiring the commodiousness of these arrangements, for I never was aboard an East Indiaman before."

"How generous you are, Mrs MacDonald, to call our doughty *Increase* an East Indiaman!" said Mr Fleming. "We are sadly accustomed to being looked down upon by the East India Company as a mere interloper."

"Interloper! That has a disreputable sound. I am sure that *Increase*, and Crawford and Fleming, do not deserve that. Surely it is only a jealous rivalry on the part of the East India Company, such as an older brother, in complacent possession of the family acres, may feel toward a bold and enterprising younger brother who has made his own name and his own way in the world."

"OBLIGE ME, pray do, you two Mrs MacDonalds, and you, too, Miss Clerk," said Captain Mainwaring when the company had reassembled on the main deck. A steward bearing a tray was offering small glasses of amber whisky. "It is mild as milk and will do you nothing but good. This is the veritable Glen Livet, the pure Glen Livet, sent to me by Lord Murray in the year 'eighteen in return for a favor in which I had been able to oblige his lordship. It was a private little matter of a quantity of Delftware—oddly packed, very oddly packed indeed—inside several barrels of Dutch butter—butter being an article of very little interest to customs agents. Glen Livet! It has been long in the wood, and long in uncorked bottles. There, you see? It has the true contraband *goût*, has it not?"

"Aaah!" gasped Catherine, having downed her dram bravely. "Yes, the true contraband *goût*, irresistible since the days of Adam and Eve."

"And then it is such an encouraging thing. Ladies who are unaccustomed to the bosun's chair sometimes do want a dash of encouragement. Now you must just skip aboard my barge, here. There you go! Neatly done."

And thus encouraged, thus inspired and inspirited, they did all succeed in transferring themselves over the gunwale once again, embarking this time in the captain's barge, a heavily built boat rigged for sail as well as for oars. There were comfortable seats in the stern, and a smart striped awning overhead provided welcome shade. Captain Mainwaring made sure that the three ladies and Grace had the best seats, and lending them his glass, pointed out landmarks on shore as they slipped past.

They set off under sail to make the best of a fickle breeze, but as the water traffic moving eastward toward Portobello became denser, the crew dropped sail and bent to their oars. They made their way among sleek pleasure yachts, broad ungainly ferries, lighters, little rowboats, and several steamers trailing plumes of black smoke. Among these, Catherine was pleased to recognise the steam launch *Dram Shell.*

"How splendid! And such an excellent vantage point!" exclaimed Mary as the barge drew toward the long beach of Portobello. For there, stretched all along the yellow sands for more than a mile, were the backs of the mounted Yeomanry and the shining rumps of their horses: nine thousand mounted men three ranks deep, spaced five feet apart, with the sun glancing bright off their polished swords, buttons, buckles, and spurs. Taking up a position several hundred yards offshore, the heavy barge rode comfortably on the deep blue swell.

"Do you too find it an impressive sight, Mrs MacDonald?" asked Mr Fleming, leaning forward to speak to Catherine. He had a most direct look—his eyes surprisingly green out here on the water—and a pleasant quiet voice, rich in timbre.

"It is a handsome uniform," replied Catherine, "and I suppose I ought to be impressed. But to own the truth, I feel as though I were in the wrong place, viewing the play from backstage instead of from a box." All those backs! she thought without saying it, all those plump gleaming rumps! Such a very posterior view! Aloud, she added, "But I suppose that from the front they must appear a formidable force."

Higher up on the beach beyond the Yeomanry seethed the dense cheerful chattering crowds of spectators, on foot or in carriages, clambering over the shifting dunes, celebrating the holiday weather. Heavy dragoons patrolling the beach repeatedly pressed back the encroaching crowd. More carriages, horsemen and walkers continued streaming down the road from town, over the grassy dunes and along the shore, seeking any remaining vantage points not already occupied by earlier arrivals. Landaus, barouches, barouchettes, curricles, gigs, open chariots, one-horse chaises, farm carts and stagecoaches lined the ridge of the dunes, all overflowing with North Britons in their best clothes. The wheeled horse-drawn parade was as motley, miscellaneous and various in its land-bound way as the ill-assorted watercraft bobbing offshore.

"I hear pipes," said Hector. "The Highlanders are coming." To shouts, cheering and jeering, the companies of tartaned Highlanders came plunging on foot down the shifting dunes to the firm-packed sands of the beach. Sutherlanders, MacGregors, Campbells, and Drummonds, they formed up, wheeled, and moved into the positions assigned to them at the far west end of the beach, some distance past the Yeomanry.

"Here he is; that's his carriage, with those eight bays," said Mr Clerk. The king alighted, to acclaim. A big strongly built gray horse was led up from one direction, and the king, plump and glistening as a peeled egg in a fresh field marshal's uniform, was led up from the other. But how was the king to mount the horse? How could such a feat of engineering be accomplished, and before a crowd of twenty-five thousand? A circle of aides, equerries and attendants closed about the interesting scene; only their backs were to be seen; and after a tense minute, the king emerged above their heads, now atop the horse. He gathered up his reins and moved the big gray forward as the encircled attendants fell back.

An appreciative cheer went up from the crowds, and the king waved; then, his mounted aides and standard-bearers drawing in behind him, he commenced his review of the Yeomanry. Eastward he galloped, drew up, pirouetted, saluted the troops with his raised drawn sword. Westward. Eastward again, passing in front of each of the three ranks of horsemen. Three times he cantered the length of the beach, returning their salute.

On horseback, thought Catherine, he did not cut too ill a figure. King, she repeated to herself. King. King King King. Like any word repeated too often, it lost its sense. What had she expected of a king? Of a king of Scotland? This was a modern king. The big gray charger, tired now, pecked in the heavy sand, but quickly recovered, and the king kept his seat. But that was enough galloping about. After a final salute, the equerries closed in, the royal dismount was accomplished, and the king stalked impressively back to his carriage.

"There, you see riding at anchor, just past that stern-wheeler? That is Captain Buchanan's *Die Vernon*, a nice little old-fashioned brig," said Captain Mainwaring, pointing it out to Catherine and Hector as they sailed back toward his *Increase* on a long broad reach, the breeze having come up again from the northeast. "I did expect he'd have sailed for Inverness by now; but your friends here, Mrs MacDonald, are glad to enjoy the pleasure of your company for an additional day or two."

Catherine could only murmur her general appreciation for his kindness; but she wished that Captain Mainwaring would not speak so freely about her private plans, not even here among friends.

"But what is delaying Captain Buchanan?" asked Hector.

There was a moment's blank pause; then Mr Fleming said, "He has been loading a cargo of baled hemp, but at a remarkably sedate pace. I hope he is salting it well, for I have heard it is far from dry. His deliberate speed may have something to do with a certain comfortable widow who lives near Stirling. . . ."

"So is it to be Mrs Colquhoun after all?" said Captain Mainwaring.

Mr Fleming raised his eyebrows meaningfully, but said nothing.

"I daresay that's likely to turn out as profitable as any amount of hemp," said Captain Mainwaring. "And didn't I hear a word or two about some difficulty with his underwriters? I do not think his last survey was just entirely satisfactory, perhaps. And ever since that business with the *Regent*, and all the scandal about fraudulent surveys and repairs, the underwriters have been more troublesome than usual. Now, worse still, we have Parliament sticking its long nose into the business, though they certainly cannot understand it, special committees or not. . . ."

Catherine stopped listening. Everyone knew about the loss of the *Regent*, which had simply fallen apart and sunk off the coast of Mauritius on her way home from India last year despite the warnings of her master, who had disembarked at Ceylon after quarreling with the captain over inadequate repairs. It was not comforting to learn that this Captain Buchanan might be in no hurry to sail; that his cargo was a dangerous one; and his brig perhaps not as sound as she ought to be.

Once aboard *Increase* again, their party went down to the cuddy cabin to dine. Catherine could not help being impressed by the dining table and its accoutrements set out by the steward in their absence. She had not supposed that even a successful merchant captain might own such a quantity of plate! Such excellent glass! Nor had she supposed that it could be kept so bright in a sea air; all was rubbed to a surprising brilliance. She was seated next to Mr Fleming; and ship's boys (rubbed as recently and as vigorously as the spoons, judging by the damp pinkness of their ears and necks) took up their stations behind each chair.

"Allow me to recommend this excellent dish of collops, Mrs MacDonald, and a bit of the walnut pickle," said Mr Fleming. "Venison collops are not often to be met with aboard ship, you may be sure, and must be given a warm welcome. And a few spears of asparagus? Of course. Now, I should very much like to know how your brother became so intimate with the principles of dynamics. Was he always thus, born to it? Or is his genius the result of diligent study?"

"Oh, *genius*! That is a strong word," said Catherine (noting the venison—such a distinctive and nostalgic taste). "*We* never supposed that Hector's devisings and tinkerings amounted to anything like genius. But he has always made a very great nuisance of himself over it. As a lad, he used to dog the blacksmith's every step. Indeed, he begged our father at one time to apprentice him, and it was a hard job to make him understand that it would not do." Catherine glanced at Hector, seated across the table, suspecting that he could hear her; but he betrayed no sign of it, for he was courteously listening to his neighbor Miss Clerk.

"Your father disapproved this pursuit of your brother's?" asked Mr Fleming; and had the midshipman standing behind them fill her wine glass, and his own.

"Oh, it was not disapproval," said Catherine. "It was only that our father feared Hector might burn down the house. Luckily, he never did, although he used to stay up late at night in his bedroom secretly making castings—strictly forbidden, of course. In his grate, you see, he contrived a sort of furnace—aye, four plates of stout sheet iron lined with firebrick. Then, as a great favor, he'd allow us—my brother Sandy and me—to creep in and operate the bellows for him. We learned to raise a superb heat, a white heat, sufficient to melt brass. That is a thrilling sight, Mr Fleming—molten metal, metal actually glowing—in the little crucible which he had from Dugald the blacksmith in exchange, I suspect, for a bottle of our father's good whisky."

"No, not our father's," said Hector, who was listening frankly now; Miss Clerk, too. "It was Sandy who furnished the whisky."

"Mmm, aye! Sandy always knew where to lay a hand upon *that* article," said Catherine. "But as for Hector, the precious commodity was metal, and never easy to get. Whenever a boat was wrecked, our Hector was there to salvage any brass fittings. I believe that considerable quantities of old harness fittings disappeared in the same way."

"Ha ha!" laughed Hector. "Do you remember when old Mrs Scott came to stay?"

"Do I not?" said Catherine. She explained to Mr Fleming and Miss Clerk: "Hector had made off with all the brass pulls from the drawer fronts of the mahogany chest in the best spare bedroom. But no one had noticed until a visitor inquired politely of my mother how to open the drawers."

"I was required to replace them, of course," said Hector. "I had already melted down the metal, to make I do not remember what—"

"My bracelets," said Catherine. "You had made three pretty bangles for me. They were very heavy, and turned my wrist green, but I loved them, and I was loathe to give them back when you wanted, to transform them into drawer pulls again."

"Was that it? I am sorry, my dear. I shall bring you some new gold ones from the Indies. But as for replacing the pulls, I made a new design of my own, and cast them myself, in the form of—what do you think?—not the usual neat gadroon-edged oval with a smooth half oval bale, no, no! *My* back plates were in the shape of a cow's head, horns and all, with the ring in her nose as a bale! And there they remain still, I suppose—my brass cows, staring out with bulging eyes from what had been a very nice new mahogany chest."

"I remember another occasion when a trunk of old military

cornets—riches indeed!—came somehow to hand, quite inexplicable," said Catherine. She raised an eyebrow at Hector in query.

"Am I to explain now, after all these years of discreet silence?" said Hector.

"Why not, after all these years?"

"Well, I will tell you this much: Those, too, came from Sandy. But he never would say how he got them, though I have my suspicions. Those kept me supplied for quite some time."

"Now, this other brother of yours," said Mr Fleming, "has he a talent for engineering as well?"

"Oh, not Sandy," said Hector. "But he did have a talent, undoubtedly, for—what would you call it, Catherine?—a talent for the clandestine. He knew the location of every still in our district, I believe."

"And recruited you to undertake certain repairs from time to time, when a metallurgical expertise was needed?" asked Catherine.

"True enough," Hector admitted. "What else had I to exchange for such desiderata as a trunkful of cornets?"

"So, a marked talent for the clandestine *and* an instinct for commerce, it would seem," observed Mr Fleming. "Such an interesting and valuable combination."

"And a very nice touch with the music, too," said Catherine. "You will grant Sandy that, Hector."

"Oh, aye," agreed Hector, "always on the pipes. While I was dogging the poor old smith for a turn at his forge, Sandy was pestering him about the pipe music. Besides his skill as a metalworker, old Dugald was something of a piper—and our first teacher, Sandy's and mine, of the great music."

"The poor man, plagued by you both!" said Miss Clerk.

"I am deeply indebted to him for his wide knowledge and his vast patience," said Hector. "And to his kind old sister, who fed the three of us many and many a dish of porridge over her smoky kitchen fire."

"She knew the old pipe tunes, too—to sing. She knew them as well as Dugald did, or better," said Catherine. "She'd correct him on the cuttings and the graces—do you recall, Hector? Her voice was old, cracked by age and use, just like her porridge bowls, but she remembered every note. I can sing some of them yet, myself, and they still run through my mind, in her voice, whenever I eat a dish of porridge!"

Catherine's plate was empty, even to the wine-dark venison gravy. How delicious! It had been a long time since Catherine had taken any pleasure in a meal. In anything.

The last dishes were removed and tea was brought in, to be poured at table by Miss Clerk. It was an excellent fragrant tea which lingered on the tongue, served in real china cups not much larger or thicker than eggshells, with *Increase* written on them in a shield-shaped cartouche. "Best chop! Best chop!" cried Captain Mainwaring, somewhat elevated now by his own hospitality. "A gift from the Hoppo of Canton himself!" To Mary, at his left, he continued, "My supply is getting low, however, and we shall have to sail soon, if only to replenish it."

"When do you sail?" asked Mary. "My husband seems unable to give me a definite date."

"Oh, a definite date. *There* is a reasonable request," said Captain Mainwaring. "My cargo is all but complete, though we have yet to finish loading the hides for the ateliers in Antwerp. And my water and stores are nearly complete as well, except for some random bits of cordage and sailcloth. And then I am awaiting the—ah, a-hemmm!—a particular private consignment. My owners and investors have not quite yet hashed out everything among themselves." Here he gave a courteous nod to Mr Clerk (who attempted to appear unconcerned, for his investment in this voyage was to have been private). "But as you ask me for a date—well, within the week, I trust. Within a week, Mrs MacDonald, you shall see the last of your husband—for a while, I mean. For a good long while."

"But I had not known that you sail first to Antwerp," Catherine remarked quietly to Mr Fleming.

"Yes, that is in fact where our voyage begins," said Mr Fleming. "Antwerp is always our port of origin, as, for all commercial purposes we are a Flemish firm. And so is this ship. *Increase* is not British; she is Netherlander, and her papers prove it."

"But why, pray?"

"You may blame the jealousy of the East India Company. As independent merchants based in Flanders, we are at liberty to buy as much tea as we can get in Canton, and bring it to market—in Europe. But if we flew the British flag, we would not be permitted to trade in tea—for that, you know, is the only commodity over which the Honourable Company still retains its old monopoly. And they protect their privilege with great zeal."

"It is wonderful that such vast trouble is taken over bales of dried leaves!"

"Oh, Mrs MacDonald! Bales of dried leaves! Tea is the most important commodity in the world! Not only to Crawford and Fleming, and to the East India Company, but also to the Exchequer of the royal personage who cut so fine a figure on that gray gelding this morning. Three million pounds each year pour into the British Exchequer thanks to China tea; the duty is at ten percent now, you know."

As the party broke up, Catherine found a private moment to say, "Pray, Hector, do not forget my present from the Indies. There is only the one thing I long for, and it is not gold bracelets. You know what it is, and I shall not be satisfied with anything else."

Hector shook his head and closed his eyes for a moment.

"Fare thee well, and come thee safely home again," said Catherine in Gaelic, and kissed him.

Then Mary said, as they parted, "Catherine, I hope you will forgive me for being so silly. My father returned your beautiful shawl yesterday, and although I intended to bring it to you today, I forgot it. I am so sorry, but I will send it at first light tomorrow, so that you shall have it before you sail. He sent you one of the copies made on his looms too, as a token of his gratitude."

Catherine and Grace were carried back to their inn before dusk.

The two shawls arrived as promised early on Saturday morning, just after breakfast. It was wonderful to compare the gossamer Kashmiri original to the weighty Paisley copy. Folded, the Kashmiri shawl made a square hardly heavier or thicker than a good handkerchief; the folded Paisley shawl made a bundle nearly as thick as a folded blanket. Catherine shook them both out and spread them across the bed, side by side. They were the same size, and the Paisley weavers had faithfully copied the intricate swirling pattern; even the colours were a good match. But while the Kashmiri shawl felt as smooth as silk, smoother than her own hair (for the under-hair of the Himalayan goat is fine and straight), the Paisley shawl was only as smooth as the best and finest Scottish wool could be combed and spun. And while the Paisley shawl still smelled faintly of sheep and dye, the Kashmiri shawl smelled of cloves, cardamom pods, and sweet tea. Catherine carefully folded the Kashmiri original and put it in her trunk with the other things Sandy had sent her: the handwritten sheaf of music and the little silver-bound ivory tea caddy. The Paisley shawl she kept out, as more suitable for wear in Scotland.

On Saturday afternoon a message came at last for Catherine and Grace from Captain Buchanan—but still it was not the expected summons, alas! Instead, he informed them, their departure was postponed once again; now he proposed to set sail no later than Monday, without fail.

Grace groaned. None of her usual pastimes retained their charms after so many days confined to so small a room. "Will you read to me?" she asked Catherine, and Catherine, also madly restless and increasingly anxious, read to Grace as much as they could tolerate of *The Life of Washington*. They could not tolerate much: " 'Run to my arms, you dearest boy,' cried his father in transports, 'run to my arms,' " read Catherine. " 'Glad am I, George, that you killed my tree; for you have paid me for it a thousand fold. Such an act of heroism in my son, is more worth than a thousand trees, though blossomed with silver, and their fruits of purest gold.' "

"The gomeril!" interrupted Grace. "I cannot believe he said *that*."

"Nor can I," said Catherine, closing the book with a slap. "If he did, he was a blockhead. And if he did not, it is a lie, and we'll have no more of it."

In bed that night, Grace told Catherine a much-improved version of the tale. In Grace's version, young George was threatened with disinheritance if he did not replace the cherry tree he had destroyed. So he set off on a voyage around the world, and brought back a hundred exotic trees from the Indies: orange, tea, nutmeg, coffee, pineapple, chocolate and ruby trees among them. His father was delighted.

Dismal Sunday passed, somehow. Monday dawned at last. Catherine and Grace waited in readiness for their summons to go aboard *Die Vernon*. Catherine observed the wind: southwest. She inquired about the tides: nothing extraordinary; an ebb beginning at about eight in the evening. Probably they would sail on that. She considered sending a message to Captain Buchanan; but what would it say? She decided not to bother him, and waited, impatiently.

No message came. Dinner came instead, brought up by the little blond maid, who was looking pale and wan, not her usual brisk self. Robbed of appetite by their restlessness, they ate anyway out of duty. Usually the serving maid came back promptly to clear up, but now the cold greasy plates remained on the table for a long time, and no one came. Some sort of fuss was kicking up down by the waterfront; Catherine heard voices hallooing and shouting, a bell clanging somewhere, and then groups of men went hastening down the street under her window toward the docks. When she noticed a column of smoke rising some distance out, and blowing off toward the hills of Fife, she concluded that something had caught fire. There was a great deal of roaring and shouting in the distance, and poppings like firecrackers, but Catherine's narrow slice of the view between buildings did not show her what the disturbance was about.

Evening drew on, and shadows gathered. Catherine was sitting near the window for the last of the light when finally there came a tap at the door. It was a serving maid come at last to clear up. It was not the little blond girl, and Catherine looked again more sharply as the maid pulled her plain shawl back from her dark sleek head. "Mrs MacDonald," said the gypsy-like foreigner in the voice and accent that Catherine had heard before. "Ma'am, the ship *Die Vernon* has burnt down to the water."

# 6

## *the most bungling Excecution*

"You! Who *are* you?" cried Catherine. "How did you find me here?"

"I am serving here, at this very good inn favored by the ship captains," said the Indian woman. She nodded to silent Grace, curled in her chair. "They are giving me a bed in the attic, with the other maids, and I am helping with the work of serving. It is a temporary arrangement only. When the king is going away, the town will become empty again. Soon I will be finding a place as a ladies' maid, and a passage back to my own country. Very soon, I think. How very surprised was I that you yourself, ma'am, were taking rooms here."

"Who are you? Won't you tell me your name this time?"

"I suppose there is no harm. My name is Sharada Swarnokar."

"It is an Indian name?"

"Oh, yes. I was born in the holy and famous city of Benares, on the bank of the Ganges River."

"My brother is bound for India."

"Yes, ma'am. Unhappily he is not needing a ladies' maid, I think."

"Quite. I, on the other hand, do need a ladies' maid. But I am not going to India." There was a silence while they both considered the inconvenient symmetry of these facts. "Why did you tell me just now of the burning of the *Die Vernon*?" asked Catherine. "Why do you suppose it is of any importance to us?"

"All the servants in the kitchen are knowing that you and this child were to be sailing for Inverness on the *Die Vernon*," said the maid as she gathered up the greasy dishes and piled them on her tray. She had shapely brown arms, and a long curving column of a neck, but Catherine could see white and pink scars puckering the tender skin on the inside of her arms. The scars ran up under her loose sleeves. She was young, probably younger than Catherine. "The Captain Mainwaring's steward was speaking of this when his master went away and gave these rooms to you," she said.

Catherine turned, annoyed. Had Captain Mainwaring and his steward nothing better to do than rattle on about her private affairs? But the harm, if it was harm, was already done, she reflected. "Well, then, Grace, my dear," Catherine mused quietly, "what are we to do now? I suppose we must find another ship bound for Inverness."

"Excuse me, ma'am," said the maid, her back pressed against the door. She was poised to push it open and take out the heavy tray of soiled dishes. "Excuse me for speaking, ma'am. But permit me to say this: Inverness is not your true destination. You will not go to Inverness."

It was quite true that Skye, not Inverness, was Catherine's eventual destination; but who knew that? "What do they say in the kitchen?" said Catherine drily. "Have you seers there? Perhaps one of them would be so good as to advise me and my daughter. It would save us a vast deal of trouble in making our own arrangements."

"Oh, no, in the kitchen they are supposing it is Inverness. Only I am supposing a different place, but I am saying nothing. Only I am thinking that you will go on a ship that is sailing to India, ma'am, to India. And I am thinking I will go on that ship with you." With that, the woman backed out the door with her laden tray, and was gone.

"Rude gypsy nonsense!" said Catherine, trying for a breezy note of dismissal, and not succeeding. She took several turns across the room and back again, agitated. Uncanny, that foreign woman's habit of suddenly appearing with predictions and dismaying warnings. The room was so very small—only two paces across. It was difficult to calm oneself here, difficult even to draw a deep breath. But when she saw that Grace was studiously avoiding any notice of her, Catherine made a great effort to settle herself. From her trunk she extricated her writing paper, pen, and ink, and sent a message to Captain Mainwaring, begging once again for his kind help in finding them another passage to Inverness.

"Inverness be confounded, begging your pardon, Mrs MacDonald. Why not sail with us instead, just as far as Antwerp?" said Captain Mainwaring to Catherine early on Tuesday morning, having downed his coffee in three gulps while standing. He had declined to sit down, though Grace's usual chair was empty, for she had fled to the bedchamber when he came in. "You would be quite safe in Antwerp, and perfectly comfortable. You would be there in three or four days—so much quicker and easier than making your way out to the western isles. You could have the apartments above the Crawford and Fleming warehouses, you and the wee lass. That is, I daresay Mr Fleming would have no objection. There are a great many Scots in Antwerp—quite likely you have acquaintance there already—and most of those Netherlanders speak French or even English, so you would have no difficulties with that. And it's such an economical place; one can live comfortably there in a quiet way at very little expense. Your return would be perfectly easy, too, once your affairs had arranged themselves in a more satisfactory train."

"As a plan, it seems to have a great deal to recommend it," conceded Catherine. "And you really know of no ships at all due to sail for Inverness just now?"

"Nothing that sails before I do, Thursday morning. You might have to wait about for some time. Poor Buchanan! Hemp, ship, and all—up in smoke! And just when things were going so well with the widow. I doubt she'll have him now. Well! You shall have the big cabin next to your brother. You'll find it quite commodious for just the lass and yourself. And a maid?"

"No. No maid," said Catherine decidedly. "It will be better to hire a maid in Antwerp, I think."

"Quite. Your trunks are here, I see. My steward is below; I shall have him convey them aboard directly. Then you and the lassie must board tomorrow evening, so as to be ready for the morning ebb. I shall send my skiff for you at the pier at nine o'clock sharp; that should be dark enough. What a surprise for your brother! We are loading our last consignment tonight and tomorrow—last but not least. Just a whisper in your ear: steam looms! Half a dozen of the newest and best design.

Your brother knows all about it. Very much in demand in Liège, you know, for nothing equals the Scottish machines. So shortsighted of the Netherlanders to try to ban them; you'd think they'd be happy to get them. Well, well, I know who will be happy to get them. But hush, not a word, and I'm sure you are discretion itself."

So the decision was made: Antwerp, not Inverness.

Aboard a ship that is sailing to India.

The trunks were carried down and put in charge of the steward; the passage money was paid; and Catherine promised to be at the pier with Grace at nine o'clock on Wednesday evening.

"One last question," said Catherine. "Do you know where I might send to Captain Buchanan?"

Captain Mainwaring did not, but he promised to inquire as he went about his business, and to let Catherine know whether he learned anything.

Catherine's supply of ready money had seemed sufficient for going to Inverness and then to Skye; and replenishing her purse from anywhere in Scotland would have been easy enough. But that same sum might not go far in Antwerp, for the captain's idea of economical living might not coincide with her own. And there might be difficulties and delays if she were to draw upon her bankers from abroad. The money she had sacrificed for two places in the Glasgow coach was gone, the price of laying a false trail. But the sum she had advanced for their passage to Inverness aboard the *Die Vernon* might perhaps be recovered. She did not like to dun a man just laid low by misfortune, but she felt obliged under the circumstances to make the attempt.

That evening, Catherine received Captain Mainwaring's note: Captain Buchanan was probably to be found at the small and inexpensive Red Bull Inn, which stood a mile or two westward along the road toward Queensferry. Promptly Catherine sent a messenger there, with a tactful note requesting that her passage money be refunded to her. It was nearly midnight when the messenger returned to report his unsuccess. He had found the Red Bull Inn, and he had found Captain Buchanan. But nothing that he or the innkeeper could do would rouse the unfortunate man from his profoundly unconscious state. The messenger had left her letter in care of the innkeeper until Captain Buchanan might be in a condition to read it.

Early on Wednesday morning, Catherine thought it best to send to her bankers. It was not until noon that she had a reply from them; or rather from their clerk, who politely advised her that both partners were gone to Newbattle Abbey for a glimpse of the king. But they would be sure to give her draft their immediate attention on the next morning.

That would be Thursday morning—too late.

Time was running short. Catherine considered what she ought to do. Could she count on Hector to have provided himself with funds, on the eve of his departure, sufficient to cover her expenses too, until she could instruct her bankers to reimburse him, wherever he might be? Perhaps. But it was presumptuous; and she did not like the idea. Hadn't she better try Captain Buchanan again? She sent downstairs for a messenger. But not even a boy could be spared, it seemed, until six o'clock at the earliest. What now? She was herself able-bodied; why not go to Captain Buchanan herself? It would not be pleasant, of course. Even if he could now be awakened, he might still be drunk. And there was Grace's safety to be considered. Catherine did not like to leave Grace alone; nor did she like to take Grace out in the town, where she might encounter Miss Johnstone's writs and bailiffs and ruffians.

Was it impossible, then? She was tempted to give up and rely on Hector for funds; then she scolded herself for weak-mindedness. Firmness, she told herself: Resolve. "Come, Grace," she said briskly. "Put on your jacket and your bonnet, and I will lend you a veil. We must go out."

"But I haven't got them," said Grace. "They are in the trunk that was taken away to the ship."

"What! Your jacket and your bonnet? Didn't you keep them out, to wear? What did you expect to wear?"

"I forgot. I didn't think I would need them."

Catherine sighed with exasperation, knowing that it was her own oversight; Grace was only a child.

"I'll stay here," said Grace. "I'll keep the door locked."

Catherine took two turns about the room, considering this. At last she said, "Don't you show even so much as one eyelash outside this room, not for any reason whatever. Do I make myself clear?"

"Not even if the place is burning down?"

Catherine glowered at her.

"I promise to stay inside, snug and safe as a little lamb in the fold, and the door bolted. I'm not a baby, Catriona."

"Expect me back within two hours. And don't call me Catriona." Then Catherine veiled herself closely, wrapped her warm Paisley shawl about her arms and shoulders; and went out into the windy late afternoon.

Catherine walked westward along the waterfront. With some distance to cover, she strode along briskly. She had always enjoyed walking, and the narrow confinement of the last week had been a hardship for her. As she moved along, she felt her mood lighten, her anxieties fall away. Yes, why not Antwerp? It was a good plan. And it would be charming to astound Hector. But perhaps Captain Mainwaring had already told Hector; he was startlingly ready at telling news that might better have remained untold. Nevertheless he was kind, always helpful, generous with his time and advice. His generosity, it seemed, could be relied upon; only his discretion was uncertain.

The water sparkled at her right hand, teeming with boats and barges, skiffs and launches; the busy town hummed to her left. The late-afternoon sun was still high, but the brim of her bonnet and her dense veil shaded her face. People glanced at her as she passed; veiled, she could look at them, too. She felt deeply relieved at being out and moving—and poised, finally, to leave Edinburgh.

Half an hour's walking brought her to the Red Bull Inn, where she inquired for Captain Buchanan. The innkeeper and his strapping wife exchanged a look laden with meaning. "I'll go and see," said the wife, and disappeared up the creaking wooden stairs. Catherine could hear her heavy tread overhead. Gratefully Catherine sat down and accepted a glass of buttermilk offered by the innkeeper. Her fashionable little pumps had thin soles and a remarkably elegant-shaped toe—too elegant for long-distance walking. She thought of her old childhood boots, thick and sturdy, so well suited to long tramps over hills, rocks and bogs. For a long time she waited. There were creakings on the stairs, and groanings of floorboards above, doors slammed, and loud voices. Eventually the landlady returned. "Well, he'll do now, I trust," she said. "Follow me, ma'am, if you please." And she led the way up to Captain Buchanan's sitting room.

The room and the man had the look of having just been put to rights. The windows were open wide, and a fine breeze off the water was doing its best to remove an unpleasant fuggy miasma made up of alcohol, sweat, smoke, and perhaps vomit. The man was newly but badly shaved, and miserably pale, his skin dull and chalky. He turned toward her eagerly as she entered; then disappointment spread over his face.

"I beg your pardon, Captain Buchanan, for intruding at a time of misfortune," said Catherine, having prepared these opening words. "I am Mrs MacDonald, Mrs Catherine MacDonald. My daughter and I were to have sailed with you to Inverness—by arrangement of Captain Mainwaring," she added, for his expression was vague and distant, as though he did not understand her. She waited, but he said nothing; he only swayed a little on his feet, and she wondered whether he were still very drunk.

"*Ochone*, *ochone*," he moaned, and collapsed onto a wooden chair, his face in his hands.

"Are you quite alright?" she said after a moment. There was no reply. She poured a glass of water from a pitcher and put it into his hands. After a moment he drank down the entire glass, and with another heavy sigh he said, "I had supposed—hoped—for a moment that you were someone else. Another person." There was something like a groan. Then he made an effort at self-command, and continued, "I fear I have no choice but to disappoint you and your daughter."

"Pray do not concern yourself with us, for we have arranged another passage. I am only here, Captain Buchanan, to ask you for the return of the passage money I had advanced. I find it is a matter of some consequence to me, or I would never think of dunning you at so unfortunate a time."

He composed himself with a noble effort. "Here is my purse," he said with a tragic air. "It is all that remains to me. You shall have it." He pressed the slack thing into her hand, and she felt that it contained very little—certainly not enough to relieve her difficulties. She would have to rely on Hector after all.

"No, no," she said, instantly giving it back. "Only when you have managed to settle with your underwriters, and received your insurance settlement—when it is convenient to you, you understand, I should be glad for the return of the sum I advanced, and I wished only to let you know where to send it."

"Insurance!" he said, running his hands through his hair and disarranging it comically. "Underwriters! Oh, I am ruined!"

A rap sounded at the door, and without waiting for a reply the innkeeper's wife opened it wide. "Mrs Colquhoun calling for Captain Buchanan," she announced, more loudly than necessary, and stepped aside to make way for the lady herself. The lady herself was well dressed and remarkably buxom; indeed, she had a snugly upholstered appearance. Composed on her face was a soft expression of feminine compassion; but this dissolved as she caught sight of Catherine.

"My angel!" cried the captain.

"Who is that?" said Mrs Colquhoun, scowling at Catherine.

"Who? Oh, this good lady? This is Mrs—Mrs . . ."

"MacDonald," said Catherine. "I have come to let Captain Buchanan know where he might send me the passage money I had advanced to him for myself and my daughter. As soon as he should find it convenient."

"Oh! How much was it?" said Mrs Colquhoun in a sharp businesslike tone.

Catherine named the sum.

"I believe I happen to have so much as that about me," said the widow, and extricated her own purse, much fatter than Captain Buchanan's.

"Oh, no, I couldn't," said Catherine.

"But of course you could, Mrs MacDonald," said Mrs Colquhoun, and pressed the money into Catherine's hand. "It is why you came here, or so you have just told me. Unless there is something else here that you wanted?"

"No, indeed, nothing of any interest to me, Mrs Colquhoun," said Catherine as meaningfully as she knew how.

"Angel of compassion, angel of generosity!" cried Captain Buchanan.

"Good-bye, then, and good luck to you, sir," said Catherine to the captain. And nodding courteously to the newcomer, she got herself out of the room. As she turned the corner at the top of the stairs, she heard Mrs Colquhoun say, "What in the world have you done to your hair, Charles?"

Not until she was down the stairs, out the front door, and into the street did Catherine laugh. The captain was probably not quite ruined after all, in the monetary sense—but there were other forms of ruin. And her own financial state was somewhat improved.

On the long walk back to Leith, Catherine came to regret her shoes, and to envy the children, workmen, and fishwives, all so comfortably barefoot. She longed to remove the smart little slippers which pinched her toes fiercely and had already raised a blister on one heel, but she could not bring herself to do it now, in town, and dressed as she was. Instead she walked quickly, so as to get back before her fortitude broke down. She consoled herself with the thought that by tomorrow she would be at her ease, aboard *Increase*. Now, with the sun quite low at her back, the water on her left hand and the town at her right, the scene was even more picturesque than before. As she drew near again to the town of Leith proper, she could make out the royal flotilla at anchor some distance out. A great deal of activity surrounded it, with supply boats pulled up in its lee, and the usual sightseeing craft circling at an interval that was more curious than respectful because His Majesty was known to be ashore.

Somewhere ahead of her were shouts, a rumbling crash, then the clatter of hoofbeats, the hoofbeats of iron-shod horses at a gallop over uneven stone pavement. There was another crash, but she could hear the galloping horses coming nearer, nearer and faster. Quickly she looked about, then jumped up to the top step of the stairs she was just passing and pressed herself against the padlocked wooden door of the stone building behind her. Just then a hack chaise with its blinds closed came careening around the corner, skidding wildly on its high narrow wheels from one curb to the opposite one. Then the chaise was away, with the wide leather straps that should have been holding on the luggage behind snapping and flapping loose like the lashes of whips. She watched the carriage fling wildly around the next turn, the iron-faced wheel rims screeching against the granite curbstones, and then it was gone. The people in the street raised their eyebrows and shook their heads at one another in a disapproving way; reckless! someone could have been killed!

Catherine had gone only a little further when she came to a knot of people in the street surrounding something, their backs blocking her view. She made her way through a gap, and craned on tiptoe to see what it was: a trunk, a traveler's trunk much like her own. It had burst open, and all the clothes and parcels inside had exploded across the width of the street. It was a lady's trunk; there were dresses, gowns, skirts, little jackets and shawls, bonnets and shoes, most in hues of ivory, and cream, with some in lavender and black. A bonnet with its own gray veil sewn on. A little lilac-sprigged muslin jacket with a pressed ruffle at the neck. There was a Spanish shawl with brilliant embroidered flowers and foliage on black silk edged by a deep fringe, now irrevocably tangled. A handsome jolly young fisherwife picked up the shawl and draped it across her own broad shoulders; her friends laughed in appreciation. She gave them a deep and affected curtsy, then danced a few steps, gypsy style. A boy snatched up the veiled bonnet and jammed it onto the red head of his little brother, who seized it, wrenching it off as a pollution and an insult, and threw it into a nearby barrel of mackerel.

A chilly heat prickled up Catherine's spine and settled at the back of her neck. She extricated herself from the rowdy, still-gathering crowd and set off, much faster now, toward the heart of Leith. She stopped a moment, took off her elegant little shoes, and, clutching them in one hand, set off again at a round barefoot trot.

From the town center someone was running, running in her direction, coming on very fast. A black-haired woman, young, light, fleet: the Indian maidservant Sharada, her long black plait flying behind her. Panting, gasping, she seized Catherine's two hands. "It was Miss Johnstone, Miss Johnstone, the American woman. She has taken your little girl in a carriage; it is going out this road. I could not stop them. I succeeded in slashing the straps, the straps of the carriage, but they were the wrong straps, and they were driving away so very fast, I could not stop them."

Staggering! The maid steadied her, still holding her hands, holding her up as the sickening truth impaled Catherine's heart. Grace, my Grace! My dearest Grace! It is all my own fault. I ought never to have left you, not for a moment. I knew I ought not to leave you alone, not for a purseful of money; not for a king's ransom.

But Catherine mastered herself after a moment. "Will you go to my brother?" she choked out, hoarse. "You will? Bless you. Tell him they have gone out westward toward Queensferry. I must try to follow them, try to catch up with them—at least I must not lose their trail. My brother Hector MacDonald! It is number twelve East Thistle Street. Of course you know that. Thank you! Bless you!" she called after Sharada, who was already away, dashing toward the center of the city.

Catherine looked wildly about; how was she to pursue them? To run after them on foot was out of the question. She might easily hire a hack chaise, or perhaps even a saddle horse if she ran back to her inn; but she could not bear to lose so much time in going the wrong direction. Was there a nearer inn? Could Captain Buchanan's inn provide her a horse or a conveyance? She remembered there was a small yard behind, but she had not noticed any horses or carriages. There must have been; surely there must. She set off again at a run, retracing her steps. If not there, then somewhere; somewhere she would find a conveyance.

She had already repassed the split trunk—now dragged to one side of the narrow street, and most of the finery already vanished—when she was overtaken by a poulterer's wagon moving along at a smart clip. "Whither away so quick?" called out the poulterer, courteously enough considering that she was barefoot and running, nothing ladylike or dignified about her except her shawl. And just now everyone in the vicinity was wearing incongruous finery, regardless of degree. Catherine was so winded that she could not answer. "Leap up then!" he said cheerfully, and, leaning back, sawing on the reins, he brought his horse to a momentary standstill. He reached down, seized her up-reaching hand, and heaved her onto the rough board that served as a seat.

The wagon was stacked three high with poultry crates of woven withies, all streaked with white and gray dung, and garnished with dingy feathers, and each containing its anxious beady-eyed turkey. Catherine sat down with a heavy bump as the horse plunged forward again. "Running fit to burst, weren't you?" remarked the friendly poulterer as he touched up the horse with his whip. In Catherine's opinion the horse really did not need any touching up; he was already nervous and Catherine, noting his twitching flattened ears and the irritable toss of his head, thought he appeared to be upon the point of bolting. The poultry crates behind made an unholy clatter and rattle, and there was something in the front axle crying out for a good dose of grease. "The extra weight's a good thing," said the poulterer. "It should settle him down a bit, especially when we come to the hill. He's new at this. And then, that collar might be galling him. My last horse was not so high in the withers."

I will fetch you back from the ends of the earth, my darling; I never will give you up, Catherine silently promised Grace, wherever she was. But to the poulterer she said aloud, "What happened to the last horse?" Her breath was coming back now, and she slipped her red throbbing feet back into her shoes.

"Foundered at last, poor creature," replied the poulterer. "Foundered, and the bone inside the hoof piercing down through the sole of it. But you needn't founder yourself, luckie. They will not be coming back to reclaim their gear, not they. You may be sure of keeping your prize. That is a handsome shawl, and hardly worn at all, is it? I picked up quite a new-looking bonnet for my wife, but I'm no judge of the fashions. There it is behind us; are you any judge of a bonnet yourself?"

"Oh, I think it is a smart one, quite the newest and best thing," said Catherine, peering back over her shoulder (and thinking of Grace's bonnet and jacket, put away by mistake too soon, inside a trunk now aboard *Increase*). This bonnet, however, was tucked down between two dung-streaked crates, and its gauzy gray veils fluttered behind like kite tails.

"I plucked it from a barrel of mackerel, and it might have just a bit of that smell. A good airing should render it fresh enough. My good wife has a taste for finery, which I did not know when I married her. And where are you bound? Where am I to drop you?"

"I had hoped to hire a horse or a chaise at the Red Bull . . ."

"A vain hope, luckie, they have no such thing. We are just for passing them, you see, and not a horse have they had these two years. I am bound for Hopetoun House myself, two miles past Queensferry. These turkeys behind you have a high and worthy destiny; they are meant for the king's breakfast at Hopetoun House. Yes, indeed! Did you not know? I wonder that anyone in Edinburgh cannot have heard. The king's last meal on Scottish soil will be at the Earl of Hopetoun's mansion tomorrow morning, and His Majesty's yacht is to be brought up overnight, for His Majesty will embark from there. Wait till you see how they've repaired the road, these last four days! Two thousand guests for breakfast! And my turkeys just ordered now, at the last possible minute, in case there should not be enough food else. That's a night's worth of cleaning and plucking. Shall I put you down at Queensferry? You should have a pretty choice of horses and chaises there. . . . Not at all; it is quite in my way, and I am glad to have the weight. The iron-jawed brute!"

ശശശ

ROWED IN TO the pier by *Increase*'s sailors finally at six o'clock in the evening, Hector noticed that the wind had changed again. Out of the east now, it promised rain, and soon. He was glad that the difficulties of the day were over. His trunk was now in his cabin; and by faithfully promising to come aboard at four the next morning, at first light and before the ebb would begin, he had persuaded Captain Mainwaring to let him sleep at home this very last night. One last night to spend in his own house, eating supper at his own table, sleeping in his own bed with his own dear wife.

But as he stepped neatly from boat to pier, cherishing these warm domestic ambitions, he was unpleasantly startled—accosted!—by this gypsy, this mysterious foreigner—this uncanny Indian woman—again! She related his sister's message—and his fond plan lay in ruins. "The Queensferry road?" said Hector. "How long ago? So long as that? We'll never catch them on land. A launch is the only thing, a crack steam launch. How the devil did my sister come to leave her alone? So careless! Here, lad; find me Captain Keith, tell him I need his *Dram Shell* directly, instantly, or I shall go aboard myself in two minutes and cast off without him! Thank providence for a tailwind when we need it, for once."

The hybrid sail-and-steam launch *Dram Shell* was moored just a few hundred yards out. Captain Keith and his crew of two, in their usual public house at the end of the pier, came immediately.

"Certainly not," Hector said to the foreign woman as one of the men untied the skiff that would take them out to where *Dram Shell* was moored in the deep water. "There is not the slightest reason for you to come any further. Here is something for your trouble and your great effort. I am grateful to you beyond words, but you certainly must not come any further."

But she pushed away the money. Though he tried again to press it into her palm, she would not take it. "It is all I have just now," he said, supposing that she objected to the smallness of the amount.

"I do not want money. I will not take it. I will come on the steamboat. I will, indeed, Mr MacDonald. Your sister will need me when we are overtaking them, your sister and the mute child also. I am coming with you." Without waiting for an answer or any assistance, she jumped into the skiff and seated herself on the thwart. Hector and Captain Keith exchanged looks, then Hector shrugged. Her manner was certainly very assured; she had remarkable self-assurance for a servant; but foreigners were so often unaccountable. "Suit yourself," he said. "I have no time to argue with you."

So the foreign woman came too.

*Dram Shell*'s coal hopper was full and her boiler was still hot, for she had just come in. Within a quarter of an hour, the little steamboat was under way again, fueled by coal, a large jug of ale, a small bottle of whisky, and the promise of a generous tip if they should catch their quarry. Captain Keith was happy to undertake a chase.

They were running nearly straight downwind, so the crewmen raised a lateen and a genoa, and set them out wing and wing for all possible speed. The shore darkened, and lights twinkled in the dusk. A crewman lit a lantern and hung it on a spreader. They passed near several boats laboriously beating their way up against the wind and, to the delight of Hector and Captain Keith, easily overtook three fishermen running downwind like themselves. The two men stood in the cockpit, feet braced wide apart, and admired the frothy wake streaming out behind them in the black water. The foreign woman huddled in the lee of the hot boiler, for her thin cotton shawl was no hindrance to a wind sweeping across a hundred miles of cold northern sea.

"You must be very cold, miss. Pray let me offer you this jacket," said Hector, coming up through the dusk after a while. "Though it is old, it is quite clean, and it will keep you warm."

"Thank you, Mr MacDonald. I do not mind its being old." The

woolen seaman's jacket was so shrunken by repeated wettings and dryings that it was nearly impervious to the wind. Gradually her shivering lessened.

Hector sat down near her; he held his hands out to the boiler and rubbed them together. "Pray tell me, Miss—Miss, ah . . ."

"Swarnokar. In English it is 'goldsmith.' "

"How does it happen, Miss Swarnokar, that you figure once again in my sister's affairs? That you act as my sister's messenger in this catastrophe?"

"Only that I was there, you see—"

"Where?"

"At the inn at Leith, sir, where your sister has rooms. I am in service at that inn, a temporary arrangement only."

"What an astonishing coincidence that of all the inns in the city, you should be in service at the very one where my sister had found rooms."

"Oh, not astonishing, sir. Is not that inn favored by all the sea captains? The Captain Dale, of the ship which brought me here, kindly sent me to that inn with his good word, knowing that I had somehow to keep myself until I could find a place with a lady going to India. My own lady had died on the voyage here, you see. Poor Mrs Guthrie, and her infant, too! She had such longing to see Scotland again, but her fate was not so kind. Thus I arrived here without place and without money, but upon Captain Dale's kind word, the innkeeper has given me a bed among the maids."

It was plausible, Hector thought—astonishing but plausible. His next question was this: "How could such a thing take place, this bold abduction of my niece in the broad day, and from a respectable inn? Were you there yourself when it happened?"

"Oh, yes, sir, I was in the next room. I saw it, but I was powerless to stop it, though I tried my best."

"Be so good as to tell me just what happened."

"Yes, sir, I am telling you. I was cleaning the next room, for the men there had just gone away and I must air the room and clean the ashes from the fireplace, and put fresh linen to the beds. First I was opening the window to let in the fresh air, and seeing a carriage halting in the street below. So curious, for usually, you see, the carriages are driving directly into the stableyard behind. The inn's boy came running out to stand at the horses' heads as his duty requires, but the driver chased him off with rude words, and instead a man who was standing nearby came to hold their heads, and this the driver permitted. So very odd it was seeming to me. No one got out of the carriage, nor got in, and that was seeming curious also, and therefore I was lingering at the window a moment. Just then I heard the door to the next room crash against the wall dividing the rooms, and I was startled, for I knew that your sister was gone out and the mute girl was in the room alone. I looked into the passage, just a narrow crack—like this—to see. And a man went running, and down the stair, carrying the child, all wrapped in the bedcover—quite wrapped, head and all, and unable to move except for kicking, nor did she cry out. In an instant I went running down after him, but he was so very quick, and everyone was unprepared. No one hampered him at all, and I saw him thrusting the girl inside the carriage. I ran up to it, but the door was quickly shut and latched from the inside. I seized the handle, and it would not open, although I was having a glimpse through the glass of the faces inside."

"And you recognised these faces?"

"Yes, oh, yes. It was Miss Johnstone, and her servant with her, who is my friend."

"Then they drove off?"

"Yes, the driver laid his whip to the horses, and the man holding their heads jumping quickly aside and running away. I had got my knife in my hand, so that I might slash the straps that hold up the carriage, for that is how the bandits in my country cripple the carriages of rich travelers sometimes. But your carriages are built differently, I think, for the straps at the back of the carriage, which I succeeded in slashing, were serving only to hold the trunk."

"And you saw them take the turn to the Queensferry road?"

"I ran after, and it was easy to see where it had passed, for people were shaking their heads and looking after it, and then there was the trunk fallen to the pavement and split open. When I came upon your sister, she sent me to seek you, while she herself went to pursue them directly."

"And how did you know where to find me?"

"I was running first to your house in East Thistle Street, where your kind wife gave me a strong drink to restore me; and she told me that you were perhaps at one place, or perhaps at another, or perhaps most likely near the ships upon the water, where I was finding you at last by greatest good luck."

Greatest good luck indeed. "Aye, thank you. That is an admirably clear account." Hector pondered in silence for a few minutes.

"How does this boat go?" asked the foreigner presently. "I see it is having sails; and having also a steam engine, but no paddles, neither at the stern nor at the sides."

"Quite. It is my own design. Instead of the usual paddle wheel, it has a device which I call a rotary oar. It resembles the screw in an Archimedean water pump, which draws up water from a ditch, you know," explained Hector, making rotary motions with his arms. "This rotary oar is entirely submerged, mounted horizontally under the surface of the water at the bow. It bites into the water, you see, and draws us forward through the water, just as a wood screw bites into a plank of wood, and draws itself into the wood. The steam engine, here, powers this piston, and the piston's motion is transformed to a rotary motion by this crank. The crankshaft's rate of rotation is increased by these gears, and this long rotating shaft, which passes through the hull there, on bearings, through a watertight gasket—well, nearly watertight—has mounted at its tip the rotary oar."

"So very ingenious," she said. "And it is your own invention?"

"Oh, many men have proposed, and even contrived, similar devices—Mr Brunel, Mr Fulton, Colonel Stevens in America, and perhaps others. But this particular design, with the rotary oar driven by steam power, is my own. Have you never been aboard a steamboat?"

"Oh, yes, but I have indeed, at home in India. The Nawab of Oudh has a steamboat which an Englishman made for him, and I have been on that boat, on the river below the palace at Lucknow. But that steamboat is having a paddle wheel."

"Aye, that has been the usual arrangement until now. Yet paddles have their drawbacks. Oh, yes—considerable drawbacks." He hesitated a moment, but this foreign woman looked so intelligent and so interested; and, after all, the subject *was* so intrinsically interesting! He plunged ahead: "The paddle structures themselves are very large, heavy and unwieldy; excessively vulnerable to enemy gunfire. And only a small proportion of the paddle structure is in the water—and therefore driving the craft—at any given time, while the large surface area above the water presents far too much area to the wind. If the ship should be heeled hard over, or pitching fore and aft, paddles may be alternately immersed too deeply or else lifted out of the water altogether, causing loss of power and of control. And then side-wheelers are so wide, which is a drawback for canal work. My submerged rotary oar suffers from none of these disadvantages."

"This boat is very fast," she said. "No doubt we shall be overtaking them."

Hector was suddenly recalled to a sense of his mission. "If only we could guess just where they were headed," he said.

"Oh, to America, certainly," she said.

# 7

## *Runnings, Variations, Allegro*

"The inn here at the pier would suit me best," said Catherine to the poulterer. "It is the Hawes Inn, I think. Yes, and thank you for the lift!" she called after him as the wagon drove off into the dusk, the horse now wringing wet but still nervous and pulling hard.

The main part of the town of Queensferry was a little further along to the west, but this inn lay near the pier where travelers boarded the ferry which ran to and fro across the Firth of Forth. Catherine doubted that Miss Johnstone would run away northward, across the Forth, but she could not pass without making sure. If the chaise had not crossed on the ferry, she could feel quite certain that they had continued westward on the road. In either case, she should be able to hire a horse here.

She hastened through the carriage gate, which opened into the cobbled stableyard behind the inn. There in the lamplight were two men tending to an unwilling horse. The taller of the two had the horse's tender upper lip secured by a twisted loop of chain on the end of a stick. He also had a tight hold of one ear, so that the threat of pain held the horse more or less immobilized. The other man, muscular but shorter, had one of the horse's hind legs pulled up and back. The man was bent over the upturned sole of the hoof, carving at it with a long curved knife.

Catherine checked herself, not wanting to interrupt so delicate an operation. Just then the horse plunged forward, dragging the taller man and knocking down the muscular one. The taller man held on, however, and brought the horse to a standstill again while the smaller one picked himself up, grabbed his knife, and kicked the trembling horse twice in the belly while uttering an oath. Then he lifted the hind foot and set to work on it again with the knife. "There!" he cried after a moment. The horse lurched and hopped, but the two men kept hold of him. "That's a nasty one. Oh, the stink! How long has he been lame on it then?"

"Oh, on and off, on and off, I could not say. Is it an abcess after all?"

"It is—a big one, full of rot and pus. Ye'll have to keep it packed with moss—or a turpentine dressing if ye've got it—until it heals."

"There's a whiff of it. Eeeuch! He can't work, I suppose."

"Impossible."

"Well, it's the knackers then. This is no hospital."

"Do I clean it and pack it or not?" said the strongly built little man irritably, holding up the hind hoof.

"Oh, go ahead then. They can decide in the morning. There aren't so many others sound just now."

The strongly built man called for a boy, who brought wads of dried moss, a bucket of turpentine, and cloths for a dressing. The man set to work again on the hoof with the knife, carving away slices of the infected tissue. Now that the abcess was open and draining, its painful pressure relieved, the horse balanced stoically on his three remaining legs with his head drooping, flinching only occasionally. The man at his head released the twisted ear. Deftly the other man packed the cavity with turpentine-soaked wads of moss. Then he ordered the boy to tear the cloth into long, wide strips, which he used to wrap the entire foot, around and around, over and under. Finally he set the big cloth-wrapped foot gently on the cobbled floor of the yard, and the horse gingerly tried a little weight on it. Straightening up slowly, the man stretched to ease his cramped back, and caught sight of Catherine at the gate.

"Where did that cloth come from?" she demanded, pointing at the horse's hoof, newly wrapped in strips of bright mustard and turkey red chintz.

The two men looked blank; it was the boy who answered. "The chaise that came through just now—they threw this cloth out in the yard and left it behind—an old bedcover rent in pieces and spoiled.

They had lost their trunks off the back, too, and hadn't even noticed until I remarked on it."

"How long ago?"

"Not much more than the quarter of an hour, I make it."

"Did you see who was in the chaise?"

"Womenfolk, I think. With a black African servant. But they never stepped out. And they had a hired driver, not postilions."

"Where were they going? Did they say?"

"Grangemouth, it was."

"At the terminus of the Forth and Clyde Canal?"

"Just so. They'll have missed the night boat across to Glasgow, and so I told the foreign lady when she inquired, for she was in a terrible haste; but she might surely hire a private boat, if she is willing to pay enough for it, and so I told her. 'Ask for Captain Curry,' I told her, 'Captain Robert Curry or his son John if old Captain Curry is out, for their boats are always ready at a moment's notice for the convenience of private travelers.' So I told her."

"How far to Grangemouth?"

"Just eleven miles precisely from this very yard."

"Well, then, I want your fastest conveyance, as quick as you can, to take me there," said Catherine, and she pressed a coin into the boy's palm for being both observant and informative.

But there was no conveyance to be had. The last sound horse had just gone out with that very carriage full of luggageless womenfolk, and there was not an animal in the yard that could be expected to cover the eleven miles without falling down. Then the men discussed between them where they might send for a horse, and which of the nearby farmers or tradesmen might part with a horse just for the night. At length they agreed that the quickest and surest course, if a horse and chaise she must have, would be to inquire at the other inn, in the main part of the town of Queensferry.

The boy offered to go there and inquire on her behalf. "Or there's just the odd chance, ma'am," he added, "if you're Grangemouth bound, that a boat here at the pier might take you up. That's a fresh east wind blowing tonight, and I trust you'd make very good time all the way. You might even beat them, if you lost no time getting started."

Catherine strode out toward the wide stone pier that jutted into the Forth. The wind whipped at her shawl, which now seemed distressingly thin. There was no ferryboat here; it must be making its crossing. Several small boats were tied alongside, creaking and bumping against their canvas fenders. Moored in the deep anchorage just offshore in the lee of the pier were a number of boats bobbing gently on the invisible black water. Some showed lights, but most were dark.

The beacon lanterns posted on the pilings at the end of the pier beckoned. Catherine walked quickly to the very end of the pier, feeling the deepening water along each side of her. Turning her back to the wind, she looked upriver toward Grangemouth. Here and there lights glimmered along the black shore, and she could sense the distant looming weight of the Fife shore opposite, seven miles across the Forth.

Where was everyone? She would have to go back to the inn itself; the boatmen must be warming themselves and slaking their thirsts in its public rooms. Every lost minute was precious, irretrievable, and boded an unthinkable defeat. She turned to hurry back to the inn—but what was that? That familiar distant rhythmic thump, carried down to her on the wind? It faded to nothing though she strained to hear it. Then it came back, stronger than before. She was peering into the wind now, her eyes tearing as she tried to see what she hoped she was hearing. Then it seemed to her that voices came down the wind, too, snatches of male voices. And then, because she knew the shape her eyes were seeking in the darkness, she was quite sure she saw it: a low sleek launch sailing down fast before the wind and bound for the pier where she stood—a boat equipped with a steam engine hissing and throbbing at full power.

Had she wished it here, an apparition? No, it was real. The sails fluttered down onto its deck as the launch approached, and it coasted smoothly alongside the pier. A seaman jumped onto the landing and cranked his painter around one of the stone stops set at intervals for tying up.

"We came inshore to find out if they had crossed here on the ferry. No? On to Grangemouth? You are quite certain?" said Hector to Catherine.

"Dead certain," declared Catherine, squeezing his strong hand, which steadied her as she stepped aboard. And here, too, somehow—but no longer astonishing—was her own dark angel, the Indian maid, huddled in the drafty lee of the boiler. Silently Catherine praised the fate that delivered them all here, now! A praise like a bagpiper's flourish: "Moladh Catriona!"—"Catherine's Praise for Her Gift."

So *Dram Shell* cast off again with no more than a moment's pause. By the time they cleared the end of the pier, the two seamen had hoisted the sails and set them thrumming, tight as drumheads. Captain Keith and the men were excited by the prospect of closing on their quarry, by the charm of taking on a new and unexpected passenger, and by several good pulls on the ale and the whisky.

ꕥ ꕥ ꕥ

INSIDE THE JOLTING carriage, Annie felt a stifled sob wrack the pale little orphan wedged into the narrow seat beside her; but the child made no sound. It was hard to tell, in the darkness, whether tears were tracking down her face; but when Annie heard her sniff, she surmised that the child was silently crying. Annie's hand stole over, seeking the orphan's hand, and found it. It grasped hers in return—surprisingly hard. Annie's mistress, bouncing on the facing seat, neither saw nor heard, for she was loudly and continuously complaining, as was her habit.

"The design of the carriage is atrocious," Miss Johnstone was saying. "My trunk should have been strapped onto the roof behind rails, as any fool can see. Besides, it's the worst-hung carriage I was ever in. I never was so jolted about in my life. At this rate my teeth will rattle right out of my head before we ever get to the canal. And the roads are shocking. The horses are the sorriest screws I ever laid eyes upon, and I'm a pretty good judge of a horse. Even Judge Grant says so. Do move your feet over, Annie. You keep jostling me."

Annie moved her feet, and the orphan sniffed again.

"That's disgusting," said Miss Johnstone. "Doesn't she have a handkerchief? Now why are we stopping? I guess this dolt of a driver has gotten us lost in the dark." She opened the hatch and barked something at the coachman.

Annie could not hear his reply. Then Miss Johnstone said, "Here? This is the Forth and Clyde Canal? But I can't see a thing. Where do we book our passages? It's pitch-dark. Driver, you do it. You can't expect a lady to blunder around in the dark looking for boats to hire. . . . What's that? Send my servant, says the man! Ha! Trust her to hire a boat? No, no, driver, you have to do it, I insist. . . . Listen to the fellow! He will not! The horses? Isn't there a boy who can hold the horses? Not a boy to be seen? Such a country! So I myself, a lady traveler, I have to get out and fix up everything myself. All because you, Annie, are so bad and untrustworthy. Give me my cloak there."

"I get out and hire that boat for you, missus," said Annie. "I glad to go and hire the boat."

"I guess you'd be mighty glad alright, if I was fool enough to hand you my purse. Stupid girl! Where's the step? That wind! Why, it cuts right through a body! Now hand me that lantern. Never a word of gratitude from anybody."

The lantern bobbed down the slope toward the dark huts and the black water, then disappeared as Miss Johnstone rounded the corner of the cluster of buildings huddled at the shore. There were distant lights, further down toward the gleaming surface of the water, and the wind carried incomprehensible shreds of men's voices up to them. Annie watched her mistress disappear, then she studied the dark line of hill, woods and sky on the other side of the carriage, away from the canal and its buildings.

Five minutes passed, and there was no sign of Miss Johnstone; then Annie slid open the hatch and said to the coachman, "The little girl want to relieve herself."

"There is a convenience under the seat," he replied.

"Oh, but she won't. She say she can't bring herself to use it. She want me to take her up to those trees on the rise, up yonder."

"Suit yourselves," said the coachman. "What concern is it of mine?"

"She say she can't wait another minute."

"Get her out then!" cried the man.

Annie and the orphan got out, and ran hand in hand up the dark hill to the thicket of trees crowning it, with the wind in their faces, and rain in the wind.

ꕥꕥꕥ

As *Dram Shell* drew up alongside the oldest and furthest downstream of the several docks at the Grangemouth terminal, Catherine was alarmed to see a constellation of lanterns gathered at the largest dock, further up the basin. What could attract such a crowd at this hour of the night? She strained to listen. There were many voices: murmuring men's voices; men's laughter, and a strident woman's voice. Was it only Catherine's imagination which made the voice sound so like Miss Johnstone's?

Catherine ached to leap ashore and run up to see for herself, but cautious Hector would not permit this. Instead, as soon as *Dram Shell* was secured at the dock, it was Captain Keith who sauntered off to assess the situation. Of them all, only he could be sure of not being recognised by Miss Johnstone, if indeed that remarkable carrying voice was hers.

Taking what comfort she could from the warm boiler, Catherine waited in the dark, straining to hear. The light rain pattered maddeningly on the water now, but she thought she could make out a few words carried down to her on the erratic gusts: "A watchman!" cried the shrill voice. "Patrollers! . . . bring the dogs, this minute!"

After a bit, the crowd seemed to dissipate; in twos and threes, men drifted away. Several mechanics passing nearby along the muddy shore met up with others newly arrived on the scene. A few words of their explanations were audible to Catherine: "Ah, no; it is only two servant lasses run away, up the hill in the rain," she heard one say loudly.

"And we're all of us to go and fetch them down this very minute! And why? Just because the old woman demands it," added another.

" 'Tis a dirty night for silly women. Let them come down when they please."

"Let her go and fetch them herself."

When Annie's eyes had adjusted to the darkness, she could see the pale oval of the orphan's face. There must be moonlight somewhere above the black clouds, for there was a kind of luminosity in the scrim of blowing swaddling mist. They huddled in the uncertain shelter of a tree, in the lee of its rough trunk. Annie's skirt had been torn by pushing through the brambles and bracken. She was trembling, and she could feel the little girl against her side trembling too. A strong gust of wind buffeted the branches overhead, and a flurry of heavy drops plummeted down on them. One struck Annie right in the parting of her hair, a small icy blow on her scalp. If she peered through the tossing bracken and brambles, she could just make out the lights of the buildings below winking in the wind, and beyond them, the black water with boats on it. Then an opaque curtain of mist came down, blotting out the entire scene.

By the time Captain Keith returned to *Dram Shell*, Catherine had already devised the outline of a plan. It was not much of a plan, but who could have foreseen this? Hector did not admire Catherine's plan either. "Will you propose something better then?" she demanded, but he could not. So at Catherine's request, he whistled a certain traditional MacDonald tune for Captain Keith to hear.

"It does seem familiar, to be sure," Captain Keith said. "No doubt I have heard it before this. But I have not just the world's best ear for a tune. I hope I will not forget how it goes."

"I will go with you also, seeking them upon the hill," proposed the Indian maid suddenly.

"No," said Hector. "You had best remain here on the boat."

"But I can help in the seeking," said the woman. "For I have now that tune in my ear. Like this," she said, and she whistled it through without a fault.

Had she learned it just now, having heard it once?

"Aye, let her come, Hector," said Catherine. "The more, the better."

"Keep up a good head of steam," Captain Keith ordered his two crewmen, who were to remain with the boat. "No lights. And be ready to cast off at an instant's notice." Then he and the two MacDonalds and the Indian maid went ashore.

Annie listened very hard. Was that the distant voice of her mistress? Or was it the baying of dogs, so soon? No, it was neither of these; there was nothing to hear but soughing wind and rain and her own blood coursing in her veins.

So this was running away. People sometimes ran away from Grantsboro Plantation. Sometimes they were caught and brought back. She could row; she could swim; she could walk all night; she could ride; she could run; she could climb a tree and remain motionless for hours. She had no plan; she had no money; she did not know where she was. And clinging to her torn skirt was an orphan who could not speak.

Turning her face to the wind, Annie considered. She wanted to be far away from here before daylight. Taking the orphan's hand, she whispered, "I take you back to the town, back to your people. Come along."

They made their way as quickly as the terrain permitted. It was rough ground—a tangle of tree roots, rocks, unexpected deep boggy places, boulders, springs, and thickets of bracken, brambles and nettles. Annie tried to keep a steady course by heading always into the eye of the wind; but how could she be certain that the wind itself did not shift?

Suddenly the orphan's breath caught. She held it, looking fixedly down the hill where there stood a thicket of coppiced birch saplings. Annie froze and listened too; she heard only wind, rain, and her own pulse. But the child was turned to stone, stock-still like a dog on point. They waited; and waited. Then they both heard it: a little tune, whistled softly; a quiet melodic phrase, a question. The child gulped a great lungful of air and whistled her reply: the plaintive answering phrase of the tune. After just a moment it came again, the first questioning phrase. And they could tell where it came from—just there, just down there beyond the coppiced birches. The child licked her lips and again softly whistled the reply. Then, gripping Annie's hand, she waded through bracken, skirting the nettles, and plunged down among the pale dense stand of trees.

There the child stopped and listened once again. Where was the hidden friend? Where was the tune? Nothing, only dark stillness. After a long minute, the orphan whistled the first phrase of the tune once more, asking.

Something moved. A dark form stepped out from the densest part of the thicket, a dozen feet away, and drew back her shawl from her head: Sharada.

"It's you! You!" panted Annie, and she placed her hand over her own pounding heart to quiet it.

"Come away, come!" whispered her friend urgently. "The MacDonalds are here on the hill, the brother and sister, and there is a meeting place—and a boat, a very fast boat! Quick, come away."

ꙮ ꙮ ꙮ

BUT THE VERY fast boat had been noticed. Catherine's heart sank, and her hand tightened around Grace's, when they returned breathless to the old dock and saw that a number of the Grangemouth mechanics had gathered about *Dram Shell.* Several of them squatted on the dock in the rain, holding up lanterns to peer at her bow, and one or two had actually gone aboard and were examining the housing and the packing of the rotary shaft where it passed through the hull while the two *Dram Shell* men proudly explained, with arm motions, how the marvelous machine worked.

Captain Keith put his fingers in his mouth and whistled; the Grangemouth mechanics drew back, making way for the passengers to pass along the narrow dock. Catherine felt the weight of their curious gazes, felt how odd the six of them must appear, looming suddenly thus out of the wet night: herself first in the dressy Paisley shawl all drooping and sodden, holding the hand of this dripping red-haired child; next the foreign black-eyed woman like a tinker; then the tall black African girl with her skirt draggled and torn; then Hector with a triumphant glint in his eye; and the captain, looking fierce.

But no one spoke as they got aboard, and Captain Keith gave the command to cast off. Smartly the launch headed downstream into the main current, with the engine throbbing. Looking back, Catherine saw the mechanics on the dock getting smaller; she imagined they were pointing out to one another the turbulent wake boiling behind the boat—the track of its underwater rotary oar. Perhaps, she thought, someone might consider it good sport to go and report what he had seen to the old mistress who had lost her servant lasses.

After a while, aboard *Dram Shell,* Grace fell asleep in Catherine's arms. Catherine felt Grace's thin taut body soften little by little, slackening gradually until at last even her mouth fell slightly open and her breath came easy and light. There was not much flesh on either of them. Catherine felt the fragility of her own bones pressed against Grace's, lighter still—light as a bird's, and inexpressibly precious.

About four o'clock in the morning, as the first faint light came up, Catherine noticed the canal steamer, a side-wheeler, in their wake far behind, heading doggedly upwind just as they were. She pointed it out to Hector, who called Captain Keith's attention to it. Captain Keith changed course; the boat far behind changed course too, now running parallel to them though still a good half mile downwind. When *Dram Shell* reverted to her original course, the pursuing boat did the same. *Dram Shell* was running without lights; so was the pursuing side-wheeler. "We can outrun them," said Captain Keith. "We're surely the faster. But I would feel happier if we'd had the time to take on a full load of coal. Well, pour it on, lads; let's lose them, and the sooner the better. A good bank of mist would be a fine thing just now."

The much-desired mist did blow down on them for a time, obscuring them from the pursuers, but they had no way of knowing whether or not they were leaving them behind. "I could put you ashore on either side if you like," proposed Captain Keith. "In this mist they would never see us do it. I could have you at Blackness in twenty minutes; or across to Inverkeithing in thirty."

"No," said Hector. "We'll run for it. We need to get down to *Increase*, down at Leith, before the ebb, and then we're safe away." So they ran down the river as fast and straight as they could.

After a time they emerged into open air again, the mist an opaque bank behind them. There was traffic ahead—small craft, and several large boats too. The fishing fleet often went out at this hour, but these were not the fisherfolk. Who were they? The rain began again, so it was harder to make out the lines and flags; but then Hector recognised the odd waterborne procession. "Isn't that the *James Watt?*" he said, "tow-ing up the king's yacht?"

"Ah! so it is," said Catherine. "Aye, of course. The king was to come up for his departure breakfast at Hopetoun House this very morning; indeed, I met the turkeys destined for his very table. Then he was to sail from here. The crew is bringing up his yacht. How are we to make our way through this melee? I suppose we must stay well clear of them, but we cannot afford to lose even a moment."

"Stay clear of them?" said Captain Keith, at the tiller. "I think not. Let us make use of them." He glanced backward again; their pursuer was not yet to be seen. The captain changed course—not away from *James Watt* and *Royal George*, under tow in its wake, but toward them, on such a trajectory as to cross very close across *James Watt*'s bows. Across her bows very close indeed. But *James Watt*, slow though she seemed, was moving faster than Captain Keith had calculated. A great gust came up and caught *Dram Shell* on her starboard bow, knocking her off just a little. Captain Keith corrected her heading, gathered his resolve, and held his course. Catherine looked back and saw the pursuing side-wheeler just emerging from the fog bank behind them. The side-wheeler did not seem to have gained on them, but Catherine did not think she had fallen back either.

*James Watt*'s plume of black smoke blew down upon them. As *Dram Shell* still did not come about nor fall off from their collision course, *James Watt* sounded a loud horn. Grace seized Catherine's hand and squeezed it hard. Captain Keith's face was grim, the cords stand-ing out at his jaw. There was the high, sharp bow of *James Watt*, with its thick planks and massive rivets; Catherine could see minute detail, far too much detail as the heavy steamer came plunging at them. Then the pitch of *James Watt*'s engine changed; and the dripping paddle wheels seemed to stutter for just a moment. *Dram Shell* skimmed under her bow and crossed safely under her very figurehead with no more than ten feet to spare.

"Ha ha!" cried Captain Keith, and snapped his tiller over to bring up *Dram Shell* into the wind. The launch was skimming now along *James Watt*'s windward beam. White faces aboard *James Watt* gazed upon them astonished, and arms gestured angrily. Then *Dram Shell* was opposite the dripping towline, as thick as a man's waist, snapping up out of the water where it had dropped when *James Watt* had checked and let off the tension. A dangerous moment drew itself out as the weight of *Royal George* fell hard on the towline. Catherine saw water snap off it, saw it reverberate like a great plucked bass string of the gods, its sound too deep to be heard by mere mortals.

Then here was *Royal George*—a very close look at the king's yacht. It was a beauty—a lovely, shining example of the shipwright's art, a pleasure craft fashioned of polished mahogany and teak and shining brass—a charming toy.

Then the rain swept down once more, a solid gray drenching curtain, like standing under a waterfall. They could not see more than twenty feet, but Captain Keith kept to his heading and, except for once changing course to avoid a mackerel boat on its way out, they encountered little further traffic.

Now they had only to get down to *Increase* at Leith at the turn of the tide. Shivering, Catherine kept watch behind. The rain continued, sometimes lighter, sometimes heavier; but she did not see the pursuing sidewheeler. Did it still stick to them? Grace and Sharada and Annie were shivering, too, and taking turns wearing the old shrunken sailor's jacket. Hector made them all swallow some of the remaining whisky. He and Captain Keith drank some too; Captain Keith needed quite a lot.

Then there was a terrible crunch and shudder as *Dram Shell* ran hard afoul of something solid and heavy submerged just below the surface in the rough gray swell. The steam piston stuttered, then lagged. The engine slowed, laboring just above a stall, while a painful juddering wracked the entire boat, a wrongful vibrating rumble. Hector shouted and threw himself toward the gasket at the bow where the rotating shaft passed through the hull. Captain Keith swore and snapped the tiller hard over. "The valve! Throw it open, there!" he cried to the sailors, meaning that they were to divert the steam pressure from the piston. But Hector was demanding their help at the same moment, to stem the black water pouring in at the badly jarred gasket through the hull. The shuddering grew worse and worse until it seemed that *Dram Shell* must wrench herself to pieces. Then suddenly it ceased. All ran smoothly once more, and *Dram Shell* continued to forge strongly ahead into the wind as though nothing had happened.

But what *had* happened?

They succeeded in stemming the leak at the gasket—it was not so bad after all. One of the sailors brought oakum and tar for packing while the other set up the bilge pump.

But Hector was scowling. Minutely he inspected *Dram Shell*'s mechanism from end to end: from steam engine to piston to crank to crankshaft to gears to the long rotary shaft, which passed through the hull and could not be inspected any further. He found nothing amiss, nothing bent nor wrenched nor twisted, nothing damaged. Still he was not satisfied. Frowning, he said, "I do not think it sounds just as it ought. Does it not seem pitched rather higher than before? The frequency of the strokes has increased; I am sure of it. But there is no more vibration than before—rather less, if anything. Yet we seem to be moving very well."

"I make it four knots," said Captain Keith. "Or perhaps a little more, which is as good or better than she has ever done, especially with such a headwind."

"I should very much like to inspect the rotary oar itself," said Hector.

"She pulls along as smooth as ever," said the captain. "The rotary oar must have escaped unscathed. Perhaps we were just snagged for a moment or two there—an old cable, it might have been."

"Mmm," said Hector doubtfully. "If only I had made the oar shippable, as I had wished to do! Then it would be a perfectly simple matter to raise and examine it."

"Not just now," said Captain Keith.

"No, not just now," said Hector. But still he was frowning. Something certainly was changed.

Slack tide passed; the ebb began, carrying them a little faster down to the port of Leith. Would Captain Mainwaring wait, Catherine wondered; for how long? Her eyes ached from gazing into the rain looking for recognisable shapes. Then they were coming down to Leith; ships and launches, smacks and sloops loomed up out of the gray mist. Where was *Increase*? Would Captain Mainwaring have sailed without them?

Captain Keith steered for where *Increase* had last been moored. She was not there; had they mistaken the place on the featureless water? Coming about, Captain Keith made for the main channel, where captains sometimes anchored in preparation for sailing. Catherine felt sick to her stomach. *Increase*, *Increase*, *Increase*?

There she lay, tall and beautiful in the gray dawn. "Ahoy there, *Increase*!" called Captain Keith as they came up under her lee rail. One after another, rigid with cold, the tardy passengers were hoisted aboard in the bosun's chair. Captain Mainwaring was on deck in his dripping sou'wester, oilskins, and tall boots as they each came soaring over the rail. "Oh, very good, very good," he was saying cheerfully. "Of course we have waited for you, Mr MacDonald; Mr Fleming would never have agreed to sail without you. Here you are, Mrs MacDonald, and just in the nick of time. Here is the wee lass! And you have brought your maid after all, I see."

"Two m-m-maids," said Catherine, her teeth chattering, as Annie came flying over the rail last of all.

**Mac Dhonaill Mor nan Eillan.** "Macdonald Lord of the Isles".

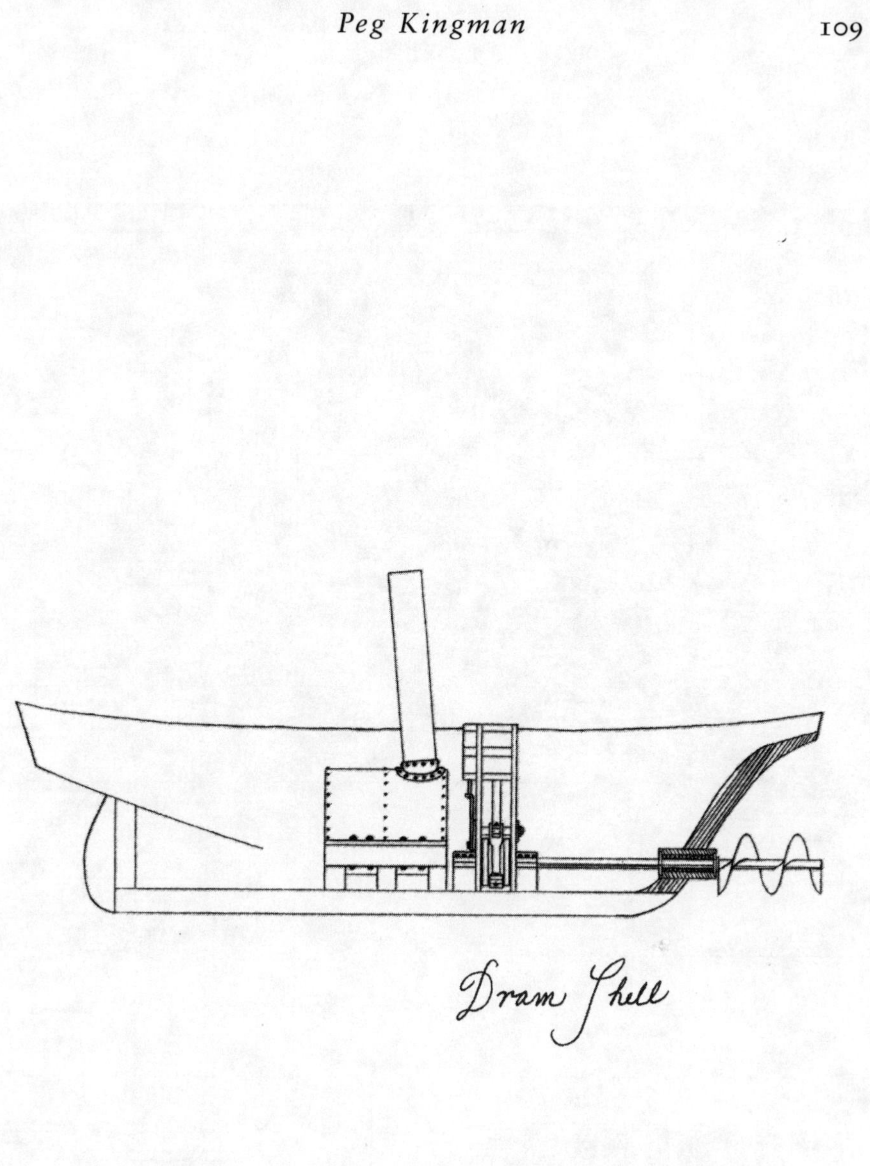
Dram Shell

AT SEA.
Spitsbergen
Edam Land
Shannon I.
GREENLAND
Jan Meyen
Iceland
Novaia Zemlia
North Cape
Lapland
Cape Taimyr
New Siberia
Arctic Circle
RUSSIAN EMPIRE
SIBERIA
EUROPE
ASIA
BRITISH ISLES
GERMANY
Moscow
St. Petersburg
Kamtchatka S.
Aleutian Is.
MONGOLIA
CHINESE EMPIRE
MANCHOURIA
TURKESTAN
PERSIA
TIBET
CHINA PROPER
Japan S.
Nipon
HINDOSTAN
Calcutta
Bombay
Madras
Ceylon
Canton
Tropic of Cancer
Azores (P.)
Madeira (P.)
Sahara
SOUDAN
GUINEA
AFRICA
Cape Verde
Ascension (B.)
St. Helena (B.)
Tropic of Capricorn
Cape Town
C. of Good Hope
Madagascar
Mauritius (B.)
Maldivas
Sumatra
Java
Borneo
Manila
Luzon
Mariana Is.
Carolinas
Gilbert Is.
N. Guinea
New Ireland
AUSTRALIA
Tasmania
New Zealand
Auckland (B.)
Campbell
Kerguelen
Amsterdam
St. Paul's
Marion I.
Bouvet I.
BRAZIL
Pernambuco
S. Salvador or Bahia
Rio Janeiro
Falkland Is.
S. Georgia
Sandwich Group
S. Orkney
Louis Philippe Ld.
Sabrina Land
Balleny Is.
South Victoria
ATLANTIC OCEAN
INDIAN OCEAN
PACIFIC OCEAN
Explanation
Places of upwards of 100,000 inh.
Places from 50,000 to 100,000
Places 10,000 to 50,000
Places below 10,000 inhabitants.
B. British Colonies.
D. Dutch
Da. Danish
F. French
S. Spanish
P. Portuguese
Sw. Swedish
Longitude East from Greenwich
Engraved by J. Dower, Pentonville, Londo

# 8

## *obvious to a Competent Judgement*

"Annie, Annie . . . Pray, what is your other name, Annie?" asked Catherine, as she folded her bulky canvaswork into a mahogany locker in her cabin aboard *Increase*. On this first afternoon at sea after their hasty unconventional departure, the sky had cleared to a pale watery blue, and *Increase* was bowling southward at a fine rate before a north-west wind, over water still gray, rough and broken.

Grace was perched on the sill of the curving window across the stern. She was rubbing the sleep from her eyes, for they had all slept half the day away. She was mesmerised by their wake unreeling behind them, rough and torn across the whitecapped North Sea. And Sharada, who knew from experience how these things worked, was transforming Catherine and Grace's beds back into their daytime guise: a pair of miniature sofas.

The cabin and its adjoining closet, occupied now by four women and a trunk, did not seem so commodious as when Catherine had first seen it empty, though the two maids had no belongings except the clothes they wore. Annie was gently rinsing the Paisley shawl in a basin of rainwater, dipping the heavy dark drooping thing up and down, trying not to splash. The shawl smelled of a wet sheep.

"What do you mean, ma'am, my other name?" asked Annie.

"Have you not another name, a family name?"

"No, ma'am, no other name—just Annie."

"How are you distinguished from other Annies and Annes, then? Were there no other Annes in your acquaintance?"

"Oh, lots of Annes—too many. Our Missus Grant, her name is Anne, but everybody call her Missus Grant. And her daughter, the little missus, she's Little Miss Anne. And then among the servants there's another Annie, always meek and mild in front of the family, but I know better than that. So the children of the family, the Grant children, they takes to calling her Annie Good; and they calls me Annie Bad, 'cause when I was very little, no older than them, why, sometimes I used to disobey them and make them cross. And so after a while the family and the servants, everybody, all takes to calling me Annie Bad."

"Annie Bad! But that *is* very bad; indeed, it is impossible. You must choose another name. Or shall I choose one for you?"

"Oh! no!" interrupted Sharada. "I beg your pardon, ma'am, and Annie Bad." Sharada straightened up, flushed from wrestling with a bolster. "But Annie Bad must not change her name, never indeed. It is surely her good name, her true good name. In our great music, our Indian music, 'anibaddh' is the word which is signifying 'unbound' or 'free'—that is, unbound by any rule of . . . of meter, of rhythm. Now she is unbound, free, by her own great courage and resolve, and by your kindness too, ma'am, so Anibaddh is surely her true good name."

"Well," said Catherine after a moment, "I suppose it is Annie's concern, and Annie's decision."

"Then I like to be called Anibaddh still, if you please, ma'am," said Annie. "I'm so used to it."

"Are you yourself again?" Catherine asked Hector, finding him bent over the miniature writing table in his own little cabin. "Did you sleep the day away, as we did?"

"A braw night, wasn't it? " said Hector, setting down his pen carefully and leaning back in his chair to stretch.

"Not the night you expected, alas! I am so sorry, Hector, that you were deprived of your last night at home with Mary and the children. I knew I ought not to leave Grace alone."

"It is not your fault. Even if you had been in the room, they might have tried snatching her, you know."

"Aye, that is true enough. It might have been much worse. Still—poor Mary! What must she have suffered, waiting for you all night!"

"I asked Captain Keith to go and tell her as soon as he got us safe aboard."

"Are you writing to her now? I will write her an apology, to enclose with your letter, if you will let me. And she will be relieved to learn how respectable a figure I now cut, attended by such a surfeit of maids."

"You have not engaged them both?"

"We agreed to make our dispositions when we come to Flanders. I am paying their passages to Antwerp in return for their waiting upon Grace and me. That is the extent of our agreement so far. The Indian maid declares she will go on to India; she expects to find an employer and a passage from Antwerp. The American girl has not settled on a plan; freedom is so very new to her. Perhaps I will engage her while Grace and I remain in Flanders, but I have also offered to pay her passage back to Britain if she prefers. In any case I shall settle a small sum on her by way of reward. We are all four of us rather surprised to find ourselves here together, and it may require some time to see how matters fall out."

"If this wind holds, Captain Mainwaring says we'll be entering the mouth of the Westerschelde in three days," said Hector.

"So soon! And then how long do you remain in port at Antwerp? *Increase*, I mean?"

"Not more than three or four days, I believe—perhaps less."

"What is that thumping noise?" asked Catherine. Above the creakings and workings of the ship itself, there was a rhythmic thudding just beyond the partition of Hector's cabin.

"I believe a newly-wed Mr and Mrs Todd have taken the next cabin," said Hector evenly.

The entire party on board assembled for the first time for their four o'clock dinner in the cuddy cabin. Besides Captain Mainwaring, the sibling MacDonalds, and Mr Fleming, there was a highland Dr Macpherson, a Mr Sinclair, and the lately married Mr and Mrs Todd. Catherine found herself seated at Captain Mainwaring's left hand; at her other side was Dr Macpherson. Sharada took up her place behind Catherine's chair to wait on her; the other diners were likewise waited on by their own servants or by the ship's boys.

"Eight at table," said Captain Mainwaring jovially. "I do like to see my table well filled. And my serving dishes and claret glasses well filled too, eh? Capital! Now you shall learn what my cook can do. He is a dab hand with the pepper once he's let loose with it, for he's an East Indian himself, from Patna, a city which is famous for its cookery. You didn't suspect it at Leith, did you? Dining on his Scotch collops of venison! But directly we are at sea, he reverts to his oriental ways. Well, that's why I keep him on. Once one has acquired a taste for spices, it is a hardship to do without them. Mulligatawnies! *Biryani*s and kedgerees! The fiery vindaloo! And those fried sweets in honey—*jalebi*, they are called. You shall try them, I promise you.

"Well! Mrs MacDonald, it is a pleasure to welcome you to my table. I trust I see you well rested and quite recovered from the strenuousness of your embarkation. It was neatly done! Do regale yourself while you can, for when you leave us at Antwerp you shall have nothing but dreary Low Country food: eels boiled with cabbages, and the like." Then, giving his attention to his soup, the captain allowed his guests to do likewise.

The soup was indeed richly peppered, quite speckled black. It was the first time Catherine had ever eaten a dish containing enough freshly ground pepper that she noticed the taste and aroma of the spice itself: rich, warm (daringly but not alarmingly so), and faintly sweet.

Across the table, Mr Todd was refilling his young bride's glass, then his own. He had an odd, arch way of addressing her; more frequently than necessary, very frequently, he would call her "Mrs Todd": "May I refill your glass, Mrs Todd?" "Won't you have a little more of the chicken, Mrs Todd, perhaps just this delicate little wing?" Or, to the company at large, "I have made the China passage before this, but Mrs Todd has never been to sea before." And each time he pronounced the words "Mrs Todd," he would cast a sidelong glance at her, one eyebrow raised, a most meaning look. To herself, Catherine accounted for this affectation as mere newlywed mannerism, but it was very odd. Thus addressed, Mrs Todd would blush and look self-conscious. Once, she allowed herself to say, "Thank you, Mr Todd. I believe I will have just a bit more of the cucumber relish, for this bracing sea air gives one a barbarous appetite." Catherine noticed that Mrs Todd did have a fine appetite; her food disappeared quickly from her plate. But Catherine was inclined to attribute it, and her rosy complexion, to other causes than the invigorating sea air.

The Dr Macpherson to Catherine's left seemed at first as tongue-tied as a boy, though he was certainly twice Catherine's age. But by the time they got to the excellent haddock, Catherine found that he would talk freely about fevers—fevers in general and fevers in particular; delicately about puerperal fevers and copiously about the fascinating malarial and typhus fevers, their related dysentaries, and the unwholesome damp tropical soils from which they sprang. Until now, his medical practice had been in Glasgow, where the only tropical fevers he had seen were long-established chronic and recurring cases, late in their course, in wracked yellow soldiers returned from India. But now he looked forward eagerly to opportunities for studying these same enthralling fevers—and treating them, too, of course—at their source.

"It is the soils which must be studied," he declared to Catherine and Captain Mainwaring while licking cucumber relish off his upper lip. "It is the soils which hold the secret. Of this I am certain. It is well known—it has long been observed—that the disease is endemic; that is to say, it occurs where particular soils are found, particular soils of exceptional moistness. Now in what consists the unwholesome principle? Samples of these soils must be collected and examined. I am in no doubt that a thorough, a really thorough study of these soils—on a microscopic level, you understand—must yield their secret, the nature of their unwholesome principle—that is, of the malarial vapours emitted by them. And then, of course, an efficacious treatment—even a cure—might be devised." Once fairly launched on this subject, he could scarcely be stopped, and his voice took on a disagreeably sonorous droning character.

How unendurable this would be all the way to the Indies! Catherine nodded intelligently from time to time as he spoke, but she could overhear other talk around the table, and all of it was better than this. At the far end of the table, Hector and Mr Sinclair were discussing the metallurgical aspects of the aquatint engraving process: "Have you a supply of the copper plates?" she heard Hector ask.

"Aye, and also the etching acids, and a case of powdered resin," replied Mr Sinclair; and they plunged into the engrossing subject of the various properties, sources and uses of resins, rosins, varnishes, and lacquers; and Mr Sinclair promised to give Hector a demonstration of the powers of wax and resin to protect certain metals from the corrosive effects of acids.

"Indeed, the sine qua non would be a preventive, or rather a prophylactic treatment," announced Dr Macpherson through a mouthful of haddock. "The current practice, the accepted practice at present, as you doubtless are aware, consists of the administration of cinchona or wormwood—Jesuits' bark. . . ."

When the doctor paused to pick a bit of bone from between his teeth, Captain Mainwaring stood: "Mr Sinclair," cried he to the young man at the foot of the table, "a glass of wine with you: To the masterpieces you will paint in the Indies!" Their glasses were filled; and they raised them to one another, bowed, and drank them down. But as a device for making the conversation general, the toast failed, for Hector immediately engrossed Mr Sinclair's attention again, on the mineral deposits and corrosive effects of salt water in steam boilers.

"Is Mr Sinclair a painter?" Mr Todd asked Captain Mainwaring as the plates were cleared away. "Does he paint heads, or is it landscapes and scenes and that sort of thing?"

"Oh, he can turn his hand to anything, I daresay," said Captain Mainwaring. "I have seen a head he did of Captain Blundell. A very good likeness, and in the background his brig *Medusa* perfectly recognisable and its rigging quite correct. There is nothing more disgusting in a picture than carelessness about such details. So many pictures are ruined by the painter's landlubberish ignorance! The ensign streaming aft, yet the sails set for a wind that is clearly dead astern! I know of a picture, much admired by academicians, in which the stays are running upward—forward and upward! Preposterous—an object of ridicule!"

"You are hard on us, sir!" exclaimed Mr Sinclair from his end of the table. "In my opinion, it is writers who are the worst offenders. I have thrown down more than one novel in disgust upon being told by the author of 'the full moon rising about midnight to cast its dappling light o'er the dim forest track.' A full moon rising at midnight! Do moons rise and set to suit the convenience of scribbling writers? Is it mere ignorance, or do writers imagine that they possess the power to set the heavenly bodies spinning out of their appointed orbits at need or at random? Directly I read such a thing, I lose all confidence in the author; my faith in his tale drains away instantly. Whereas a moment before I had been willing to ride upon the magic carpet of his art, suddenly the magic fails and I am cast unceremoniously to the ground—a very unpleasant fall."

"But may not the full moon rise at midnight, from time to time?" asked Mrs Todd. "I daresay it may; it is so very changeable. . . ." Here she trailed off as her husband laughed at her.

But Captain Mainwaring gravely answered, "No, no, Mrs Todd, it cannot; it never has and it never will. You shall have an astronomy demonstration four nights from now, if you like—you and Mr Todd and anyone who likes, for that will be full moon. Then I shall undertake to show you why the full moon must always rise opposite the setting sun, and a moon which rises at midnight must be waning; and no painter or writer can change it to suit the requirements of his tale."

"Forgers must have a hard time of it these days, what with all this scientific knowledge about," said Mr Todd. "Not so easy anymore to carry off a hoax, I daresay."

"It is certainly a factual age, Mr Todd," said Mr Sinclair. "Though it seems to me that our connoisseurs and collectors are as credulous, and greedy, as ever. But they are only too likely, when evaluating a painting or a poem, to fix upon its pedigree, its certifications of origin, while closing their eyes to its artistic merits; to the intrinsic beauty of the thing itself—like sailors who stuff their ears with wool so as not to hear the ravishing songs of the Sirens."

"Thus we steer clear of credulity, I hope," said Mr Fleming with energy. "We rely upon facts for their virile power to reinforce—or else to contradict—the seductive eloquence of beauty."

"Aye, facts," said Hector thoughtfully. "But, alas, we are so likely to be deceived in our facts. How frequently do we stumble, cursing, across a fundamental discovery while blundering about in determined pursuit of some error!"

"The challenge then," said Mr Fleming, "is to appreciate the significance of what has tripped us up, and not stupidly to curse it. We must perceive the import of those very uncharted rocks and reefs, so to speak, upon which our theories are dashed."

Dr Macpherson shook his head as though to disagree, but he was unable to speak because he had just put half of a large juicy pear into his wide mouth, and so he lost his chance.

"Well, I have sometimes wondered," ventured Mrs Todd, "how are adventurers to discover all these—these uncharted rocks and submerged reefs!—if not by running onto them?"

This silenced everyone for a moment, and Mrs Todd flushed and began to look faintly alarmed, uncertain whether she had said something clever, or very stupid indeed. Her husband was just about to enlighten her, but Captain Mainwaring spoke first. "Only well-charted waters for us," he said positively and loudly. Just then the tea was brought in, and the cloth withdrawn, and the subject changed: Catherine inquired about shipboard methods of catching and collecting rainwater, and Captain Mainwaring was happy to explain in some detail.

The weather continued clear and windy, so that by evening *Increase* was sailing comfortably with the wind abeam, with little for the crew to do. The broad clean deck where the passengers walked and sat together was heeled over only so far as to excite but not disconcert the inexperienced travelers among them; and the regular smooth swell was now a dark blue, as slow and heavy as slag. Other sails could be seen, other ships and boats making their way up or down the wind, but there was no sight or sound or smell of land—only dark water in every direction to the horizon.

"A soldier's wind," said Mr Fleming, joining Catherine where she leaned on the broad windward rail at sunset.

"What do you mean?"

"When the wind is abeam like this, strong and steady, sailors call it a soldier's wind because . . . perhaps you can guess." His dark hair was blown back from his high forehead, and the last of the sunlight gleamed in his eyes—now darkest blue like the sea. Hadn't they been green before? Did they change as the sea changed?

"Because even soldiers could sail a ship in such a wind?" Catherine ventured.

"Precisely."

"Pray, how did you feel, Mr Fleming, the first time you went to sea?" asked Catherine. "How did you feel to see your native shore sink to an invisible nothing behind you, the deep blue sea surrounding you, and nothing but six inches of oak planking to hold you safe from it?"

"Ah! I was but two weeks old for my first sea voyage, an infant in my mother's arms, so I cannot report my sensations on that occasion. But when next I went to sea, at the age of fifteen, I felt free and light for the first time in my life. Have you dreamt that nightmare in which you must run, though you are mired in a bog? That is what land-bound life—all the life I had known—had seemed to me, all slow heaviness. I had supposed it was the lot of humankind to trudge. Imagine then my exhilaration at this novel sensation of movement and gliding ease! I remember marveling at the seabirds coasting above our fantail, hanging on the wind without effort. I fancied that their freedom and lightness was hence to be mine as much as theirs. So I have stayed at sea as much as possible ever since."

"But to leave the place of your birth . . . ?"

"The place near Sluys where I was born was lost to the sea many years ago when a dike broke. The entire district was flooded, and it has never yet been reclaimed, for it was of only marginal value as farmland."

"Near Sluys? That is in Flanders?"

"Yes, we shall pass near it, if not quite above it!"

"So you are quite literally a Fleming by birth, not just in name."

"No," he said, smiling. "I am quite literally a native of this sea."

"Ah! Well, I will admit that being abroad upon your native sea is not so dreadful as I had feared," Catherine said. "This ship does seem so very solid."

❧ ❧ ❧

IN THE MORNING, Sharada, humming quietly under her breath, came in carrying a tray, and set it on the little gimbled stand beside Catherine's sofa bed. Seeing that Catherine was awake, Sharada adjusted the blinds at the big stern window to let in the early light. With a murmur Grace turned away from the brightness, but she did not awaken. Catherine sat up enough to see out: blue sea, blue sky. Sharada deftly arranged a bolster and two pillows behind her back, to lean against.

Then she disappeared, still without speaking, into the tiny compartment beyond which she shared with Anibaddh.

The tray bore a teapot; two cups; a milk pitcher. Catherine filled a cup, splashed in milk, tasted. Excellent tea. She had slept deeply and long, gently rocked by the easy regular motion of the ship. She pressed against the pillows at her back. As she swallowed the fourth mouthful of tea, there washed through her like a change of tide a perfect ease, an unexpected sense of well-being.

Presently she found herself thinking of the exquisite little Indian paintings in Mr Clerk's collection, upstairs in his handsome Edinburgh house. The lovers in those paintings disported themselves among exquisite silken embroidered cushions and brilliant damask bolsters. The feather pillow at her back was covered in serviceable bleached linen, wrinkled now but formerly well pressed, the flax fibers still flat and shining from the heat and pressure of the flatiron. In her imagination Catherine transformed this pillow into a wide soft bolster covered in gold silk with a saffron fringe and blue embroidered birds. She adjusted the scene: a bolster, a nest of soft brilliant cushions in a pavilion set in a teeming green garden, in a warm soft dusk. Someone is coming; the beloved one is coming, with music. Here, he arrives at last!

But where his face should be, there is only a blur, a blank.

There is no one. The face of the beloved is lost; it cannot be remembered. Nor even imagined. The damage is done.

Catherine blinked away this disturbance and resettled herself against her rumpled white linen pillows, but the quill of a feather kept pricking her.

Beyond the thin board partition, someone was humming quietly: Sharada, of course. She was humming the traditional MacDonald tune they had taught her in the steam launch at Grangemouth; the tune that had brought Grace safe. Grace stirred once more, and Catherine saw her eyes open, pale lashes blinking at the sunlight.

❧ ❧ ❧

SHARADA APPEARED AND disappeared like incense smoke, humming quietly to herself almost all the time, sometimes audibly and sometimes under her breath. She was always at hand when required: she fetched warm water for washing, brought boiled eggs and bread with cheese and ham for breakfast, combed Catherine's hair in the morning, waited on her at dinner, helped her undress at night, carried away the pot from under the sofa bed. But at other times Catherine had no idea where Sharada was or what she did.

Anibaddh liked to take her work up on deck, where she would sit upon an enormous coil of rope with the wind in her face, the sun on her back, sewing in her lap. There was always work to be done. Her own dress, savagely ripped in the nettles, she had neatly repaired. The gown that Catherine had been wearing that night had been washed too; and now Anibaddh was replacing its ribbon trimmings, which she had had to remove, launder and press separately. Grace had quickly become Anibaddh's pale silent shadow, helping when she could.

Grace had her meals in their cabin, privately. Anibaddh would bring food on a tray, then retire to the adjoining closet so that Grace could eat alone.

ꕥ ꕥ ꕥ

TOWARD EVENING OF the fourth day at sea, after dinner, Catherine noticed that the waters were becoming distinctly crowded. Considering that no land was in sight, there seemed a remarkable number of boats. Many were broad-beamed fishing boats flying triangular-rigged sails in a vivid orange hue; others were scantily manned small trading brigs and sloops, all making their way busily somewhere, or from somewhere, but where? She scanned the horizon, searching for land, but none was to be seen. There were only masts and sails. Behind her, Mrs Todd was seated out of the wind, painstakingly working over a drawing pad, with the tip of her tongue caught between her teeth.

"Oh, Mrs MacDonald," said Mrs Todd presently, looking up from her work. "The captain mentioned it, and I have been wanting to ask you—is it true that your Hindu maid will not remain with you in Antwerp? That she hopes to make her way to India?"

"She intends to return to India as soon as she can get a passage," said Catherine.

"Pray, do not think me impertinent. But you see, Mr Todd and I made our preparations so quickly that I could not engage a maid before sailing; I expected to manage for myself until we get to India. But then I thought, why not take your maid, if she is not to remain with you in any case. And if you have found her satisfactory."

How desirable and convenient an arrangement, both for Sharada and for Mrs Todd! But Catherine found herself saying instead, "My destination is not . . . not fixed with absolute certainty. It may be that . . . in short, it may be that my maid may continue in my service after all." She was not ready to say aloud, But I am thinking of proceeding to India myself. She had not till now quite realised how seriously she was considering this: To India, herself! Because sometimes she did not quite believe what she had been told about the fate of her sly, slippery darling, her twin.

"Oh! I beg your pardon," said Mrs Todd. "I must have misunderstood the captain. Well, here is another thing I've been wondering: Do we go first to Antwerp, then to Anvers? Or the other way about? I cannot make it out from what everyone says."

"But," said Catherine, "but they are the same, you see. They are only the two names of the same city. Antwerp is its Flemish name, and Anvers is its Walloon name—that is to say, its French name. Mostly I think it is called Antwerp."

"Oh, dear! I've gone and betrayed myself again! Now you know what an ignorant goose I am, if you didn't before. Mrs MacDonald, you won't mention it to Mr Todd, will you? He is just a little annoyed with my—my foolishness. I haven't had great opportunities come my way. But I have resolved to make use of my time during this voyage to improve my knowledge and acquire some ladylike accomplishments. I thought of trying my hand at drawing; here is a sketch of that picturesque Dutch fishing boat we have been overtaking. It is only a first effort, of course, but what do you think?"

Catherine kindly looked at the drawing pad offered for her inspection. "I am no judge," she said, "but it seems to me that you have succeeded in capturing the feeling of—of movement."

"I thought I might ask Mr Sinclair to give me a few tips and pointers."

"I expect that Mr Sinclair would be happy to be of use."

Before dusk, Captain Mainwaring set *Increase*'s crew to cleaning her channels and washing her sides, as though landfall were imminent. Still there was no land to be seen. Then Catherine realised she had been looking much too high; she had been scanning the horizon for distant hills, hills like Scotland's. The Netherlands had no hills. What she had taken for distant masts and sails resolved themselves instead into steeples and windmills arising directly out of the water, or so they first appeared. Then arose trees, towers, and dikes. And finally, as it grew darker, she could make out flat, smooth green land itself, low and sedgy.

But as they came closer inshore, it seemed to Catherine that they must have mistaken their landfall; this was only a long blank low piece of coast. Then, looking around, she realised that they had already entered the Westerschelde's broad open mouth and were already passing over its shallow shoaled outfall, over choppy muddy water. The mouth of the river was broad—as wide as the mouth of the Forth—but slow, shallow, sluggish, phlegmatic. *Increase* and the beamy Flemish fishing boats converged, taking advantage of the last light and a favorable tide to make their way up the sluggish channel. It seemed to Catherine that she was looking down onto the fields; the low wet green land was much lower than her high vantage point, and seemed even lower than the level of the water itself.

After dinner, as night came on, *Increase* steered a little out of the main shipping channel and hove to. At the same time, Catherine noticed a particular fat little Dutch boat coming down the estuary, drawing apart from the general traffic in the channel. It drew near, was hailed, replied, then came in under *Increase*'s lee quarter.

"Who is this?" asked Catherine of Mr Fleming, the only other passenger remaining on deck. "What is that boat?"

"That will be our pilot coming aboard; he will bring us up the channel to Antwerp," he replied.

"What an odd-looking boat," said Catherine. It was deep, round, and broad, with a marked curve to both stem and stern.

"It is called a 'poon,' and a very worthy and handy little craft it is for inland work."

Catherine saw an active little man come aboard, climbing up *Increase*'s side ropes as easily as a spider climbs its web. He was met by Captain Mainwaring, who took him along to his private cabin. After a moment, Mr Fleming went away, too, leaving Catherine to observe the *poon*. She thought it would cast off again directly, but instead it remained alongside, its crew in it. And she expected that *Increase* would brace up her yards and get under way upriver again, to make the best of the favorable tide and fair wind. But no one seemed to feel any urgency.

The moon was high and near full. It made a wide silvery track over the wrinkled water. There was a brackish smell of tidal mud, very different from the pure air of the open sea; and mixed with it was tobacco smoke from the pipes of the sailors in the boat at *Increase*'s flank who sat smoking in complete silence. Looking down, Catherine could now and then make out the glow of a tiny orange ember.

"Now that is an excellent smell, an excellent healthful smell," said Dr Macpherson as he poked his head up through the hatch and emerged on the main deck. It was his habit before bed to come up and smoke a last pipeful, while taking a few turns up and down the deck. He had tried each night to get Hector to try some of his excellent tobacco, and Hector had invariably declined. "Good evening, Mrs MacDonald," said Dr Macpherson. "A beautiful evening, beautiful. Whose tobacco do I smell? Ah, the Dutch sailors'. The Dutch have excellent tea and fair tobacco. Fair, I say, but not as good the Virginia leaf my Glasgow merchant gets for me. Your brother must try it; I have told him so. It will do him good. It is my only indulgence, and an expensive one, it must be admitted; but then it is so healthful."

As Dr Macpherson talked, Catherine became aware of some activity deep in *Increase*'s cargo hold. Someone came up to remove the gratings from around the capstan, then disappeared.

"Simultaneously a relaxant and a stimulant, a benign and harmless kind of stimulant, you understand, Mrs Macdonald," Dr Macpherson was saying, "with the capacity to sharpen the mental capabilities, to whet the wits if you like. . . ."

Several of *Increase*'s sailors came up and rigged a pair of tackles in the dark, tailing them through a snatch block and to a windlass. Then they let down the heavy iron hook into the hold.

"But can you find the smoke itself anything but unpleasant?" asked

Catherine while she continued to observe the sailors. "I cannot bring myself to enjoy breathing smoke. Even a smoky chimney always makes me cough, and coal smoke is said to be unhealthy."

Dr Macpherson's reply was lengthy, and referred to the essential differences between fumes of vegetal origin and those of mineral origin: "And thus it is that smoke of vegetal origins actually has a healthful influence upon the pulmonary and bronchial systems—that is to say, Mrs MacDonald, in laymen's terms, upon the lungs themselves. Indeed, tobacco smoke is proven to have a pronounced preservative effect!"

"Oh, indeed?" said Catherine when she noticed that he was waiting for this pronouncement to have its due impact. There were six men at the windlass, and in response to a signal from below they bent to it. She heard the creak of its working.

"Oh, yes, quite proven. But it is a principle with which you, Mrs MacDonald, are already well acquainted, I daresay. Just consider, if you will, the ham—the simple country-cured ham. Now, what preserves it from putrefaction? I shall tell you. . . ."

Catherine saw a large crate slowly emerge, rising from the dark hold, dangling, then rotating queasily as it cleared the cargo hatch. Someone steadied it with a gaff and a guy line. Catherine could tell even in the dark that the man was Hector.

"And that of course is the smokehouse. Now, the healthful preservative effect of the smoke operates upon our tender pulmonary tissues, just precisely as it does upon our hams—not to say *our* hams, but hams in general, of course. They are hardened and toughened by the smoke, and thus are they rendered far less susceptible to the harmful effects of damp, of infection, of rot and putrefaction!"

Catherine saw the inboard tackles eased, the outboard ones taken up; and the enormous crate was slowly maneuvered out over the rail and above the waiting *poon*. On command it was gently let down and, with a faint bump, eased onto the deck of the smaller boat.

"I venture to predict that the smoking of a quantity of tobacco every day will soon be recognised as the best, the most efficacious of treatments in cases of consumption! It is not too much to hope that it may perhaps even prove valuable as a preventive in those families with a history of unsatisfactory lungs."

The hook was disengaged, and the tackles were hauled inboard again, drawn up, and made fast. The gratings were replaced around the capstan. The Flemish crew on the *poon* quickly secured the crate with cables and draped it with sailcloth. Then they set the sail and cast off just as Captain Mainwaring gave the command to brace up the yards and get *Increase* under way again.

"So you see, Mrs MacDonald, you might try your influence with your brother, for the sake of his health, particularly in damp conditions such as one invariably encounters on a long ocean voyage. Why, there is your brother now, up on that deck with Captain Mainwaring. I wonder where he has been all this time and what he has been doing. It is a pity that I have nearly finished my pipe already this evening! Pray excuse me, Mrs MacDonald; I must go and speak with him."

Catherine could see her brother and the captain and the active little pilot up on the quarterdeck in silhouette. Was that Mr Fleming up there with them? Left alone again at the rail, Catherine watched the *poon* glide away, watched it sail up the silvery track of the moon across the wide water until she lost it in the darkness. *Increase* lurched gently; then, slowly gathering way, water chuckling now against her hull, resumed her stately progress up the estuary.

In the morning Catherine awakened before dawn. The cabin felt close and stuffy, so she put on a wrapper over her nightdress, and a cloak over the wrapper, and went up onto the main deck. A thick fog shrouded the ship; the tops of the masts overhead were invisible. Peering upward, Catherine noticed that *Increase* was again hove to, her main yards braced sharp 'round with main-topsail backed, and making no way at all. She saw that the gratings around the capstan had been lifted and the tackles rigged. There was an air of hushed surreptitious business as half a dozen crew members awaited orders near the windlass. Catherine went to the lee rail and saw what she had seen before: a *poon* riding there on a couple of long spring lines—the *poon* she had seen last night, or its twin. How deeply interesting, thought Catherine.

She settled herself on a neat stack of spars, and watched. She saw again what she had seen before by moonlight: a great crate hauled up from the hold; the tackles belayed to lift it out over the lee rail; the crate lowered onto the deck of the *poon* and deftly secured there. The active little Flemish pilot who had come aboard last night lightly swung himself over the rail and climbed down to the *poon*. Someone else climbed down after him, awkwardly. It was Hector, with a satchel slung over his back, the strap diagonally across his chest. The *poon* cast off and made sail, disappearing silently into the fog. After a few moments, *Increase* was making way again too. The leadsman in the bow called his soundings.

Mr Fleming came past—startled, Catherine saw, to find her there. "You are awake very early, Mrs MacDonald," he said. "A pity the fog is so thick. There is so little to be seen."

"On the contrary," she said. "I have seen a great deal, and I am full of questions. I wonder if you will answer them for me."

He murmured that the full extent of his little knowledge was entirely at her service.

"What is that boat that just went away from us, and our pilot with it?" she asked. "Have we finished already with our pilot?"

"Oh, by no means. That boat has brought us another pilot. Look, there, you can see him on the quarterdeck with Captain Mainwaring."

"The large man, smoking like a—like a Dutchman?"

"Yes, that is he. He will bring us up through the locks into the harbour."

"But why not the first pilot? Is it usual to change pilots at this point?"

"Oh, no. No, it is not just the usual thing. It was necessary in this case, however, because the first pilot was found to be drunk. Quite drunk. So he has been sent away, and a sober man brought in his place."

Catherine considered this explanation, and found it wanting in several respects. Even as improvisation, it fell short. On the whole, she thought, Captain Mainwaring's voluble indiscretion was to be preferred. "Oh, quite. That explains everything," she said blandly, and he excused himself and went on his way. Catherine returned to her cabin, and her sofa bed, and gazed into the blank mist from her big window in the stern.

Later, after breakfast, Sharada came to help Catherine dress. Catherine sat in front of the tiny rectangle of looking glass mounted on the bulkhead to have her hair unplaited and combed. Sharada was humming under her breath, a slow tune, a tune timed to the stately motion of the ship. Was she even aware of breathing music all the time?

"I wonder," said Catherine, "what was the spice in that sauce for the leg of mutton at dinner yesterday? It was a most unusual flavor, most savory. I don't know if I have had it before."

"Were you enjoying it, ma'am?" asked Sharada.

"Yes, it was delicious. Do you know what spice was in it?"

"Many spices: *dar cheeni*, *zeera*, *elaichi*. You are calling it, ah, cinnamon, cumin, cardamom. Also black pepper, cloves, and nutmeg. These are the heating spices, so very necessary in this cold misty climate."

"Oh!" said Catherine. "But how can you tell which spice was in it? Merely by the taste of it?"

"Oh, no, ma'am. I made it. I was toasting the spices myself, and grinding them, and making the sauce."

"Is that where you spend your day, then? In the galley with the cook?"

"He is a countryman of mine, from the great city of Patna."

"I see," said Catherine; she felt her thick unruly hair smoothed again, as Sharada hummed. Catherine found herself thinking of Sandy, remembering times when the two of them would venture out on the sea loch below the house in a little flat-bottomed skiff that belonged to their father. Once, a sudden mist had descended on them, as thick, as opaque as a sheep's fleece. They promptly had lost their bearings. Which way was land, and which was the open sea? The gray flat water, windless and waveless, gave no clues. Stilling their rising panic, they had held their breath and listened. Distant voices pierced the mist; they heard the old songs of the old women herding cows upon the faraway hill; and these songs were their beacon, drawing them safe through the blank mist, back to the solid rocky shore. Our own Hebridean sirens, Sandy had called them, adding ungratefully, but why must they be so old and ugly?

As this reverie receded, Catherine became gradually aware again of the tune that Sharada was softly humming under her breath. Its tempo had quickened. It was familiar, intimately known; it was shockingly, stunningly, personally familiar. Catherine listened hard to be certain, expecting to find herself mistaken. But it was no mistake; she knew it well. No wonder she had been thinking of Sandy. Sharada had finished combing and was now pinning the heavy coils of hair at Catherine's prickling nape.

With a feeling that she was plunging headlong, Catherine laid firm hold of her courage and asked, "What is that tune you are humming?"

"Oh, I beg your pardon, ma'am, was I humming? It is an old habit. I will try not to do it."

"But what is the tune? Where did you hear it?"

"It is . . . I cannot say, ma'am. It must be a tune I have heard sometime. Tunes come into my ears and remain forever after. Always there is music sounding in my head, always. I beg your kind pardon." She smoothed pomade into the curly short hair at Catherine's temples. Catherine could not see Sharada's face in the small mirror, only her deft hands and her arms, the undersides marked by fading white and pink scars.

Presently Catherine said, "Mrs Todd asked me yesterday if it was true that you intend to go on when I stop in Antwerp. She hoped to engage you for the remainder of the passage to Calcutta."

Sharada's nimble fingers stopped. After a moment she said, "And what was your answer to Mrs Todd? If I may be asking, ma'am."

"I told her that my destination was not yet fixed with complete certainty, and that you might remain with me after all."

"Oh, indeed, ma'am?" Sharada's note of inquiry hung in the air for a long moment.

Then Catherine said, "But now, this morning, I find that my mind is made up. I shall tell Mrs Todd that I am not stopping in Antwerp after all, that I intend to remain with the ship for the entire passage. I shall tell her that I am going on to India."

Sharada's hands fell away from Catherine's head, and Catherine heard her deep intake of breath, her great sigh. "Yes, certainly, ma'am," said Sharada at last. "I was sure of it. I said, you will go to India." After a moment she resumed dressing Catherine's hair, threading a pale green ribbon around the heavy coil at her nape, and finishing with a neat bow on the left. There—coiffed, at last.

The tune Sharada had been humming was known to only a few people in the world. Catherine knew it; and so did Hector.

This maid knew it.

And so did Sandy, whose tune it was. But Sandy was drown'd.

Or else he was not. Not yet.

# 9

## *A very agreeable Vicissitude or Variation*

"Ha ha!" laughed Captain Mainwaring. "A drunken pilot! You are most observant, Mrs MacDonald; we must teach you to go aloft so we can post you in the foretop to keep lookout for us, eh? So tell me then; if you could not believe in Mr Fleming's drunken pilot, what did you make of what you saw? What explanation did you contrive for yourself to account for what you had observed?"

"I concluded that you were unloading the steam looms, the last cargo you loaded in Leith—Scottish looms that are not permitted into the Netherlands. And I supposed that my brother has gone to see them properly installed and working."

"Did I speak of steam looms at Leith? I don't remember it. But if you say so, I suppose I must have let a word or two slip."

"You said half a dozen steam looms, for Liège."

"Did I? I said as much as that? Fancy your remembering it. Well, you are quite right, perfectly correct. Your brother and the looms are in Liège by now, or so they ought to be. It is not like smuggling, you know. It is just, just—trade, and brings nothing but good to all involved. Why should the Netherlanders not have the best looms they can get? No harm is done. . . . Your brother will rejoin us at Antwerp, at the port itself, so you shall see him again there before we sail. Never fear, we will be in time for you to take a proper leave of each other."

"Hmm. That is the other matter. Captain Mainwaring, I have decided not to stop in Antwerp. I wish to remain aboard your ship for the entire voyage to India. To Calcutta."

"Do you, by Jove? To India, after all? Well, no one will pursue you so far as that, to be sure! So you have had a taste of shipboard life and find that it suits you, eh? It is splendid, is it not? I find I am never better than when I am at sea. Some ladies do not like it, but then some do, many do. Captain Hunter's wife has gone to sea with him every voyage these last twenty years. I believe that by now she could command his ship as well as he can. Or, being a wife and accustomed therefore to command, rather better! Well! Of course I shall be very happy to have you—you and your little party. You are comfortable in the big stern cabin, I suppose? You are most welcome to it. How fortunate that no other party had engaged it from Antwerp. We are very well thus, eh? Very well thus."

Early in the afternoon, as *Increase* made her way up the wide Westerschelde, the steward brought to Catherine in her cabin a small folded note:

> *Mr Fleming begs that Mrs MacDonald will honour him with her company after dinner; that she will give her opinion of his Wuyi tea; and that she will allow him to apologise for his reserve in replying to her inquiry of this morning.*

Catherine accepted this invitation; how was it to be refused?

When the time came, after dinner, Sharada smoothed Catherine's unruly hair once again. "Are you wanting your shawl, ma'am?" she asked.

"Yes, just the light India one will do," said Catherine, and Sharada turned to fetch it. Catherine waited, rubbing the rough edge of her fingernail. For a long moment she waited; then she turned to see Sharada standing quite still in front of the open press, holding the forgotten shawl against her breast.

"Oh! I beg your pardon, ma'am!" Sharada said, suddenly coming back to the present moment. "Here is the Kashmiri shawl. But these other things—shall I put away those papers in a safe place?"

"What papers? Oh, all that bagpipe music? It is safe enough where it is, with that caddy of tea. Now, where is Grace? With Annie? She has had her dinner and her tea, I suppose? Very well. So, then." And with a little trepidation, she went to Mr Fleming's cabin, thirty feet away, to drink his tea and receive his apology.

"I might as well admit to you at once, Mr Fleming," said Catherine, "that my opinion of your tea, or of any tea, is little worth having. I am sure it is very good tea because it is yours, and because you say so. And even if I thought it were not—supposing I were qualified to form any opinion about it—well, I must not say so."

He smiled and said, "Well, then, Mrs MacDonald, I will frankly tell you at once that *my* opinion of any tea is considered well worth having. Furthermore, the oolong which I will give you this evening is the best you have ever tasted, so you may just enjoy it in complete confidence."

"So I shall."

"Here, you see, in this specially fitted cabinet, are my stores of teas. This is Yun Wu, which means 'clouds and mist' and ought to appeal to Highland Scots in particular. Here is a splendid Qihong, which the Chinese think fit only for western barbarians. And here is some very fine Lung Ching, the famous 'dragon well.' This is the Wuyi Dahongpao which we are to drink this evening. And then here, in this next cabinet, are my stores of water, my own bottles filled at particular springs noted for the excellence of their water, especially for the brewing of my tea."

Catherine noted the contents of this cabinet: dozens of tall rectangular stoneware bottles fitted snugly into their racks. Each was stopped with a cork, and each cork was covered with a wax seal, and labeled with a date and the name of a spring.

"But is not Captain Mainwaring's water satisfactory? I had thought it very good indeed," said Catherine.

"Oh, yes, very good and perfectly wholesome; he pays particular attention to the ship's water. But I always get in my own stores of water and of tea. This particular tea is plucked from some venerable old bushes grown on the steep red-soil slopes above a famous spring high in the Wuyi mountains. And the water just now coming to the boil is from that same spring." A small spirit stove hissed; it was suspended in a gimbeled stand at Mr Fleming's elbow, and the water in the kettle above it was just beginning to send up steam.

How precious! And faintly absurd; Catherine felt slightly embarrassed for him as she took her seat.

The steward came in and laid out the tea equipment: a tiny melon-shaped red clay teapot and two tiny red clay bowls on a bamboo tray. The vessels were unembellished and unglazed. "But this is tiny, fit for dolls!" she exclaimed. "Is this miniature bowl meant for a cup?"

"It is. This evening we shall have our tea in the true Mandarin style," said Mr Fleming. "These pieces are made by venerated potters near Yixing."

"The Chinese tea sets I have seen were quite different from this, much larger," said Catherine. "They were white-glazed porcelain and painted with oriental scenes, and the cups had handles. My sister-in-law has been yearning for one particular set, painted with red and blue dragons, which she saw displayed in an Edinburgh shop. She took me there to admire it at least three times. I daresay she has made my brother promise to bring her just such a set."

"Ah, yes, that would be export ware. It is made for the European taste—very different from what the celestials consider elegant enough for their own use and refined enough for their own taste."

As he spoke, he deftly removed the neat calyx-shaped lid and filled the teapot—nay, overfilled it—with boiling water. It overflowed into the bamboo tray, which, Catherine now saw, was fitted with a rack, so that the spilled water ran into a hidden catch basin below. He did the same with the two cups. Then, opening the tea caddy, he reached in, frowning, and pinched a finely judged quantity of the long twisted black-edged leaves between his thumb and his first three fingers. With his free hand he emptied the hot water from the now-warm teapot, dropped the leaves into the pot, replaced the lid, and shook the pot. Then he paused for a moment. "To allow the leaves to expand," he explained, noticing Catherine's quizzical look.

She nodded, and waited. Removing the lid again, he passed the teapot under his nose, sniffing first the leaves inside the pot, then the inside of the lid. He reached across the table without a word and passed the leaves under Catherine's nose, too. She inhaled the aroma, as he had done: two deep breaths through her nostrils. It was like . . . like what? Like roasted chestnuts coming out of the shell. Certain lilies at night. New hay in a stone barn.

He filled the pot with steaming water, put the lid on, swirled the pot once—then quickly poured out the pale liquor into a waste basin. Then he immediately filled the pot again and placed the lid on it. "It is best to rinse these oolongs," he said. "Yes! Where were we? Your brother can order an entire tea set for his wife, with her name or her initials on it, or dragons or anything she likes, at Canton. It can be completed in a week or two if it is nothing very unusual."

"But I don't suppose my brother will have any occasion to go as far as Canton," said Catherine.

"I beg your pardon; he certainly will go to Canton," said Mr Fleming. "Would we sail without our engineer on our maiden voyage with his new steam engines? Oh, he certainly will be aboard, I assure you, on the first voyage from Calcutta to Canton."

"I had supposed that Hector's steam engines were destined for riverboats in India," said Catherine.

"They will run their trials on the rivers, no doubt, and will be certainly very useful there, because they can go up against the current as easily as down. But their true superiority will be in the country trade, on the fast coastal runs between Calcutta and the China ports. That is, after all, the one really profitable route for independent traders such as ourselves."

"Oh, I did not know!" said Catherine, feeling that she should have known.

Mr Fleming emptied the hot water from the two little tea bowls and filled them with tea from his tiny pot. Immediately he refilled the pot with more hot water, covered it, and set it aside to steep again. The liquor in the cups was thin, pale, sparkling; each cup sent up a twisting plume of fragrant steam.

Following his example, Catherine took up her tiny cup, cradling it between her two palms, enjoying its heat, its smoothness, and the aroma of the tea. She tasted it. It spread over her tongue, simultaneously wet and astringent. She held a few drops cupped in the center of her tongue for a moment, drawing air over it to inhale its full fragrance. Then, after she swallowed, a sweet flowery aftertaste spread across her mouth and throat. "Ah," she said, quite involuntarily; and Mr Fleming smiled. "It is not like my sister-in-law's tea," she said.

"No," he said. "But not everyone can appreciate the difference."

"It needs no sugar, nor milk."

"No indeed!" They both drank again.

"And is there adequate fuel for steam-powered boats on the

coastal run between Calcutta and China?" asked Catherine, setting down her cup.

"The tropical forests furnish an inexhaustible supply of wood; the only difficulty is in maintaining a reliable labor force to cut it," said Mr Fleming.

"Yet the wind costs nothing," observed Catherine. "Is steam power really so superior as to justify so much expense and trouble?"

"Oh, but you see, Mrs MacDonald, it is a perilous run to China, and our cargo is exceedingly subject to seizure. Not only would the Malay pirates like to relieve us of it, but so would the Chinese customs officers, who are charged with preventing this particular trade, despite the fact that they make their private fortunes by allowing it, clandestinely. But with the superior maneuverability of steam power at our command, we shall have a great advantage, upwind, downwind, or no wind at all."

"But what is your valuable cargo, so subject to seizure?" asked Catherine, feeling once again that she ought already to know the answer to this question.

Mr Fleming refilled their two cups, and then refilled the tiny teapot for a third infusion before replying. "It is the best Patna opium."

"Oh!" said Catherine, and drank her tea. This second cup was more flavourful than the first, and more distinctly astringent. She said, "I had supposed that the East India Company controlled all the Indian opium trade."

"So they do. Only the Company may produce it and sell it. But as the emperor of China forbids the introduction of the pernicious drug into his empire, and as the Honourable Company is loathe to incur the emperor's wrath, the Company takes no official part in the import—or some might say smuggling—of the article into his domains. No; they only grow it; and manufacture it; and sell it at auction to independent merchants such as ourselves. The terms of the auction require payment in silver, you understand. Then it is up to us, the independent merchants, to run the risks associated with carrying the forbidden article to China. If we are caught, the Company simply shrugs its Honourable shoulders and disclaims any responsibility." He shrugged, elegantly expressing the Company's superb unnotice, and continued. "Meanwhile, the Company takes this silver—the silver we've paid them for their opium—and carries it to China, where they buy tea with it, for the Chinese, you understand, will take nothing but silver for their tea. And as the Chinese, in their turn, have a monopoly on tea, they may impose what terms they please. So that is how Indian opium is transformed into Chinese tea—by the alchemic virtue of silver—and carried thence to all the good housewives in Europe."

"We are not obliged to buy their tea, I suppose," said Catherine.

"It is theirs or none, however, for tea grows nowhere else in the world. And tea has become as necessary to Europeans—and the duties on it as necessary to our national exchequers—as though it were opium itself." And he filled their cups for the third time.

"Could not tea plantations be established elsewhere?" asked Catherine, lifting her cup and inhaling its steam, which no longer seemed so fragrant. Was her nose becoming jaded, or was the enchanting perfume dissipated by now? She felt remarkably alert, yet deeply calm. Her mind had time, space, clarity, as though she could see a great distance across purple mountains while also perceiving in uncommon detail the very spores speckling the bracken at her feet. The tea, quite strong and more astringent than before, now left a markedly sweeter taste on her tongue after she swallowed.

"As was done in the case of nutmeg, you mean?" said Mr Fleming. Catherine was flattered, for of course that is what she would have meant if she had known anything about it. "It was a favorite ambition of Sir Warren Hastings, back in the 'seventies," he said, "and there has been enthusiasm for the project from time to time among the botanists of the Asiatick Society. Seeds and seedlings have been smuggled out of China, but no one has succeeded in growing them. No, we remain in thrall to the Chinese for tea; and they remain in thrall to us for opium." He filled their cups once more.

"Are the Chinese unable to grow their own opium?"

"Oh, yes, the peasants grow a poor grade of it, and always have. A great deal of the Turkish stuff ends up in China too. But for purity, potency and profit, there is nothing like Patna opium. And no other commodity can induce the Chinese to part with their silver."

"I see." And for a moment, she did understand it all.

"Now, Mrs MacDonald, I have answered your questions without reserve or self-justification, so as to make some amends for my evasiveness this morning when you asked about the cargo you saw taken off so early. This is my apology; and I hope you will accept it."

"With all my heart," said Catherine, and meant it.

"I think my teapot has given its utmost," said Mr Fleming, removing the little lid and peering inside. "A fifth infusion would only disappoint us both. It is best to stop at the fourth with this Dahongpao." By now, his obsession no longer seemed an absurd affectation; clearly he was quite in earnest about it.

He reached inside the pot, drew out a single leaf, limp and bright green with mahogany red edges, and ate it. Then he offered the pot to Catherine, his mobile black brows arched in invitation. To eat tea leaves! It had never occurred to Catherine; but she tasted one. It was succulent and faintly bitter, and left a sweet aftertaste. Mr Fleming smiled. "In ancient times, the Chinese ate tea as a health-giving vegetable."

"With salt and pepper and a knob of sweet butter on a hot bannock or a potato, it would be a Highlander's treat," said Catherine. "I wonder that no one has thought of it. It is tastier than sea-tangle. Have you eaten sea-tangle gathered off a Hebridean shore? No? Tea leaves are certainly superior, pleasantly free of any sand to grit between the teeth."

She looked around the neat little cabin. Every bit of bulkhead not given over to stores of tea and water was lined with books, the neat rows of octavo editions held fast by mahogany bars across their spines, and the bars secured at each end by bright brass fastenings. There were the usual volumes of Virgil, Homer, Milton, Dryden, Shakespeare, Molière, Pope and Johnson. But there were also many unfamiliar titles: *Hitopadesa*, *Sakuntala*, *Rig-Veda*, *Ramayana*, *Bhagvat-Geta*, *Mahabharata*; as well as a Sanskrit grammar and a large handsome atlas. One cabinet held rolls of creamy thick paper, tied up in silk ribbons. "What are those rolls?" asked Catherine.

"Ah, my Chinese scrolls," said Mr Fleming. "If you are not careful, I will make you admire them the next time you come and drink tea with me."

"It must be very pleasant to have your books with you," she said. "I brought only two, not expecting to stay away from Scotland for long, and I fear I cannot get any more in this city in any language I can read."

"You must make use of mine. But of course you must; I am quite in earnest. Choose something to take away with you. I know them all by heart, or nearly so; they are all my old shipboard companions. There's not one that I've read fewer than a dozen times, so you may choose anything you like without depriving me in the slightest."

He succeeded at last in making her borrow a translation of *Ramayana*. "As you are bound for India after all," he said, "you might as well begin to steep yourself in the particular flavour of the place, the *rasa* of the place. I will be most interested to know what you make of it."

When Catherine had thanked him and returned to her own cabin, she examined the book. The embossed morocco binding smelled not only of leather but of Mr Fleming's cabin; of sandalwood and varnished mahogany and tea. The text was printed in two languages, two scripts. On the left page was the original Sanskrit text, she supposed, in a script so strangely unintelligible; it looked like laundry hung from a line to dry. Facing it, on the right page, was the English translation in the familiar alphabet. The paper was thin and translucent so that each script showed faintly through the other in reverse.

Kind of him to lend it. Catherine still felt invigorated and alert, still felt the soft, wide, far-seeing stimulus of the tea. She had enjoyed that. She would not mind drinking tea with him again.

❧ ❧ ❧

THE NEXT AFTERNOON, Catherine went looking for Anibaddh and found her in her accustomed spot on the main deck. She was hemming a pillow slip in the watery sunshine, and Grace sat in her lee as usual, sewing a long seam on her lap.

Catherine still could not bring herself to say Annie Bad. "Annie," she said, "it is time, you know, to determine where you will go and what you will do. *Increase* will remain in Antwerp for only a few days, and if you would return to Britain, or to America—Boston or Canada or some safe place—it must be from here. Captain Mainwaring will find you a return passage if you are determined to go back. And remember you are to have the sum from me, which is yours to invest or to use as you please. Or perhaps you might prefer to remain in service for a time at least. In that case, Mrs Todd has asked whether you would wait on her and continue with her to India."

Anibaddh set her sewing on her lap and looked away from Catherine. After a moment she said, "I never decided anything important before."

"Oh, but you have, Annie. When you rescued Grace. When you ran away from that woman."

"Mmm, I guess I did, then. Well, Mrs MacDonald, ma'am, I've been thinking about Africa. And I've been wondering, is this ship going to pass near by it?"

How could this poor, uprooted, ignorant tall child be turned out to fend for herself in the wide world? But Catherine said only, "Let us go and consult an atlas."

Anibaddh folded her sewing and stood up. Grace made to do the same, but she found that her length of calico would not come free of her lap. She tried again to lift the doubled wrong-side-out length of calico, but her skirt lifted too. Understanding dawned; she had sewn her skirt into her long straight seam. Jumping to her feet, she danced a few steps, brandishing the absurd tangle of cloth and skirt, and laughed, a long, free peal of laughter, her transparent skin suffused by warm delight.

Catherine laughed too, but then tears came instead and she had to turn away. Not since that accident had Grace laughed aloud.

Anibaddh took up scissors; "Hold still, now, child!" she said. "Look at you, hopping about like a kid goat!" And after a moment she succeeded in cutting Grace's skirt free.

At Catherine's request, Mr Fleming opened his atlas on one end of the big table in the cuddy cabin and leafed through its heavy broad pages to a map of the world. He smoothed the pages flat.

"Oh!" said Anibaddh, awed, and Grace craned to see.

"Here is where you began," said Catherine, pointing to the eastern coast of the North American continent. "Virginia."

"That's where I was born, right there," said Anibaddh, touching the spot with her fingertip, for she did indeed know how to read.

"And you sailed with your mistress from . . . what port, do you know?"

"Alexandria, there! And all across the Atlantic Ocean, I know that, too—aha! to Scotland, way on up north, in the cold!"

"Here, you see, is Greenock," said Mr Fleming, "just outside Glasgow, where your ship must have come to port. Was the cargo tobacco, do you know?"

"Tobacco and wheat."

"Then you would have come into Greenock, I am sure," said Mr Fleming.

Catherine said, "And then you and your mistress came by land to Edinburgh—just here, you see, across this narrow neck of land. And here is where we all got aboard *Increase* and sailed out the Firth of Forth, and southeast across the North Sea, coming up the Westerschelde, up to Antwerp, here."

"We're at Antwerp now?"

"Aye. There, far to the east of us, is India. And this great continent, around which we must pass to get there, is Africa."

"All that is Africa? It's mighty big. Will this ship stop there?"

"Yes, as it happens, we will," said Mr Fleming. "There, at the Cape of Good Hope, at the southern tip of Africa. We are to take on a particular cargo here in Antwerp, a consignment of Flemish mares to be carried to Cape Town, destined for the stud of Lord Charles Somerset, who is the governor of the British settlements there."

"So if there's lords and gentlemen at Cape Town, then I guess maybe there's ladies too?" said Anibaddh. "And I guess maybe those ladies needs maids to do their heads and look after their clothes?"

"I suppose they do," said Mr Fleming.

Anibaddh studied the map again in silence. Then she said, "I just want to get to Africa somehow or other," she said. "I'll wait on Mrs Todd, I guess, far as Cape Town."

✣ ✣ ✣

"YOU SHALL HAVE your astronomy lesson this evening, Mrs Todd, if you and Mr Todd will come to the quarterdeck at sunset," promised Captain Mainwaring at dinner. "Anyone who likes to come is welcome; the full moon of August is always splendid, and it is well worth seeing its rising through a good glass, if you have never done so before."

Having nothing else in particular to do, most of the company, excepting Hector and Mr Fleming, did assemble there. A few clouds still hung in the east, for it had rained earlier in the day.

"Now, Mrs Todd," said Captain Mainwaring, "you must not look directly at the sun, not even now as it sets. It is too bright and will harm your eyes. Oh, yes, it is quite capable of doing permanent harm. The moon is another matter; there you may gaze as long as you like in perfect safety, for its benign light is only reflected. Those clouds will clear away soon, I think. We cannot expect to see moonrise just yet, but do watch. It will rise just beyond those masts there—the masts of those yachts."

Mr Sinclair, elbows on the rail next to Catherine, said, "So you will sail with us to India after all, Mrs MacDonald. I was glad to hear of it."

"To India after all," said Catherine lightly. "Mostly so as to suit the convenience of my Hindu maid, who wants to return there."

"Ha ha! Your maid is the one who sings under her breath all the time, I think?" asked Mr Sinclair.

"You have heard her?" said Catherine. "Let me apologise for her, but I do not think she is even aware of doing it."

"What does she sing?"

"Anything, everything. It is not just Indian songs but Scottish tunes too, even those she has heard only once or twice. She is amazingly quick to pick up a tune. At first, when I heard her strange Indian melodies, I thought that she was simply an unskillful singer, that her pitch was not true, for she would sing such strange notes! But when she sings Scottish tunes, her pitch is exact—quite exquisitely just. So perhaps it is only that oriental music uses different notes, new notes."

"New notes! Hmmm; more likely they are the old notes," said Mr Sinclair thoughtfully. "All the unused notes that fall between the keys of the pianoforte, lost to us now."

"How odd to think of losing notes, of discarding them!" said Catherine. "Like losing colours. Are there lost colours somewhere, to be recovered, do you think?" She nodded at the sky, an improbable aubergine, darkening as the moments passed.

"Ah! I should so like to astonish the world by rediscovering some lost colours! India will be the place to look for them," said Mr Sinclair. "If they are to be found anywhere, it is there."

"There! There it is!" cried Dr Macpherson loudly, taking his pipe from his mouth and gesturing with it at the thicket of masts to eastward. "Lo, the moon appeareth!"

" 'Lo, the moon appeareth'?" repeated Mr Todd in a quiet sneering tone, aside to Mr Sinclair.

" 'Shew thy face from a cloud, O moon; light his white sails on the wave of the night!' " declaimed Dr Macpherson, his unpleasing pedantic voice at its most irritating pitch. "Oh, there is no one so sublime as Ossian for a moonlit maritime scene. Here's another: 'Rise, moon, thou daughter of the sky! Look from between thy clouds, that I may behold the gleam of his steel, on the field of his promise.' And there's a great deal more, you know, a great deal."

"Ossian, is it?" said Mr Todd a little more loudly. "Ossian Macpherson, The Great Sham? Rise, Member for Camelford and Arcot, from thy oft-filled shells, and shed thy great beams and motes in the eyes of the credulous."

Mrs Todd laughed, then quickly covered her mouth, but Dr Macpherson affected not to hear this sally.

"Don't, sir. It's a shame," said Mr Sinclair quietly to Mr Todd, and tried to turn him away by the elbow. But Mr Todd, somewhat elated by his after-dinner wine, would not be hushed. "There's a great deal more of *that* too, I assure you," he said. "Here's another: Hide thy broad beaming self, oh moon, for thy kilt is blown awry by the whistling blast that issueth from thy shadowed darknesses!" And here Mr Todd succeeded in emitting on cue a loud fart.

Seizing Mr Todd's arm in an undeniable grip, Mr Sinclair instantly led him away. As they passed, Catherine heard Mr Sinclair saying, low but vehement, "For shame, man, you might forbear; do you forget he is a Macpherson himself, near kin to the very man, and educated by his generosity?"

After a moment's embarrassment, Mrs Todd made Captain Mainwaring a little curtsy and followed her husband to their cabin below.

Captain Mainwaring remarked calmly to no one in particular that persons who had indulged rather too freely in the joys of the shell were best ignored. He tried to put his telescoping glass into the doctor's hand, begging that he would feel free to make use of it.

Dr Macpherson had been slow to take offense, slow to recognise the insult and ridicule directed at him; but as conviction dawned, he had ruffled and swelled up glaring like an angry cock turkey. He had not had an opportunity to retort, but he complained now to the captain: That was a low churlish fellow! It was a trial to be thrown into such company! And who was the fellow after all, with such a name as Todd! Certainly incapable of appreciating the beauties of an Ossian! Beneath the notice of his betters!

"Quite, Dr Macpherson, quite," said Captain Mainwaring. "Now, pray look through my glass, Doctor, for I have got the instrument focused to the most exquisite degree. You will notice in particular what cannot be so easily seen with the unaided eye—the great, shadowed craters between the Mare Tranquillitatis and the Mare Fecunditatis, in the southeast quadrant, there. It is a very fine instrument; I had it of a most frighteningly learned man in Prague some years ago."

The sensation of the heavy polished wood and glass instrument in his hand returned Dr Macpherson to the present. "A fine instrument indeed," said he, putting it to his eye—and losing its exquisite focus by tapping it.

❧ ❧ ❧

HECTOR, RETURNING TO *Increase* early the next morning, disapproved of Catherine's decision. "Oh, Catherine, no. No, no, I will not hear of it. Of course you must remain for a little time here in Antwerp, and then you will go back to Edinburgh and stay with Mary. It has been all settled. I have seen the house here, the house and warehouse belonging to Crawford and Fleming; you and Grace will be perfectly comfortable there."

"No doubt we would be comfortable, Hector. But it is not a question of comfort."

"What, then? You have not given me any rational explanation for this absurd change of plan."

"But I have explained to you as well as I can," she said. It was noon; they were on the main deck of *Increase*, which was tied up at one of the two modern gigantic French-built docks in the commodious port of Antwerp, so that the half-dozen Flemish mares destined for Cape Town could be easily brought aboard. The big stolid mares walked aboard placidly, quite unimpressed by their surroundings. "I have thought about it a great deal," Catherine said, "and I feel quite certain that it is right for Grace and me to go out to India."

"Quite certain! Based upon what? You have not given me anything resembling a cogent reason, Catherine. Come, what are your reasons?"

"Shall I tell you my reasons so that you can argue them with me?"

"Or will you conceal them, so that I cannot?"

She had her reasons: Sandy was not yet drown'd; wasn't that the meaning of the message he had sent her? Hector had seen that page of music too, titled in Sandy's handwriting, but Hector's mechanical mind would not consider it evidence that Sandy was still walking on the earth among the living. Then her maid had hummed that very tune—so uncanny! Somewhere, sometime Sharada had surely heard Sandy play his tune—perhaps only once, at some distance, across some Indian town at dusk. But for Catherine, hearing Sharada hum that tune was like hearing the old women singing on the hill, when she and Sandy had been adrift on the water in the mist. To Catherine it meant, come this way; this is the way. She could try to explain all this to Hector, but he would never consider these sufficient reasons to go to India.

Indeed, she herself knew these to be preposterous reasons to go to India. Nevertheless, she was going. To India, where one might find the things that were lost: lost notes, lost colours—perhaps even a lost brother.

"Well?" he said.

"Well, what?"

"Catherine, you are most exasperating. Is it that woman? Do you suppose that dreadful American woman will pursue you here, you and Grace?"

"Oh, no; we have seen the last of her, I daresay. And she, of us."

"What, then? I only hope you are not still . . . cherishing fantastic hopes . . . imaginings, about Sandy."

"No, my dear, I am quite innocent of fantastic imaginings. I am mired in grim doubt, as mired as you could wish." And this was true; she was as full of doubt as of hope. "Now let us change the subject. Let us discuss . . . oh, let us discuss, perhaps, smuggling—the justifications for smuggling contraband steam looms into a country, a foreign kingdom which has banned them. Just for the sake of argument, how might a promising young mechanic, a practitioner and devotee of natural philosophy, justify his participation in such an enterprise? Is it for money? Is there a great deal of money to be made?"

"Catherine, you are infuriating! You were always infuriating."

"Well? And will you tell me your reasons so that I can argue them with you?"

Hector did not reply, only frowned and looked out at the Flemish city, fingertips drumming on the broad rail.

"Or will you keep your own counsel," said Catherine, "and permit me to keep mine?"

"These are separate matters; you must not muddle them up together. I would be shirking my duty as your brother, and as head of the family, if I failed to solemnly represent the dangers of allowing your rampant impulsiveness to get the better of you."

"I give you my word that no rampant impulsiveness has got the better of me. There. You have done your duty as brother and as head of the family. Are you satisfied?"

Hector scowled but did not speak, so Catherine continued. "And perhaps you will allow me, your sister and the wee bairn of the family, to inquire whether you are equally satisfied that no rapacious greed has got the better of you?"

"Oh, fie, Catherine! It is only steam looms!"

It was on the tip of her tongue to ask him whether opium was only opium, but he went on. "And there is very little money being made in the undertaking, certainly not enough to compensate for the risks we run. It is mostly a gesture of goodwill, a generous and brotherly sharing with an old acquaintance of Mr. Fleming's—that may at some future time blossom into a mutually profitable manufacturing partnership in flax and hemp. There! Are *you* satisfied?"

"Why must the looms be smuggled, then? Why so furtive?"

"Because the king of the Netherlands wishes to shelter his neophtye mechanics from the harshness of competition while they figure out how to build steam-powered looms as good as ours. It is a mistaken precaution, however, a faulty notion; why should they struggle for years, decades, and replicate all our own early difficulties? Why should the weavers not have the fruits of our experience now? Flemish trade and manufacturing will benefit immediately. The Flemish mechanics will soon copy our machines, and learn a great deal from doing so. No doubt they have taken one apart already. Not the least harm is done; everyone gains."

"Well," said Catherine, "let us each attend to our own conscience, then. Apparently each of us has been endowed with one of our very own."

# 10

## *more cultivated Geniuses*

"That doesn't look like any straw hat I've ever seen," said Catherine, gazing up at the famous portrait by Sir Pieter Paul Rubens.

"No, it's probably a mistake," said Mr Sinclair, "a persistent mistranslation. It should be called *Le Chapeau de Poil*—of felt—not *de Paille*—of straw."

"Oh, a felt hat! Yes, it might certainly be a felt hat," said Mrs Todd. Mr Todd sighed noisily, shifting from foot to foot.

Their little party stood before Rubens's famous painting in the gilded leather-paneled drawing room of a handsome Antwerp house, having already passed through a vast reception room hung with sumptuous tapestries. The house, and the noble collection which filled it, had belonged to a notable merchant banker of impeccable taste and fathomless resources, now recently deceased. His worldly goods were to be auctioned in a few weeks' time, so prospective bidders (and those, like themselves, who had not the slightest prospect of bidding) had come to see the collection before its dispersal into the hands of new owners. Small groups of well-dressed people sauntered about the room, talking quietly or shrilly, considering the pictures in turn. Catherine heard comments and exclamations in French and Dutch, German and Italian.

The lady in the painting was all neck and hands. The deep neckline of her dress framed translucent plump flesh; and her fingers were long, tapered, be-ringed. Her chin was tucked demurely down, but her gaze was unabashed. Her face was illuminated by reflected light (reflected from where? wondered Catherine) even under the wide brim of her black hat. "It does seem amazingly familiar," said Catherine, "as though I had seen it before."

"Perhaps that is because it has been very much copied," said Mr Sinclair. "I have done several portraits just like it, for it is a composition which suits every woman."

"I should so like to try it myself!" cried Mrs Todd. "If only I dared. But who would sit for me?"

"You might do it as a self-portrait. You would need only a looking glass for your model," said Mr Sinclair.

"Oh, Mr Todd, do say that I might," begged Mrs Todd prettily. "It will be just the thing to occupy my mornings when we sail. Only pigments and a canvas—and of course I shall require a wide-brimmed hat, of any colour. The colour doesn't signify in the least, as I can paint it as I please."

Catherine wandered away from them so she could look at the great man's collection without distraction. Each picture was worth seeing: a Diana at her hunt; a barefoot Eurydice with a viper of malicious appearance; a horribly accomplished Crucifixion, from which Catherine quickly averted her glance. What manner of man found it edifying (or worse, stimulating) to contemplate so gruesome an image?

She came to a set of eight smaller pictures in watercolour, framed alike and hung together. They were only sketches, she realised, and unsigned, but they showed a certain mastery. They might be composition studies, she thought, for they were imbued with vigour yet lacking in the polish or painstaking finish of the other works in the collection. Why were they here? Reading the French captions set into the painted border surrounding each picture, she realised that the series portrayed the life and career of Alexander the Great. Here was the hero before the high priest; here he was wounded at the battle of Issus; here he was in his magnanimity granting clemency to the family of Darius. And then there was the scene of his victory over Porus, king of India. Macedonian Alexander had gone to India; why shouldn't she? She looked closely at the painting itself. The great Alexander was left-handed, for he held his sword in his left hand, and his shield on his right arm. Catherine's own Alexander, her own dearest Sandy, had been left-handed too.

But something about this picture nudged her memory. It gave her an uncomfortable twisted feeling; and wasn't it like something she had just seen, just now?

She returned to the magnificent reception room hung with tapestries, which they had already passed. Yes, here was the same composition woven as a great tapestry, eight feet high and twelve feet long: Alexander's defeat of the Indian king Porus at the River Hydaspes. But it was a mirror image of the little watercolour sketch in the other room. In the tapestry, Alexander was right-handed; he held his sword in his right hand, his shield on his left arm.

Mr Sinclair appeared at her shoulder. "A superb collection, isn't it?" he said. "The man was endowed not only with the collector's compulsion but with the connoisseur's eye as well—and, rarest confluence of all, the means to indulge them."

"A happy combination!" said Catherine. "But then I have not seen many collections—only Mr John Clerk's, in Edinburgh, and some dark old paintings in one or two gloomy old lairds' houses when I was too young to notice them properly."

"Ah, you have been in Mr Clerk's house! Pray, what did you think of his collection?"

"Oh, I am in no way qualified to judge; you must excuse me," said Catherine.

"I beg your pardon, Mrs MacDonald, but I must contradict you. You have eyes in your head for seeing, and a mind inside it for judging and considering what you see. And I have observed you here, doing what very few people do, which is to really look. I am quite sure that anyone who looks intelligently can form an opinion worth airing."

Catherine smiled, flattered in spite of herself. "You almost induce me to speak," she said.

"But did you not admire Mr Clerk's Rubens? You do not recall noticing it? A plumpish but pathetic *Callisto*? And yet he has it in a place of honour—or so he had, when I saw it several years ago. And in a dazzling carved and gilt frame; and he would draw the attention of all his visitors to it, for he was excessively proud of having secured so valuable an object."

"Alas, I certainly do not remember noticing it. I did admire the portrait of his father—a sober, old-fashioned picture painted by Sir Henry

Raeburn. And I was much struck by a set of Indian pictures; tiny, brilliant paintings like jewels. Those I see still in my mind's eye from time to time. In any case, Mr Clerk was drawing our attention to other things: an old pipe music manuscript he had just acquired; and a tiny working model of my brother's steam engine. It is a sorry admission, but I am proof that the untutored opinion—the natural taste of the sublime savage, if you like—is of little value after all."

He laughed, quite clearly delighted. "No, no, Mrs MacDonald; in fact you have proven just the contrary; for the pictures you describe—the Raeburn portrait and the Indian miniatures—are genuine, and very good examples of their type. Whereas Mr Clerk's *Callisto* is a fake, and a sorry daub as well."

"Is it? Surely not! How can you be so certain?"

"Because I painted it myself, in my impoverished student days. You doubt me! I was astonished beyond words when I first recognised it hanging in Mr Clerk's cabinet. It was like meeting an old enemy unexpectedly at point-blank range. I owned only the one canvas in those impecunious days of my youthful ambition, so I painted it over and over again as I traveled about Europe on my student pilgrimages from one great collection to another, and copying, copying, everywhere I went. For of course you must copy the masters if you are to learn to paint; there is no other course. My one and only canvas was now a still life, now a Venus, now a Flemish portrait, now a Renaissance allegory, and the paint thicker upon its surface at every new incarnation. I parted with it at last in Paris to a compassionate Jacobite expatriate only slightly less poor than I, who wanted a present for his wife to hang on the wall of their lodgings. I had just copied the *Callisto* in Brussels, though my supplies of paint were so scanty by this time that it was really just the thinnest film of a picture, with the shadow of my previous effort—a *nature morte*—almost showing through if you knew how to look. But I got enough money to pay for my return passage to Scotland, and my kind friends were happy to have the picture, or so I believed then. Thus I parted with the much-abused single canvas of my student days and thought no more about it. So you can imagine my astonishment upon coming face to face with it in the house of the eminent Edinburgh collector! He was very proud of it, for it was then his newest, proudest acquisition."

"His newest thing is always his favorite, I think," said Catherine.

"Just so. And he was filled with the glee of having snatched it from under the very nose of another collector. He told us how he had accomplished this canny feat, but I was unable to attend, for I was sadly distracted. At first I was not absolutely certain, as some time had passed, and it was painful for me to believe that even in my student days I could have produced so unconvincing a piece of work—for really, it was not an admirable thing at all. But then I managed to maneuver myself into a position to discern the proof—that is, the traces of the *nature morte* that I knew underlay my *Callisto*. And there it was! Pears, dead hares, and guns. Thus I knew it was mine."

"What did you say? Or do?"

"Nothing, at that time, in company. But later, when Mr Clerk and I were alone together, I led him, as artlessly as was in my power, to see the outlines of the pears and hares. He had never noticed them before. But even this new discovery did not cast any shadow of doubt over the chastity of his cherished *Callisto*. Not even an Iago could have had any success with our Mr Clerk! On the contrary, he was inclined only to congratulate himself on having got two Rubenses for the price of one. He was unable to hear any suggestions of another nature, and went so far as to imply that my doubt was only the incompetent's base envy of a master's skill."

"And how did you bear such aspersions?"

"Poorly, I am afraid. We did not part friends. But I had assuaged my conscience. It was never my intent—indeed, it had never occurred to me—that my bungling journeyman copy might deceive anyone. But some people will not be undeceived. So I told myself, 'He that is robb'd, not wanting what is stol'n, Let him not know't and he's not robb'd at all.' "

"As for this collection," said Catherine, gesturing about the tapestried gallery, "I suppose it harbours no cuckoos of yours?"

"Not a one, alas!" Mr Sinclair said with a laugh. "Though several of these paintings have long been the objects of my ardent admiration. And of my most sincere compliment, too, in the form of faithful imitation. I have appropriated more than a few of these pictures—copied, reworked, adapted, and used their composition and their elements again and again. The classical column, the balustraded terrace, the scarlet drapery arranged handsomely behind the sitter—these are the standard settings for a great many portraits by any painter. No, if I may claim any artistic genius, it lies in an ability to recognise what is worth copying. Well, and I claim also a certain hard-won felicity of execution."

"Speaking of copying, I see that the little watercolour sketches in the next room are copies of these tapestries. But why are they in reverse?"

"Very noticing of you—but backward still! Let us go and look at them. The tapestries in fact came after, for the little watercolours are the designer's original sketches. So astute of this great collector to have got them. From these original designs, then, a full-size cartoon was next made, also backward, to be placed under the loom for the guidance of the weavers in producing the tapestries. The weavers work from the back of the tapestry, you understand. Occasionally one sees errors where a designer has forgotten to reverse some important element, so that a finished tapestry might have odd left-handed figures or inscriptions with some backward letters. The weaver, of course, simply copies what he is given."

"How very confusing it must be to draw in reverse, in mirror image!"

"There is a certain knack, a versatile way of seeing. It is a knack that all good engravers must have. And there are tricks, too—tracing and mirrors and the like—but I must not reveal the secrets of my trade."

An elderly footman belonging to the house approached them, bowed, and asked a question in Flemish. Mr Sinclair answered briefly in the same language; then, as the footman went away again, he translated for Catherine. "He says a foreign maidservant is below, seeking a Meester Mikdinell, or something like that; he was not quite clear about the name, but he did clearly convey a distinct disapproval of uncivilized foreign names. The foreign maidservant carries an important letter but refused to give it to him. I told him to bring her to us. Do you know where your brother might be found?"

"Hector has a knack of evaporating just when he is wanted. But he did say something this morning about a playhouse. He wondered whether there might be a play worth seeing."

"Ah! It is nearby. But here she comes, the barbaric foreign maidservant." They could see Sharada at the far end of the enfilade of the formal rooms following in the wake of the elderly footman. She had not yet seen them; as she passed through the magnificent galleries, she took the opportunity to look about her. A party of vivacious Italian visitors was making its way out, and the footman stood against the gilded embossed-leather panels lining the narrow passage that separated one gallery from the next to give them room to pass. Sharada, just behind him, moved to one side as well to make way for the Italians. But then, it seemed, she sprang forward again, nearly colliding with one of the dark gentlemen in the Roman party. He laughed, steadying her by the shoulders. With a remark to one of the ladies in his company, they continued on their way, the ladies laughing now and fanning themselves. The elderly footman looked extremely annoyed, however; he frowned heavily at Sharada and addressed some words to her. "That was a rebuke, I make no doubt," said Mr Sinclair. "But why such a leap—like a deer?"

"I daresay she suddenly saw the leather paneling on the wall behind her—saw that she was in danger of actually touching it. And if there is one thing she cannot bear to touch, it is the hide of a cow. My trunk is a handsome leather-bound thing—I confess I have always been ridiculously proud of it—but she cannot bring herself to touch it. I have seen her use a cloth so as not to touch it, and then she must launder the cloth! Sometimes she will get Annie to handle the trunk instead."

"Oh, aye!" said Mr Sinclair. "She is a Hindu, I suppose, to whom leather is horror, defilement, an unclean abomination. Now, we Highlanders, too, are fond of our cattle, but then we are as likely to honour it on the plate as on the hoof."

The footman made his bow to them, made it deeply expressive of his disapproval, and went away. Sharada, flustered, placed her hands together and bowed her head instead of her usual little curtsy. "Ma'am, I beg your pardon," she said. "Here is an important letter of great urgency from Mr Fleming for your esteemed brother, but no one knew where he was to be found. So I am carrying it to you in hopes you are knowing where he has gone."

In a few minutes they had settled their plan. Mr Sinclair would take Mrs MacDonald in search of her brother. And Mr Todd would take Mrs Todd to buy a broad-brimmed hat.

"The theatre, then," said Mr Sinclair, as he and Catherine stepped into the street, Sharada close behind. "And as it lies on the most direct route back to the quay, your maid might as well follow."

They reached the theatre, and found Hector in the foyer, just as a rain shower began.

"It is only 'The Young Werther,' in French," reported Hector. "Would it amuse you this evening to observe the Young Werther sinking under his sorrows?"

"Oh, Werther! So petulant," said Catherine.

"It is hard to muster any sympathy or even patience for a character who is so incompetent," said Mr Sinclair. "There is nothing unusual about his troubles, and we must not all go about shooting ourselves if we find ourselves crossed in love."

"The playhouse does not inspire confidence either," observed Hector.

"It was the Tapestry Hall in former days of glory," said Mr Sinclair.

"That would explain why there are so many filthy old tapestries hanging about. We had best stay inside until the rain lets up, and I will show you an interesting one with a piper in it."

Clerestory windows high up near the stepped roofline of the old building admitted gray light onto the dirty tapestries hung along the building's water-stained walls. "Look," said Hector, "here stands the piper atop this overturned barrel, and the peasants all dancing about—the ones who aren't feasting or misbehaving themselves or being sick. It must be a lively tune, to judge by the animation of the dancers. I see only two drones to his pipes; and that is just what we had in Scotland, too, in the old days."

"Not very splendid, is it?" Catherine said. "I am disappointed. Somewhere I had acquired the delusion that old tapestries were fairy confections woven of silver and gold."

"But you see here only those which survived the occupation of the Buonapartists," said Mr Sinclair. "The valuable ones, the ones with gold and silver thread, proved too great a temptation when the troops were rioting for their arrears of pay. Those were nearly all burned to recover the value of the metals in them."

"Yet the Flemish speak affectionately of the French occupation! It is astounding."

"Inexplicable are the workings of the merchant mind. Nor were these from the best ateliers. Falsified town marks—all marked 'Brussels' no matter where they were made. Badly faded, and not from sun and venerable age but just because the dyers didn't know their trade, or cheated and used indigo instead of the costly woad—that sort of thing. *Afzetter* work and forgeries."

"What is *afzetter*?"

"Oh, literally it is 'offsetter,' but it means cheater, swindler. Come, here is an example of *afzetter* work." He was peering closely at the face of an oriental soldier in the background of a large soiled and faded tapestry depicting some ancient military victory. "You see the contours, the shading under the cheekbones of this barbarian soldier, this Mongol? Any buyer of a tapestry is entitled to expect that the design of the tapestry is woven, not painted, is he not? Yet this shading is not woven, not a result of weft threads first dyed the desired shade, then woven over the warp threads. No, it is powdered chalk brushed onto the finished tapestry to correct it, to heighten the design, to compensate for poor draftsmanship or poor dyes. This is the dishonourable touch of the *afzetter*. One finds it usually on minor background characters. More care is usually taken with the principal figures, such as this barbarian general, whomever he may be. Who is this meant to be, do you suppose? Genghis Khan?"

"It is Lord Timur, sir," said Sharada unexpectedly. "Tamerlane, you English are calling him."

They had forgotten that she was there. "I beg your pardon, sir. And ma'am." Sharada put her hands together and bowed her head.

"Tamerlane! Is it indeed? And how can you be certain? Have you seen this tapestry before?" said Catherine.

"I have seen one very like it in the palace at Allahabad; it was a gift to the first emir from *feringee* merchants in the reign of the Emperor Akbar. Also in that palace is hanging another *feringee* tapestry. I think it is just like the tapestry in the grand house where I found you just now, showing the victory of the invader Sikander at the Hydaspes River."

Was she in the habit of frequenting imperial palaces, this ayah? Catherine tried to see her face, but Sharada was looking at the floor, her face averted behind the hem of her shawl.

"Sikander? Oh, she means Alexander!" said Hector, looking up from his letter.

Such an old name, so many variations. Sikander; Alexander; Alasdair. Sandy.

Catherine said, "Now, Hector, what is this exceedingly important letter which we were so good as to bring to you?"

"It is from Mr Fleming, and he encloses another letter in Dutch, or Flemish. As far as I am able to make out, they are having some difficulties in Liège with their new looms. No doubt they have disassembled one and cannot put it together again."

"I am at your service, sir, as a translator," offered Mr Sinclair.

"It is very kind, but I had better go along and ascertain Mr Fleming's views. He says he will be at the warehouse. You had best return to the ship, Catherine, for here is your maid to go with you. But Mr Sinclair, sir, you might find it worth your while to come with me if you are so disposed, for our Mr Fleming has some interesting things. Books and ancient fragments—rather miscellaneous to my eye, but worth seeing nevertheless, I suppose."

Catherine said to Sharada, "Grace is with . . . ?"

"With Anibaddh, who is teaching her to play at chess."

Chess! There was an unexpected accomplishment in a slave girl. "Well, then, Hector," Catherine said, "I should like to see the warehouse, and Mr Fleming's collection. I rather like to see the treasures that people gather around them. Their plunder."

Hector looked as though he might oppose this proposal. He drew a breath, but then he merely shrugged and said ungraciously that she could come along if she liked.

And so it was settled; Sharada returned alone to the ship, as she had come, and thus was able to conduct a few matters of her own business along the way.

The massive iron-bound carved wooden doors fronting the Crawford & Fleming warehouse—a handsome stone building like all the others in the old prosperous merchant town—were not open. Instead, Hector knocked at a small door to one side, and a little iron-grated spy hole slid open. An unblinking brown eye inspected them for a moment; then a sturdy Flemish servant admitted them.

He led them without speaking toward the rear of the building through several dark rooms and passages. They emerged into a vast hall lit by expanses of glazing near the dark carved and gilded ceiling. Bales of goods were ranged about the walls in promising array. The air was a heady blend of foreign scents, both sweet and acrid, mixed with the smell of tidal mud.

Enormous doors stood braced open, showing a stone-paved loading dock outside, still glistening with rain, and a narrow brackish canal lapping sluggishly below. A stout block and tackle was rigged on a thick frame of timbers on the dock just outside the door. When Catherine got close enough, she saw that a barge lay on its spring lines against the stone pillars of the dock. And there was Mr Fleming himself, just turning away from directing his crew as they lowered a heavy canvas-wrapped bundle from the dock to the waiting barge. Six men moved three huge timbers used for rolling out the heavy cargo. The timbers made a deafening rumble across the stone floor, drowning out Mr Fleming's first words to them.

"I hope you don't mind, sir," said Hector loudly, "but I have told my sister and Mr Sinclair that you might be so good as to let them view the wonders of your cabinet while you and I contrive some sort of reply to these weavers in Liège. I fear they have got themselves into a sorry muddle. It is just what I expected, despite my best precautions."

Mr Fleming agreed graciously. He gave instructions in Flemish to his servant, who then led Mr Sinclair and Catherine back through the dark ground floor of the building and up a set of stairs. They crossed a handsome landing, with a tall window overlooking the street, then passed through a pair of carved heavy doors, into a suite of high-ceilinged rooms, well furnished in the newest French style.

Here they were given over to the care of an immaculately aproned housekeeper, her manner as stiffly formal as her snowy starched linen coif, in the style of the country. They were seated before a fire in well-upholstered chairs; then, impossibly quickly, tea was brought on a polished tray set with handsome china, and arranged before them. The housekeeper offered to pour, but Mr Sinclair assured her in Flemish that they could manage for themselves. After she had pointed out the door that opened onto her master's cabinet, she left them.

"Agreeable, to be sure!" declared Mr Sinclair, looking about. "Now this! This is the famous domestic comfort of the Netherlands."

"Exceedingly handsome," agreed Catherine. She and Grace would certainly have been very comfortable here. The tea, as she expected, was of superb quality. The fire burned vigorously, as all fires should. Everything in the room shone with polish and cleanliness and excellence. "Why would the Netherlanders ever venture out of their houses, I wonder?" she said. "One might suppose they would be ruined for the rigors and harshness of the world by such comfort at home."

"But that is precisely the purpose of comfort," argued Mr Sinclair. "It is not just softness and ease. It is *conforter:* to strengthen, to reinforce, to make strong. To fortify, in fact—to fortify against the slings and arrows of fate, against the blows and buffets dealt by the wide world."

"Of course you are quite right," said Catherine. As she gazed into the fire and drank her tea, she thought of her housewifely sister-in-law, whose well-run house was so comfortable, so strengthening that Hector was sufficiently fortified to venture forth and leave it all behind for years at a time.

She considered her own domestic history, too—the houses she had lived in, and the houses whose comforts—or discomforts—had been her responsibility. She remembered well a vast baronial fireplace that couldn't be made to draw, its finely carved marble chimneypiece permanently soot-stained. She remembered succulent roasted joints of aged beef dripping with juices; exquisite collops of venison from the hill; flaky tartlets filled with wild berries gathered above a wee burn. But she also remembered unpleasant cooled soup served up with floating gouts of congealed fat. The freshest sweetest butter, but only bitter rye-flour bread to spread it on. Freshly aired eiderdowns and ancient soft linen sheets; but also rough woolen blankets riddled by moths, and sharp quills stabbing through pillows. Old silver candlesticks, heavy and handsome still; but bent, tarnished black, greasy with tallow. Mr Sinclair was engrossed in his own thoughts, for he had found a book lying open on a table and was intent upon it, one finger tracing the captions under the engravings.

"Will we go and look at this collection of Mr Fleming's?" proposed Catherine presently. "And perhaps you will be so good as to explain to me what I am seeing, and what I am to think of it."

"I beg you will excuse me for a few minutes more, Mrs MacDonald; this book is one I have been seeking for a decade. Pray go and see the collection, and I will follow you in five minutes."

"Of course. Please do not hurry yourself in the least," said Catherine. And so she opened the door and crossed the threshhold to Mr Fleming's cabinet.

But what had she expected?

Not this: a Pompeian cameo glass vase, larger, lovelier, a darker sea-blue than the Duchess of Portland's, the translucent creamy goddesses most exquisitely carved, most elegantly disposed around its surface; of unsurpassed delicacy. But both arching handles snapped off, missing, the remaining stumps jagged, raw.

A broad Greek *kylix*, red figured on a black ground. A masterfully painted scene of Perseus slaying the monster, and Andromeda, of a comeliness well worth Perseus's effort, bound by her wrists to a pair of shapely little trees—an olive and a laurel. The rim was decorated with palmate and key patterns, but the whole was cracked across the middle—between Andromeda's lovely breasts—and clumsily repaired with rusted iron staples.

A darkly glittering old tapestry—Adam and Eve in the garden, a scene of rich and bosky orchard, verdure, shadow, stream. Oddly, there was a gleaming city in the distance, gleaming because the threads were of gold, real gold. The forbidden fruit was rendered in gold as well, and the snake, though dark with tarnish now, was surely of woven silver. But the lower right quarter was missing, and the ragged edge unmistakably scorched. Water stains rose as high as Eve's rosy thigh.

A painting: a most exquisitely painted lady in Florentine dress, with grave countenance. But other figures which once surrounded her had since been cut away. From the edge of the canvas, a plump baby's arm, disembodied, reached toward the breast of the solemn lady. A beringed hand, a man's hand, lay lightly on her shoulder, connected to an arm which extended off the canvas. The man's shoulders and head were excised, and only some of his damask coat showed behind the lady. The richly carved and gilded frame could not relieve the disturbing effect of these disembodied limbs extending out of the picture.

A Mughal dagger, its blade of watered steel, its hilt of pale carved jade in the shape of a horse's head, with inlaid rubies for eyes and emeralds for a bridle. But where the hilt met the blade, only empty gold settings remained; the gemstones themselves had been pried out. What stones could those have been? Had the rubies and emeralds not been worth taking too?

There was a great deal more of this kind.

There was a chair. Catherine sat down, and considered what might be the character of the man who had gathered these things.

She heard voices in the other room through the door. Mr Fleming had come; he was speaking to Mr Sinclair and Mr Sinclair was praising the rare books. She heard Hector's voice too. Then the door opened and Mr Fleming came into the cabinet.

"Ah, here you are, Mrs MacDonald, keeping company with my exquisite widows and orphans," said Mr Fleming. "My ravishing cripples and amputees. Dealers on three continents know how they can dispose of their damaged goods; they need only let me get a sight of them. They must do it as offhand as possible, and they know it. And so here it is, my magpie's nest."

"They are beautiful," said Catherine. "But painful, too. Painful to see shards of glass here, where the handles should be. As though my own arms had been broken."

"Ah! You feel it, then—a physical sensation, quite singular," he said, and his gaze met hers for a moment.

"Perhaps the pain heightens the beauty, makes it more poignant," said Catherine. "More moving, somehow, than admiring perfect things, strangely enough."

"Sometimes I have wondered," said Mr Fleming, turning away to pick up the Mughal dagger, "if my circumstances permitted me to acquire objects in perfect condition, not damaged in any way, would I love them as much as I do these? When I come across something like this dagger, something formerly exquisite but now flawed through no fault of its own, I feel a clawing at my heart. No serious collector would treasure so damaged a thing; but I find it irresistible."

"I guessed I'd find you here," said Hector, walking in. "Didn't I tell you, Catherine? Look at that horse-headed knife! What were the missing stones, do you suppose, Mr Fleming?"

"They would have been diamonds—large, uncut ones, judging by the size and shape of the settings," said Mr Fleming.

"Diamonds! That size! I do hope a few of those might have been overlooked and are still lying about India when I get there. . . . What are we waiting for?"

"Nothing more, as a matter of fact. That barge we have just finished loading carries the last of our Indies-bound cargo: good Norway spruce fit for spars, and heavy canvas just fallen from Jacob Raes's widest looms. And there remains room enough on the barge to carry you three back to the ship, if you desire; the master is ready to cast off within this quarter hour."

"Excellent. Nothing could be better. Will you come now, yourself?"

"Tonight," said Mr Fleming. "There remain yet a few matters requiring my attention."

The master of the barge made them comfortable, seating Catherine on a cushion on a plank under a flapping canvas awning. The barge glided down the canal drawn by a pair of heavy horses trudging along the towpath in tandem, their coarse blond tails blown against their hindquarters by the wind. With the wind aft, the barge was unwieldy, but the bargemen, with their dripping slippery poles, deftly held it off the bank. Hector and Mr Sinclair stood, watching the city glide past. On this bank were houses, warehouses, docks, shops, heavy-planked beamy boats. And on the far bank, windmills.

The wind had come up during the time they had been inside, enough to turn the windmills, enough to make them creak and groan as the vast heavy vanes turned over, over and over. "Like souls in travail," said Mr Sinclair.

"But how does the wind actually make them turn?" asked Catherine. "I have never quite understood that."

Hector was best qualifed to answer this, but he remained silent, contemplating the windmills. "It is just like a child's pinwheel," replied Mr Sinclair, glancing to Hector for confirmation.

"Aye, that much I see," said Catherine. "But why should the vanes *turn*? Surely there is just as much air behind the vane as in front of it. I do not understand the mechanical principle that makes it move."

"I have always understood—I have supposed—that it functions on the principle of the Archimedean screw, only in this case the movement of the fluid—that is to say, the air—acts to move the screw, rather than the screw acting to move the fluid," said Mr Sinclair, but without his usual assurance. "Is that not so, Mr MacDonald?"

"Yes, more or less," said Hector. "It is at least a useful way of thinking of the forces in operation. And yet our actual trials do not always bear out our suppositions. I am thinking of my rotary oar—in essence another Archimedean screw—of which I have recently received some baffling news. You must remember, Catherine, that last night aboard *Dram Shell*—"

"I am in no danger of forgetting," said Catherine.

"We ran afoul of some submerged object, and I feared that the rotary oar had been damaged?"

"But apparently it was spared," said Catherine, "for it continued to propel the boat as well as ever."

"Aha! A fair conclusion. But untrue."

"What do you mean?"

"I have had a letter from Captain Keith, who tells me that upon subsequently hauling out *Dram Shell* to examine her hull and oar, it was found that the forward half of the oar had indeed been broken off entirely, the shaft snapped quite through. Where there had been originally two complete turns, or spirals, of the thread, only one full spiral remained."

"Yet the performance of the boat seemed not at all impaired," said Catherine.

"Not only was the performance unimpaired, but in the trials which Captain Keith has run since, using that same damaged oar, *Dram Shell* has achieved consistently greater speeds than before."

"How can that be?"

"I am baffled. I had supposed that the greater the biting surface of the oar through the water, the greater its pulling power—like a screw driving into wood. Yet it appears that I have overlooked some fundamental mechanical principle; there is apparently some interference for which I have not adequately accounted. It occurs to me now that a vane arrangement similar to that on those windmills might be worth trying."

They had come out into the wide harbour, and a steam-powered tugboat fitted with side-wheels took their barge in tow for the short trip down to where *Increase* now lay at anchor. A beamy Flemish *pleit* beating up to windward passed close across their wake, then came about, shifted her big-bellied triangular red sails, resheeted, and crossed their wake again, the wind now across her other bow.

"To be frank," said Catherine, watching all this, "I don't quite see how boats can sail upwind either."

"Undoubtedly they do it, however," said Hector. "It is so fascinating to observe mechanical principles functioning quite independent of our comprehension of them."

"Divine principles, too," said Mr Sinclair.

# 11

## *the particular excellency of this Grace*

"What is that?"

A wailing, an unearthly wheezing, a dying breathy gasping. Some creature in the galley below was being slaughtered with a dull knife. It expired, a merciful release from suffering.

Then it took a deeper breath and wailed again. In agonies, choking, then sighing, then silence.

It inhaled, a long deliberate measure; now it shrieked in a new powerful voice: loud, rude, and uncannily thrilling, a broadsword, a claymore of a voice, bursting out of unbearably narrow tight dark dense wood and reed.

"Oh, that Hector," said Catherine to Grace and Mrs Todd. "I didn't know he had brought his bagpipe. He hasn't played in years, as anyone with ears can tell. What will Captain Mainwaring say?"

Gladly they put aside their employments—canvaswork, sketchbook, sewing—for it was too bright, too dazzling, to be working on the main deck in the middle of the broad blue Atlantic on a brilliant September afternoon. They descended into the dimness below.

Captain Mainwaring had already arrived in the galley. He was pointing at the ungainly device squatting on the cook's big stove, and Mr Sinclair answered his question while Hector bent over the machine to anoint it with grease from the cook's can of drippings. The foreign cook stood in the passageway to his inner storeroom, perhaps guarding it.

"It was a wager," explained Mr Sinclair to the captain. "I had bet Mr MacDonald a shilling that he couldn't contrive a steam engine that could blow a set of bagpipes. And you see he has won his wager. Although I helped a good deal, didn't I? Against my own interest."

"Against your own interest indeed!" said Hector. "It was entirely in the cause of our common interest. And curiosity."

"Your machine can blow, to be sure, but I can't say I admire its playing," said Catherine.

"No, not particularly musical, is it? But what can one expect of a machine?" said Mr Sinclair.

"How does it work, Mr MacDonald?" said Mrs Todd very seriously.

"Is the principle of steam engines familiar to you, at all?" asked Hector.

"Not in the slightest," said Mrs Todd. "But I am most eager to learn."

"Are you? Here you see an ordinary copper boiler; it is the cook's second-best boiler, which we have borrowed of him. It is half full of water, boiling briskly, thanks to this good fire going under it. No, you cannot lift off the lid to see, for we have riveted it on tight—for purposes of this experiment—and sealed it with tar and oakum, in the same way as the ship's seams are sealed, except for this pressure-relief valve, just as a precaution. No, no, captain, we are using seawater, not your precious freshwater.

"So here we have a sealed copper of boiling seawater, which produces steam under pressure. And the steam passes out through this tubing to this Y-shaped valve, you see, which I operate by hand to direct the steam pressure alternately through these two tubes—first to one end, then the other of this bilge pump, which we borrowed of the mate. So we have got the bilge pump operating rather like a piston, up and down, thus moving its handle—this long lever—up and down. And the moving handle, you see, operates the bellows, which we borrowed of the smith. And the bellows blows air into the bagpipe through its mouthpiece, here, sealed as snug as possible."

"Oh! How strange to see it all moving—so steadily, so vigorously—and yet untouched!" said Mrs Todd. "But would it not be simpler to put the steam directly into the bagpipe?"

"Steam in my bagpipe! Oh, no, Mrs Todd, that is no way to treat a set of pipes. I could not do that, not even for science," said Hector.

"Oh, is steam so very . . . I did not think of that. So that is a bagpipe! Just how does it produce that very—that very particular sound, pray?"

"Have you never examined a set of Highland pipes?"

"Never at such point-blank range. I am from Newcastle, you know, and lived there all my life, until—until I met Mr Todd. Of course I have heard pipers play, but I have never exactly seen how a bagpipe works."

"This is the mouthpiece, through which the piper—or in this case the steam-powered bellows—blows air. Ordinarily the piper's arm keeps a steady pressure on the air in the bag. But for our experiment I must press the bag against the deck with my foot, you see, because we haven't got enough airtight tubing to raise it any higher. There is the chanter, on which the piper plays the tune—just the nine notes, you know. And these are the three drones which ordinarily stand over the piper's shoulder—a bass and two tenors, all tuned to A, the bass an octave lower than the others, it being twice as long, you see. Oh, yes, each of the drones has its own reed; and the chanter has a double reed. That is why so much air pressure is needed."

"Can it play a tune?" asked Mrs Todd. "Some simple little tune?"

"Well, that is a difficulty, because I must operate this valve here while also pressing my foot on the bag there to moderate the pressure in it; so I cannot reach the chanter, and I have only one hand free in any case."

"I can reach the chanter," said Mr Sinclair, "if I lie down here and dispose myself thus, on my side. There! Now you can operate the valve and press the bag with your foot; and I shall lie here and play a tune on the chanter."

"The truth emerges at last," said Hector. "You are a piper yourself? You did not admit so much before."

"A bit, just a wee bit of a piper. A tune or two. Let us try it."

Hector freshened the fire under the boiler; tapped the pressure-relief valve; greased the bilge pump again; checked the seal between bellows nozzle and mouthpiece; and set his foot upon the bag. The drones stiffened, raised themselves, became erect—and howled.

"Harder," shouted Mr Sinclair, his fingers lightly covering the holes of the chanter.

Hector pressed harder with his foot, and a shriek came from the chanter. Mr Sinclair played a little phrase—two bars of "John MacKechnie," before the bag slipped under Hector's foot and lost pressure. Hector adjusted its position and tried again. This time Mr Sinclair played a whole measure of the reel. Mrs Todd's hands covered her ears, but Captain Mainwaring wore a look of pure gleeful delight at the loudness of the sound. Grace had retreated into the passage.

"You're hideously out of tune," shouted Catherine, but her words were inaudible. She reached out to the bass drone and stopped it with a light touch to the top; then stopped one of the tenors in the same way. Now only one drone accompanied the little melody that Mr Sinclair was playing on the chanter. Hector kept pressing the bag and operating the valve. Catherine used two hands to twist the drone downward, shortening it just a little. Its pitch brightened slightly. Catherine listened to it against the slow tuning phrase that Mr Sinclair was now playing—base; fifth; third; octave—then shortened it a little more. There; that was precisely right. She flicked a finger into the top of the other tenor drone to restart it, and shortened it, too, listening to the wow-wow-wow waugh-waugh-waauugh-waaaauuuugh, slower and slower as the frequencies came closer, then stopped when the two drones were playing exactly the same frequency, both playing exactly the same pitch as the chanter's A. That was better; she could feel the sound ringing inside her body now. Then she started and tuned the tall bass drone, which by chance had to be lengthened, not shortened, lowering its pitch, dropping down into tune with the other drones; the same note an octave lower, exactly half their frequency.

Mr Sinclair nodded approvingly at her—a quick lift of his eyebrows—and played a little spring, a brief ornamented phrase, then repeated it with a more elaborate ornament. His fingers were light and easy on the chanter, entirely at home. He tried a few more practice phrases, then played the first line of "Alike to the War or Peace."

Catherine smiled, taking it as a particular compliment to Hector and herself, for they knew the tune by its other name: "The MacDonalds' Gathering."

Grace reappeared in the doorway, with Sharada behind her.

ꟹꟹ ꟹꟹ ꟹꟹ

"HECTOR," SAID CATHERINE one afternoon a week later while stitching steadily at her canvaswork (fine crimson wool for an outsized strawberry peeking from under a leaf) and ruminating on domestic comforts, "why did that chimney at home suddenly take to smoking?"

"What? What do you mean?" said Hector, his reverie interrupted. He was reclining on a coil of thick hemp rope and gazing upward, where the blue clear sky was filled by luminous curved sails, masts, yards, and an unintelligible system of halyards, sheets, shrouds, stays, lines, cables, and other miscellaneous and mysterious ropes.

"The great fireplace in the hall, behind the table where we always dined. Our father had that great carved marble chimneypiece carried in boats all the way from—I don't know where. It was when he was building the new east wing on the house. But as soon as it got its handsome new chimneypiece, that old fireplace began immediately to smoke and balk, though it had always been so well behaved before. It smudged the beautiful marble a filthy black, don't you remember? And impossible to clean; the maids tried scrubbing it with coral sand until the carving began to wear away and our father put a stop to it. The other chimneys didn't take to smoking—only that one. Though it was swept and was straight and unblocked, still it would not draw unless we kept open the door across the room—not at all pleasant with snow on the east wind."

Hector laughed. "I do remember," he said. "And I told our father the reason, too, but he refused to believe me. It had nothing to do with the elegant carved marble chimneypiece, of course; it was because of the new wing he'd built. Those new walls were too high and too close to the top of the old chimney, which was in their lee. So whenever a wind blew—and when did it not?—the air would eddy about the top of that chimney; nothing could get up it. I told him, but he did not believe me. He could not see how turbulent eddying air at the top of the chimney could disrupt its ability to draw at the bottom. I . . . but . . . oh! oh! Catherine! I wonder . . ." He was gazing fixedly at the broad curving sails overhead. Then he abruptly leapt up from his comfortable coil of rope and hastened away without any explanation or apology. Catherine, more amused than amazed, watched him disappear through the hatch, his hand running distractedly through his hair. This kind of behavior was not without precedent from Hector; this conduct was in fact quite typical of Hector in the grip of a new idea.

❧ ❧ ❧

"I WISH I HAD a twin," said Grace to Catherine in the dark one night.

"Do you? Why?"

"To play chess with me when Anibaddh is too busy."

"Aye, chess. How did Annie learn to play chess, I wonder?" asked Catherine.

"A boy in that family in Virginia made her learn so he would have someone to play against. She always had to let him win, no matter what silly moves he made. But it is so very maddening when she has to break off—at the trickiest moment!—to wait on Mrs Todd. If I had a twin, you see, there would always be someone handy to play with me."

"Perhaps the twin might have views of his own about that."

"Did you and Uncle Sandy sometimes disagree?"

"Oh, aye, very often. Nevertheless, he was always my choice companion. And I, his, too, I suppose. It is true that he was always handy, for play or for quarrels."

"The twins in Sharada's stories don't quarrel. Kusa and Lava—they are the twin sons of Queen Sita, and they can sing all of Valmiki's great song about Rama, which takes up many days. And I like to hear of the Asvins, the celestial twins who never can be defeated."

"Never can be defeated, is it? That must be pleasant."

"Well, they are heroes, you know, not just people. They drive a chariot drawn by falcons through the sky, and sometimes they come to the aid of mere mortals in dire straits and rescue them."

"Has Sharada a great many stories, then?" asked Catherine.

"Oh, aye, a great many, and very good ones they are. I like her singing, too. I like her. She is brave, I think, like Queen Sita," replied Grace.

"Brave! Hmmm. I suppose you are right."

"And she knows things. The very first time I ever saw her, she told me my fortune, and some of it has already come true. You remember, at Uncle Hector's and Aunt Mary's house, when she brought the parcel from Uncle Sandy."

"What? What do you mean?"

"That very first time when she delivered that parcel for you. With the tea and the Kashmiri shawl. And bagpipe music. You know."

"It was Sharada who brought that? She delivered it that night?"

"Of course. Oh, Catriona, surely you knew that."

"But why in the world did you never say so?"

"No one ever asked me."

"Aunt Mary said she asked everyone in the house, and no one knew a thing. It was the great mystery."

"She never asked *me*. No one ever speaks to me at all."

"Of course they don't; you never answer anyone."

"But I remember it perfectly well. It was when you and Uncle Hector went to Mr Clerk's ball, the night of the bonfires when the king finally arrived. The footman was out, the baby was howling because of his tooth and Aunt Mary was with him, and the maids were craning out the attic windows at the great bonfires on the hills instead of attending to their duties. There was no one to open the door but me, so I did. And the woman asked if Mrs Catherine MacDonald lived here, and I nodded yes. Then she showed me the package with the writing on it. Of course I could not make it out, but I did not let on; I just held out my hands to take it. And she took my hand—this hand—in hers, standing there in the open doorway with the rain pouring down, and turned it over and over and looked at it. And told me my fortune. Then she gave me a coin, pressed into the sweet spot in the center of my palm, and handed me the parcel to give to you. So I put it on the table, upstairs in our bedroom."

"So you did. And what did she tell you of your fortune?"

"Mmmmm. I would rather not say just now. But a bit of it has already come true. And I would show you the coin if you like. I think it is from India. Afterward I thought that I should have been the one to give her a coin, for bringing the parcel, but I did not think of it at the time. Besides, I had no coin to give her."

"I think it is alright," Catherine assured her. "I do not think she expected you to pay her."

"No, I suppose not. She is not much like other servants, is she?"

"Not much," agreed Catherine.

After Grace had fallen asleep, Catherine turned over and over in her mind this new fact about the mysterious parcel—and this mysterious maid who was so unlike other servants. Be resolute, Catherine admonished herself. It is time you found out the truth about this woman. She is only a maidservant. Ask her.

In the morning, Sharada came as usual after breakfast to help Catherine dress. Grace had already gone. The day was gray and overcast, and a steady wind blew that made the ship lean. There were big steel-coloured swells, too, and every few moments the ship's bow would meet one of them at just such an angle that the impact made the entire ship shudder, then hesitate a moment before plunging down into the trough beyond. It was just such a suspended moment, thought Catherine, as the best Highland dancers could achieve at their most whisky-inspired.

Sharada was unusually silent.

"It's cold," said Catherine. "I'll have a shawl. The light Indian one will be enough, I think. There; that's better." Sharada arranged the shawl around Catherine's shoulders, and Catherine toyed with the fringe as Sharada attended to her hair.

"This shawl, you know, was in that parcel you brought me at my brother's house in East Thistle Street," said Catherine casually.

"Was it indeed, ma'am? Also, I am guessing, perhaps the ivory tea caddy and the written-down music, which I have seen among your clothings? Yes; it is Lucknow work, that ivory box; and this is a very handsome Kashmiri shawl, in the newer style."

"What newer style is that?"

"In the old days, ma'am, the design of these goat-hair shawls was woven; but nowadays they are embroidered. This one, you see, is embroidered. The design is stitched onto its surface; it is not the weaving of the cloth itself. These shawls are gifts of great honour in my country, and it is usual to be giving them in pairs."

"Alas, I was given only the one," said Catherine lightly. "But that parcel, now—I have been meaning to ask you: just how did the parcel come into your hands, into your charge?"

"It was my late mistress, poor Mrs Guthrie, who was carrying it home to Scotland—carrying home several parcels as a favor for her *feringee* friends in India. But she died of fever off Madagascar, and next the little baby, too. In Edinburgh then I carried her belongings to her people. Nothing more could I do, save taking charge of those parcels and seeing them safely delivered—a last service to perform, to honour the deceased." Was there a catch in Sharada's voice? Had she been so very attached to this poor Mrs Guthrie?

"Had you served Mrs Guthrie for a long time?" asked Catherine.

"Not long, no. I came to serve her only when she was leaving Ghazipur, for her previous ayah would not go with her, not over the black sea."

"I see," said Catherine. Who had she been, that unfortunate Mrs Guthrie, who was now beyond all questioning and explaining? Had Sandy known her well? Or hardly at all? People often did carry home letters and parcels from abroad as a favour. It was just a thing one did if going home: offer to carry things, sometimes bringing quite large or valuable consignments—even from people one knew only slightly—to people one knew not at all.

Presently Catherine remarked, "And now here am I, straightaway carrying it back to India again. How curious . . ."

"It is so very curious indeed. The twists and turns of fate are most marvelous," agreed Sharada fervently. She folded Catherine's night-dress and put it away, then said, "I am troubled in my mind, however, ma'am. Tea and shawls may easily be replaced; but if the written-down music is lost, it might never again be recovered. I am troubled, seeing those papers undergo again the risk of an ocean voyage. What a pity they are not lying safe ashore in Scotland!"

"So they would be, if only my plans had come aright."

"But if I may be suggesting . . .You—or I, if you are permitting it, ma'am—might copy that written-down music and send back the copy by any Scotland-bound ships we are meeting, at any opportunity, so that a copy, at least, might lie safe in Scotland."

"Oh, but that is a great deal of trouble for a manuscript which cannot be of any great value or antiquity. Indeed, I recognise the handwriting as my brother's. My late brother's. I have not looked much at it, but I daresay he has just written down some of the old marches that pipers play. In any case, I fear my supply of paper would be insufficient for such an undertaking."

"Oh, but fortunately, ma'am, I got in a large quantity of paper while we were in Antwerp, and pens, and ink as well."

"Did you indeed?" said Catherine, and searched out Sharada's face, above and behind her in the little looking glass. But Sharada had turned away just then to plump the bed pillows and make up the sofa beds for daytime.

ꕤ ꕤ ꕤ

"Mr Todd did buy me a hat, the smartest broad-brimmed hat I ever saw," Mrs Todd was saying at dinner, "and a selection of most delicious ground pigments. And some exquisite brushes made of sable, Cossack sable; I dread the prospect of spoiling them by dipping them into paints. But just fancy! Mr Sinclair tells me I have forgotten the most important colours of all: black and white! And I have already used up nearly all my paper on copies. But that is not the worst of it; for somehow I was so absentminded as to forget to buy any canvas!"

As his spouse prettily recited her follies, Mr Todd drained his glass and nodded for the boy behind his chair to refill it.

"Oh, as for canvas, Mrs Todd, there can be not the slightest difficulty," said Captain Mainwaring. "If there is one commodity which this ship carries in abundance, it is canvas. Six thousand yards, more or less, just in the aft hold. I shall be happy to furnish you with as much canvas as you can possibly cover with a brush!"

"Oh, sir! I had never thought . . . but would ship's canvas be suitable, I wonder, Mr Sinclair?"

"It will do, certainly. Artist's canvas is of a finer weave than ship's canvas, and is usually of linen, so that properly speaking we ought not to call it canvas at all. True canvas is hemp, properly speaking; it is called canvas from its Latin name, *Cannabis*. But ship's canvas will do very well. And as for the black and the white pigment, there is no need for despair there either. Indeed, if you were going to forget a colour or two, these two are certainly the best to have forgotten, for we can make them ourselves. Now, if you had forgotten your ochre or your sienna, your lapis or your terre verte, we would have been sadly at a loss, for these are earth pigments, simply not to be had at sea! But as it happens, both black and white are well within our means, even aboard ship. No doubt we can lay our hands upon a piece of ivory; and a lump of lead."

"White from ivory, I suppose; and black from lead?" said Mr Todd.

"A reasonable assumption, but in fact it is quite the other way about," said Mr Sinclair. "We char the ivory to produce ivory black, and fume the lead over vinegar to produce flake white. You, Mr MacDonald, might like to see how it is done—the flake white in particular. I shall be happy to undertake the making of black and white for you, Mrs Todd, when the time comes. You will not need them soon, however."

"No? How discouraging! And I had supposed I was making such excellent progress!" she pouted prettily.

"You are doing very well. Your drawings have improved amazingly. But you have a great deal of copying ahead of you, before we begin the spoiling of Captain Mainwaring's canvas."

"Am I to be set to copying forever? I warn you, I have used up nearly all my paper during these last three weeks, both sides of it. Now I am scribbling in the margins and the corners."

"I can furnish you with paper, Mrs Todd," offered Catherine. "As it happens, my maid laid by an ample store of paper in Antwerp. We shall copy side by side; for I have myself just begun a tedious job of copying out a manuscript of old bagpipe music."

ꕥꕥꕥ

"WELL, HOW DO you and *Ramayana* get along, Mrs MacDonald?" Mr Fleming asked Catherine one evening after dinner. "Perhaps if the adventures of King Rama and Queen Sita are not to your taste, you would like to trade it for some other book."

"I like King Rama and Queen Sita very well," said Catherine. "But it is not easy reading, and I wonder if it may be partly a case of faulty translation."

"Nothing could be more likely," said Mr Fleming. "I expect the halls of Hades are teeming with translators. But if you will kindly come and drink some tea with me, I will try to shed any light I may possess. I am no great scholar of Sanskrit, but greatness is not always required."

Catherine agreed to come and drink his tea with him. The windows of his cabin were open, and a fresh light breeze washed through. Once again, the steward set out the tea things. Catherine took a seat, with *Ramayana* on her lap, and sighed comfortably. This cabin did not feel crowded, though it was smaller than her own. There seemed to be a place for everything. On Mr Fleming's worktable lay half a dozen of the ribbon-tied Chinese scrolls she had noticed before. One of them now was unrolled across the table and weighted with an inkstand and a small box to hold it flat. One edge of it, she noticed, was water stained, but most of the rectangular Chinese characters were still legible. Nearby lay sheets of paper, closely written over in a handwriting that Catherine took to be his own.

"Is the Chinese language among your accomplishments?" she asked him.

"Hardly," said Mr Fleming. "I have somehow managed to scrape a bare acquaintance with merchants' Cantonese. But that is quite inadequate, I am afraid, for translating this venerable old classic. Nevertheless, that is the task I have set myself for this voyage, and a very intractable one it is proving. Here, we are ready to pour, I think. This is a nice delicate Yun Wu, which I have been saving for a special occasion such as this." He said this without looking at her, and filled her cup.

Was this a special occasion? Catherine chose to take no notice of this remark. But she observed his long tapered fingers, deft and knowing, handling the smooth porcelain. Then she looked away and said, "But this exquisite scroll—what is it?"

"It is a part of *Cha Ching,* which means Tea Classic. It is the book of knowledge about tea, and it is very old, the work of a scholar named Lu Yu, who lived in the eighth century."

"What does it say?" she asked, glancing at his closely written manuscript. Mr Fleming's handwriting was like himself, like his eyebrows: sinuous, neat, definite, black. His translation was much lined out, amended, interlined with corrections and additions.

"This particular scroll tells us how simple it is to manufacture tea: the leaves need only be picked, steamed, pounded, shaped, dried, then sealed!"

Catherine laughed. "So simple as that! Anyone could do it!"

"But then, it seems, the venerable Lu Yu drifts off into poetry—or deliberate obscurity perhaps—with remarks about the boots of Mongols, all shrunken and wrinkled, and windblown mushrooms, and—if I am not mistaken—something about the jowls of wild oxen. I rather think I must be mistaken. I hope so; for if my translation is correct, it does not get us any further in our study of how to manufacture tea."

"Is that your purpose?"

"In part. Several of my friends have urged me to try my hand at it; and it is the sort of text that is of interest to the Asiatick Society."

"And who, or what, is the Asiatick Society?" asked Catherine. The Yun Wu tea seemed to open doorways in her mind—doorways into spacious vaulted halls, well lit and quiet. It was a deeply pleasant sensation.

"Oh, just an assembly of odd fellows in Calcutta, all of us afflicted by a common inquisitiveness about any number of things—oriental sciences, horticulture, literature, medicine, and all that. We get together and read one another papers about things, and sponsor expeditions to collect curiosities and specimens, and publish translations, and so forth. The society have published a number of these old oriental papers. If you like, I will take you to meet these people when we get to Calcutta, for they are my friends: Dr Wallich and Dr Carey and others."

"This Dr Carey?" asked Catherine, touching the *Ramayana* in her lap.

"That Dr Carey indeed. But you had a fault to find with his translation, had you not? What is it?"

"I had; but now that I know him to be a friend of yours, I will moderate my tone. Here I have marked the passage—where it says that 'the Danuvas and the Yukshas have born all.' Does this mean that they have given birth to all, or that they have tolerated all?"

"Let us refer to the original Sanskrit, here on the opposite page. So good of Dr Carey to have printed it, for this Devanagari script is most troublesome to set up in type. Hmm . . . yes," said Mr Fleming, following along the line of upside-down-looking letters with his finger. "Ah! of course it is 'tolerated.' 'The Danuvas and the Yukshas have tolerated all.' No, no, they certainly have not given birth to all! I might have translated it a little differently myself—perhaps 'suffered all.' "

"Is it quite literal, this translation of Dr Carey's?" asked Catherine.

"Very nearly so."

"That is best, I daresay, and simplest."

"Ah! I am not sure it is best, and a literal translation is not so simple as one might suppose." He refilled their cups; after sipping at his own, he said, "How, for example, would you translate this simple word: 'taste'?"

"Oh, taste! Well. It is . . . what is the context? Are we speaking of the sensation on the tongue, or of a connoisseur's nice discrimination and appreciation?"

"Of some implied process of judgment, of selection, overlying an assumption that some sensations are superior to others? Even an implied consensus about what constitutes the most refined judgment, the superior sensibility?"

"Just so," said Catherine, laughing at him.

Perhaps he liked her to laugh at him, for with a leap of his sardonic eyebrows, he went on: "And from what language are we translating, and into what language? From English to French, our task is simple, for *goût* in French contains both the meanings you have identified for 'taste' in English. But suppose we are translating, as the good Dr Carey has done, from Sanskrit. There is in Sanskrit an important word: *rasa*. And it means—oh, a constellation of meanings! But its most basic meaning might be translated as 'taste' or perhaps 'flavour,' even 'juice.' But it suggests a great many other meanings as well. It means the experience which the well-prepared observer derives from contemplating a work of art—hearing music, seeing a play, gazing upon a painting or a sculpture. It is aesthetic emotion. And this aesthetic emotion—the learned Sanskrit commentators tell us—occurs in nine flavours, nine tastes, nine *rasas* which are sufficiently noble to inspire art. Now, how is all that to be translated? In a word, if you please?"

"Ahem," said Catherine, laughing again, "I find I do not want a literal translation after all. Will you allow me to wish for a sensible and intelligent paraphrase?"

"Alas, your wish must be much qualified. First of all, what would you have your conscientious translator do about meter and rhyme?"

"Ah. I suppose he must not be allowed, as Dr Carey has done, to ignore them?"

"Oh, fie, Mrs MacDonald! And do you still expect poetry to result? Would you have him ignore the exquisitely complex meter that characterises Prakrit poetry, for example? You might as well omit the leaves from the pot of tea and serve up mere hot water instead. You might as well pour gin and call it whisky."

"That would never do," said Catherine. "It would never retain Captain Mainwaring's 'true contraband *goût*,' would it?"

"Ah, the exquisite flavour of the forbidden! No, it would not. And then there are the broader questions of tone and style. Let us suppose instead that you wished to refresh your acquaintance with Homer, comfortably, in English. Would you have Pope's elegant but quaint paraphrase? Or would you prefer James Macpherson's misty and Ossianic *Iliad*?"

"James Macpherson's *Iliad*? Did 'Ossian' Macpherson translate Homer, too?"

"Yes, I am afraid so, about ten or fifteen years after his *Ossian*. People laughed at it. It was very like his *Ossian*, all 'shades of heroes untimely slain' and so on. But I don't think it had his full attention. He was much engrossed just then in the writing of pamphlets against the Americans for Lord North's government. That really was his strength, I think—pamphlet writing. Then he got a seat in Parliament, where he represented—whom do you think? Not his constituency in Wales—no, no!—but the interests of the Nawab of Arcot! So much more profitable! And fathered five natural children in his spare time—I beg your pardon for mentioning it—and by two or three different mothers too. But he was a generous patron to many a young kinsman, let us not forget. Including our Dr Macpherson."

"Our Dr Macpherson, aboard this ship?"

"Himself. He has told me that his studies of medicine at Edinburgh were funded by a bequest from 'Ossian' Macpherson, who had been his uncle or great-uncle, I am not certain—perhaps a cousin at some remove."

Catherine returned to her cabin at last quite refreshed, even exhilarated. She supposed it was an effect of Mr Fleming's tea; and perhaps also of his unaccustomed energetic style of talk, his wide-ranging knowledge and information, great spiraling arcs of connection and analogy. Her maid undressed her and put her to bed, and there she lay, perfectly calm but profoundly awake, for hours, while Grace slept.

Catherine thought about turtle soup; and the map of the world; and of Mary, in Edinburgh with her children. Then after a while she found herself at the threshold of James, her poor lost James. Don't think of that, she usually admonished herself. Too painful, that wound; too raw, that loss. But on this long calm alert night, she could venture even across that threshold. She whispered his name in the darkness of the cabin, with the soft Gaelic lisp and lift: Seumas. Seumas, dearest. Just as she had used to whisper it behind the curtains of their bed.

ꕥ ꕥ ꕥ

CATHERINE LEANED BACK in her chair and stretched to ease her cramped shoulders, for the chair pulled up to the big table in the main cabin where she sat at her copying was not quite a convenient height for the work. The light was fading now too; but Mrs Todd had left her drawing things scattered about in the best place close under the window; and the folio of engravings from which she had been copying was set up on a high easel, where it obscured much of the scant remaining light.

"Hector!" said Catherine as her brother came down the passageway. "You are just the person who can help me. What a vile hand Sandy always had. I can hardly make it out. Does this say 'Cruinneachadh Chlann IcIllEathain'?"

"What, the name of this tune? You'll need a lamp in here. Let me see . . . yes, yes, that is it. And he has it in English, below, too: 'The MacLeans' Gathering.' "

"But Hector, look at the tune itself. That's not right."

He hummed the first line of music, following along with his finger on the manuscript page. "No, that's not right. That's not 'The MacLeans' Gathering.'"

"It's 'Black Donald's March,' " said Catherine.

" 'Piobaireachd Dhomhnuill Duibh,' " agreed Hector.

"Certainly Sandy knew that," said Catherine.

"Well, he made a mistake then."

"How could he? The tunes are nothing alike."

"Even Homer nods; and heaven knows Sandy made a mistake or two in his time."

"I think it is very curious," said Catherine. It seemed to her a familiar mistake, one that she had noticed before, elsewhere.

Mr Sinclair came clattering down the passageway, bringing with him the distinctive scent of salt wind, and sporting a bright pink spot on each cheek. "Oh, there is my Leonardo!" he said, and tenderly gathered up his folio from the easel. His glance fell across Mrs Todd's drawing, lying on the table. He raised his eyebrows, then after a moment turned over the sheet so that it lay facedown.

"Pray, Mr Sinclair, let us have your opinion as a piper," said Hector. "Do you know 'The MacLeans' Gathering'?"

Mr Sinclair thought for a moment, an upward-and-backward remembering look on his brow, and then lightly sang the first phrase.

"Yes, yes. Just so. Now look at this, sir, if you will."

As Hector had done, Mr Sinclair sang the music off the page, quietly. "Oh," he said, "but that is 'Black Donald of the Isles' March to Inverlochy.' "

"Of course it is. I am sure it is a simple error, Catherine," said Hector. "You must correct it in your copy."

"Is this the manuscript you spoke of copying, Mrs MacDonald?" asked Mr Sinclair. "Interesting. But I cannot agree, Mr MacDonald, that your sister ought to correct mistakes. It is bad enough that errors of transcription will creep in of their own accord, no matter how careful one is; but if one is copying, one must not make any deliberate change of any kind, no matter how trivial it may seem and no matter how obvious the original error."

"I did not expect so scientific a rigour from you!" said Hector. "Perhaps she might write '*sic*' in the margin?"

"A reasonable compromise. May I ask, Mrs MacDonald, why you have undertaken so onerous a task?"

"Because my maid tells me I must," replied Catherine lightly. "I suppose she thinks I need some useful work to do."

"Checkmate!" rang out Anibaddh's triumphant voice through the thin partition separating the main cabin from the adjoining cabin. "Checkmate at last! You led me all around the bush this time, child! You're going to beat me one of these days, and it won't be long."

ON A BRILLIANT day of mid-Atlantic autumn sunshine, just before dinner, most of *Increase*'s passengers were on the main deck enjoying the fine weather. A light but steady wind filled the topsails, but there was only a faint breeze down at deck level. The sea was smooth and the darkest blue except where the ship's aqua wake stretched straight back to the northeast horizon. Catherine worked in the shade of a sail at a small makeshift table contrived from a board laid across two chair backs. Taking the *piobaireachd*s in order, she had now arrived at the seventeenth—of a total of 126 *piobaireachd*s. It was a surprisingly large number. How and when and where had Sandy learned so many?

Nearby sat Mrs Todd, drawing with red chalk on paper. She worked on a small board on her lap, copying a picture from a book of Mr Sinclair's. The book—a handsome collection of Italian engravings—stood on an easel also belonging to Mr Sinclair. Grace was trying her hand at drawing, too, copying the same picture as Mrs Todd.

Mr Sinclair was walking his daily half mile, forty perimeters of the main deck, while reading a small book. He had done this so many times that by now he stepped automatically over the prisms set into the deck to bring light below. Each time he passed the steps leading up to the quarterdeck, where he had previously laid out forty large dried beans, he picked up one of them—without looking up from his book—and dropped it into the canvas bag that he had commissioned Grace to sew for him. By this system he was relieved of the necessity of counting his laps.

Hector lay comfortably on his favorite coil of rope, gazing upward at the sails, pondering their shape.

Dr Macpherson smoked his pipe—ruminating—downwind from the others but within earshot.

Where was Mr Fleming? In his cabin, Catherine supposed, toiling over his translation.

For once, no one was talking.

Delicious smells wafted up from the galley, which vented just here: onions; cinnamon; garlic; the unmistakable aroma of roasting lamb or, more likely, mutton.

"They are all gone, Mr Sinclair," cried Mrs Todd, for Mr Sinclair was feeling blindly for yet another bean as he read, not realizing that he had completed his fortieth lap, and no beans remained.

"Oh, so they are," he said mildly, looking up from his book at last.

"I have been waiting quietly these last three turns, knowing that you had nearly finished, and not liking to interrupt you. But do come see what I have done, sir, if you please. And you must be sure to praise me, for I am sure it is the best thing I have done yet."

Mr Sinclair came as summoned, tying up his bag of dried beans and tucking his book under his arm. He stood behind her, looking over her shoulder as she held up her work for him to see. After a moment, he said, "Well, really, Mrs Todd, that is not bad at all."

"Not bad at all!" she said. "Do hear him, Mrs MacDonald: 'Not bad at all.' And this is the highest praise I have ever been able to wring from him. Well, sir, pray go on: what is not bad about it? What will you single out as being particularly not-bad?"

But Mr Sinclair did not smile. He said only, "The accuracy of your draftsmanship is improving. And you are discovering the uses and virtues of chalk at last. You are no longer attempting to use it as though it were merely a blunt quill."

"The virtues of chalk! I have got it all over my sleeves, the dirty stuff. My maid will have something to say about that. But what do you think of my elegant outline, here? And the convincing shadows? I have worked very hard on the shadows in particular."

"Yes, so I see. But do not be discouraged; more practice will give you ever greater ease and facility."

Mrs Todd's response was a merry peal of laughter, to show that she was much amused and certainly not discouraged.

Then Mr Sinclair went to see what Grace had produced. Grace sat drooping over her board so that her messy, windblown plaited hair lay across her work, like a pale broad stroke of red chalk. Mr Sinclair moved the long braid to one side and looked, without saying anything, for a long moment. Then he said, "That is remarkable. Quite remarkable."

"What? Let us see, Grace, do. Hold it up so we can all see, like a good girl," said Mrs Todd. But Grace was too bashful for that, and leaned over her board again, sheltering it from view.

"May I, please?" said Mr Sinclair gently, and coaxed her into giving it up to him. "Do you realise that you have drawn it in reverse? You have made a perfectly accurate mirror image. You would be worth a great deal in an engraver's workshop, my lass."

"Whatever do you mean?" inquired Mrs Todd. "Why would such a trait be of any interest to an engraver?"

"Images to be engraved must be drawn in reverse on the plate," explained Mr Sinclair.

"Let me see," said Dr Macpherson, coming to look. "Aha! I have encountered this sort of phenomenon in the past, though it is fairly rare. And it tends to run in families, I suspect; a father and his son of my acquaintance, in Kingussie, wrote their names from right to left. Not only the order of the letters but the letters themselves were reversed, as though one were seeing it in a looking glass. They were joiners, the both of them, very clever artificers, and nothing deficient in their intellect was to be observed in the ordinary course of things. Yet they shared this peculiarity. As for any other writing of theirs, whether it ran backward or forward I do not know; for they both avoided any occasion of writing to the extent that their trade and their way of living allowed, only sometimes being compelled to write out an account, I daresay. And then again, when I was studying medicine at Edinburgh, a distinguished faculty member described the case of a boy, an orphan, who was unable to distinguish right from left, or clockwise from counterclockwise, though his intellect was not only unimpaired but markedly superior in other respects. And the most interesting point was that this boy's elder brother, and his two younger sisters, also orphans of course, and from infancy fostered and brought up in different towns where they never had seen one another since the first breaking up of the family after the death of the parents, also manifested just the same peculiarity. So it could not be supposed, as might be argued in the case of the joiner and his son in Kingussie, that the parent had simply taught his child his own peculiar way of writing their name. Instead one is led to the inescapable conclusion that there is something inherent in the familial organism which produces this result. It is most interesting, most suggestive. Pray, Mrs MacDonald, is there any degree of this reversion, as it might be called, of this tendency to reverse, in yourself or your other kin? Or does your daughter's peculiarity derive perhaps from her father instead?"

"But Mrs MacDonald is not actually Grace's mother!" cried Mrs Todd. "No, no, indeed not, Dr Macpherson, did you not know? Bless us, sir! No, no, Mrs MacDonald is her stepmother, you see. They are in fact no flesh-and-blood kin at all, not in the least."

"Oh, I beg your pardon then, madam. I had naturally assumed that you were the child's mother. I am sure that I was told you were her mother, and then there is a physical resemblance, both of complexion and of feature, which might certainly support the assumption. Well, well! So I suppose that this tendency to reversion might have come from either her father or her mother, but we must not expect to see it expressed in yourself. Well! It is a pity we are prevented from tracing the peculiarity any further."

"I do not like that man," said Grace to Catherine in the dark that night.

"Who?"

"That Dr Macpherson."

"Oh, my dear, his is neither a genteel manner nor an admirable character. Your judgment is quite just. But I do not think he means any harm. It is only an unpolished manner, and an unfortunate temperament, I trust. And he has struggled with misfortunes all his life. Let us try to keep charitable hearts."

"Still, he is not a good man. If I were ill, I would not let him come near me."

"Let us hope then that you do not fall ill."

❧ ❧ ❧

"CATHERINE? OH, HERE you are," said Hector early one morning. "I awakened this morning with the most marvelous tune running in my head. Let me sing it for you, and you can tell me what it is."

"If you think I might recognise it," she agreed; and he hummed it for her.

"It is a pipe tune, I suppose," she said.

"I think it is. Yes, in my head I hear it as pipe music. It would fit on the pipes, I am sure. But what is it? Do you recognise it?"

"No, not just precisely. I could not put a name to it. Here comes Mr Sinclair. Ask him."

"Good morning, sir," said Hector. "Do you recognise this tune, this pipe tune? It goes like this . . ." Hector sang it again, and Mr Sinclair listened intently, with his head cocked to one side.

"Hmmm. I cannot just say that I recognise it. Where did you learn it, then?"

"I do not know. I awakened this morning with it running through my head, and it has been with me ever since. I have been trying to put a name to it."

"So, it might be your own. Perhaps you have made it yourself."

"So it might; but each time it runs through my head, it sounds more familiar, and then I doubt its being my own."

"Oh, aye. An image once appeared in my mind's eye—complete, compelling, and, so far as I was able to determine, of the most complete novelty. I could not remember having ever laid eyes upon it, not in all my studies or travels. What was it? Oh, just the eyes, seen very close, the direct gaze of a stag. So I drew it, peering out from the foliage at the border of the title page decoration I was then engaged upon, a decoration for an edition of *The Lady of the Lake*. A very handsome and striking effect it had, peering from the oak leaves and the pine sprays of the border—you know that unblinking, direct gaze of the wild animal when it thinks it has not been seen?—and very proud I felt of my own original invention. It was not until a year or two later that I happened across what must have been my inspiration, from my earliest childhood. I was visiting my brother and his young family, and while reading to my little nephews from a book of old tales from the Black Forest—a book that had been in our own nursery before it passed to my brother—I came face-to-face with a woodcut print of the virtuous poor woodcutter who figured in the story. And in the bosky decorative border I saw a badger peering out from a tangled hedge—just his eyes, his face, and in the eye that same fierce, intent regard which I had succeeded in putting into the eye of my stag."

"Were you disappointed?"

"Crestfallen. But I resolved then to guard against the false pride of originality. Of the thousands of drawings I have made, there are some whose sources even I do not know. But I try not to pride myself on having originated them, for it is far more likely that I have simply not yet remembered what previously seen images inspired them."

"Thus in science, too," said Hector. "Even my spiral oar, you know, which first came to me in a dream I had about mining, and which I regarded at first as entirely my own invention—why, a very similar design was proposed by Mr Nasmyth, the eminent mechanic, and artist, too, you know, at just about the same time. Had I seen or heard of his proposal at one of the Mechanics Institute lectures perhaps? I do not know; I do not remember hearing of it, but perhaps I had. Yet ideas are free to us all."

"Nevertheless, this tune of yours—"

"Which may not be mine at all—"

"Nevertheless you must write it down, just as you have sung it for us. Too often tunes disappear without a trace, departing as they arrived. Sooner or later you may come across the original, or—if not—you may eventually feel confident that it might be your own, at least in part. Meanwhile, we are all the richer for the arrival, somehow or other, of a tune which is new to *us*, at least."

"Here is some paper, with staves already drawn," said Catherine.

An appalling sound issued from behind the thin wooden partition, from Mrs Todd's little sleeping cabin—a sound which the three of them in the main cabin pretended not to hear. "Well, I shall go write it down while it remains fresh in my mind," said Hector, and went away. A few moments later, Anibaddh came out from Mrs Todd's little cabin, carefully drawing the door closed behind her. She was carrying a basin, with a towel draped across the top to cover its contents. Though she hastened quickly away, a faint smell of vomit lingered in the room. Catherine's glance met Mr Sinclair's for just a moment.

"And the sea as flat as a billiard table this morning, too," he said.

ꕥ ꕥ ꕥ

JUST BEFORE BEDTIME, Catherine made her way to the main deck for a breath of fresh air; and for a brief and rare draught of solitude (or near solitude, for the helmsman was at his helm as always, the binnacle light glowing muted on the compass and on the spokes of the great, heavy wheel and its cables). Sheltered by the black night, she felt free to try out Hector's favorite place, free to recline on the thick coil of hemp rope with its view of the full-bellied sails and the black fathomless sky beyond them. There was no moon, only starlight, and the stars were spilled in a great dizzy careless swath across the velvety deep blue-black sky.

The pale sails faintly glowed. They reminded Catherine somehow of strong horses leaning into their collars, powerful pulling shoulders and haunches of sail. And Catherine heard, issuing from somewhere deep in the ship itself, from the warm, steamy, spice-scented galley, a voice—a low, long, deep tone. Then another, and then song of incomprehensible words, pure voice—a strange song of most ardent longing, of endless, hopeless lament. It was Sharada's voice—not (for once) modestly humming under her breath, barely audible or perhaps even unconscious, but actual song, the open-throated voice, the full voice with all the resonance and flesh-and-blood timbre of the chambers and bones in the skull, the throat, the chest.

It went on for a long while; then a drum spoke, too (or, more likely, a big kettle, drummed upon perhaps by the cook whose kettle it was, and who was after all of the same district as Sharada, or so she had said, and who might be supposed to know the same music). The drumming, although regular and even, seemed to Catherine casual; of a pattern which remained unintelligible for a long time. Catherine lay back and let the plaintive song stream off behind her, streaming away and left behind forever like the ship's wake, like the air they passed through and passed upon. Eventually she noticed that there was, after all, logic and meaning in the drum—such logic and meaning, and in the song it accompanied. The singer and the drummer knew what they were doing after all, it seemed.

Catherine was borne along by their music, filled and moved by it, just as the ship was borne on the breast of the ocean by the wind pressing the sails into their amplest shape, and their wake streaming out behind like time itself. When the song stopped, it was as though the wind had died: Her spirit lay becalmed, slack.

Yet *Increase* sailed on her course. Arising after a while, chilled, Catherine made her way down to her cabin, where Grace, she supposed, would have gone to bed some time ago.

But the cabin was not dark; a shaded lamp still shone, and Grace was not in her bed. "What are you doing?" Catherine said. Grace was seated close before the little looking-glass fastened to the bulkhead. She held a book—it was *The Life of Washington*—open to the looking glass, its binding against her thin chest. Peering over her shoulder, her glance met Catherine's. She was flushed, her translucent skin glowing and eyes glistening. Catherine shut the door carefully behind her.

"I *can* read," whispered Grace. "Again. After all. In the looking glass, I can make it out, ever so slowly."

# 12

## *an ackward Pitiful, Clownish Fellow*

Dr Macpherson was consulted; he called upon Mrs Todd, interviewed her privately, examined her still more privately. Then within a very short time the nature of Mrs Todd's sudden illness was known to all aboard *Increase*. There was certainly no cause for alarm; all was well in train.

"Ha ha! *Increase* indeed!" said Captain Mainwaring, and sent in an offering of his cook's daintiest and most wholesome custard flavoured with saffron and rosewater, using the last of the milk from the failing cow. The captain also promised Mr Todd that his steward would seek out a freshened cow as soon as they should drop anchor at Porto Praya in the Cape Verde Islands, a landfall expected within a fortnight's good sailing if the wind remained favorable.

Mr Todd had to eat the custard himself, however; Mrs Todd could not bear the sight of it, and called it a nasty quivering thing. She had Anibaddh bring her plain biscuit, and washed it down with plain water. Upon this diet her nausea abated, though she lay weak, pale and petulant, and complaining of a headache, which compounded itself with each passing day.

"The headache keep her abed, not her stomach," Anibaddh confided to Sharada.

"Headache, is it? And what is saying the doctor to that?"

"He say she must eat a egg each morning, well boiled. The cook, he boil a egg for her breakfast each day, and I carry it to her soon as

Mr Todd has got dressed and gone out. And she eat it. I coax her to eat it, though it smell of fire and brimstone. But the headache still is bad as ever."

"Hmmm," said Sharada. "And she is drinking her tea?"

"Oh, no, that doctor don't allow no tea," said Anibaddh.

"No tea?" said Sharada. "Why is that?"

"He say no tea until she take regular exercise again."

"But that she will be unable to do; the headache must go first. Well then. I will be curing her headache, Anibaddh, this very hour. Come, let us ask the cook to boil us some sweet water for a strong tea. You will be seeing."

"But I am not permitted to drink tea," objected Mrs Todd twenty minutes later as Anibaddh helped her to sit up in her bed.

"You will relish it so much the more then, ma'am, for being not permitted," said Sharada, pouring out the first steaming cupful from the pot.

"But this is green tea," said Mrs Todd. "I always have black."

"This will be so very healthful, ma'am, in your condition," replied Sharada. "Just tiny sips, one sip following the other."

"Is there no milk for it? " said Mrs Todd.

"No, ma'am, no milk," said Sharada. "The poor cow has gone dry. Cows are not happy going over the black water. But there is sugar."

Mrs Todd drank a cupful, slowly. Then Sharada refilled the cup.

"It tastes very odd," objected Mrs Todd. "And smells odd. What is that smell?"

"There are three slices of the root of *adrak* in the pot too," said Sharada. "It is very healthful, the gingerroot, for it has properties of soothing the stomach and settling the digestion."

Mrs Todd drank the second cupful. "Anibaddh, I want another pillow behind my shoulders," she said. "And do open the shutter so I can see out. Why, it is a brilliant day, a sparkling day."

Once more Sharada refilled the cup, and Mrs Todd, sitting now quite upright against her pillows, drank her third cup without complaint. The brilliant equatorial light glancing in the little window no longer hurt her eyes. She rolled her head forward, left, right, back; and her neck no longer felt as though she had been hanged. Her skull felt big enough to hold her brain, at last. Her spine, which had felt as though it were dissolving into her blood, had stopped aching and seemed to have reconstructed itself properly. She pressed her palms to her forehead. "Where is Mr Todd?" she asked.

"Up on the deck with the other gentlemen, ma'am," said Anibaddh.

"What time is it? So late as that? Why, it will soon be dinnertime. Perhaps I could manage to eat a few mouthfuls today. I do believe I am feeling quite rejuvenated. I will get dressed and go up for a few turns on the deck in the sea air at least. And later, Anibaddh, I shall want freshwater to wash my hair."

They dressed her and sent her up the hatch to the main deck. When she had gone, Sharada explained to Anibaddh about the tea-sickness. "You must make her drink a cup or two of strong tea every day or the headache will be returning," said Sharada. "The sahibs and memsahibs are addicted to tea, every one of them. They must be having it, as any opium smoker must be having his opium, or they suffer from headache and ill temper. I have known of some babus in Patna who took up *feringee* ways and adopted the *feringee* habit of drinking tea; they also were afflicted by headache when their fortunes changed and they could no longer be buying the expensive leaves from Canton. Yet as it is otherwise harmless, except as sometimes making them excessively excitable and unable to sleep—and making a great deal of water, so inconvenient!—so it is well worth the trouble of making sure there is always tea, a sufficiency of tea. But I would not drink it myself, no."

ꕥ ꕥ ꕥ

"NOW, MRS MACDONALD, what is all this about Ossian?" inquired Mrs Todd confidentially one afternoon some days later when the two of them sat together on the main deck using up paper. "Pray, just refresh my memory a little about Ossian, for if I ever learned about it—or him?—I seem to have forgotten the details. Wasn't Ossian an ancient poem, or perhaps a poet, like Homer?"

"Oh dear. I am not so very clear on the details myself," admitted Catherine, leaning back and gazing up at the sails. "But the gist of the matter is this, I think. Back in the 'sixties there was a young Mr James Macpherson, from Kingussie, who astonished the world by publishing his translation—from the ancient Gaelic—of an epic poem which he had recorded in our Highlands, a remnant of the old tradition. The poem—or I suppose it must be called a collection of fragments—commemorated the wars and loves of the great Celtic heroes Fingal and Oscar, who lived in—oh, the second or third century. And this epic was said to have been composed by their contemporary, the great bard Ossian. So it made a great splash, this epic poem of Ossian's, but not everyone quite believed in it. Some said it was a fabrication of Mr Macpherson's—a forgery, in short. And the world—or the part of it which reads books and has opinions about them—divided into two camps over the authenticity of Mr Macpherson's Ossian."

"Have you read it yourself?" asked Mrs Todd.

"I made a brave dash at it when I was a girl. But even my young romantic taste found it heavy going. Forlorn hills, howling storms, shrieking torrents, bloody battles, too—a great deal of that—and silent, sorrowful ghosts drifting about. In truth I did not succeed in appreciating it."

"But was it authentic, or was it a forgery?"

"I cannot say. If only he had published his Gaelic sources with his translation! He might easily have done so—if any such sources existed—but he never did."

"How dreadful it must have been for the poor man if it was authentic!" said Mrs Todd. "How painful to come under attack as a forger!"

"Dreadful, too, if it was a forgery," said Catherine. "How unbearable to hear his Ossian lauded! How jealous he must have felt to hear the rude native genius praised to the high heavens and be unable to claim any of that undeserved glory for himself."

"Oh! Jealous of his own success!"

"But worst of all must have been to hear its authenticity asserted on the grounds that he, Nobody Macpherson, was certainly incapable of producing such a masterpiece himself."

"Poor man! Whatever became of him?" said Mrs Todd.

"You need not pity him overmuch. Ossian made him famous—as famous as he'd made Ossian—and so he met all the great men and got himself into politics and died rich."

"It is wonderful that so much fuss can arise about a mere book, and after all these years," observed Mrs Todd, shaking her head. She rubbed out a mistaken chalk line with her finger, then said, "I wonder if Mr Todd would agree to name it Oscar if it is a boy? Oscar Todd . . . it has a grand ring to it, has it not? Or even Oscar Fingal Todd? But perhaps that might be a bit much."

ꙮ ꙮ ꙮ

"HECTOR, DO COME and look at this," said Catherine one evening between dinner and tea.

"At what, my dear?" said Hector, who was feeling mellow, for he had just been adding another installment to his serial letter home to Mary.

"Come and look at this tune in Sandy's collection."

"This one? 'The Aged Warrior's Sorrow'? Never heard of it."

"No; you must sing it."

He sang the first line.

"Go on," said Catherine. "The second line."

He sang it, quietly. "Hmm," he said. Then he sang the third line. "You found it, then. And I'd hoped the tune was my own! I was beginning to think of a name for it. But do you know, Catherine, I like my version better, with *dari* here, not *barludh*, as he has it. I wonder where I ever heard this. We never played it. I can only have heard it played somewhere, by someone. How odd that it stuck in my head—to emerge now, of all times! And I always had such difficulties learning by heart. The harder I tried, the less able I was to memorise any tune. Yet Sandy could memorise anything, having heard it only once or twice. You, too."

"Anything but multiplication tables."

"Merely a question of diligence. But have you progressed so far as this? More than one-third done? That is good progress. You are simply working straight through, copying them in order? Is there any particular order?"

"Not alphabetical, nor geographical, nor chronological. By what other principle might they be arranged? Hector, I have been thinking, but I have hesitated to mention it to you. You are such a scoffer."

"I, a scoffer? I preserve a nice skepticism, that is all."

"Hmmm . . . Well, do you remember that curious mistake I showed you where 'Black Donald's March' was miscalled 'The MacLeans' Gathering'? Aye; well, it is not the first time we have seen that particular mistake. It was thus in Joseph MacDonald's *Compleat Theory*, too. Don't you remember, from Sandy's copy of that book, his prize copy? Only one brief phrase from the tune is given as an example of something or other, I cannot remember what, but that phrase is wrongly named."

"No, I don't remember anything of the sort. But if so, it was most likely a printer's error."

"No, it was not, for when Mr Clerk showed us the original manuscript itself that night, and was all agloat over his newest prize, I noticed it there, too, as I looked over your shoulder. If it was a mistake, it was made by Joseph MacDonald himself, not the printer."

"Mmm. Well, I will own that it is a curious coincidence. But this is undeniably Sandy's hand. Who could ever mistake that?"

"Yes, it is certainly his writing. But Hector, might he not have copied some other collection?"

"What collection would that be? Oh, Catherine! Are you imagining that sixty years after it went missing, Sandy found the collection of the Great Music that Joseph MacDonald was supposed to have compiled in India? And where is this precious manuscript now, pray? Why did he not send that along home, if ever he had got his hands on such a thing? Catherine, you of all people should know better than that. You know what Sandy was like, his taste for tricks. And his own tune tucked into it, too—a cuckoo in the nest! How delighted he would have been, at having put this one over on you! It is a sad weakness you have, my dear, for fantastic imaginings."

"How do you account for it then, Mr Clear-sighted? How do you account for these one hundred and twenty-six tunes, and so many of them tunes that we never learned? And then this mistake, so very like that little slip in MacDonald's *Compleat Theory*?"

"I do not pretend to account for anything Sandy ever did. For all I know, he made up these tunes himself, with just the prettiest touch here and there of pretended mistakes, for verisimilitude, so as to take in the credulous, such as yourself. It would have been just like him."

"If Sandy made up these tunes himself, his genius far surpasses anything we ever suspected," retorted Catherine. "You may flatter yourself upon 'a nice skepticism,' but I call it scoffing." Then she did not speak to him again for an entire day, which he did not notice.

ꕥꕥꕥ

THEIR FAIR WIND continued, and the Cape Verde Islands materialised during the very night when Captain Mainwaring had predicted they would. The first sight at dawn of the distant smouldering peak of del Fuego caused a sensation among the passengers. It pierced the sky impossibly high and sharp, suspended above a low bank of haze. Far off to the east of them, another ship was beating its way northward, homeward, too far off to hail or to recognise, but the first vessel they had seen in the four weeks since leaving the heavily trafficked Bay of Biscay.

*Increase* threaded her stately way past craggy guano-frosted desert islets, to the big island of Saint Jago, and anchored near the watering place at Porto Praya. Then all the passengers, who had been leaning their elbows on her rails since dawn, tore themselves away from the sight of land (feeling so thirsty for the mere sight of it!) and hurried below to their cabins to prepare to go ashore (for if the mere sight of land was so gratifying, what pleasures might it not afford beneath their feet?). They changed their clothes, chose their hats, and finished and sealed their fat letters to be sent home—distracted all the while by thunderings, rumblings, and crashings below their feet, for the water butts were being rolled out of their places in the hold and raised, one by one, to be sent ashore and refilled.

Catherine and Grace and Hector came up on deck, ready to board the pinnace and be carried ashore on its next return from ferrying water butts to the watering place. Mr and Mrs Todd were there before them, waiting at the rail. Mrs Todd wore her wide-brimmed hat, the one her husband had bought for her in Antwerp. She had it tied with a broad ribbon under her chin.

"You look ridiculous in that hat," said Mr Todd, not quietly. "Do you make a spectacle of yourself on purpose, pray? Or is it merely the effect of ignorance and faulty taste?"

"My hat, a spectacle? But why did you not tell me sooner? I shall go and change it if you do not like it," said Mrs Todd.

"You take an interminable time to dress," he said. "Look, and here is the pinnace already. The MacDonalds are ready to go ashore. Dressed in a seemly manner, too. I shan't wait for you. And I won't be seen with that hat."

"I shall fly!" promised Mrs Todd, and ran off to change her hat, untying the ribbon under her chin as she went.

The pinnace tied up alongside, and one by one the passengers wanting to go ashore were lowered briskly to its deck in the bosun's chair. Mr Todd went last, but Mrs Todd still had not returned. "You may cast off," Mr Todd said to the second mate in charge of the pinnace as soon as he was safely aboard.

"No, by no means; we will wait a moment or two," said Hector. "We have no objection to waiting for Mrs Todd. There is no hurry."

Mr Todd scowled but did not reply. The sailors rested on their oars, and the mate, a Mr Griffiths, dried off the seats for his passengers. Within two minutes—an awkward, silent two minutes—Mrs Todd came sailing over the rail in the bosun's chair, and was let down next to her husband. Mr Griffiths steadied her by the arm, extricated her from the bosun's chair and handed her to a seat next to her husband. She wore a neat close bonnet now. The sailors leaned to their oars, and as the little boat skimmed toward the shore, Mr Griffiths politely pointed out various landmarks of interest: the governor's house, the jail, the main watering place, and the principal inn.

But the Todds were inattentive. Mr Todd, still frowning, muttered something sharp to his wife, and Catherine could not help hearing her reply, for Mrs Todd never could achieve a discreet tone: "Oh, a glimpse of my stockings! But it is out of my power to prevent it, you know, my dear, if I am hoisted aloft in that frightful machine. I'm sure no one thought anything of it. Only you, dearest. My jealous one! Still jealous!" and she made a private little move, a wiggle, closer to his arm, tried to slip her arm under his own as she sat next to him, tried to hold it to her plump bosom. But he would not suffer his arm to be taken. He shifted away from her, made some space between them, and turned his back to her as much as the narrow boat allowed, turning away to have a good look at the little town looming closer now on the shore.

The landing place was a wide beach of loose rounded pebbles. The crew of the little boat rowed them right up until the keel ground on the beach. Then four sailors leapt over the gunnels and hauled the little boat up onto the shingle, beyond the reach of the little licking waves. Mr Griffiths helped his passengers out, high and dry, and told them when he would be back to take them aboard again. Then the sailors pushed the little boat back out until she floated once more, pivoted neatly, and was rowed smartly away.

"But I have forgotten how to walk!" said Mrs Todd, laughing while attempting to keep her balance as she toiled up the steep bank of shifting pebbles. Grace was light enough to skip easily up the long slope of loose rock, but Catherine found that she and Hector did better if she took his arm. Even so, their progress was slow. "Oh, do wait for me, Mr Todd!" cried Mrs Todd, last of all. "I cannot go so fast as you do. I am ever so out of breath!" He stopped where he was, ten yards ahead of her, and stood; but he did not offer to go back to help her. Instead, Hector reached out, offering his free arm for her to lean on; and at last they all made their way laboriously up to the top of the slope, where Grace awaited them.

"I have never felt so utterly ponderous, so earthbound!" panted Catherine as they stood to catch their breath. "The earth rises up so solidly underfoot, meets one so firmly, after the experience of being buoyed along for weeks, borne so lightly over water!"

Catherine and Hector and Grace walked through the streets of the little town, and had soon seen all there was to see. There were boarding-houses and warehouses and residences of every description, from respectable mansions to jumbles of small shacks leaning against one another. The further up the hill they went, the smaller and more squalid were the shacks, until the cobbled street gave way to dirt, and the dirt became a track into the parched wasteland above the town. Some distance up the slopes of the mountain, however, Catherine spied several handsome villas standing in verdant gardens like oases in the desert, nearly smothered behind vast tumbling flowering vines. These mansions, she supposed, were the houses of the more prosperous traders, consuls, or company agents.

It was a hot thirsty place altogether, and had not nearly enough shade. The best boardinghouse was large and new, built of the native volcanic stone, with a white-painted wooden veranda across its front. It had blue louvered shutters closed against the heat and glare, and window boxes filled with flourishing scarlet flowers. The several warehouses were cavernous but well filled, Catherine could see, with stores of every description: spars, chains, rolls of canvas, coiled cables, and barrels of provisions. In the streets behind them stood rawboned horses harnessed to wagons, empty or laden, their tails switching, hooves stamping, and eyes shut against the greedy, stinging assaults of flies.

And then the people! There were shiny black people and green-eyed Creole people. Their speech was boisterous and incomprehensible—a corrupt variety of Portuguese, Hector said. Bold children stared at Grace, who gazed back.

"Aha! there you are!" cried Captain Mainwaring, coming up the street behind them. "I am just going to call on Mr Harvill—the consul, you know. You must come with me and be introduced. Yes, but certainly you must. You will be entirely welcome, for these consuls always do keep an open house. Everyone goes to the consul's house, though we must get a conveyance to take us up there; it is that white villa, up there on the ridge above the town, you see. Oh, and there are Mr and Mrs Todd! They must come with us, too. Oh, Mr Todd! We are just going to call on the consul! How fortunate that we should all meet here. Mrs Todd will like to rest in the shade of his loggia and have something cool to drink, I am sure. What time is it? Well, we shall be too early to be offered any dinner, I suppose."

Captain Mainwaring quickly engaged conveyances for them all: saddled mules for the gentlemen and covered litters for the two ladies; Grace was carried with Catherine. It was a rough, jogging passage up the hill, but the view of the town and the harbour as it spread out below them was enchanting, and Mrs Todd poked her head out of the curtain of her litter to exclaim how charming it was to look down from such a vantage point and see *Increase* at anchor among the other ships.

The fragrance of tropical flowers met them at the garden entrance of the consul's villa. A bowing Creole butler showed them into a high room—very dim and quite cool because all the shutters were closed—then went away. A few minutes later, another servant brought a tray of tall glasses of iced sweet lemonade. Catherine felt most grateful for it; and glad it was not steamy milky tea.

Mr Todd cast himself into one of several cane-backed reclining chairs set about the room; he sat slumped down in it, his head back and his eyes closed. Catherine thought he looked remarkably sullen and unpleasant. "Oh, Mr Todd," said Mrs Todd, "you must try this lemonade. It is so exceedingly refreshing! Shall I bring you a glass of it?"

His reply was a long, loud sigh.

Mrs Todd cast an arch look at Catherine with an indulgent half moue, and carried a glass of the lemonade to where Mr Todd lay, his eyes still closed. "Here," she said brightly, "I shall set it just here on the flat wide arm of this chair, by your hand. What a very convenient design for a chair. You will like to drink this, I am sure. Ice! I wonder where they get ice, and how they keep it in a climate like this one. What a luxury. I did not expect to find it here."

Mr Todd did not stir, or reply, and Mrs Todd turned away again. To Catherine she said, "We have been walking about the town, and Mr Todd was thinking of inquiring for a fresh cow to be brought aboard for the rest of the voyage—for my health, I mean—but apparently there are none to be had, for there has been a terrible drought here. Just fancy! It has not rained these eighteen months! Not a drop, the man said. There is not a cow in milk on the entire island, no milk to be had but goat! Or ass!"

There was a shattering crash. They all turned; Mr Todd's glass of lemonade had smashed on the wooden floor. It puddled against the edge of the Turkey carpet and had splashed across the back of Mrs Todd's dress. He still did not open his eyes, but now one leg was slung over the arm of the chair where the glass had been, and he swung his booted foot insouciantly.

A servant looked in, and came back a moment later with a basin and a cloth to clean up the sticky mess. Mrs Todd laughed her silly laugh.

Just then Mr Harvill entered, and apologised for not coming to them sooner, for he had been ordering repairs to the cistern. "You will give us the pleasure of your company at dinner, I hope; indeed, you must," he said. "There is a Captain Appleton coming, of the *Minerva*—

no doubt you saw her in the harbour—with his officers, a most gentlemanlike set of men, and my neighbor Mr Mashiter, our eminent commercial man. Of course you must; it is far too hot to go out now, you know, especially for the ladies, and Mrs Harvill has made me promise to secure the pleasure of the ladies' company in particular."

Grace was taken to the nursery to play with Mrs Harvill's children. And as soon as Captain Appleton and his officers arrived and were introduced, they all sat down to dinner. Mrs Harvill was a small sallow woman with dark circles under her eyes, but she was prettily dressed. She had also a pleasing manner, an easy flow of agreeable conversation, and, apparently, a cook who knew well how to comfort homesick Britons. There was an excellent turtle soup. Then came the fish, of some flavourful and firm-textured kind that was not likely ever to be seen or caught in Scottish waters. When the joint of mutton arrived (or was it goat? remarkably mature flavoured, and stringy), the general talk, which had been maritime and mercantile in the extreme, turned to the news from home and to the king's recent visit to Scotland.

"But did she not accompany the party, then?" asked Mr Mashiter, the mercantile man.

"Oh, no. They say Lady Conyngham was sulking at the Sussex seaside. She had been hoping for a little jaunt to Florence instead, and would not go to Scotland," said Captain Mainwaring.

"There was a rumor that he was tiring of her," said Mr Harvill.

"Well, it is an odd way of expressing it then—this showering of pearl necklaces, and belts of diamonds and sapphires, and Florentine marquetry tables," said Mr Mashiter.

"Pray, Mrs Todd and Mrs MacDonald," said Mrs Harvill quite brightly, "will this be your first crossing of the line, of the equator?"

"Yes, indeed," said Mrs Todd, "and Mr Todd has been frightening me with dreadful tales of the ordeal I must expect to undergo."

"Oh, no, you will be excused in compliment to your sex, to be sure. And any gentleman who does not like to undergo the ceremony of ducking and shaving must simply pay the forfeit—it is just a ration of grog for all hands."

"Oh! Mr Todd! Mr Todd! He does not hear me. I shall be sure to give him the hint, however. It is a peculiarity of his to dislike extremely any sort of ridiculous situation. It puts him quite out of humour. You should have heard him this morning. He did not like my hat, and he quite ordered me to change it! In the lordliest tones, too."

Catherine noted that Mr Todd, seated across from his wife, applied his fork and knife to his mutton with some vehemence.

Mrs Harvill said, "I doubt Mr Harvill has ever in his life formed an opinion about any hat of mine. I daresay they all appear equally ridiculous to him, unless they are actually invisible. In fact, hats are rather ridiculous, if one stops to think of it. And so, did you change your hat?"

"Certainly I did. I am exceedingly obedient. I did not even advance the argument that he had himself just bought me the very hat! Indeed he had, in Antwerp. Yet when he uses that lordly tone, that masterful way of speaking, well, I am quite helpless; I must obey. I am tempted to mention it now, however, now that he is no longer so hot and cross. Oh, Mr Todd? Mr Todd!"

Unable to turn a deaf ear to her importunity any longer, Mr Todd gave her at last his stony countenance.

"I was just telling Mrs Harvill what an exacting husband you are, and now you must tell her what an obedient wife I am." And she reached across the table and tapped the back of his hand playfully with her fan.

Mr Todd drew away his hand, and then, throwing down his fork and knife, he sprang to his feet. His chair overturned with a crash on the floor behind him. Mrs Todd shrank back into her chair, frightened at last by his violence and the stony expression of hatred on his face. Silence fell over the table. After a frozen moment, Mr Todd turned to Mr Harvill, bowed stiffly, and without speaking stalked out of the room and out of the house.

A painful minute passed; it was broken when the butler carried in a brilliant trifle of tropical fruits and custard. The trifle was spooned out by Mrs Harvill, and the plates were carried around the table by the silent black servants. The talk turned to the exotic fruits and vegetables which grew so lavishly in these low latitudes. A plate of trifle was set at Mr Todd's empty place, as though he had been called away on some brief business and might be expected back at any moment. But no notice was taken of his absence, least of all by Mrs Todd, who had numerous questions about the cultivation of pineapples in the open garden, and who told at some length of having once eaten one that had been grown in a Sussex greenhouse.

In due course the ladies rose and retired. They visited Mrs Harvill's nursery, well-stocked with four little girls and an infant boy, where silent Grace had been offered an infant ration of porridge. Catherine took Grace's hand and brought her down to the drawing room, where tea was promptly brought in, followed soon thereafter by the gentlemen. Mrs Todd had looked up eagerly when she heard their heavy footfalls on the hall landing, but then, Catherine noted, managed creditably to conceal any appearance of disappointment.

When shadows lengthened across the garden, Mr Harvill conceded that the worst heat of the day was past, and soon the party broke up. The saddle mules and the litters were brought up to the gate (Mr Todd's mule was nowhere to be seen, however) and the farewells soon made. The ride down the hill was even rougher than the ascent, but accomplished more quickly.

When Mrs Todd emerged from her litter at the landing place on the beach, her face betrayed that she had given way to tears behind the privacy of the vehicle's curtains. Nevertheless she was soon her usual cheerful self, laughing as she held Hector's proferred arm and they made their precarious way down over the rocks to meet the boat. Catherine, sliding over the slippery pebbles while hanging on to Hector's other arm, still privately censured Mrs Todd's silliness, but had to credit her, too, with a style of courage she had not previously recognised in her. Mrs Todd sustained her high spirits, her rather hectic spirits, until they had boarded *Increase* once again. But upon finding that Mr Todd had not returned to the ship, she retired to her cabin.

Hector shut himself up in his little cabin, too, to put the finishing touches on his long letter to Mary, for Captain Appleton's *Minerva* was Portsmouth-bound and had offered to carry their letters home. Catherine gathered up the first forty tunes which she had finished copying from Sandy's manuscript; and tied them up in oiled muslin and twine, to send back to Mary for safekeeping. It made a thick parcel. When she took it to Hector to be sent with his letter, he rolled his eyes, but he did not try to dissuade her.

Captain Mainwaring was in his own cabin overhead with his steward, dealing with bills and receipts, but upon hearing that Mrs Todd was unwell, he kindly sent her a medicinal offering of his special whisky, the whisky which was so notably endowed with the true contraband *goût*. Anibaddh carried trays of tea and food to the little cabin. Mr Sinclair, Dr Macpherson, and Mr Fleming all had gone ashore.

When at last Mrs Todd fell asleep, Anibaddh was at liberty to settle down with Grace to their chess game, set up on a little stand in one corner of the main cabin. This hard-fought game had been continued over a period of several days despite numerous interruptions; and had at last arrived at that distilled interesting point where every move of the surviving pieces was heavy with consequence. Catherine sat stitching diligently at her canvaswork (a creamy dove in a dwarfish tree), but she heard Anibaddh say "Check!" and a few moments later, heard her say it again. Then there was silence for a long while, and Catherine threaded her needle again, now with a length of moss green worsted, and the ship rocked gently and creaked.

After a while there was a commotion above of familiar voices and footfalls. Then Mr Sinclair and Mr Fleming came in, followed in a moment by Dr Macpherson. Hector emerged, his fingers stained with ink and a smudge on his forehead. Mr Fleming stood over the bent heads of the chess players and studied the game. Then he went above again to the captain's cabin; Catherine heard his footsteps overhead.

"Is Mrs Todd asleep?" asked Dr Macpherson in a low voice, far more discreet than his usual braying tone.

Hector said that she was. "Did you happen to come across Mr Todd at all?" he asked.

"Oh, aye, we did," said Mr Sinclair.

"Could you not persuade him to come aboard with you?"

"He was in no mood for persuasion, sir," said Mr Sinclair.

"Roaring drunk," said Dr Macpherson. "Disgusting. Making an appalling row on the veranda of this filthy town's filthiest brothel, sir. And then he presumed to mock me. If I thought him in a condition to be responsible for his words, I should have demanded satisfaction immediately. As it is, and in consideration of what must be the feelings of another person, I am inclined to be satisfied with a full apology as soon as he shall be competent to produce one."

Mr Fleming returned. "Captain Mainwaring expects to sail as soon as the watering is finished, no later than ten o'clock tomorrow morning," he said to the other men in a low tone. Catherine continued to train her gaze upon her needlework.

"Sly girl! You learn too fast," murmured Anibaddh. Catherine could see Grace hugging herself with delight, squirming in her chair with the excitement of the contest.

"He will be unconscious long before that," said Mr Sinclair.

"The second mate, with four stout seamen, will go ashore and collect him, but not until the middle watch, sometime after midnight," said Mr Fleming. "We shall have him aboard before breakfast. He can be put in a hammock in the infirmary for as long as necessary."

"I guess I teached you too well," said Anibaddh when Grace made her next move: a bishop.

"It is extremely unpleasant to be forced to tolerate such low, such vile company," said Dr Macpherson, his tone rising again. "It is the great evil of a sea voyage—this enforced proximity for so extended a period. The language he used to me, sir! Could ever any gentleman bear to be addressed so, and before others?"

"Oh, Dr Macpherson, I certainly heard no particular language. Indeed, his speech was hardly intelligible," said Mr Sinclair.

"I beg your pardon, Mr Sinclair. It was intelligible, quite intelligible. Did you not hear him call me a pitiful, clownish fellow?"

"I did not attend to his utterances, Dr Macpherson, not at all. I do not recall hearing any such offensive words."

"He did, though; he said 'awkward, pitiful, clownish fellow.' "

"No doubt he was referring to himself, referring ruefully to his own situation, Dr Macpherson. I daresay you misunderstood his reference."

"Well, well! Do you think so?"

"I am quite certain of it, doctor," Mr Sinclair assured him.

"He did cut a sorry figure. His linen all awry, a bottle at his lips, and that poxy harlot on his lap! Oh, well, it is fortunate that I have laid in a good supply of tincture of mercury. . . ."

"Checkmate!" cried an exulting childish voice, a voice unfamiliar to all but Catherine. Hector, Mr Sinclair and Mr Fleming turned, astonished; and Dr Macpherson's talk trailed off when he saw he had lost their attention—for Grace had wrested her victory at last from Anibaddh.

# 13

## *Such a Contemptible Notion*

Of the male passengers, only Hector, Mr Sinclair, and Dr Macpherson could not call themselves sons of Neptune; only they had never yet crossed the equatorial line. Consequently, it was explained to them, they must expect upon their first crossing to undergo the time-honoured rite of ducking and shaving, or else pay a forfeit, set at the cost of a ration of rum for the crew.

"What! An additional allowance of rum?" said Dr Macpherson. "To be added to their usual ration? Indeed! I must be excused from any participation in so barbarous a custom. No, indeed, gentlemen, you must excuse me. My grounds for objection? But they are several. First of all, upon medical grounds. The allowance of rum granted to the sailors even in ordinary circumstances is so great as to be detrimental to their health, and I cannot in conscience as a medical man, as a man of Hippocratic principles, sir, contribute to so unwholesome a practice."

"Ah! just what one expects from the man of hypocritic principles," murmured Mr Todd, not quite audibly.

"I beg your pardon, Mr Todd?" said Dr Macpherson.

"I said, sir, if you will not pay the forfeit, then you must undergo the ducking, that is all," said Mr Todd.

"No, no, Mr Todd. Again I must insist upon being excused. Upon what grounds? Oh, sir! Do you ask? Do you press me? Well, I do not like to speak of what ought to be a private matter of conscience, but as you inquire I will answer, for I am not ashamed. It is upon conscientious grounds, sir—moral grounds. While other men's consciences may permit them to indulge in play-acting pagan rites, I cannot myself submit to anything of the kind. I am a son, I hope, of the Almighty, and of my father and my mother, but I am none of pagan Neptune's, sir. And while others may do as they please, my conscience will not permit me to undergo such an unholy travesty, sir, not even in jest."

Mr Todd emitted a snort.

Dr Macpherson bowed stiffly in his direction, and continued. "Mr Todd is amused, I daresay, at hearing such old-fashioned principles avowed. It is not fashionable, I am only too aware. Nevertheless it is a private matter of—of righteousness, if you like. So I must insist upon being excused." With this, the doctor rose from the table and walked out of the cabin.

" 'Unholy travesty' and 'pagan rites'!" sneered Mr Todd as he refilled his wine glass, spilling a little. He rearranged himself in his chair and, as the ladies had gone, he tugged indelicately where his fashionably cut trousers gave him no ease. "That is just the illiberal sort of conduct that gives Scotsmen in general a bad name in the world," he declared, then drained his glass and refilled it once more. "A man who will begrudge the crew a guinea's worth of rum, and pretend it is out of concern for their health! Yet he does not deny himself any of the captain's good wine, you will surely have observed. And then, fearful of rough handling of his righteous self, to pretend that he cannot submit to it as a matter of moral principle! Oh, we have got a precious soul aboard, I fear—a saint! Let us hope that the Almighty waits to gather him to his bosom until we have all got shafely asore. Safely ashore," he corrected himself carefully.

"Perhaps he has not got a guinea to spare thus," suggested Hector.

"A man ought not to embark upon a voyage without a few quid to spare for King Neptune, and such other incidental expenses as fall upon gentlemen, or those who expect to pass for gentlemen," said Mr Todd. "He ought to have figured it into the cost of his passage."

"Oh, but he has his passage in exchange for serving as the ship's doctor during the voyage," replied Hector. "I daresay he has in all truth not got sixpence to spare."

"Suppose another man were to pay the forfeit in his name," proposed Mr Sinclair.

"Might he not be extremely offended?" said Hector.

"Perhaps it could be done privately, without his knowledge."

"A man who cannot afford a drink for the men must not suppose he can afford pride," Mr Todd drawled.

"Oh, Mr Todd, sir!" said Mr Sinclair. "Who among us can relinquish pride?"

It was about noon the next day when *Increase* was hailed by a royal personage or, more correctly, by a deity. Alerted by a hint from Mr Fleming, Catherine and Grace had been whiling away the warm morning on the main deck, and were well positioned to see it all.

"Ship ahoy!" cried the foretop watch. Then, as soon as the captain's permission had been sought and secured, a dripping wet grinning red face suddenly appeared at the rail. King Neptune himself clambered up from beneath the forechains and swung himself nimbly over the headrail. He strode to the center of the foredeck, where he struck a noble pose, as regal and dignified as though the water were not running off him in rivulets, a puddle rapidly spreading around his bare feet. Within two minutes all his court had swarmed aboard too, through the gunports and over the hammocks: a score of hearty mer-men, all equally dripping, grinning, and most outlandishly costumed and painted.

Among them they bore several buckets of grease and tar. King Neptune himself wore royal robes of heavy wet canvas garlanded in seaweed, and he brandished a sceptre (which bore a remarkable resemblance to a flattened iron hoop from a barrel). Above his long, sopping beard, made apparently of frayed hemp and oakum, could be discerned the features of one of the foredeck hands, a man who had had some playacting experience before his impressment, and who would sometimes amuse his watchmates by reciting Falstaff. One of his attendants played a flourish upon a pennywhistle; then the god of the seas cried in an impressive voice, "What ship is this, who is her captain, what is her nationality, and where is she bound?"

"This is the merchant ship *Increase*, under the command of Captain Mainwaring, of Antwerp in Flanders, and bound to Calcutta, may it please Your Oceanic Majesty," replied the officer of the watch, making a deep and solemn bow.

"Oh, Captain Mainwaring, is it? An old, old friend of mine, always welcome in my domains," cried King Neptune. "I would go ten degrees out of my way for the pleasure of his company. Be so good as to take me to him." Blithely mounting a gun carriage, the deity royale was drawn aft by his attendants to the quarterdeck, where Captain Mainwaring presided.

Captain Mainwaring bowed like a courtier and delivered an address of welcome, which Catherine did not attend to very closely, as it went on for a long time: "Most Honoured Sovereign, it is with sincere pleasure that I once again welcome you aboard this good ship *Increase*. . . . Your benevolent tolerance of our passage . . . the beneficent currents of your realm that bear us on our course . . ." He finished at last with a flourish: "And now you will wish no doubt to exact your rightful tribute from those who are for the first time trespassing on your domains. Allow me then to transfer command of the ship to your majesty for the duration of the ceremony."

With rowdy shouts of joy, then, the god's suite undertook to turn upright on the main deck the smallest of *Increase*'s boats. The fire engine was deployed to fill it with seawater; and the light tackle was rigged above it. So quick, efficient, and enthusiastic were the courtiers that this was the work of two minutes. Brandishing his sceptre, King Neptune and a half dozen of his attendants then climbed into the little boat full of seawater, and the burliest of the courtiers were instructed to bring one by one anyone who had not yet paid his tribute.

Among the crew were perhaps a dozen men and boys who had never before crossed the line. One by one these were seized upon, their faces smeared as for shaving with the slippery mixture of grease and tar, and then, seated upon a sling descending from the tackle, they were lowered with shouts and cries into the boat, where King Neptune and his attendants shaved them, not too gently, with the bent barrel stave sceptre. Then after a couple of duckings to get them good and clean, they were set staggering on their feet again to enjoy the spectacle of those who came after them undergoing the same treatment, or even to help administer it. Some of the initiates resisted valiantly, submitting only by compulsion; others reveled in the spirit of the occasion and begged to be ducked over and over again, calling for soap and sponge; but all underwent their ordeal in good heart.

Two of the midshipmen, mere boys of twelve or thirteen, had certainly never yet encountered a razor at close range. The smaller of the boys was seized upon first, and his downy chin was slathered with tar and grease, at which he squealed most unmanly until a seaman stopped his mouth with the mixture. Catherine felt Grace shrink close against her side. Spitting, the boy was mounted on the sling and lowered briskly into the boat while his mates made sure to point out to him the high honour of receiving his very first shave from so exalted a personage. The personage made sure to shave him exceedingly thoroughly, and to douse him very thoroughly, too, and bade him wash behind his ears. When at last he was heaved out of the boat to drain on the deck, he lay panting for a moment before leaping up to serve his fellow midshipman just as he himself had been served, or perhaps a little rougher—for his ears were glowing scarlet.

After the initiation of every half dozen neophytes or so, King Neptune and his suite renewed their strength with a draught of grog. By the time all the neophytes among the crew had been duly initiated, the royal entourage was not so thorough nor so efficient in their ceremony as they had been.

Now the attention of the watery god turned to the officers and the passengers, as was his undisputed right, for no officer or passenger, be he ever so exalted in the hierarchy of mortals, could pretend to any rank which could exempt him from the god's jurisdiction.

Of the ship's officers, only Mr Griffith, the second mate, had never yet crossed the equator. Although he had made several lengthy voyages in the Mediterranean, and had crossed the Atlantic to and from the West Indies half a dozen times, never yet had he crossed the great line itself, not during his six years as midshipman nor during his two years as second mate on a merchant ship. It was a virginity he was eager to lose. When summoned at last into the presence of the watery god, he came promptly and made his bow with a flourish "for the pleasure at last of paying my respects, ahem, my respects *and* my forfeit! to your Oceanic Majesty, for whom I have always felt the deepest—ha ha! *deepest*! regard." He was ready with his purse and paid the tribute demanded with good grace, and the initiates—now including every sailor aboard—gave him a cheer of appreciation as he retired, and his contribution was entered into the accounts by the chancellor of the Exchequer.

At last King Neptune's heralds were sent to address the passengers.

Despite the quantities of rum these envoys had consumed, their deportment was respectful. They preceded themselves with music—the pennywhistle again—and drew themselves up in a semicircle like actors turning to their audience at last. "His Oceanic Majesty sends his royal compliments to the ladies and gentlemen who have dared to enter upon his domains!" proclaimed their leader, a smallish man endowed with a surprisingly large voice. "He furthermore has authorised us, his envoys, to inquire as minutely as should be necessary as to the credentials which any of the gentlemen may carry which should constitute their claims to be his adopted sons as a consequence of having previously traversed this particular latitude of his realm." Here his voice dropped to a more usual speaking pitch: "Always excepting Mr Fleming, who is an old hand well known to his Majesty, and of course the ladies *and* their maids, who *being* female, can't be *sons* of King Neptune nor of no one else, and so are naturally exempt from the ceremony." This gallant speech was accompanied by another deeply respectful, not to say theatrical, bow—a gesture reciprocated by gracious curtsies from Mrs Todd and Mrs MacDonald, while Grace retreated behind Catherine.

Then, prompted by a hint from the man at his side, the chief envoy turned to the gentlemen, among whom Mr Sinclair stood foremost. "His Watery Majesty bids me inquire with all respect, sir, whether you have ever passed this latitude before."

Mr Sinclair readily admitted he had not.

"And will you choose to undergo the initiation ceremony which you have seen performed, or will you prefer to pay the forfeit, which his Majesty levies in the amount of a pound, sir—about enough for a ration of grog for all hands?"

Mr Sinclair chose to pay the forfeit, and handed it over to the sailor who acted as treasurer, the crew expressing their appreciation with a hearty cheer.

Hector promptly offered up his forfeit as well, looking sheepish, for he was—Catherine knew—always shy and easily embarrassed and did not enjoy amateur theatricals. He was similarly rewarded by the crew's expression of gratitude.

Mr Todd in his turn asserted that he was already a son of Neptune, and under questioning about the dates and name of the ships and their captains, succeeded in establishing to the satisfaction of the embassy that he had indeed traversed these latitudes on a previous passage to and from Calcutta.

"But where is the doctor? Where is Dr Macpherson?" Mr Todd then asked loudly. The doctor had been here, observing the shavings and duckings; but now he was gone.

"Fetch him up, bring him up!" was the cry from the crew. "Harpoon him and haul him in!" And a deputation surged down the hatch to go and seek the doctor.

"I hope he does not suppose that they will let him off without the customary emolument," said Mr Sinclair, and he turned to Mr Fleming.

After a few minutes the soggy deputation emerged again. They had succeeded in fetching up Dr Macpherson, but their deportment was noticeably soberer than when they had gone down. Dr Macpherson walked among them, but he stalked as stiffly as a dog surrounded by a strange pack, his spine bristling with defiance. The seamen surrounding him wore something of the same punctilious carefulness, and a hush fell as the convoy drew up in front of King Neptune, who, having tired of the water-filled boat once the shavings and duckings were over, had climbed out and reseated himself unsteadily on his throne atop the gun carriage.

The herald looked about, considering, and decided that his safest course was to follow established protocol. "By the authority vested in me, sir, by His Oceanic Majesty, I am to inquire—ah, to inquire with all *respect*, doctor, whether you have ever passed this latitude heretofore."

"Certainly not," said Dr Macpherson with a marked hauteur, a palpable disgust.

"What's that? Speak up; we cannot hear you!" cried a few voices.

"Certainly not!" shouted Dr Macpherson, looking as black as a monsoon sky.

"Well, then, doctor, sir, this is about the size of it," explained the herald quietly. "You can just pay the forfeit, you know, if you do not choose to be shaved and ducked. It is just the custom, you know, doctor."

"No, no, indeed," said Dr Macpherson. "You must excuse me from any participation in this charade of yours. I insist upon being excused. I decline to participate in any form." And he turned as if to walk away;

but there was a solid wall of sailors around him, and they did not make way for him to pass.

"Come, doctor, it is only a draught of rum!" said someone.

"What is your fee for a consultation, then, doctor?" cried another.

"Will it be the fine, or will it be the ducking then? For one or t'other it maun be!"

"And a man who will not ante up has chosen the ducking by default!" The sailors knew the law of Neptune well; but still no one among them was quite ready to be the first to lay hands upon the doctor. He turned about in his little open perimeter, glaring fiercely. They glared back, some of them quite as fiercely.

Catherine glanced over to where the other passengers—her brother and Mr Sinclair, Mr Fleming, and Mr Todd—were conferring. Mr Sinclair was speaking, gesturing. Mr Fleming shook his head in a decided negative. From his quarterdeck, Captain Mainwaring observed, quite still; but he did not appear poised to intervene.

"Will they go so far as to seize him by force, do you think?" whispered Mrs Todd to Catherine.

"I think they might," replied Catherine.

"Why does not Captain Mainwaring stop them?"

"But why will he not fall in with their custom? It is so entirely harmless," said Catherine.

"His dignity will not allow it, poor man," said Mrs Todd.

"But it is his dignity which stands in grave danger."

At just this moment Dr Macpherson made an ill-judged attempt to push his way between two of the slighter seamen who surrounded him. Even these small specimens were far more solid than they appeared, however, and upon the instant that their genteel hesitation about employing physical force upon the doctor's person had been breached—by the doctor himself!—all was over. Twenty hands seized him; a cry went up, and the mob swept him along to their buckets and their boat, like a wave washing over the deck. It was a moment's work to slather his face with tar and grease. A great deal of it found its way into his nose and eyes and onto his coat, too, because, far from submitting meekly, the doctor fought back as well as he could despite a score of restraining hands. King Neptune toppled off his gun carriage, but none of his subjects noticed. The struggling doctor was lashed to the sling and lowered into the boat with a great splash. The barrel stave which had been used for the shaving could not be found, but someone brought a ship's scraper, and this served for a razor.

Dr Macpherson was scraped and scrubbed, and finally hoisted out and set upon the deck to drain. For a moment he lay quite still, only panting and gasping; apparently he was not actually drowned. Then he raised himself, turning away his face, his hands to his eyes, perhaps to wipe them clear of seawater and greasy tar. His thin shoulders heaved. Was he sick, or weeping? Water still sluiced off him. Why would he not stand up like a man, and laugh or roar like a man, like other men? The moment drew itself out painfully.

Then Hector plunged down the gangway. "Valiantly contested, good doctor!" he cried in a hearty voice, putting his arm around the man's wet shoulders and drawing him quite forcefully to his feet. Hector had his handkerchief ready in his hand, offering to wipe the tar from the doctor's eyes. "A man who will not be daunted by such odds as those is an example to us all! Let us have a cheer for our doughty doctor!"

And the sailors, grateful for the suggestion (for they had begun to feel just a little abashed about what they had done), raised their voices in a hearty huzzah three times over. Some eloquent speaker among them cried out, "Not but what we're glad to drink up the forfeit if that's how any gentlemen passengers choose to pay, but ain't we just as glad or gladder to have to do with a gentleman who is a good sport, a gentleman who is not afraid of saltwater and a razor!"

"Hear him! Hear him!" cried a dozen voices.

"The doctor is a good 'un!" cried someone else.

"A true Son of Neptune forever, and a brother to us all!"

And under the cover of this noisy appreciation, and behind the curtain of Hector's handkerchief, the doctor succeeded in somewhat mastering himself; in standing up on his own feet; in clearing his eyes of tar and of tears (if indeed there were any). This was good enough. Then, still unable to speak or look about him, he took himself away, and down the hatchway, down to the refuge of his cabin.

Thank you, good, dear Hector, thought Catherine when her eyes met his over the heads of the sailors.

Dr Macpherson did not appear at dinner, where not a word was said of the day's doings. But Catherine noticed later that Anibaddh had somehow got hold of his coat—perhaps his only coat—and was applying all her considerable energy to the task of redeeming it.

It was hot, hotter than Catherine had ever experienced, the oppressive, heavy, drowning heat of the tropics. Even the breeze that still puffed out the sails was hot and singularly unrefreshing, a breeze of a type never even conceived of in Scotland. But they were not to complain of the hot breeze, said Mr Fleming; they were to rejoice in it, for it too often happened in these equatorial latitudes that there was no breeze at all. Too often ships lay becalmed for weeks. They had been lucky, marvelously lucky in their passage, particularly for this unusual and unpredictable season. This hot miserable travesty of a breeze was to be appreciated and praised, for light though it was, still it bore them steadily along day and night, southward to where they might expect to pick up the reliable westerlies which would take them past the cape and all the way to India—or to Australia even, if they failed to strike off in time.

No fresh cow had been found at Cape Verde, but a beautiful goat with long drooping ears and her twin kids had been brought aboard instead to provide milk for Mrs Todd in particular. Mrs Todd found this milk repulsive, however; it smelled horribly of goat, she said, and told Anibaddh not to bring her any more of it. Anibaddh tried to argue that it smelled no more of goat than cow's milk smelled of cow; but Mrs Todd insisted that cow's milk smelled only of milk, smelled only just the way milk, real milk, ought to smell; that only cow's milk was real milk, and the fluid produced by the goat was counterfeit stuff. Arguing was of no use. She flatly refused any milk. Consequently the other passengers—and the twin kids—made free of it. No butter could be made, because *Increase* had no separator, and the ship was never still enough to allow the cream to rise, goat's milk being particularly slow to separate, and likely to spoil first in the equatorial heat. Goat's milk turned out, however, to be an excellent binding medium for the pastel crayons which Mr Sinclair now taught Grace and Mrs Todd to make.

He showed them how to grind their pigments very fine in a mortar, then to mix them with a little milk to make a brilliant paste. These pastes would be set out on separate plates to dry a little until they reached a consistency suitable for shaping. Then this pigment dough could be formed into little balls, and these balls flattened and rolled out like worms or snakes and left to finish drying, which they did remarkably quickly in the harsh, bright sun. Then Grace and Mrs Todd had the satisfaction of drawing with these crayons that they had themselves made: the delicious ochre jaune; rich, gorgeous siennas both raw and burnt; exquisite vermilion; ethereal terre verte; cobalt. They were delighted at the beauty, depth, and brilliance of the colours they had made, as delighted as though they had indeed invented the very colours. They would never have looked so attentively at these colours, never have seen them so thoroughly, if they had not had to make the crayons themselves.

In the mornings, Catherine copied and Grace drew. Mrs Todd drew, or often dozed.

Mr Sinclair walked his circuits of the deck with a book before his face, halting often to check the drawings and advise.

Hector was thinking something through. He would sketch and scribble feverishly in his notebook. Then for long, languid hours he would lie pondering, sighing, frowning up at the sails against the dome of blue sky. He was in the grip of an idea, Catherine could tell. It apparently was a tight, uncomfortable, pinching grip, and gave him little rest. Sometimes he sought the distraction of music; he would take out his violin and play Italian tunes, or Scottish ones, until his fingers were sore. Worse yet, he would work on the briefest phrases of three or four notes, playing them over and over, trying out infinitesimal differences in phrasing, timing, and emphasis. It was excruciating to listen to. Knowing this, he would banish himself as far to leeward as he could on the ship, in courtesy to his fellow passengers, so that the faint hot breeze would carry the sound overboard straightaway. Nevertheless, these feverish practicings were often audible in the heavy slow air, seeming to pursue them, eddying in their lee.

Mr Todd was irritable. He sulked and complained and criticised. He did not like the sultry breeze; he did not like the glare of the sun, nor the close stuffy air under the awning. He did not like to lie all day and night without taking any exercise; he did not like walking about; he did not like to swim, nor read, nor draw, nor write letters, nor play music, nor hear it played. He did not like the pale yellow yolks of the eggs produced by the hens; and when one of the two kid goats was butchered for dinner, he did not like the smell of its roasting. He did not admire his wife's drawings, nor her little jokes, nor her pretty ways. But sometimes after dinner, and a quantity of Captain Mainwaring's wine, he would rally sufficiently to try to engage the others in a game of whist or dominoes.

"Come, Sinclair, do," said Mr Todd. "For any stakes you choose, a halfpenny a point if you like. We are so dashed slow, I do not see how anyone can bear it."

"You must excuse me, Mr Todd. I have promised Mrs MacDonald that I would advise her about some matters of composition and colour for her canvaswork."

"Mr MacDonald then. Surely you are not entangled in women's work."

"I am hopeless at such games, you know, Mr Todd. I cannot oblige you."

"Well! I suppose it is no use asking our doctor. He never will play for any stakes at all, I am sure. And I have made it a firm rule never to play unless there is a stake, no matter how small. It is such a bore to play when there is nothing to be gained or lost."

Dr Macpherson faintly nodded his head in acknowledgment; but neither of them would directly address the other, and Dr Macpherson went out.

To Hector, who still remained in the cuddy cabin, Mr Todd said, "I wonder if the good doctor would agree to be ducked and shaved again for a quid? Ha ha! Did you ever see such an amusing sight! I am much obliged to him for the entertainment! It has turned out a dashed quiet and sober voyage. A stupid, priggish lot. Now, on my previous passage, going out on the *Ariel*, we were a pretty company. Among us were several gentlemen of fashion, and one in particular who was known for a wit and had been the particular friend of a noble personage before his marriage. There was a pair of pretty young widows, too, quite fresh and attractive. Ah, that was an agreeable voyage! We had some romping and some roaring! Of course I was not much more than a raw boy then, and not used to fashionable company. At first their pranks and raillery quite astonished me. But I got the hang of it, and pretty quick, too."

"I am sorry you are disappointed with the tone of the present company," said Hector. "Yet on the whole it seems to me we have been pretty tolerable. I am going above to take a turn or two on the deck. Will you come, sir?"

"Shall I have to hear Dr Macpherson urging the benefits of tobacco?" said Mr Todd. But in default of anything better to do or anyplace else to go, he went.

On this occasion Dr Macpherson was not arguing the merits of tobacco, but those of his kinsman and patron James "Ossian" Macpherson instead. "He certainly offered to display his original manuscripts and transcriptions at his booksellers for minute examination by any who might choose to avail themselves of the opportunity," the doctor was declaring to Catherine and Mrs Todd.

"But why did he not publish them in the original Gaelic?" said Catherine. "A volume, with the original Gaelic on the left and his elegant translation on the facing page, just opposite—now, that would have been a most valuable document. That is just the arrangement of the *Ramayana* translation which Mr Fleming has lent me, and a most logical and convenient arrangement it is."

"I believe he had such a volume in preparation at the time he died. He was not born to wealth and leisure, Mrs MacDonald; he was never one of your dilettantes. No, he never had the luxury of freedom from worldly cares. He had no advantages of place, position, or patronage. Nor had he any more of name or family than belongs to any Highland gentleman, no more than I have myself! Despite this, he built a towering and durable literary reputation—before he had reached the age of thirty. And then he went on to make himself exceedingly useful in the political sphere as well. Exceedingly useful."

"He was a marvel of determination and energy, I am sure," agreed Catherine. "Nevertheless I do maintain it is a pity he never published his Gaelic originals. Nor did they ever appear after his death, when an executor might have found them among his papers and brought them before the world."

"Oh! Ossian is it, still!" exclaimed Mr Sinclair good-naturedly, walking up and joining them under the awning. "Well, well. Old jewels in new settings are still jewels."

"But why not present the jewel to the world in its genuine old setting?" said Catherine. "Why reset the jewel at all?"

"Because tastes change, of course," said Mr Sinclair, "and the old-fashioned setting may prevent us from perceiving the beauty of the jewel itself."

"And who among us can even read the old Gaelic character these days? I would have an easier time with Greek, myself," said Hector.

"Always supposing it *is* a jewel, and not mere glittering glass," said Mr Sinclair.

"But do you mean to say, sir, that Fingal is glass?" said Dr Macpherson. "Do you deny that Fingal is great poetry?"

"Glittering glass in a setting of brass," muttered Mr Todd, singsong to himself.

"Oh, sir, I am no judge of poetry," said Mr Sinclair. "Yet I cannot feel just exactly confident about Fingal, and Ossian, and all that. It is just like the curious feeling that I have sometimes when I am looking at a painting. The more I would *like* to believe in it, the less certain I feel that I am justified in doing so. Yes, that is it. For there we were—what was it, fifty years ago? a little more—there in particular were we, the Scots, the Gaeltach, smarting still from the ravishment of the Union and a couple of failed rebellions and a harsh and demeaning Disarming Act. And not just the Scots, you know, sir, but all of us, all Britons, sallying out into the great world. It was a credulous, anxious, ambitious age, men hungering for something that would prove us as splendid as the Greeks and Romans; or splendider if it could be managed, or their worthy heirs at the very least. Then lo and behold, a Mr Macpherson appears and presents us with a vernacular epic of our very own! And in the best classical style, too! It couldn't have been better if we had had one built to order. And that is precisely why I am just a little skeptical, you see."

"Hmph! But what do you say, Mr MacDonald?" asked Dr Macpherson. "You are a Gaelic speaker from the cradle, I believe."

"Oh, doctor, I am a mechanic, and must confess to having shirked my studies of literature at every opportunity. But if I were to consider the question from a scientific standpoint, I might reason as follows: If it is great poetry, then I suppose it must have been the work of a great poet. Now from all that I have heard and read of your good kinsman, sir, I believe that his abilities lay more in the realm of the political and the polemical. With all due respect, I am not convinced that his soul was that of a great poet. I conclude, therefore, that if Fingal is great poetry, it must be the work of some other man."

"But of course it is!" cried Dr Macpherson. "There is your proof; it is the genuine poetry of Ossian himself, only translated for the modern reader by my great-uncle."

"Still, sir, I have heard songs and tales of Fingal and Cuchullin, of Oscar and the others all my life, and all in the old Gaelic," said Hector. "Yet my impression of them is quite different from what Mr James Macpherson has given to us. Now, I do not pretend to much poetic sensibility. Even when I was very young, my head was full of infantile ambitions about metals and levers; and perhaps I did not pay closest attention. Perhaps it is my own fault that I never noticed much of misty romance, pathos, love, or sublime sorrow in those old ballads. A fair amount of fiery martial sentiment I do recall, more gruesome than heroic. What I remember best, I'm afraid—due to the defects of my own taste—were the bawdy and ridiculous bits."

"Oh, who gives a fig? Who cares whether he translated 'em or made 'em up himself?" said Mr Todd, and he threw himself into a low chair.

"A society which ceases to concern itself with questions of truth, authenticity, and legitimacy is in decay," announced Dr Macpherson in his most didactic and irritating tone. "Such a society is diseased; it lies susceptible to fraud and deception of every description."

"Legitimacy! Diseased!" cried Mr Todd, rearing up in his chair.

"Yes, Mr Todd, *legitimacy*, I say," declared Dr Macpherson. "In accordance with the established rules, standards, and accepted principles of society. The regular and orderly descent of name, title, property, and power, as known and witnessed and understood by all, open and true for all to see and attest to."

"This from the very man who mistook Mrs MacDonald for Grace's mother! Do you set yourself up as a judge of legitimacy, sir!"

"I do not 'set myself up' as anything, Mr Todd. That is an offensive phrase."

"Oh, he is speaking merely of provenance, Mr Todd," said Mr Sinclair.

"Providence! I'm damned tired of his precious pratings about morality and righteousness and Providence!"

"No, no, *provenance*," said Mr Sinclair, and set himself between the two men, blocking their view of each other. "Dr Macpherson is only referring to what is sometimes called provenance—knowing where a thing has come from, the path a thing has taken." Mr Sinclair thrust his hands in his pockets and assumed a leisurely stance as he continued. "Let us consider a painting, for example: Who are all the men who have owned it since it came from the brush of the painter? Whose are the hands through which it has passed? When this is known, the authenticity of the painting, the question of its origin, can more easily be assessed. That is what we mean by provenance. But let us leave off; it is tedious talk for a hot evening. Let us have something airy, something breezy."

"Tedious talk! It is damned offensive talk, sir! All the men who have owned it! The hands through which it has passed! And this before her very face!" he cried, gesturing at Mrs Todd.

"The man is drunk," said Dr Macpherson, peering around Mr Sinclair's shoulder at Mr Todd, who was now attempting to rise from his low chair.

"And you are—you are—" But Mr Todd was prevented by Mr Sinclair and Hector from delivering his opinion, even if he had eventually succeeded in finding the words to express it, for he was certainly quite drunk. He struggled out of his chair and launched himself bodily at Dr Macpherson—without, however, actually landing any blow. With the help of Mr Griffith, the second mate, who quietly appeared from somewhere, they managed to take his arms, his body, and remove him, nudge him, herd him, carry him, help him, push him down the gangway and below, to his cabin. "Diseased! He said I was diseased!" he cried as they inserted him through the hatch.

"Oh, no, Mr Todd. He certainly said nothing of the sort, never at all," Mr Sinclair assured him.

# 14

## *Deviation from the Proper & native Style*

The quarrel could not be made up.

Dr Macpherson solemnly asked Mr Sinclair to act as his second. "As second? Oh, doctor!" said Mr Sinclair. "I make no doubt that this little matter can be adjusted without resorting to the use of arms and the employment of seconds. There is no need, I am sure. But if I can be of any use in removing the misunderstanding that has unhappily arisen between Mr Todd and yourself—why, that I will do if I can."

Mr Todd solicited Hector to act as his second. "I cannot undertake to perform any such duty," said Hector. "But if you wish, I will speak with Dr Macpherson. Surely there is no ground for so grave a view of the matter, and no doubt we shall be able to remove the causes of this unfortunate misunderstanding."

So Mr Sinclair and Hector found themselves closeted together, if not as seconds, exactly, then as spokesmen, negotiators, diplomats. There was a great deal of private talk, low-toned and not so low-toned murmurings behind thin partitions; a great deal of to-ing and fro-ing on the parts of the diplomats as they shuttled between the principals and their own private conferences.

But the quarrel could not be made up.

Dr Macpherson maintained that neither his words nor his actions required any apology; that on the contrary he had suffered enough and more than enough of Mr Todd's jeering and fleering, gibing and taunting; and he would be happy to meet Mr Todd upon any field whatsoever, be it ever so small a rock in the middle of the ocean.

*Increase* did not happen across any rocks in the ocean, however.

Mr Todd, for his part, was convinced that Dr Macpherson had insulted him, his wife, and his unborn child by public insinuations upon their lineage and morals; and furthermore had publicly made the false claim that he, Mr Todd, suffered from a venereal infection. He was firmly resolved to demand satisfaction of the doctor and settle the matter once and for all so soon as any landfall should offer the opportunity, and the sooner the better.

Dr Macpherson held that he was himself the injured party and had the right to choose the weapon; and he chose pistols. Mr Todd, however, declared positively that the injury was his, and that his was the right to choose; and he insisted upon swords.

The atmosphere in the cuddy cabin became heavy and close, due now not so much to sluggish airs and oppressive heat—for *Increase* continued to make good progress in her southerly course, sometimes as much as two hundred miles in twenty-four hours, and with every degree of southward progress the air became appreciably cooler and fresher, and the loyal breeze sprightlier—but due rather to the utter breakdown of the fragile little society. Mr Todd, who had never been an early riser, now remained in his cabin until just before dinnertime. And as soon as dinner was over, Dr Macpherson, an early riser, would withdraw to his own cabin, or to the main deck to smoke. They both sat at the table for dinner itself, but their places were moved so that they did not actually see each other's faces. They sat both on the same side of the table, with Mr Fleming between them, and rarely did either of them speak more than a word or two throughout the meal.

Everyone else did their best to take no notice. Mrs Todd conducted herself as though nothing had happened, but hints reached Catherine, through Anibaddh and Sharada, that she had implored her husband by turns sternly, prayerfully, and tearfully, to apologise to the doctor.

The principals became impatient with their seconds, even angry. The seconds, who had never agreed to serve as seconds at all but only as conciliators, became disgusted with the principals. Finally, one evening Hector, in yet another private conference with Mr Sinclair, said, "I am convinced that false vanity and dangerous *amour propre* are more concerned in this affair than wounded honour; or we should have been able to effect a reconciliation by this time. I intend to express my opinion to Mr Todd and to withdraw from any further involvement in this matter."

"I am of the same opinion," said Mr Sinclair, "and I am on the very point of tendering my resignation to Dr Macpherson. It is time for an end to this."

The diplomats accordingly withdrew from any further involvement in the dispute. Dr Macpherson looked black and implied that it was most irregular. Mr Todd, breathing brandy from some store of his own, reserved apparently for private morning use, muttered a few words about a thrashing being good enough for a man who will not fight. Then nothing more was said about the matter, but the mutual ill-will of the two antagonists continued to poison the atmosphere in general.

"What? Mrs Todd's black maidservant to remain in Cape Town? But she certainly will not find any of her aboriginal people there! Oh, no, I should say not!" said Dr Macpherson positively. He was speaking with Catherine and Hector at dinner. "They are Hottentots at Cape Town, but it is apparent that she is not of that Hottentot race, not at all. But of course I can be quite certain. First of all there is her height; she must be five feet nine inches tall at the least, and perhaps has not even yet attained her full height, for I have the impression that she is young still. The Hottentots, however, are of excessively small stature. And then there is her anatomy, her conformation. The Hottentot females—well. Of course there has been no occasion, no opportunity for an actual examination. Nevertheless I feel confident in asserting that your Annie does not exhibit the—the anatomical peculiarities so typical, so notable, in Hottentot females. I have had occasion to observe the so-called 'Hottentot Venus,' sir. Perhaps you recall that female aborigine from Cape Town who was brought to Britain and taken about for viewing?"

"It was a Marine surgeon who brought her from the Cape some ten or twelve years ago, as I recall," said Captain Mainwaring.

"Yes, about then. A surgeon by the name of Dunlop, William Dunlop. I saw her in Manchester. Then those abolitionists brought an action to have her released from her patrons. Do you not recall? But in court she said she had come of her own accord and stayed of her own free will, so that was the end of that. But I did have an opportunity, as I said, of observing for myself her very peculiar anatomy, which, I may add, manifests itself only in the females of the race; the males are formed in accordance with the normal appearance. Yes, astonishing—the steatopygian buttocks being of course the most striking and obvious feature. There is another peculiarity as well, which I shall not describe. Nevertheless, I feel entirely confident in asserting that your Annie is certainly not of Hottentot descent. Of course there may be other races at Cape Town as well; I do not know what they are called, nor what might be their anatomical peculiarities. Perhaps your Annie may be one of those."

Within two hours of *Increase*'s coming to anchor in Table Bay below Cape Town, two of the governor's personal servants came aboard: his land agent and the head groom of his stud. They came to inspect the Flemish mares and to supervise their being taken off—one by one, each borne up by a wide sling under her round belly, a blindfold tied over her head, her strong heavy-boned legs safely hobbled. The mares were unloaded and taken away without mishap. Before two more hours had passed, there came a general invitation to the ship's officers and passengers to spend two or three days at the governor's hunting lodge. The officers and gentlemen would drive out for the shooting; and any ladies and children were welcome to see the vineyards, the kennels, the tame ostriches and zebras. Apparently the Flemish mares exceeded all expectations.

Captain Mainwaring declined for himself and his officers due to the press of ship's business, but Mr Fleming and the other passengers were prompt to accept this flattering mark of attention.

"The native horses here at the Cape were not a bad type at all," explained Mr Fleming in the boat which carried their party ashore the next morning. "They were of oriental lines originally, Arabic and Turkish. But the breed has been much improved these last ten years or so by his lordship's introduction of the finest English bloodstock—a dozen or so of the best Thoroughbred stallions that money could buy. Crossed with the native oriental mares, they have produced a really superior stock, excellently suited for racing, hunting, polo and such sports, so dear to Lord Charles Somerset's heart. But I suppose that, as cavalry mounts, they were found perhaps a little lacking in size and bone. Thus the Flemish mares, of course—so notable for their size, substance, bone, girth. Heavy dragoons require heavy mounts, you may be sure."

"It is surprising to hear of any great demand for cavalry in so maritime a setting as this, at the tip of the continent," commented Dr Macpherson.

"It is a vast continent, though, doctor, and there is always trouble with the tribes. Oh, yes, indeed, several invasions by the Zulus; and the Xhosa to contend with; and trouble between the Bantu and Suto and Chuana, not to mention the Bataung, the Griquas and the Korannas. Well, you will understand that a larger, heavier cavalry type is wanted along the eastern frontier. You remember the settlers coming out two years ago, do you not? It made a splash at the time. Oh, yes! Five thousand British men, women and children made their way to the interior to carve out new farms. Virgin river valleys, for wheat, mostly. But we are beginning to see quite a lot of other trade too: everything from ostrich feathers to ivory—many tons of ivory each year—and of course the famous sweet wine. You shall be offered some, make no doubt."

Mr Todd brightened slightly at the mention of wine, sweet wine. He had been silent and sulky, out of sorts, and his brow was pinched and drawn, as though the brilliant November midsummer sun glancing off the bright water pained him. He frowned and squinted at the peculiar-shaped, aptly named Table Mountain, which hung above the town. Mrs Todd had tucked herself in close to his side, solicitous—annoyingly solicitous—of his comfort.

A couple of old-fashioned open carriages, like wagons, driven by silent Dutch farmers, met their party at the landing place. When Mr Fleming addressed them quietly in their own language, these Boers brightened perceptibly and became willing to help arrange parcels and hand up the passengers. By some invisible force, it happened that Mr Todd and Dr Macpherson found places on separate conveyances. At last the convoy drove off. They passed through the old Dutch-built town with its distinctive baroque curved fronts. Soon they left the town behind and ascended gradually, hugging one edge of a wide valley whose center was graced by a broad tame leisurely river. There were vineyards and wheat fields, pastures and orchards, strange fat-tailed sheep that looked as if they might tip over backward as they grazed, so heavy were their tails.

"I should so like to see a hippopotamus!" declared Mrs Todd. "I should like it above all things."

"No, lady, you would not," said the driver unexpectedly. "Very dangerous."

"Oh! Are they dangerous? What do they do?"

"They kill peoples. Do not worry, all are dead now. No hippopotamus in this river, no more. All dead. All shooted."

"Oh! Oh!"

"Many crocodiles still."

"I should so like to see a crocodile!"

And eventually Mrs Todd got her wish. From a high vantage point where their horses drew up to recover their wind, the driver pointed out logs lying on the riverbank below, screened by towering grasses. Picking up a stone, he lobbed it accurately into the river beyond them—and the logs plunged into the river, a half dozen of them instantly converging upon the splash of the stone, their sudden animation astonishing.

Lord Charles Somerset's hunting lodge was called Newlands. It was not rustic in the least, no more rustic than Lord Charles himself. Nor was his lady rustic. They, and all their belongings, were in the very best, newest and most admirable English style. Never had Catherine felt so provincial, so Scottish. The house was handsome and modern, set in a large park tastefully and expensively planted. Its furnishings, too—the tables, the plate, the napery, the china, the enormous dark Turkey carpets—expressed refined taste and ample means. Yet because it was a hunting lodge, zebra skins lay on the floor, overspreading the Turkey carpets, and mounted heads hung on the walls amid the family portraits. There were heads of antelopes and wildebeest and lions; and on each mantel, over each fireplace in each handsome room, was a pair of vast elephant tusks, purest gleaming ivory. Catherine could not help stroking one when no one was looking. Oh the smooth, warm curve of it! Oh the colour of it! The exquisitely tapered tip of it, both sharp and blunt!

"And you, Mrs MacDonald?"

"I beg your pardon, Lady Charles; I did not hear you," admitted Catherine to her hostess. It was after dinner; the ladies had withdrawn to a pretty little sitting room belonging to Lady Charles, where tea was brought in to them by servants.

"I was asking whether you and your daughter would like to see the farm tomorrow while the men are out shooting."

"Yes indeed," Catherine answered. That sounded most delightful, and she would like it above all things. While Mrs Todd chatted with Lady Charles, Catherine had been observing the stony, silent black servants. Such various physiognomies! One female servant of very low stature, hardly taller than Grace, brought food for Lady Charles's little dog. This servant had the widest mouth Catherine had ever seen on any human being, extending almost from ear to ear, though there was nothing smiling or cheerful about that mouth. Her body was thick and bulky. Another maid, carrying the heavy tea tray, was remarkably tall and thin; there was a loose, slack marionette look to the way she moved her lanky limbs, and a drugged dullness in her heavy-lidded eyes. The nurse who brought Lady Charles's baby for their inspection and admiration was extremely fat; she waddled painfully, great pads of flesh wobbling about her vast hips and thighs. Her lips protruded a considerable distance from her face. Lady Charles spoke English to these servants, who presumably understood, although they did not betray the slightest understanding by any expression of feature or in their glittering black eyes.

Catherine found these servants frightening and appalling, but she reminded herself how startled she had been at first by Anibaddh's blackness. Yet when Catherine looked now at Anibaddh, she saw not blackness but the bold, silent, critical intellect gazing out from those dark eyes. Catherine recalled also the various types of Scottish faces she was accustomed to seeing at home: red and florid; sandy; pale as straw; Spaniard dark; broad, sonsy, freckle-speckled. The tall and lanky, the short and stout, old, young, bent, and occasionally, the handsome, beautifully formed, the tall and broad chested. Sadly rare.

When all the servants had left the room, Catherine said, "I hope you will advise us, Lady Charles. A black ladies' maid, formerly a slave in America, who has been traveling with us—waiting upon Mrs Todd, in fact—thinks of remaining in Africa. I will be sorry to lose her, for she has been entirely satisfactory, and I will give her a good character."

"Oh, yes, she is very clean and nice," said Mrs Todd.

"But is there any likelihood of her finding a good place here as a ladies' maid?" asked Catherine.

"As a free servant? Indeed, no, Mrs MacDonald. That would be exceedingly unlikely," said Lady Charles. "And then it is so disturbing to the rest of one's people to mix free servants among them."

"Do you tell me that yours are not free servants?"

"Oh, my! All our servants are slaves here. Did you not know?"

Catherine certainly had not known.

"Of course you will think very ill of us. But it is a painful legacy here, a dilemma left us by the Dutch. When the old masters go away, what are the new masters to do? An emancipation plan will be devised very soon, Lord Charles says; and in the meantime we must just go on as before, keeping custody of these people entrusted to us. It is not a problem that lends itself to drastic solutions, you know. These people cannot be simply turned out to starve, any more than one can turn out one's little dog to earn his own living. But it is no place for a free black ladies' maid—not here, certainly not just now. I could not recommend it at all."

"I heard something of an African settlement of free blacks, an effort undertaken by the Americans," said Catherine. "Is that anywhere nearby?"

"Oh! There is a disaster! Some reports have reached us here. Yes, a couple of years ago the Americans landed a shipload of freed slaves—a great distance north of here, on a miserable, low Portuguese part of the Ivory Coast, near a place called Freetown. All swamp, a most unhealthy situation. They could hardly have chosen worse. About ninety souls, and at least a third of them died of fever within the first three weeks! That region is still much preyed upon by slavers too. The local kings and chiefs along that part of the coast have always derived the greater part of their revenue from selling their enemies into slavery, you know—any captives they could get.

"Then last year, not to be chastened by experience, the Americans tried again: two shiploads, or so I heard. They have got themselves settled on a miserable island, which they have named Perseverance, of all things! My husband tells me they have had nothing but disease and fighting ever since. Fever, and fighting amongst themselves and against the local natives, who are Dey and Bassa, and not well pleased to make way for this invasion of strangers. In short, that is no answer for your maid—nor for the freed American blacks either. It will never answer.

"What is to be done? It is not easy, you see. Clearly something must be done, but what? Well, well. Come, come here, Cato, precious, bad dog; that is my scissors case. Give it me, darling," she scolded her little dog, who retreated under the sofa with his prize.

The gentlemen drove out before dawn the next morning for their two days of shooting. The ladies who were left behind breakfasted much later on peaches, coffee, and an enormous omelette made from a single ostrich egg. Then Lady Charles ushered them out, saying they must make their tour early before it grew too hot.

It was already hot and bright. While the sun dazzled them, then baked them, then stupefied them, they trudged about and saw first the kennels (oh, the noise and the stench!); then the dusty ostriches irritably pacing the fences of their paddocks; then the flocks of newly imported fine-wooled Spanish sheep in their tight-fenced pastures; and finally the neat corrugated dark green tiers of grapevines and the stone-built winery. They entered the winery at last, a cool dim haven smelling of molds and yeasts and dampness, so welcome after the dazzling midday heat outside and the vertical blazing sun. They loosened the ribbons of their bonnets and fanned themselves; and Lady Charles ordered sweet cold wine brought to them in elegant little glasses. Raising the glass to her lips, Catherine closed her eyes to breathe in the scent, and was briefly, gladly, in a tiny private universe of yeasty honeyed sweetness. On the tongue, the wine was treacly and viscous. Though it was cool, it did not quench the thirst but only whetted a desire for more. They drank more.

"Now you have tasted our famous Constantia, and at its very source," Lady Charles told them. "It is generally conceded that our Constantia is superior to anything else grown at the Cape. Lord

Charles's father, Lord Beaufort, takes several pipes of it every year. The foxhounds you just saw are from Lord Beaufort's kennels, you know, and the Beaufort Hunt have always been widely acknowledged to be a really superior bloodline. Lord Beaufort has always been most interested in the breeding of his hounds, and everyone admits they are the best in England—which is to say, the best anywhere. But he was eager, most delighted, to trade his most promising youngsters to Lord Charles in exchange for a few pipes of our Constantia."

"But what do you hunt? Are there foxes?"

Lady Charles laughed. "Nothing so homely as foxes, I assure you! No, no, we hunt jackals; we are quite plagued by jackals. Won't you have just a little drop more of the wine, Mrs Todd? Mrs MacDonald? You who are not accustomed to our dry climate must be sure not to get overheated."

"Thank you, I will," said Mrs Todd, and she did.

"You will certainly want to see the zebras," said Lady Charles. "But it is too hot now. My poor little Cato, in his fur coat! Is he terribly, terribly thirsty? Let us return to the house to rest. I will take you to see the zebras after sundown."

As they walked back to the house, Mrs Todd said confidentially to Catherine, "If it is a daughter, I shall name her Constantia. 'Constantia!' A lovely sound, is it not? I never had a wine I liked so well. So refreshing! I should like to urge Mr Todd to lay in a good supply while we are here."

After sundown, the ladies ventured out again. The sky was a pale lavender, a dove gray. All the soil and trees and grass and animals seemed to exhale, at last, now that the punishing sun was gone. Heat still radiated up from bare red dirt, from plowed fields, from rocky roads, from stark rocky escarpments in the hills above them; but now the irrigated pastures and the dark green grapes and the groves of fruit trees exhaled a cool damp breath. The airs mixed, turned, blended, settled, rose here, drained there. Catherine could feel warm upwellings and cool downdrafts as she walked.

The stables were situated some distance from the house. "Downwind, of course," explained Lady Charles, "but uphill, I am sorry to say." Grace, wearing her childish laced boots, skipped; the grown ladies stepped gingerly in their little slippers. A cloud of insects gathered 'round them and progressed up the hill with them—no worse than Highland midges, but Catherine was glad for the shawl which covered her arms.

The stable block looked like any well-built stable block associated with any prosperous mansion in any county in Britain, with velvety, well-fenced pastures and roomy paddocks stretching away on the far side. But the horses! Some of them *were* horses, in the usual horse colours, various shades of gold, brown, black, and gray. But these others! A little herd of zebra mares and foals grazed at the far end of the largest pasture. They raised their large heads as the walkers approached, and pricked up their large ears—not neatly pointed like horses' ears but round and fringed, like furred funnels. The smallest foals moved behind their mothers. Then one of the mares barked, a harsh, strange challenge like the barking of a hoarse-voiced dog, and another answered.

"Look, Grace, stripey horses!" cried Mrs Todd. "What lovely stripes they have! What lovely black muzzles, like velvet. And the babies! Oh, the babies! Are they tame at all?"

"Oh, far from it," said Lady Charles. "They are just the wildest things. They will not be tamed."

"Even the babies, if they are raised by hand and fed from a bottle?"

"We have hand-raised at least a dozen. They are docile enough when young, but as they mature it becomes increasingly difficult, even dangerous, to handle them. Nevertheless, Lord Charles has high hopes for some of his yearlings. And he has got the coachman working with several three year olds, getting them broken to harness. Quite likely we shall be in time to see them working; they generally train in the evenings at this season, after the heat of the day is past."

And so it was. Their little party came around the corner of the buildings into the large yard, to see a strange sight. In heavy chain cross ties between two stout pillars stood a stocky full-grown young zebra, a handsome gelding. He stood shifting his weight, rocking oddly forward and back like a rocking horse, for a pair of hobbles bound his forelegs and another pair bound his hind legs. There was a stout iron muzzle strapped over his black velvet mouth, and a blindfold tied over his eyes. His groom, a tall broad-shouldered young Boer, carried a tangle of harness from the carriage house and hung it nearby, keeping a wary eye on the zebra.

The head coachman directing these operations nodded to Lady Charles and her party, but his full attention was for the zebra, which had somehow sensed their arrival; his head jerked up, his funnel-like ears pointed unerringly at them; they could hear him snuffling the air through the muzzle. In a moment, another groom led out a horse, an ordinary brown cob, who was put in cross ties at another pair of pillars across the yard. The cob, a sedate old creature, wore neither hobbles nor muzzle nor blindfold, and he stood at his ease, one hip cocked.

"Should you like to stay and watch?" whispered Lady Charles to them. Mrs Todd silently nodded yes, certainly; Catherine and Grace glanced at each other but said nothing.

The old cob was soon bridled and harnessed. He stood contemplating the situation with the lines and traces doubled up and tucked out of the way over his haunches while peaceably chewing his bit.

Then it was the zebra's turn. Both grooms approached him warily from either side, avoiding the perilous zones directly before and behind, where he could strike despite the hobbles. The coachman directed them tersely from a safe distance. The zebra laid his ears back flat as he sensed the grooms' approach, but they managed to buckle the collar around his thick neck, then strap on the hames, ease the saddle with its turrets into place, and gingerly fasten the belly strap. Positioning the crupper was a most ticklish operation which had to be undertaken from the side. Despite the hobbles, the young Boer had his foot painfully trampled before the crupper was buckled home. Fortunately the zebra was unshod, for what farrier could shoe such a creature?

Last was the bridle. The elder groom unbuckled the iron muzzle; as he slipped it off, the zebra lunged, his black velvet mouth open to bite and bite hard. The young Boer forestalled him with the bit, perfectly positioned to slip between his teeth, and the headstall over his ears, and over the strong halter, which they certainly did not dare to remove. The elder groom deftly slipped the iron muzzle back into position, and the two of them refastened it over the zebra's now-bitted mouth. He chewed angrily on the bit, salivating copiously; then, coiling back onto his haunches, he lashed forward with his hobbled front hooves. Blindfolded, he struck only air; and the groom punched him twice in the jaw with his fist. Furious but chastened, the zebra stood still while they ran the lines through the turrets, and the strapping young groom nursed his knuckles.

"But what if you were to use one of your hand-raised youngsters instead of this wild creature?" whispered Mrs Todd to Lady Charles.

"This *is* one of our hand-raised youngsters. And gelded at the age of eight months!" whispered Lady Charles.

"Oh, my!" said Mrs Todd.

"Grace and I will walk back to the house, Lady Charles," whispered Catherine.

"Oh! Will you not stay and watch? When he settles down, we might even have a little drive," murmured Lady Charles, but Catherine shook her head, smiling to reassure her hostess; and she took Grace away.

"Look, Grace," said Catherine as they walked back down the handsome avenue toward the house. "See the egrets out there in the pastures? I suppose they are hunting little frogs and snails, but I always think they look like hunchbacked angels, drooping there in the fields."

"You need not hurry me away from such sights, Catriona," said Grace.

"What sights?"

"Oh, horses and harnesses and carriages and that sort of thing. They're going to have a wreck, I daresay. That zebra will wreck them if he can."

"It's not a thing I want to see myself," said Catherine.

But when they heard the clatter in the stableyard behind them, they could not help but turn and watch. The heavy training brake swung out of the yard, taking the first corner at a hectic pace. The zebra was hitched on the near side, and the brown cob off. The two grooms were clinging to their perch behind like piglets at a sow. The coachman had a tight grip on the lines and on his whip, and even at this distance there could be discerned a grim set to his shoulders. The brake made for one of the carriage tracks that led up into the hills surrounding the pastures. "Uphill first, to tire them out and settle them down, I suppose," said Catherine.

But at the beginning of the incline, at a tricky spot between a bank and a ditch, where the old veteran leaned into his collar and dug into his work, the zebra balked and shirked instead. The coachman gave him a brisk word and a touch with the whip. The zebra resented it extremely, and did not mind who knew; but he plunged forward a few yards before balking again, to the annoyance of his harness mate, who now laid back his ears. Again the coachman rebuked him, more harshly this time, and touched him with the whip. At this the zebra reared, pawing the air in front of him. Everyone leaned forward. The coachman lashed him hard—one, two, three—on both sides of the neck, and shouted, but the beast would not go forward. He bounced down for a moment, only to rear again, higher this time, head back, higher and higher, until he toppled straight over backward, quite deliberately, or so it seemed. He landed with a heavy crash against the dashboard of the brake, then rolled off to the left, bringing down the bay cob, too, in a tangle of leather, iron and splintered wood, and overturning the brake into the ditch.

The two grooms had leapt off their step as the zebra fell. Instantly the burlier of them darted into the wreck and sat heavily on the zebra's head, immobilizing him. The older groom got to the brown cob and held his bridle, wary of the zebra's threshing hooves, while the coachman slashed with a stout knife at the cob's traces to free him. The traces were made of several layers of the strongest, thickest leather and did not part easily, but after a few moments the cob was freed and, at the command of his groom, heaved himself to his feet. He was led off to one side, limping heavily on the near fore.

The heavy groom on the zebra's head had taken off his waistcoat and used it to cover the animal's eyes. He was bent over the zebra's fringed ear, perhaps speaking soothing words or, more likely, a virulent stream of Dutch curses. Every so often the zebra would try to raise himself, but with his heavy head pinned to the dirt he was unable to heave himself over and get his feet under him. Still, he tried.

At this very inconvenient moment, another wagon appeared at the crest of the hill and came clattering down toward them at a good pace, its sweating horses sitting back solidly against their breechings and the driver leaning on his drag as much as he dared.

"Isn't that the shooting car?" said Catherine. It was, certainly; and it was to have stayed out until tomorrow. The driver drew up his horses, halting them a hundred yards from the wrecked training brake, and several of the passengers leapt out and cautiously approached the downed zebra. Hector and Lord Charles were among them, Catherine saw. Between them they succeeded in getting three of the zebra's legs leashed, then cutting its traces. The Boer got off the zebra's head, and the animal lunged to its feet, the waistcoat falling free. It made as if to dash away, nearly pulling Hector off his feet, but was brought up short by the reins and the tethers on its legs. The zebra stumbled but scrambled up again, both knees torn open now and bleeding. Warily the Boer approached the trembling animal and succeeded at last in getting his waistcoat over its eyes again, this time tying it securely.

At last the two animals, both lame, were led off to the stables by the grooms. The other men righted the shattered training brake and pushed it clear of the track to make room for the wagon to pass. Catherine and Grace saw now that Lady Charles and Mrs Todd had cautiously approached, too, as unsure as themselves whether to try to help or to stay out of the way. Now, at a gesture from Lord Charles, Lady Charles hurried forward. He addressed a few quiet words to her, with a nod at the cargo area of the wagon, and her hand went to her mouth. Catherine now noticed for the first time a long, linen-wrapped bundle laid out flat in the back of the wagon and secured by leather luggage straps. And where were Mr Todd and Dr Macpherson?

It fell to Catherine to comfort the new widow. Catherine sat at Mrs Todd's bedside, in a room darkened as though for fever, and orchestrated the bringing of broth, and of wine—iced Constantia laced with laudanum. She held Mrs Todd's hand, and gave her fresh handkerchiefs, and stroked her hair back from her forehead. Eventually, as Mrs Todd began to think of questions, Catherine answered them as gently as she could, drawing on what little Hector had been able to tell her.

"Oh, I so feared an accident when he drove off this morning," said Mrs Todd. "I have had a feeling of dread all day long, a fearful sense of foreboding. You must have noticed that I was not myself today; indeed I was not, not at all, though I tried to conceal my fears. Oh, Mrs MacDonald; it was an accident, I suppose? A terrible, terrible accident?"

"Most terrible indeed."

"But an accident? Or, or . . . ?"

"No one saw it, my dear; it happened in one of the hunting blinds set up along the riverbank, and Mr Todd's bearer was not with him just then."

"Oh, but couldn't they have been kept apart? Your brother and Mr Sinclair and Mr Fleming all knew of the bad feeling between them. Why, oh why, would the two of them be sent off to the same blind, alone together? I do not understand . . ."

"They had been taken out to separate blinds, each accompanied by a native bearer, quite a considerable distance apart, my brother says, along the riverbank where the springbok come down to drink in the evening."

"He was so tender to me this morning at our parting! Oh, our last, last sweet parting. He had not lately been . . . well, Mrs MacDonald, not always quite so gentle, not quite so patient as, as formerly. But this morning! His last, sacred kiss! I shall always treasure the memory. Ah, extinguished! I cannot bear it." Mrs Todd broke down again, sobbing, with her handkerchief over her face, and Catherine held her hand, patting it. After a moment or two, Mrs Todd mastered herself, and her sobs subsided. "Oh, forgive me, Mrs MacDonald. Don't leave me, pray don't leave me alone."

"No, no, I will stay with you. As long as you like, my dear."

"But, oh! I cannot bear it. How does one bear it? Oh, Mrs MacDonald, you have borne it yourself. How does one bear it?"

"Come, my dear, have another sip of the wine. It can do you no harm."

Obediently Mrs Todd drank down the wine. "But, but, I do not see how . . . how could they have encountered each other then? Do you say that these two blinds were within rifle shot of each other? There was an . . . an accidental discharge?"

"No, the blinds are separated, I understand, by a large outcropping of rock, where the river makes a sharp bend around them, and they communicate only by a narrow path cut into the bank below the curving rock face. It is thought that one of them for some reason left his own blind and, making his way along this path, approached the other."

"And was mistakenly fired upon, for game?"

"Oh, it is not at all clear what happened, my dear. Come, you must not torture yourself with these painful speculations. A little more wine."

Mrs Todd drank what was offered to her. Her blank gaze rested upon Mr Todd's portmanteau, lying open against the far wall. "It was when I saw, this morning, that he had taken all his money that the dread came upon me," she murmured quietly. "And then his farewell was so much kinder than usual, quite his old cheerful self, as he used to be." She held out the glass for more wine, and Catherine refilled it for her. "It was no accident, was it?" she said after a few moments.

Slowly, Catherine shook her head; no, it had been no accident.

"And it was Mr Todd who went along the path to Dr Macpherson's blind?"

"Just so. He was found there, inside, but too late, of course. It must have been over very quickly, my dear. He did not suffer."

"And the doctor?"

"Gone. Into the bush, they suppose, probably making his way toward the eastern frontier. Lord Charles sent one of the trackers after him, but only to follow him so as not to lose him. They will go after him with several men and fetch him back to appear before the magistrate."

"Gone. Run away. Lost his nerve."

"It will make it much harder for the doctor to plead self-defense or accident, certainly. Affair of honour or anything of that sort."

"Oh! Honour!" cried Mrs Todd, and her face screwed up painfully, not pretty now but distorted and blotchy. "Honour! What do I care for honour! Is a woman to cherish last words about *honour*? What of love? It was nothing but pride, Mrs MacDonald, merest pride, mere self-love. It always was with him. And what did he care for *my* honour! And now he has fallen after all, defeated after all by that terrible man, that doctor, and left me behind with nowhere at all in the world to go. And with child! And me not even a proper widow!"

Having said this, she focused with some difficulty on Catherine's face, as though to judge the effect of her words. This time she refilled the glass for herself, sloppily. "Did you hear me? Did you hear what I said?" she demanded.

"Aye," replied Catherine.

"Not even a proper widow. He promised to carry me over the border to Gretna Green, where we could be married straightaway.

Straightaway, he said! Oh, such a man for the promises! But then, the bridge was washed out . . . and we could not get there. . . . There was one difficulty after another, one delay after another."

"But you could have been married anywhere in Scotland, you know; not only at Gretna Green," said Catherine.

"Is it so? Anywhere? Perhaps he did not know. Or . . . perhaps he did. After a while it did not seem to matter very much. 'Mrs Todd,' he called me, before others, before all of you. His little joke. Very amusing, for him. He promised to look after me. 'As long as I live, my heart is your own, I swear it.' That's what he said to me. 'As long as I live'! And do you know, it was the truth, wasn't it! For once, he was telling the truth!" She closed her eyes and lay back against her pillows, still holding her glass, empty again. After a few moments she began to snore gently, and Catherine breathed out a long sigh. Tactfully she eased the empty glass from Mrs Todd's plump curled fingers and set it on the little table beside the bed.

With a hiccup, Mrs Todd came awake again. Her eyes flew open, and she said, "And he did take care of me, in his way. He was kind of me, careful of me. He was glad about the child, he said. Once he knew the infection was upon him, after Porto Praya, he did not touch me. But, oh, that doctor! He refused to call in that doctor, and only dosed himself as well as he could, and it did prey on his mind that if the infection were not quickly cured, it might lead to some permanent harm. He intended to consult some medical person at the Cape. When are we to arrive at the Cape, do you know?"

"This is the Cape; we are here," said Catherine.

"Ha ha! I had forgotten! So we are! Here we are at the Cape after all! And no medical person to be consulted! Ha ha!" And with this, Mrs Todd's eyelids closed again, and her mouth gently dropped open.

# 15

## *quite opposite to the Original Design*

As *Increase* sailed clear of the channel leading out of Table Bay below Cape Town, Hector was peering back over her stern at the small boats fishing in the rich shallows just outside the channel. They fished close in under the headlands, where the wind came in gusts and bursts. He saw a small boat knocked down by the force of a strong invisible downdraft pouring over the cliff from above. The little boat in question was carried clear of the perilous spot by an impetuous current and was righted by its crew. But the next boat to pass the same place was nearly knocked down too, in just the same way. Hector watched until the little fishing boats could no longer be discerned, and *Increase* had set all her sails to ride the steady force of an exuberant wind driving across the open sea—toward India.

Then Hector asked Mr Sinclair to spare him a sheet of copper so he could make some experimental models. The two of them disappeared into Hector's cabin. For two days there was conferring and sketching; cutting, filing, and hammering; and finally a foray down to the ship's smithy to do some brazing. By their fifth day at sea, Hector and Mr Sinclair were ready to test Hector's new theory, and Mr Fleming was invited to observe.

Catherine was curious, too. She was accompanied by Mrs Todd, who at this time did not like to be left alone. In the cuddy cabin, Hector had set up three large glass beakers of seawater, and mounted in each of these was a mechanical device made of copper. Each device differed a little from the others.

"It is a matter of turbulence, I think," said Hector, taking up a bottle of grenadine syrup which stood at hand and idly twisting its cork as he spoke. "I had assumed that an oar of two spirals must exert twice as much propelling power as an oar of only one spiral. Then, by mischance—or good luck—the oar on *Dram Shell* snapped in two, leaving only a single spiral. Yet the oar's power actually improved! I could not understand why. I have been pondering it for these three months. But when you asked me, Catherine, why our old chimney would not draw after our father built the new wing near it, I realised then I had to understand not just the action of the fluid upon the upstream plane of the oar but also its action behind the plane—the eddies and currents at the top of the chimney, so to speak, and the pressures—or the voids—exerted there. It has been valuable to observe the action of wind upon the sails all this time, for air and water are both fluids, and their action is similar. When I saw the effect of the wind pouring over the cliffs outside Table Bay, I understood at last how to redesign my spiral oar. And so this is what I have been making, you see: three small models for testing. Here is my rotary oar as I originally designed it, with two full spirals. This next one has only one spiral. And this third model is an entirely new design, with four quarter-spirals, all mounted shoulder to shoulder, so to speak."

"It does not look like a spiral oar at all," said Catherine. "More like the vanes of those windmills at Antwerp."

"Aye, only rather broader and shorter, as water is a denser fluid than air."

"Now, on your steam engines below, in the hold—" said Mr Fleming.

"Those rotary oars are the original design, with two full turns," said Hector. "But if trials were to prove one of these newer designs more efficient, it would be a simple matter to forge new ones and mount them to the engines. No modifications would be required to the engines themselves.

"Now let us begin. I have devised these rawhide loops to act as drive belts upon this spit, borrowed from the galley, of course. Perhaps you, Mr Fleming, will be good enough to turn it—as steady as possible, if you please. There they go, the three of them—a pretty sight! Now, into the water, just in front of each rotor, I inject with this baster a dollop of the grenadine syrup. Ah! Look!"

The crimson syrup bloomed in the beakers, swirling in ribbons and streams churned by the moving rotors. Within a few seconds, though, the syrup had dissipated throughout the seawater, and the distinctive patterns of turbulence caused by each of the three devices could no longer be discerned.

"We'll do them again," said Hector. "One at a time now." Pouring out the pink water, then pouring in clear water from a bucket, he started over again. And again, while he intently studied the swirling patterns of turbulence and diffusion, sketching notes and memorising the differing patterns produced by each of his little rotors. Over and over. And over. Eventually Mrs Todd sighed and wandered away, but it wasn't until the steward came in, seeking to set the table in the cuddy cabin for dinner, that Hector released his assistants and ceased his experiment at last.

ANIBADDH HAD DYED black Mrs Todd's shoes and her three muslin gowns, and Catherine had given her two pair of black kid gloves which she had laid by, no longer needing that colour herself. Mrs Todd's broad-brimmed Antwerp hat—the one which had aroused Mr Todd's derision—was trimmed now with black silk ribbon and several crape roses, also salvaged from Catherine's mourning clothes. Mrs Todd would absently twist and roll the ribbon as she sat and talked to Catherine under the canopy rigged over the maindeck in the long afternoons.

She liked to speak of Mr Todd. She talked of his virtues, and the kind consideration with which he had always treated her. She liked to reminisce about how they had first met, and how he had admired her and courted her, was bowled over by her charm and beauty, from the very moment he had laid eyes on her. Catherine was fairly certain that a great deal of this was made up (indeed, she recognised particular scenes and phrases from certain popular novels), and wondered, as the stream of words flowed past, what purpose could be served by this making of fiction, this energetic falsifying of the past. Mrs Todd never again referred to any irregularity in her connection with Mr Todd; nor did Catherine ever allude to it. Catherine was not certain that Mrs Todd was even aware of having once given away this secret.

About the first of December, when they had been under way again for a week, Mr Todd's personal effects were sold by bid as usual, with the second mate acting as auctioneer. The proceeds were given to the widow. It made a little store of ready money, in addition to what Mr Todd had been carrying. Of his belongings she kept only his gold-and-ivory toothpick.

"I have every confidence that Mr Todd's dear friends in Calcutta will open their arms to me, for his sake," Mrs Todd assured Catherine, torturing her black ribbons, "but it is a comfort to have a small sum laid by for contingencies which may arise. Oh, yes, especially one particular and inevitable contingency, which is certain to arise only six months from now! Ah, such a bittersweet memento of himself he has given me!" And she laid a hand just below the sash at her bust, plumper now than ever.

Out of compassion, Catherine schooled herself to let Mrs Todd talk, though she could not really listen. But as she sat and stitched doggedly at her canvaswork, she found that Mrs Todd's reminiscences, embellished and imaginative though they must be, triggered a deep remembering in herself. It was a fluent upwelling of long-held memories, and they came upon her in astonishing vividness and detail. While Mrs Todd talked, Catherine remembered everything.

Every thing. But they were not so very painful now, these memories. Though clear and exquisitely detailed as a miniature portrait on ivory, they seemed small and far away. For she herself was now very far away. Now, here, she could afford to remember.

James MacDonald, her own darling. Tall and grave, she had thought him. So sad at first, mourning still his wife. Then the evening when he had first sought her own quiet company rather than sprightlier others. The fine man he was! The deepening pleasure of learning the qualities of his character; and of knowing her own qualities esteemed by such a one as he.

Not just esteemed, then, but loved. Beloved. Oh, the exaltation! the exultation!

The joy of going to dwell in his house, to be his wife.

There, her tender care of his griefs (aye, still), and of his silverware. There, fostering his little pale daughter; fostering the spring peas in his garden.

This vast piece of canvaswork, spread even now across her lap. Stitch, stitch: a golden tulip forming now under her fingers.

The heather-scented linen sheets of their bed, and the curtains hung 'round it: she could see clearly the sprigged muslin of their lining. Their bed.

His kindness to her, and his delight in her. His pride, his virtue, his uprightness in his dealings with all men and all women.

His pride in his horses, and his masterful but tactful way with them. That one wicked mare, so lovely to look upon: a bright chestnut with perfect markings and a gait like the doe on the hill—

"Will you spare me a length of dark worsted, Catriona, my dear?" said Grace, appearing suddenly at Catherine's elbow in a most startling way. Bunched in her hand like an old dishcloth was her grubby sampler, a thing she had always loathed. "I beg your pardon, Mrs Todd," Grace added belatedly, for Mrs Todd had been talking.

"Aye, I will," replied Catherine. "But what makes you want it after all this time?"

"I am going to stitch my name. Look, Sharada has written it for me on this paper: 'Grace.' That is how you write Grace in the Devanagari script. Perhaps I will stitch the whole Devanagari alphabet. It is curious that it does not get muddled up in my head like our alphabet does, still."

"Perhaps it is because you have never yet dashed this new alphabet to bits by pitching onto your head."

"Nor do I intend to. It was most disagreeable. Look: this is 'ga,' the first letter of my name."

"It is very pretty and graceful. Just like yourself," said Mrs Todd.

Grace smiled upon her, truly pleased, then asked Catherine for a new needle, as her old one had rusted.

In Catherine, memory welled up again . . . The wicked beautiful mare had been killed, too, bolting over the cliff in harness. Catherine regretted this; she would have liked to shoot that mare herself.

❦❦❦

"DO YOU LIKE Mr Fleming?" Grace asked Catherine suddenly as they lay drowsy in their beds one night.

Catherine was struck dumb, for a long moment. Of course she liked him; he was well bred and perfectly amiable. But what did Grace mean? And what would her reply mean to Grace? And as she considered the childish question, it broke quite suddenly upon Catherine that she liked him very, very much indeed. "Oh, aye, I do like him," she said at last.

"I like him, too," said Grace. "He lent me a book, a Sanskrit grammar, which was kind of him, though I doubt I shall ever look at it."

"No? Why not?"

"Sharada says that no one knows Sanskrit anymore except the priests and the singers. She says that Hindi and Bengali will be far more useful to me."

"I suppose Sanskrit is the language of the cultivated class, of scholars, just as Latin and ancient Greek are for us," said Catherine.

"Sharada knows Sanskrit herself, though, because she knows the old songs. This evening she sang some for me so I could hear how it sounds."

"Ah, was that it? I thought I heard her singing. But I could not walk away from Mrs Todd while she was talking to me."

"She is the loveliest singer, Catriona. Did you know that she was a famous singer, and a musician, before she became an ayah?"

"Was she?"

"A musician by profession, she told me. She knows how to play ever so many native instruments whose names I cannot remember. Her father taught her, for he was a very famous musician himself, though he was blind. And she used to play and sing for the great prince and his nobles, she said, at court. At the full moon, everyone would go out in boats upon the river, and she and the other musicians would sing and play for them all night by moonlight on the water."

ꕥꕥꕥ

DURING THE NEXT four weeks, Sharada taught Grace the Devanagari alphabet, and some Hindi and Bengali phrases—and Hindustani chess while she was at it, a game called *chaturanga*.

Catherine referred to Mr Fleming's Sanskrit grammar from time to time, for she was still making her deliberate way through *Ramayana*.

She had copied two-thirds of Sandy's manuscript by now, and from Cape Town had sent a second batch of copied pipe music back to Mary in Edinburgh via a homebound ship. She still made a point of devoting to it an hour or two each morning, hoping to finish by the time they arrived at Calcutta. Sometimes Mr Fleming inquired about her progress, and she would report what number she had been copying. She asked him in turn about his translation of the Chinese tea scrolls; they were slow going, apparently—obscure and troublesome.

In the afternoons, sitting on the deck with her canvaswork across her lap while Mrs Todd talked, Catherine continued remembering everything about her time with James. It no longer hurt, not very much. She had been quite happy in those days, while she was married, before her heart had been so grievously maimed . . .

"Mrs MacDonald, are you quite well?" insisted a voice. It was Mr Fleming. How long had he been standing over her? She had been very far away.

"Perfectly well, sir," she croaked with great effort, for her tongue felt thick, and as she whisked back a stray corkscrew of hair from her cheek, she dashed away the tear she found there, and mustered a smile to reassure him. Mrs Todd was sound asleep in her chair, a few feet away, her mangled black ribbons still twisted between her fingers in her lap.

He looked searchingly at Catherine nevertheless. "I am just going to treat myself to the last of my Yunnan," he said, "and I beg you will do me the honour of drinking it with me. Pray do, Mrs MacDonald. You will be doing me a great kindness. You cannot conceive how tired I am of human endeavor. I do not complain of your brother; only, only . . . Come, it will do us both good. A change of scene is not to be had, alas, aboard ship, but perhaps you will settle for a change of company. You have had a long, hard watch since we left Cape Town. She can spare you just now," he added quietly. "We both have earned some respite, some relief from demands."

"I daresay we have. . . . Am I to understand that Hector is being imperious?" she asked as she rose from her chair.

"Well, not to say imperious, precisely, but alarmingly enthusiastic. He now proposes to cut those rotary oars from those engines stowed below just as soon as we arrive in Calcutta and to replace them with new ones of another design. Another design, which, he assures me, will prove far superior."

"But you are just a little skeptical about these new rotary oars of superior design, I think?" asked Catherine.

"They are entirely unproven. They do not even exist except in your brother's imagination."

"Aye. To him, however, they are quite real. I think it must be very agreeable to be a mechanic, for, unlike ordinary people, they are never abashed by their mistakes. Quite the contrary, they are exhilarated by them, because they learn so much from making them. A practical person such as yourself cannot take the same view of the matter. You, of course, need a design that will assuredly do its job, and you have no time for mistakes, no matter how inspiring. Well, Mr Fleming, I wish you luck in dealing with any brother of mine. We are obstinate and arrogant, we MacDonalds! You will have an interesting time of it."

"Are you both like this, then?"

"Oh, aye," she said. "We never give up. And then, so often, we turn out to be right."

"I daresay it will be interesting then," he said. "We Flemings are just the same way. I consider myself warned. Still, I would be glad if you will come and drink some tea with me."

"I will," Catherine said. "Only I must go and put away this tiresome needlework first."

This she did, stuffing it into the narrow closet in the bulkhead of her cabin. And there, in the back of the dark recess, she saw the little ivory box of tea which Sandy had sent, his last present. She withdrew it and removed the ivory sliver that served as hasp, then opened it and inhaled deeply of the malty scent. The large, twisted brown leaves were dashed with golden tips, and the caddy was still nearly full, for she and Mary had drunk only a little of it. She took it with her across to Mr Fleming's cabin.

The steward was already there, tending the kettle. "Sitakund water, this time," said Mr Fleming, and set a chair for her. "From Queen Sita's well. Your wee lass startled me this morning. She asked me—in quite passable Hindi—whether I knew how to play *chaturanga*."

"Oh, dear," said Catherine. "From one extreme to the other. She talks every waking minute now in any language. Well, and what did you say to her? *Do* you know how to play *chaturanga*?"

"I did not admit to it," he said, setting out his cups and polishing them with a cloth.

"It is a corrupted form of chess, I gather."

"Oh, not corrupted in the least, I beg your pardon, Mrs MacDonald. It is in fact the pure, original form of chess—the game was invented in India. Later the Persians learned it, and the Moors got it from them, and the Europeans from the Moors. But it originated here, in India. Now what tea will you have? I can give you that bohea from Yunnan which I mentioned, or a Lung Ching, now unfortunately a little past its prime."

"Neither one, if you please. I have brought you some tea this time," said Catherine, and presented him with the little ivory box.

"Handsome," he said, examining the box before opening it. "It puts me in mind of some of the finer Moghul work." He peered at the tea inside, and sniffed it. Then he shook a few leaves into the palm of his hand, turning them over lightly, and held them under the window for a close look. He smelled it again; then he tasted one dry leaf. "What is it?" he said. "Where did you get this?" He took a pinch of the leaves, dropped them into his teapot, and poured the steaming Sitakund water over them from quite high up, making a splash. Then he covered the pot with its lid.

"It was sent to me by my brother—my late brother, Sandy, from India," said Catherine.

He suddenly stared at her very oddly, intently. But it was as though he did not quite see her, as though he were looking through her instead, beyond her, to someone or something else. "Sandy MacDonald . . . Alexander MacDonald?" he said slowly.

She nodded: yes.

"You did mention, long ago, I think, that you had another brother. Your brother Alexander was in the Company's service?"

"Aye, for nearly four years."

"Civilian or army?"

"Civilian. He took part first in an exploratory expedition to the eastern hills; and afterward the Company posted him to a district called, I believe, Ghazipur, where he superintended some aspect of the Company's opium production. Until, they tell us, he met with a fatal accident during last year's monsoon flooding."

Mr. Fleming blinked hard several times. His expressive eyebrows rose, and he took both her hands in his, saying, "But my dear Mrs MacDonald, what a blockhead I have been, all this time! I knew your brother!"

And then the story spilled out: "I met him in Calcutta at an Asiatick Society dinner in the year 'twenty. By merest chance we fell into conversation, and quickly discovered in each other a congenial mind and temper. What a delight it is to meet a new friend! At my invitation, he afterward paid me a visit at Serampore. A genuine friendship soon formed between us, perfectly effortless. . . ." He fell silent for a moment, remembering, and then went on: "This was after his return from that expedition to the Assam Hills, and he told me a little about what he had seen there. He stayed with me for perhaps a fortnight while awaiting his next instructions from his superiors. I was so glad to have his company and his conversation. Dear Mrs MacDonald, I liked your brother so very well! How sorely you must miss him."

"I do," said Catherine, trying to will away the tears that welled up in her eyes.

"And then you are so very much like him! In feature, complexion, and bearing, of course, but also in the tenor of your mind and conversation; and in your sturdy independence, your self-reliance and dignity. It is no wonder that you have seemed so—familiar, somehow, to me. So like a friend I have known for a long time. . . ." He released her hands and went on, "When Alexander received his orders to proceed to Ghazipur, I was very sorry to lose the pleasure of his company. He was much disappointed, too, for it was not the posting he had requested. Twice I wrote to him at Ghazipur, but I never had a reply. Possibly my letters or his went astray. I was at Macao during the monsoon season of 'twenty-one, and did not hear of his terrible accident until I passed through Calcutta again in September. Dear Mrs MacDonald, what a sad loss! I am so very sorry."

Catherine stroked the smooth ivory lid of the little tea caddy, and almost said something—but what?—about her doubts. Then the moment passed, for Mr Fleming spoke again: "By that time I was on my way to Britain, where I hoped to engage a mechanic capable of applying steam power to our China trade ships. In my researches, I had heard of certain promising trials of a fully submerged spiral oar; and before I ever met him, the reputation and successes of a Mr Hector MacDonald had already made him a person of interest to me. I sought him out at the Mechanics Institute in Edinburgh, where I was introduced to him by Captain Keith last January. Perhaps I am amazingly stupid, but it did not occur to me even to wonder idly whether the Mr MacDonald I then engaged in Edinburgh might be related to the Mr MacDonald I had liked so well in Calcutta."

"Oh, no, why should you?" said Catherine. "Hector scarcely resembles Sandy and me. And then, one meets with MacDonalds everywhere."

"True, I have encountered MacDonalds all over India, and in China, and the Antipodes, and in America, too, without supposing that they must be your brothers. Still, to discover only now . . . And so it was Alexander who sent you this tea." He lifted the lid from the pot, sniffed inside the lid, then replaced it and poured into their two cups. He tilted his cup, examining the red liquor—its clarity, its colour, its sparkle. Then he sipped. Catherine watched him roll it around inside his mouth, watched him draw air into his mouth over it. He had a faraway, considering look. He swallowed; closed his eyes. Catherine waited. He tasted again.

"I have tasted this tea before," he said finally.

"My sister-in-law didn't know what it was," said Catherine. "We drank some."

He inverted the steeped leaves into the lid and raked them out with a finger, peering at them. "This iridescent coppery colour is not often seen. It's beautiful though, isn't it? The breadth and colour of the leaf bring to mind some of the red teas from Yunnan, in the south. Yet it is not Yunnan. Your brother, you know, was very interested in tea. In fact . . . He swore me to secrecy about this, Mrs MacDonald, and I have never told anyone. But no harm can befall him now if I entrust to you the secret which he confided in me then . . ."

"What?" said Catherine, rigid.

"In Assam he had found a plant, native to those hills, which he considered was certainly the true tea plant, and he had collected specimens of it. Then in Calcutta he'd found a native of Fu-jian who had let him into the secrets of the manufacture of tea itself. This is that tea. I am quite certain of it."

"But why must this be so deep a secret?"

"Your brother had little interest in the politics and economics of trade, and did not seem to fully understand the implications of what he claimed to have found. Some months before we met, he had sent a confidential proposal to the Honourable Company's board of directors for establishing tea plantations and manufactories in India, near the border with Assam. At the time when I made his acquaintance, he was expecting to receive the directors' approbation and instructions to proceed. But their reply, when it finally came, was a sore disappointment. The directors only rebuked him for his presumption, and directed him to proceed immediately to their opium plantations."

"But why should the directors not have embraced such a proposal?"

"Oh, Mrs MacDonald, you *are* just like him. First of all, they did not believe him, for their own experts have always assured them that tea cannot be grown outside of China. And then, of course—do you not see that it would be the end of the East India Company?"

No; she did not see this.

"Tea is the Company's only remaining monopoly," said Mr Fleming. "If they lose that, they have nothing left. Everything but that has already slipped from their grasp."

"Surely not, Mr Fleming! Might not the Company establish a monopoly over tea-growing in India—just as they have done with opium—and shake off at last the necessity of dealing with the Chinese ever again?"

"To assert a monopoly upon a plant which grows wild throughout the hills—poppies or tea—is an ambitious undertaking, even for the East India Company," said Mr Fleming. "One might as well claim a monopoly on air, or water, or salt. It will prove impossible to defend for long. But they will try, very hard, for there is a great deal of money at stake. My last advice to your brother, when he went up to Ghazipur, was to attract as little attention to himself as possible."

Once again Catherine felt the impulse to confide in Mr Fleming her doubts, her feeling that Sandy was alive. But no, she argued with herself; that could wait. She would like to think it all through first. Hector did not believe in this intuition of hers; why should Mr Fleming? She valued his good opinion and was in no hurry to lay her faintly founded hopes before him. She did not wish to see them knocked down by sober reason; nor was she eager to demonstrate to him any fond foolishness, any silly self-delusion.

But when she returned to her own cabin at last, she carefully put away the precious tea again. She had a great deal of important new information to ponder. Instead, though, she found herself thinking about how her hands had felt, enfolded for a few moments, in his.

ꕥ ꕥ ꕥ

ONE DAY, *Increase* crossed the equator again, northbound now. No one took any notice.

ꕥ ꕥ ꕥ

"OH, DO, SHARADA, pray do. Just one game," Grace begged winningly one afternoon shortly before Christmas. "Chess or *chaturanga*, whichever you like. We'll play *chaturanga*. I'll remind you what's what. Your bishops, here, are elephants. They do look a little like elephants, with those big domed hats like an elephant's head. And the rooks are chariots. And both queens to the left of their kings. There! Counselors, I mean, not queens. You begin."

"No long strides for your foot soldiers, then!"

"No, no, only one square for the pawns. You begin, Sharada, do."

Sharada sighed and, sitting down, moved out a pawn. "It was more peaceable when you were remaining always silent," she said.

"But tedious for me," said Grace, and she advanced a pawn of her own. After that they both fell silent for some time, except when Sharada reminded Grace that her counselor was not a queen and had no right to dash arrogantly about the board. "Check," said Grace eventually. Then there was silence again, except for the working of the ship. They both were braced uncomfortably against their chairs, for the cabin floor was far from horizontal, but at least the heel of the ship remained fairly constant.

After a while Anibaddh came in, windblown. She had been above decks, and she brought down with her the smell of salt and wind, and of some new element, too. Sharada inhaled through her nostrils a deep hungry breath, then looked up eagerly—for that was the smell of India.

Anibaddh studied their board. Finally Sharada made her move, an aggressive game-ending move, or so it appeared to Anibaddh; but then Grace's king astonished her by leaping out and away from the attack, knightwise. Anibaddh opened her mouth but succeeded in smothering her remark. She drew Grace's attention nevertheless. "It's not *chess*," Grace explained loftily. "It's *chaturanga*. It's how the game is played in India."

"Checkmate!" said Sharada.

"Oh! Oh, Sharada! I did not see that. I let myself be distracted. That is the problem with *talking*. Well, you must give me a rematch, and the sooner the better."

❧ ❧ ❧

ON CHRISTMAS DAY, Captain Mainwaring presented each of his passengers with a bottle of his cherished contraband whisky, and a particularly good dinner of turtle soup and roast kid, the last one. But even more delightful was the delicious sight of land rising up beautifully from the sea, to the west, and riding there all that day: the fabled island of Ceylon. They did not pause even for water, but continued running northward very fast, up the Bay of Bengal, and the island soon sunk itself again in the sea behind them, Atlantis-like.

❧❧❧

In the course of packing up her belongings, Catherine returned to Mr Fleming the books he had lent: *Ramayana*, and the Sanskrit grammar.

"But I am in no immediate need of them," said Mr Fleming, "and I daresay we shall encounter each other at every turn. I suppose you will stay with your brother at our Howrah establishment, and I shall be there very often. It is just across the river from Calcutta, and you will be amazed at what a small place Calcutta is. So you are welcome to keep the books until you have finished with them."

"But I have finished with them, I thank you. I turned over the last page last night, and was astonished to realise that this is only the first volume! But then my maid told me how the story ends. What an admirable wife Queen Sita proved! But I cannot forgive King Rama's treatment of her after all she had suffered—such a cruel return for her loyalty! My maid says the story is still current here, and often sung and acted, and she sang me some verses from it. Apparently she has been a professional musician at some court—at Lucknow, I believe she said."

"At Lucknow!" said Mr Fleming. "She must be most accomplished, then. How curious that she has ended up as a ladies' maid. I wonder how that happened. Lucknow is reckoned the most splendid court in India these days."

"Is it? Not Delhi?"

"Oh, no, Lucknow is the place. Well, I am glad you found *Ramayana* interesting. I shall make sure that you meet Dr Carey. He is not only a translator and a linguist but a missionary, a botanist, and a publisher—in short, a most admirable man, and he would like to know you, and Grace, too. He would be intrigued by her quickness at learning the oriental languages and scripts. He has an agreeable house and an interesting garden not far from my own."

"Have you a house here, too, then, aside from the Crawford and Fleming premises at Howrah?"

"Just a bungalow up at Serampore, about fourteen miles above Calcutta. Not large, but pleasantly situated overlooking the river. We will certainly make an expedition up there one fine day; it is a most agreeable outing."

"For a man who claims no country as his own, sir, you keep a considerable number of houses, it seems to me."

"Oh, yes—like the coconut, attempting to send down roots wherever I wash ashore," he said lightly.

"And have you another collection here, at this India house, of exquisite objects? Another collection of damaged beauties, perhaps?"

"Damaged beauties? . . . Ah! Just a thing, or two . . ."

ꕥꕥꕥ

ON NEW YEAR'S Eve, just below the mouth of the Hoogly River, the pilot schooner was encountered at last, and a pilot taken aboard with his budget of news and newspapers. Instantly the native supply boats had swarmed about *Increase's* flanks too, like clouds of mosquitoes. The steward and the cook had deliriously yielded to temptation, buying limes, oranges, coconuts, plantains, yams, eggs, chickens, pigs, lambs, oddly shaped fruits, and ice.

Bearing a little dish of spiced meat, Sharada entered Catherine's cabin and said, "Ma'am, the cook asks will you taste the Scottish pudding he has made for the New Year."

"The cook has been making a Hogmanay pudding? A black bun?"

"It is made from the—the offal of a sheep," said Sharada dubiously.

"Oh! A haggis!"

"Ah, yes, ma'am! Haggis! But he found it lacking in savor when he prepared it first according to the receipt given him by your brother, so he has been presuming to season it as seemed proper to him. But he asks if you will kindly be tasting it, before he is putting it into the casing."

"But what seasonings has he used?"

"Just the spices for a dish of *kheema matar*: onions and garlic to be sure; and grated gingerroot, and hot chiles, and ground coriander and cumin. Also garam masala and salt and ground black pepper. And also the juice of lemons and the fresh leafy cilantro."

Catherine laughed and said, "I daresay it must be the most delicious haggis ever made. Aye, I will taste it. It smells most appetizing. And will you taste it yourself? Do, Sharada."

But Sharada declined. And then, not wishing to give offense, she explained, "Only it is my day for fasting, memsahib—ma'am—or I would taste it."

"Fasting! The entire day?"

"Oh, yes, ma'am. It is the eleventh day of the fortnight, the widows' fast."

"Oh!" said Catherine. Was Sharada a widow? But she did not ask. "Well," she said, "you may tell the cook to proceed; he may put it into its casing. I do not know if it *is* a haggis, but it is undoubtedly delicious."

Their New Year's supper boasted all manner of delicacies: a whole roasted piglet stuffed with nuts and mushrooms and spinach; fowls in delicate sauces made from tomatoes and cream; green, gold, and pink ices of melon, mango, and strawberry; and chilled champagne for drinking toasts. Catherine supposed that Mrs Todd might retire early from this jollity; but she remained, gallantly downing her full allotment of champagne. Instead, it was Captain Mainwaring who had to retire early, for his place, as they entered the channel of the Hoogly, was upon his quarterdeck, at least until the pilot had proven himself competent. Nevertheless, he came down briefly from time to time, and as midnight struck at last, he offered a handsome toast to all the company, and most especially, he said, to the estimable Mrs MacDonald: "Grant me the honour of being the first to wish you joy of your birthday, Mrs MacDonald," said Captain Mainwaring to Catherine with a courtly bow.

"You are very kind," replied Catherine. "Only you must reveal who told you it was my birthday."

"Your brother, of course."

"Oh, Hector!"

But Hector was unavailable for rebuke just then. A dreadful honking was heard in the passageway outside the cuddy cabin. It was tentative at first, then in a moment the drones settled in as they ought. Then came the blast—the brilliant E of the chanter. Quickly tuning (oh, close enough! who can tell but another piper?), Hector piped in the haggis. The doorway was so low and so narrow that the pipes could not pass in; Hector had to sidle in sideways, at a squat, a most comical, undignified, unpiperlike posture; and the chanter shrieked in protest when his thumb slipped off its proper hole. Once inside the cuddy cabin, he still could not stand, for the ceiling was too low to admit the full height of the bass drone. He sidled to one side of the door to make way for Mr Sinclair, who, holding high the platter, ceremoniously bore in the haggis, if it *was* a haggis. He made a triumphant tour of the cabin with it before placing it on the table. Hector had dropped to one knee and played the rest of the tune half kneeling. Most of the company had covered their ears with their hands, for it was a large sound in a small low cabin, but there shone only glee and excitement on every face. Hector finished his tune with a flourish, and the company all rose and clapped their hands, and cried their applause of the haggis and of the piper; except for Mr Sinclair, who, being a piper, had a remark or two for Hector about his tuning. Hector retorted that Mr Sinclair was entirely at liberty to pipe the tune next year and that he, Hector, would be just as happy to carry in the pudding. This was tasted by all the company, and pronounced to be if not exactly a haggis, certainly a great improvement on one.

Catherine suddenly found that she had had enough noisy merriment and made her way up to the main deck. After the din of the close hot cuddy, it was marvelous to climb into the airy quiet huge night under the now-familiar planes and angles of sail and the vast, starry black dome of sky. The wind—cool, light, and steady—smelled of tidal mud. It stirred her hair and cooled her flushed cheeks.

"That is Sagor Island to starboard," said Captain Mainwaring from his quarterdeck, up behind her. "In daylight you would see the little temple there, just above a pretty white sand beach, and the palm trees all about."

"It sounds a perfect spot for a picnic," said Catherine.

"Oh, yes, if you don't mind man-eating tigers. It was just there that Captain Munro was carried off by a tiger in broad daylight, and his companions could do nothing, for they had foolishly come out unarmed for their picnic."

"Is this the very spot! Can a tiger simply carry off a full-grown man?"

"The beast seized his head in its mouth and carried him off just as a cat carries her kitten."

"Astonishing, and on an island, too."

"Oh, these tigers hereabouts swim just as well as the sharks. I much prefer sharks, myself," said Captain Mainwaring.

"At least sharks have the decorum to remain in the water," said Catherine.

"Just so. And only in saltwater, at that. But you must not be alarmed; Calcutta itself is quite free these days of the more dangerous animals. Mr Fleming has told me, however, of some alarming predations committed by the crocodiles up at Serampore. It seems his lady's little dog was snatched off the riverbank by an enormous monster one evening, in full view. The guards hunted it down and killed it and slit it open; it was the work of five minutes, and there was the little dog inside, quite entire but stone dead. The poor lady was prostrated, I understand, until Mr Fleming brought her a new little terrier, which she now never lets out of her lap."

"Oh!" said Catherine. "How shocking!" She was shocked less by the fate of the little dog, however, than by the news that there existed such a person as "Mr Fleming's lady."

Mr Fleming's lady!

Was she a Mrs Fleming? Surely not! Or how in the world could she have gone unmentioned, unalluded to, for all these months? But what was she, then, this "lady" who lived at his house at Serampore? Catherine thought of drinking tea with Mr Fleming in his comfortable cabin, of their two heads bent over his Chinese scrolls, of his taking her hands in his own the other day. She had come to like him so much. She had felt glad that he liked her, and glad that she would continue to see him often in Calcutta, that she still could expect the pleasure of his company, his stimulating conversation, his pleasant manners, his kindness to her, the whole companionable unreserve that had gradually established itself over the course of the voyage. In truth, that had been her greatest pleasure while at sea. That had been in fact the only pleasure she had felt in a very long time. And now! Now, it seemed that frank friendship had not been so very frank after all. She felt a shaming flush rising through her; she had been made a fool of. She had made a fool of herself.

Master yourself! she thought. He was only . . . a friend. A shipboard acquaintance. Nothing more.

But perhaps she had misunderstood the captain. There had been a prim elderly housekeeper at Mr Fleming's apartment in Antwerp, Catherine remembered: a starched, proper, matronly female who kept the place in polish and brought refreshments on a tray. Perhaps the captain referred only to a similar person who looked after Mr Fleming's villa here.

To whom he made presents of little lapdogs?

Well, and why not?

"A scorpion in my boot, a fine fat fellow," Captain Mainwaring was saying. "So now I generally sleep aboard, for nothing can suit me so well as my own cabin, where scorpions never do find their way into my boots."

"I shall miss my comfortable cabin too," said Catherine, making a great effort to put away her private distress. "It has come to feel amazingly like home."

"Just so, just so. It has been a wonderfully fast and excellent voyage—favorable winds at every point, never a storm, never becalmed, a most excellent passage—well, except for that unfortunate incident at the Cape. And certainly not quite the voyage you yourself had contemplated back in Edinburgh! But I am very glad you have been among us, you and the little girl. Do you know, she actually spoke to me the other day. 'Good morning, Captain,' she said to me, clear as eight bells. Well, and to arrive on New Year's Day—that is a pretty thing, isn't it? And your birthday. It would have been your twin brother's birthday, too, I suppose, bless his soul."

"Oddly enough, it is not. We were born twenty minutes apart. He was born ten minutes before the stroke of midnight, and I was born ten minutes after it."

"Ah! So his birthday is New Year's Eve, and yours is New Year's Day. Born not just into different days, but into different years!"

"Not just into different years, sir, but different *centuries*. He was born in the last minutes of the year 1799; I in the first minutes of the year 1800."

"Now that is a marvelous thing! I wonder what the native astrologers would make of it. Perhaps some astonishing fate awaits you."

"Oh, I trust not," said Catherine.

Cruinneachadh Chlann Domhnuill. The Mac Donalds Gathering.

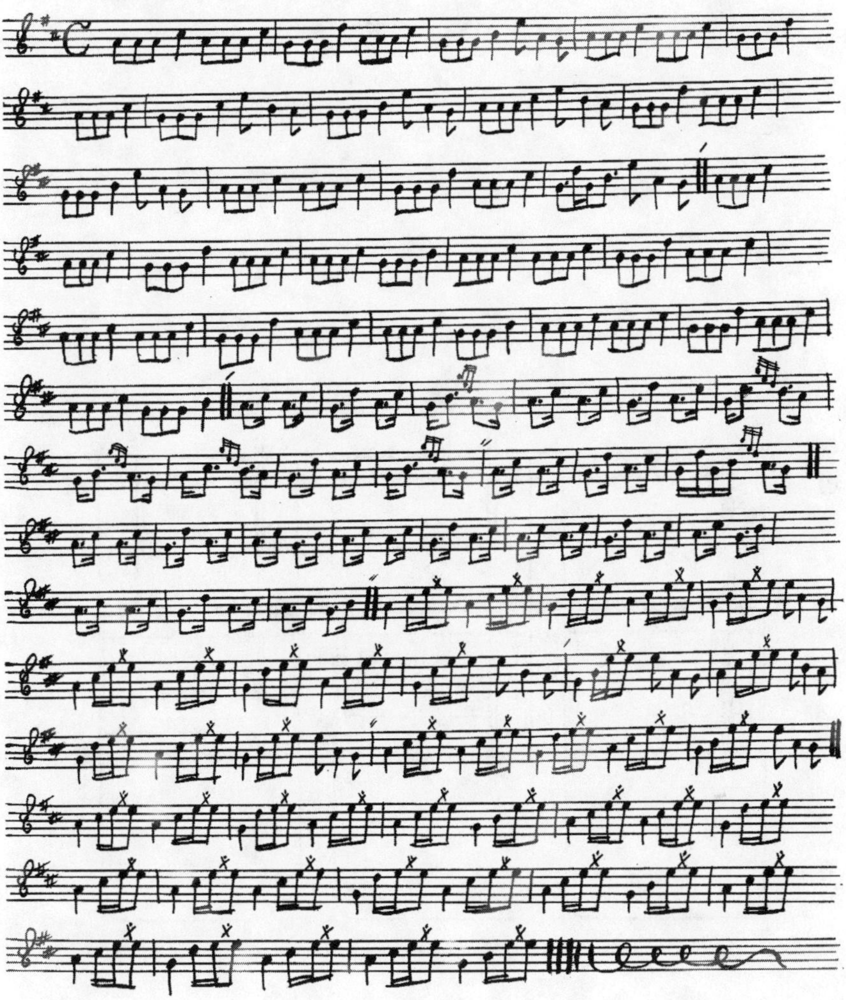

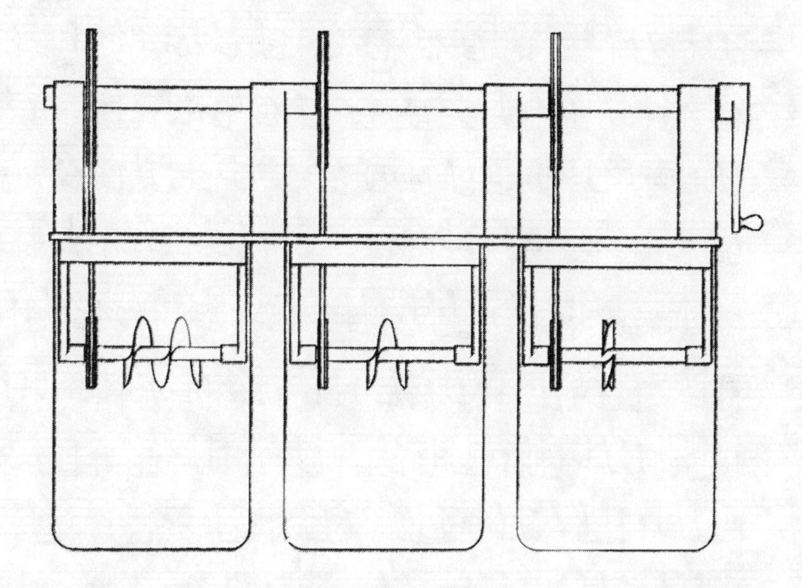

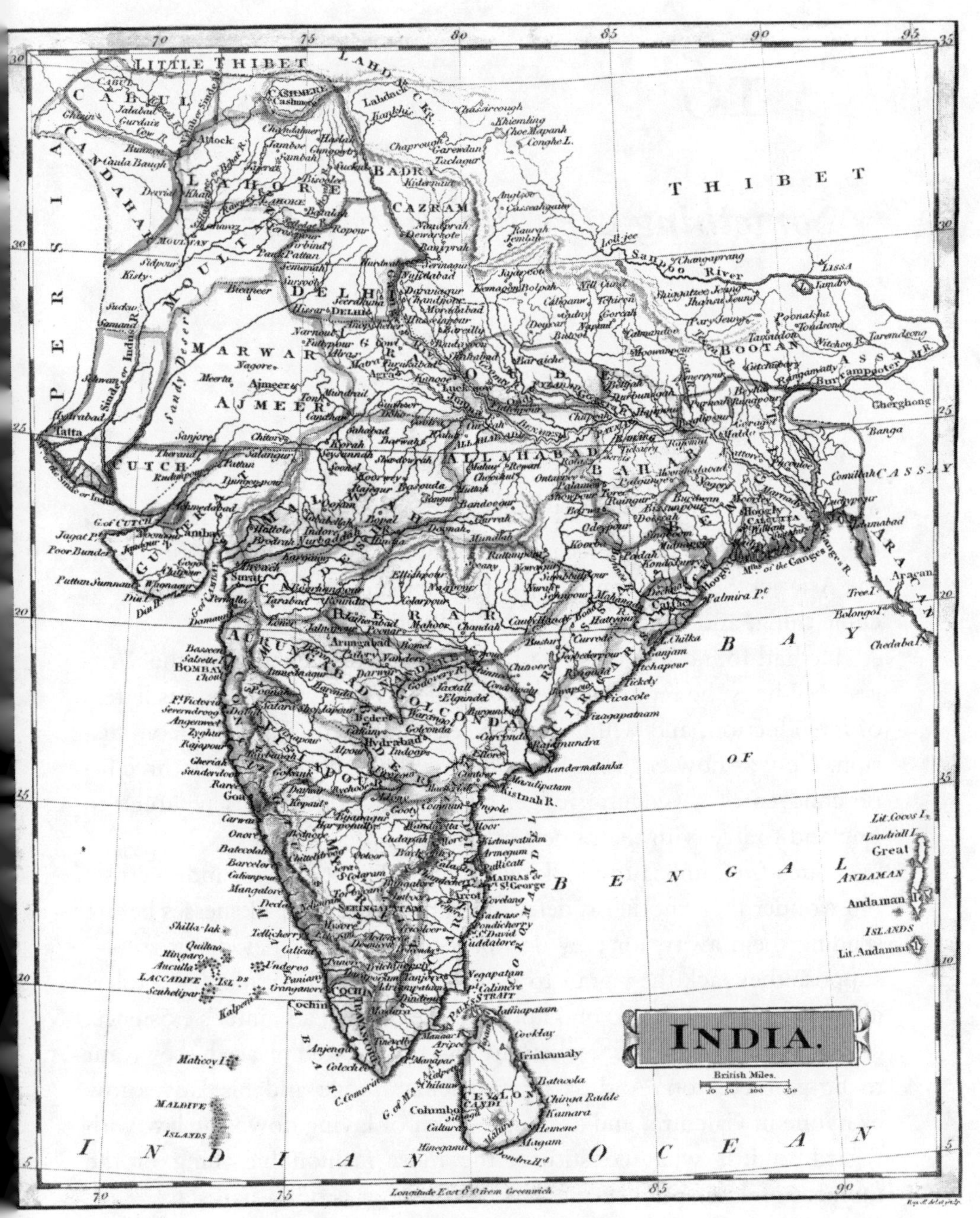

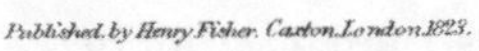
Published by Henry Fisher. Caxton. London 1823.

# 16

## *Something very Peculiar in the Taste*

"Mr Sinclair! How very glad I am to see you here!" exclaimed Catherine. She was attending a reception given one evening by the trustees at the Asiatick Society's museum. A familiar face in Calcutta was a welcome thing, and Mr Sinclair was equally glad to see her.

He had found lodgings in a pleasant part of the city near the Writers' Buildings, he reported. He had made his calls, presented his letters of introduction, and within three weeks had secured his first commission. He was now engaged in producing the likenesses of the three little children of a Calcutta judge, who were soon to be sent home to England to live with their uncle and be educated.

"Such thin, unhealthy-looking children!" he told her, "and so cross! No wonder their mother is determined to secure their likenesses before sending them away, for they do not look thriving. They do sit still—I suppose they lack the vigour to do otherwise—so I am making a tolerable job of it. Children, you know, are the bane of a painter's existence, except as an entrée. Then, when the parents are well pleased, they want to be painted, too. And as my particular judge and his lady know everyone in Calcutta, and are in the habit of laying down the law with regard to just what constitutes the most fashionable thing of the moment and what constitutes the best taste, it is not a bad start."

"I am glad you are so fairly launched," said Catherine. "Have you seen Mrs Todd? No? I met with her at the races one bright day last week, in blooming looks and surrounded by new friends, all young officers and civilians."

"Ah! She was sure to land on her feet. Is she in lodgings?"

"No, she has been invited to make her home with a friend of Mr Todd's, an attorney in private practice and his very young wife, to whom I was introduced. Apparently she and Mrs Todd have become entirely necessary to each other. They are inseparable friends and go about everywhere together, arm in arm. And Mrs Todd talks of starting a school for Anglo-Indian girls."

"Mrs Todd a teacher! Only imagine the polish she could impart to her young ladies."

"I daresay it will not come to pass. Her new dear friend will not hear of it, cannot think of doing without her. They seem very well matched, these two; and Mrs Todd seems to have recovered all of her old gaiety and assurance. Or perhaps even more than all."

"Very resilient of her. And what of yourselves? How does the Howrah side of the river suit you MacDonalds?"

"We are comfortably lodged in the buildings belonging to Crawford and Fleming, but I seldom see Hector. He is at the shipyard or the ironworks from dawn until after dark every day. He goes about with furrows engraved on his forehead, and forgets to eat. He and Mr Fleming have had great controversies about whether to build Hector's newly redesigned rotary oar and install that, or keep to the original design as already built."

"Is any resolution possible?"

"They have reached a compromise: Hector is permitted to build his new design and graft it onto *one* of the two engines; on the other, he must leave well enough alone and keep to the original design. Then they are to run trials on the river to show which is superior."

"And how do you and Grace amuse yourselves? You have nothing like the Esplanade or the Maidan, I suppose, on your side of the river. Where do the sahibs and memsahibs on the Howrah side go in the evening to take the air and stroll about and gossip?"

"I am afraid it is not a fashionable neighborhood; very little air is taken nor reputations ruined on the Howrah side. But we have had some interesting explorations, Grace and I, amongst the shipbuilders' yards and the foundries and warehouses. The great piles of coals are a worthy sight in themselves."

"It is a rare lady who delights in piles of coals."

"Odder still, we particularly enjoy visiting the logs," said Catherine.

"What logs are these?"

"The logs floating on the river—great herds of them. It is the timber for the shipbuilding—teak, sal, *Shorea robusta*, or so I am told—all crowded up close to the bank and secured by a cable to prevent their being carried off by the tide. They remind me of the cattle at home when they're brought down to market, all crowded together in the enclosure and lowing and complaining."

"You do make it sound so much more interesting than driving about the Esplanade three times and lifting one's hat to everyone. Is your brother here this evening? I have not seen him."

"No, he remained at Howrah, frowning at papers, or perhaps writing again to his wife. Mr Fleming brought me here. There he is, talking with that tall dark man."

"Ah! I think that is Dr Wallich himself; he is the curator and superintendent of the museum."

Mr Fleming and Dr Wallich looked up and came to join them. Mr Fleming performed the introductions. Dr Wallich was a man of aquiline appearance, courtly reserved manner, and a just-discernible Danish accent. "Have you admired our silkworms, madam?" he said to Catherine, for the occasion of the reception was to mark the acquisition of a collection of those useful insects. "These are some fascinating specimens; I am so happy to have them. I see that you yourself are already a devotee of the insect. Oh, I mean only that your sash is made of silk. *Bombyx mori* silk, I daresay. That is the silk produced by the insect which feeds exclusively upon the leaf of *Morus*, both *alba* and *nigra*—the mulberry tree, that is."

"Oh!" said Catherine, who had never thought of her sash as having been produced by insects.

"This case contains our specimens of *Bombyx mori*. Here are the eggs. Then we have the preserved specimens of each instar—each larval growth stage. Yes, in only a month's time they proceed from this tiny black thread you see, at first instar, to this enormous white-headed, soft-bodied fifth instar, dotted black along the sides. Such a large, regular, handsome cocoon they spin! The pure white cocoon is most highly prized for its ability to take up any dye. And these are the adult moths, male and female."

"Such marvelous dark, feathery eyebrows they have! Like Madame de Pompadour," said Catherine.

"Those are called antennae. You may argue that *Bombyx mori* is of Chinese origin, but in fact it has been cultivated for millenia in the region of Manipur, above the valley of the Brahmaputra River, and therefore we have included it in our collection. Next we have the purely indigenous Indian silkworms. You have heard of *tussore*, of course."

"Of course," said Catherine, exchanging a glance with Mr Fleming, who only twitched one eyebrow.

"This is *tussore*, also called *tasar*; we naturalists call it *Antheraea pernyi*. It is native to Bengal and is found in the central uplands as well, where it feeds upon any of several widely distributed jungle trees, of which the jujube and certain oaks are preferred. And of so magisterial a size! Look at this well-grown caterpillar; it is fully four inches in length and such a striking shade of green, set off by the lateral stripe of yellow, edged with red. Naturally they are much preyed upon by birds. Here is the cocoon, spun inside an envelope of jujube leaves. The silk is relatively coarse but quite astonishingly strong. It is highly valued by the natives, who consider it particularly unpolluted and not requiring ritual washing before use. The moth remains a full nine months in the pupa state, then emerges—thus. The females commonly exhibit a wingspan of eight inches; the males about five or six."

They were indeed worth seeing; Catherine found herself bent over the display case, quite entranced by the elegant colouring of the creatures.

"Now let me show you here the silkworm called *Bombyx cynthia*, which is reared upon the leaves of *Ricinus communis*—that is, the common castor-oil plant, which the natives called *arrindy*. This is the caterpillar which the natives call *eri*. You see, it is a plain pale green and attains a length of only three inches or so. The cocoons are remarkably soft and fine—so delicate, in fact, that they cannot be unwound, and so must usually be spun, as cotton is. This caterpillar is remarkable for remaining in chrysalis for only twenty days; so that eight generations may commonly be raised in the course of a year. The cloth made by the natives from this silk, although loosely woven, is of astonishing durability, as long as it is not subjected to hot water. It is commonly used for hangings and canopies, which are passed from parent to child."

"Remarkable," said Catherine. "And what is this one?"

"Ah! That is *muga*, the marvelous *Antheraea assama*. It is found only in Assam and eastern Bengal, where it feeds upon *Machilius bombycina*, which the natives call *som*, the divine nectar. The cloth is never dyed, but is prized for its natural lustrous golden colour. The ancient kings of Assam reserved all *muga* cloth for their own use, but now of course it is a subject of commerce, like everything else. Those are the specimens that cost our benefactor his life, I fear."

"How is that, sir? And who was the benefactor?"

"The collection is the bequest of the late Captain Edwards, who gathered nearly all the specimens himself. He was so unfortunate as to tread upon a sharpened bamboo spike set into the rough ground outside a Naga village. The spike pierced quite through his boot and into the sole of his foot. Infection set in immediately, or possibly the spike had been dipped into that poison for which the Assamese mountaineers are so notorious. In any case, he was gone within twenty-four hours in spite of anything that his companions or a copious application of leeches could do."

"Do you mean Captain Walter Edwards?" asked Catherine carefully.

"Yes, that was his name. Were you acquainted?"

"How extraordinary. He was engaged in conducting a survey for the Company of the natural resources of the Brahmaputra Valley, was he not?"

"Just so."

"My brother Sandy was one of his party. My late brother, I should say. Mr Alexander MacDonald."

Dr Wallich made a little bow. "My sympathy. Was your late brother an entomologist as well?"

"No, Sandy was assisting the expedition's surveyor. But he seems to have developed a particular interest in the plantation and cultivation of tea outside of China."

"Yes, a highly interesting object to us all. I cannot tell you how many times hopeful collectors have brought me specimens which they feel certain must be the tea plant itself, the true *Thea chinensis*. It never is, of course. Usually they are laurels, or various native camellia. At the botanical garden I have several specimens, which were brought to me from China, of the true *Thea chinensis*; it is useful for identification purposes, or rather for disproving wishful misidentifications. There is in fact an Assamese camellia . . . I beg your pardon, madam; did I understand you to say that your brother was lost on Captain Edwards's Assamese expedition?"

"No, sir, he survived the expedition. He was one of those who carried the collected specimens back down to Calcutta and finished Captain Edwards's report. The Company sent him afterward to the opium fields at Ghazipur, and it was there that he lost his life in the floods."

"I am so sorry to hear of it. But will you tell me his name again, pray?"

"Mr Alexander MacDonald."

"Madam, I feel certain I have met your brother. I shall review my accession notes. I believe it was he who brought me the Assamese camellia of which I was just speaking. In fact we have planted out those very specimens at the botanical garden, and they were thriving when last I noticed them. Have you visited our botanical garden?"

"Not yet, sir."

"You must certainly do so."

"I should be glad to take you there, Mrs MacDonald," said Mr Fleming. "It is a very pleasant outing, just a little below Calcutta, on the bank of the river, and very well worth seeing. I should like to go there again myself. You must come with us too, Mr Sinclair, if you can spare the time."

"I should be happy to meet you there and show you the camellia which your brother contributed to our collection," said Dr Wallich. "It is a handsome thing, but not, alas, tea."

❧ ❧ ❧

"WHAT IS THAT tremendous row?" Catherine asked Grace.

"It is Uncle Hector and Mr Fleming having a disagreement."

"Oh, another disagreement. But why must they have it so loudly?"

"Mr Fleming says Uncle Hector should have consulted him first."

"First before what?"

"I don't know," said Grace. "But Uncle Hector was offering to make a tremendous wager, for a hundred pounds."

"Hector hasn't got any hundred pounds for wagering."

"Aye, that's what Mr Fleming said. So then Uncle Hector said he would stake his commission from Crawford and Fleming. And Mr Fleming said there was not likely ever to be any commission to stake if they were to miss the entire trading season due to delays and preposterous second, third, and fourth thoughts, which ought certainly to have been thought of before now."

"Oh, dear," said Catherine. "Has Hector changed the design again?"

"I think he has," said Grace. "I think he wants to make it run backward now."

"Oh, dear," said Catherine, and went downstairs to find out.

Hector had indeed changed the design again; and was so inspired, so enthusiastic, so confident of his new insight that already, without consulting Mr Fleming, he had caused the shipbuilders to cut a new hole in the hull for the new placement of the shaft for the cambered-vane oar. The great innovation was this: The cambered-vane oar was to be mounted at the stern of the vessel behind the rudder, not at the bow. It was to push the vessel through the water, not draw it.

"But no modifications to the engine itself are required, you see, sir; none at all," explained Hector, quite mild and innocent in his confidence. "We simply mount it in reverse, with the shaft extending out the stern rather than the bow. Except for the direction of rotation, very trivial. And then the benefits are so great; the oar is far better protected from damage—so important a consideration in these shallow shoaling waters, or where constantly shifting sandbanks make navigation uncertain, or in unfamiliar and uncharted waters. And then the profile of the vessel itself is certainly cleaner and therefore faster. Stronger, too, with the full integrity of an intact stem. And the vessel is so much less vulnerable to leaks around the packing if the gasket is at the stern—far safer. I wonder I did not think of it sooner."

"I wonder you did not!"

"We lose no more than a day. A mere matter of twenty-four hours. And there is so much to be gained!"

"Twenty-four hours for your Leith workmen perhaps; it is more likely here to require a week! You promised me yesterday that both vessels would be ready for launch by next Saturday."

"Give me until Sunday then. And I warrant you this, sir—they both will beat any steam vessel on this river—side-wheel, stern-wheel, center-wheel, or what you will. And the stern-propelled one will perform better than the bow-drawn one. You may count on it."

The two vessels in question were twins—each a hundred feet long, of 132 tons burden; handsomely formed and stoutly built, of the best teak all through—keel, frames, planking, and all, the better to resist the insidious shipworm *Teredo navalis*. The hulls were already complete, or nearly so, when Hector's steam engines arrived. There had been some misunderstanding about the configuration of the supports and mountings which the heavy engines would require, and the necessary modifications took longer than Mr Fleming thought reasonable. It was not that Mr Fleming sought the distinction of launching the Hoogly's first steamships, although he was well aware that a paddle-wheel vessel was under construction at another yard on the river. Rather he was anxious not to miss a trading season if it could be helped. And it would be essential to conduct trial runs on the river and the Bay of Bengal before the new vessels could with any confidence be laden with so valuable a cargo as opium and then be expected to carry it safely so far as China. And it was off the coast of China that he expected the vessels to prove their real utility—namely, their ability to outmaneuver and outrun pirates and the emperor's coastal patrols—upwind, downwind, or no wind at all.

The boats were not ready for launch on Sunday. Nor were they ready on Monday, nor Tuesday, nor Wednesday.

On Thursday, however, late in the afternoon, the first of them was launched, the one whose propeller shaft passed through her bow. And on Saturday morning, her sister ship, the one whose propeller shaft passed through her stern, joined the first one on the Hoogly.

They both floated.

Hector was pale and thin; the transparent skin around his eyes was deeply shadowed. A servant had been carrying his meals to him at the docks. Catherine had seen to it that a cot was set up there for him in a shed, because he no longer would come to the living quarters in the evening and waste entire nights on mere sleep.

The fitting-up proceeded at a great pace now. The decks, the cabins, the superstructures, the holds for fuel and for cargo were all completed. Shipwrights and carpenters and metalsmiths swarmed over the vessels and the docks. The little ships had to be rigged with masts and spars and sails, too, with their shrouds and their stays, for when the wind was fair or when fuel was not to be had. Then there were chains and anchors and water barrels and stores. In fact, when all was fitted and done, the two doughty little ships did not have a great deal of cargo space. But then, best Indian opium was not a bulky cargo, and even a small quantity safely transhipped to the right Chinese buyer—payment received in silver—made for a very profitable voyage.

DURING THESE HECTIC weeks, Mr Fleming did not forget about the outing to the botanical garden. He invited Catherine and Mr Sinclair, and the new factor now in charge of Crawford & Fleming's premises in Howrah, a young Mr Morris. Also of the party were several other pleasant-seeming people to whom Catherine was introduced, and whose names she promptly forgot. The only other lady of the party was a married woman accompanied by her husband. Catherine still had encountered no sign of that disturbing and perhaps fictitious person, called Mr Fleming's lady.

Mr Fleming had arranged for a native pleasure boat, a *budgerow*, to carry them down the river. There was a pleasant airy cabin with windows all around, and on its roof was a commodious platform with chairs and tables for the entire party, all shaded by a pretty pink-striped canvas awning. The day was warm and clear and sunny. The air wafting off the river was deliciously cool and scented by the luxuriant flowering and fruiting trees and vines which grew exuberantly down to the water's edge all along the shore, setting off the elegant and picturesque villas which adorned the whole long extent of the Garden Reach. It seemed to Catherine a perfect earthly paradise, and setting aside her usual awareness of time-running-short and Hector-must-eat, she gave herself up to the enjoyment and appreciation of the scene gliding past: a holiday.

At the botanical garden's landing place, Dr Wallich came down to greet them. "You must see the rhododendrons first of all," he called to them even before they had attained solid ground. "For twenty-three years we have been waiting for the *bhutanensis* to bloom; it is shy of flowering even in its native mountains. It has never before bloomed for us here; we did not know if it ever would. Now at last, however, our patience is rewarded; and you are here to see it! The first bracts opened this morning. Come; this way . . ."

Catherine was disappointed at the rhododendron from the Bhutanese mountains; such a graceless thing, pale and paltry! She preferred the billows of magnificent crimson blooms on the common Himalayan rhododendrons, now flowering so vigorously as nearly to hide the leathery green leaves drooping below. The hill men, said Dr Wallich, liked to suck the juice from the petals, claiming that it had an intoxicating effect. He himself had never experienced the effect, perhaps due to the low altitude here.

Mr Sinclair, who had brought his colours and his folding easel, offered to record the rare *bhutanensis*. Nothing could have pleased Dr Wallich more; for, he said, the man who usually did the drawing had been incapacitated for nearly two weeks by a fever—unfortunate for him but also excessively inconvenient just now. Mr Sinclair set up his easel and his palette with an obliging alacrity, and was left there to work while Dr Wallich conducted the others through the rest of the garden.

It was richly endowed with noble trees, including old natives—neem, peepul, mango, and banyan—which had been growing there even before the garden was begun forty-some years earlier, as well as younger exotic specimens. These had been collected by Dr Wallich himself and by his far-flung network of collaborators and colleagues, not only from the relatively nearby Nepal, Pulo Penang, Sumatra, and Java but from faraway Brazil, Australia, Africa, and the South Sea Islands. Catherine and the others admired what was shown them: a tender nutmeg tree, carefully swaddled against even the mild Bengal chill; a striking avenue of sago palms rising overhead like the nave of a Gothic cathedral; a grove of gigantic plantains that made everyone feel dwarfed; and even a wretched little oak, miserable and sickly in this climate, perpetually too warm and too wet to promote health or vigor.

"But do not think I have forgotten, Mrs MacDonald," said Dr

Wallich at last. "It is the camellias you have come to see, and the Assamese camellia in particular. I have looked over my accession notes, and I have confirmed that it was indeed your brother, Mr Alexander MacDonald, who brought us these very interesting specimens. This way, if you please . . ."

"When was that, sir?" asked Mr Fleming, who followed.

"When? Let me think. It must have been about two years ago. Yes, that is right. He had just returned from Captain Edwards's expedition up the Brahmaputra. It was just about the time the Burmese had stepped up their incursions into Assam. He had not yet completed his report for the Company; I was able to help with several identifications of certain specimens, both botanical and entomological. Ah, let us take a small detour here for Mr Fleming's sake, as it is on our way. These, Mr Fleming, these are my prized specimens of the tea plant, *Thea chinensis*. This, Mrs MacDonald, is tea itself, and practically unknown outside of China!"

"However did you get them?" asked Mr Fleming.

Dr Wallich winked. "Oh," he said airily, "these small specimens here were grown from seeds sent to me by a friend whose name I must not mention. And these larger ones were brought privately to me as young plants by another friend, whose name I must also not mention, as both these friends wish to continue to trade at Canton."

The little shrubs were only about two feet high, rather attenuated, rather slender and yellow tinged, as though, thought Catherine, they were a little jaundiced, a little unhappy about the climate in which they found themselves. The leaves, alternating on thin straight ungainly branches, were substantial and slightly puckered, about two to three inches long, oval with a pointed tip, the edges finely serrated. The shrubs grew branchy and low; a few still had small white blossoms, rather shy, facing downward under the leaf axils. Most had finished blooming, however, and a few had set seedpods, quite large and covered with green scales. It was a plain, homely little shrub.

"They would prefer a sharper-draining soil, I believe," said Dr Wallich. "I am thinking of having them taken up and reset in a higher situation."

"Have you made tea from them?" asked Mr Fleming.

"We plucked some leaves during the last rains, but the plants, as you see, are not robust, not very substantial yet, and we have hesitated to take too much."

"How did it taste?"

"I fear we have not yet quite mastered the teamaker's art. It was not, ah, not exactly what a tea wallah might call distinguished. Here, perhaps you would like to taste a leaf. And you, Mrs MacDonald?" Dr Wallich plucked two small leaves, giving them each one. Mr Fleming put his in his mouth and chewed it thoughtfully; Catherine did likewise.

It tasted like a leaf. Green and juicy. Tough, a little acidic. Still following Mr Fleming's example, Catherine spit out the chewed green shreds. A pleasant sweet aftertaste spread over her tongue. She looked at Mr Fleming, whose awareness, she saw, was at this moment inward directed; his universe just now seemed to consist entirely of the taste on his tongue. "Hmm," he said at last, returning to an awareness of their presence. "How interesting. And they have been manured with goat dung, I see."

"Yes. In the China gardens they use the night soil, I am told. But let us proceed. Pray come along this way. Over here begins our collection of camellias, which Mrs MacDonald has come to see."

"Oh! how beautiful!" exclaimed Catherine, surprised by their size—like young trees!

"The *japonica*s you will have seen before now, in English and Italian gardens. These tall rangy specimens along here are quite certainly *reticulata*, and there is *rusticana*, from a higher altitude, a colder climate. The blooms on those *lutchuensis* are worth putting your nose into, for they have a distinct fragrance; most of the others have none at all. Along here we have *sasanqua*, and those on that bank are *saluenensis*. Now, come along. Here we are: this, Mrs MacDonald, is the *Camellia assama*, which your brother was so good as to bring us from Assam. They were small plants then, hardly six inches high. But look how they have grown; they are quite thriving."

They were indeed quite thriving, like a big robust version of the homesick tea plants they had just seen. The leaves were larger, some near five inches long, and of a much deeper, healthier green, but they were of the same shape and had the same finely serrated edges. Their white blossoms with a cushion of golden stamens in the center, also nodded shyly downward from their discreet seats in the axils, but they were proportionately larger than the blossoms which they otherwise so exactly resembled on Dr Wallich's tea plants. Their green-scaled seed-pods were likewise a larger version of the ones on the tea plants. They were less bushy, less branchy around their young stems or, rather, young trunks; more treelike, less shrublike.

"Pretty," said Catherine, and bent to put her nose into a blossom. "And fragrant."

"May I taste a leaf?" inquired Mr Fleming.

"What? Of this *assama*? If you like; I daresay it will do you no harm," said Dr Wallich.

Mr Fleming plucked a small new leaf for himself and one for Catherine. It also tasted like a leaf—green, juicy, and bitter. It had the same sweet aftertaste spreading over her tongue, perhaps sweeter, perhaps broader, a little more grateful to the tongue perhaps.

"Rich in complex alkaloids, all these ericaceous plants, of course," Dr Wallich was saying, "but none of these camellias is known to be particularly toxic. That one, the *assama*, is said to be sometimes cooked and eaten as a vegetable by the hill men. Or used medicinally, as was reported to us by your brother, Mrs MacDonald. You can see that although it does slightly resemble my *Thea chinensis* in some respects, it is certainly not the same plant. No, no; it is quite distinct by virtue of its colour, leaf size, growth habit. Your brother was deeply disappointed to hear that I could not concur in his opinion that it was the same species; but no, this is undoubtedly a camellia—certainly not tea itself. He was most unwilling to hear it, most unwilling to be convinced."

"He always was very strong minded, my brother," said Catherine.

"I do not think he went away satisfied with my answer," continued Dr Wallich. "I think he sought another opinion after mine. I have the impression that he went so far as to consult with Dr Carey, up at Serampore, for Dr Carey later mentioned to me that he had some specimens, too."

"But why could these Assamese plants not be tea?" asked Catherine. "Of course I see the differences, as you have pointed them out, but might these not be a natural variation within the species itself, just as horses may be any of several colours and a considerable range of sizes and shapes, and still be horses?"

Dr Wallich smiled gently and made her a deferential little bow. "Of course, dear lady," he said. "But at some point you have got an ass or a zebra instead, or perhaps a mule; but certainly not a horse at all. Taxonomy is an art *and* a science; but it is necessary to guard against wishful thinking. There is a great commercial desire, as I am sure you know, to discover that growing tea is viable outside of China. But we must not allow our commercial desire to cloud our scientific judgment. I told your brother I could not support his identification of the plant as a native variety of tea, that if asked by the agriculture commissioner, I would have to identify it only as *Camellia assama*. He did not go away happy. I am sorry for it, but what else could I do?"

"It is a knotty question, I am sure," said Catherine, "this business of taxonomy. And yet you did not hesitate to refer to the cocoons of all those different caterpillars as silk, despite their having been produced by caterpillars of quite different species."

Dr Wallich smiled again, with some brittleness this time. "Madam, you have your brother's rhetorical skills," he said. "Yet 'silk' is not a scientific term."

"Is 'tea' a scientific term?"

"Yes, Mrs MacDonald, it is. It refers to the leaf of the *Thea chinensis* plant only, and to no other."

"I see," said Catherine, though she saw only his testiness. They walked back the way they had come, and found the others. The steward had called the bearers to bring out tables and chairs and refreshments; all were seated under the shade of a magnificent old peepul tree to eat sweets and drink tea.

Tea.

Mr Sinclair had finished his task of recording the rare rhododendron and presented the portrait to Dr Wallich. Everyone admired it: the lifelike appearance, the delicate colouring; a complete simulacrum to life. After their meal, the entire party made their way back to the landing place, and reboarded the *budgerow* in time to ride back up to Calcutta on the boisterous afternoon tide.

Mr Fleming seated himself at Catherine's side, and she smiled at him. "It was so kind of you to arrange this outing for us all," she said. "I know your energies have been much occupied by this matter of steam engines."

"Very true, which is why I was much in need of a holiday—for gliding on the river and strolling in a garden—in pleasant company," he said.

"And an opportunity to investigate the doings of yet another of us MacDonalds."

"Ah! Our clever and determined Alexander does not seem to have made a great friend of Dr Wallich."

"No, nor did I," said Catherine ruefully. "I am afraid I was rather argumentative."

Mr Fleming laughed. "He did not much enjoy the sharpness of your argument, did he? It was interesting to hear how assured, how positive he was. I do think that just a dash of diffidence—even pretended diffidence—is more becoming in anyone. But I hope you will agree to another outing soon—upriver, to Serampore? I should like to show you that. And I should like for you to meet my friend Dr Carey, who is a very different kind of expert."

"I shall look forward to it," replied Catherine.

ANIBADDH HAD SET her heart upon a gold bangle, just such a one as adorned the wrist of every woman in India. As for money, she had not only the sum which Mrs MacDonald had paid her, but also her quarterly wages from Mrs Todd. Until now, Anibaddh had never thought of owning an ornament; until now she had never seen nor even imagined the warm gleam of gold against dark brown skin. But now she *had* seen it, and she was determined to acquire a gold bangle of her own.

"Very well," Sharada had said, "I will take you to the goldsmiths in the bazaar." So on the day when the MacDonalds had gone down to the botanical garden, and when Mrs Todd had gone with a large party to the last race meeting of the season, Sharada called for Anibaddh at the attorney's house, and the two of them went on foot through the narrow crowded streets of the native district to the old bazaar.

"What's all those painted figures?" asked Anibaddh, for they were everywhere. Large trays in the stalls displayed identical little clay figures, brightly painted: a hideous dancing black-skinned, bare-breasted woman with long witchy black hair, her mouth wide open, her tongue thrust out, wearing garlands of skulls about her neck and her hips, and her several hands brandishing decapitated heads by their hair, and bloodstained knives.

"That is Kali, the black goddess. The small figures are for a special festival two days hence, a *burra din* in honour of Kali, who is the particular goddess of this place, you see."

"A goddess! These are idols, then?" whispered Anibaddh. She had heard preachers rant about the sin of idolatry, but she had never expected to lay eyes upon an actual idol, nor meet an idolator.

"They are not yet being consecrated, these little figures," said Sharada. "But householders are buying them in preparation for the festival. Then a brahmin, a priest, will be consecrating them. It is part of the festival, you see. Afterward, the figures will be given to the holy river, the Ganges."

"Where do they come from? Who make them?"

"The idol makers, the holy artists. It is their livelihood."

Anibaddh was profoundly shocked and thrilled. She stopped and watched as a pretty woman wearing a brilliant pink sari and accompanied by her two small daughters negotiated a price, then bought one of the idols from the shopkeeper. She gave the little figure to the older of her two girls, who dandled it gleefully by the arms and stuck out her tongue at it, mirroring the goddess' grimace.

Was that any way to treat a goddess? Or a figure that would soon be consecrated a goddess?

"I can buy one? They lets me buy one?" asked Anibaddh.

"Yes, certainly, if you like. I will be speaking for you." In Bengali, Sharada struck a bargain with the shopkeeper. "Choose," she said to Anibaddh. All the little figures were nearly the same, but the individual strokes of the artist for eyes, nostrils, and brow made their expressions individual. Anibaddh chose; Sharada handed the coin to the man, who stared quite openly at Anibaddh. He offered her a shy smile and *namaste*, and said something to Sharada, who did not translate. The little goddess was wrapped up in a leaf to make a neat parcel, and they walked on.

"What did he say?" Anibaddh asked.

"He was saying you are like the black goddess herself."

"Is she evil? She look evil."

"Not evil. Very powerful. She vanquished the terrible demons when no one else could do it."

"Where are we now? Who are these folks?"

"This is the quarter where the Chinamen are living, the men from Canton. Many Chinamen these days now in Calcutta; they come here on the ships of the country trade. They have silk and tea and opium. . . . Come this way. We are entering now into the quarter of the goldsmiths. See how strong and close they make their houses? Not even a grain of gold dust can go astray."

"So many goldsmiths!"

"Fortunately you are having me for your guide. You shall have the very best gold bangle in Calcutta, the purest metal, the finest workmanship. Come." Without hesitation, she led Anibaddh to the ironbound door of a certain shop, and rang; after a brief exchange, they were admitted. The gray-haired babu bowed to them, brought them through a passage into a narrow garden courtyard, and invited them to be seated on cushions. After Sharada explained what they wanted, a silver tray with a dark blue velvet cover was set before them. The babu ceremoniously lifted back the velvet cover; and there, gleaming, was a treasury of gold bracelets, each one different from the next.

The sight of these made Anibaddh feel as though she was melting inside. She murmured once again to Sharada, reminding her of the sum she could spend. Sharada nodded; she knew quite well. Minutely Sharada examined the bracelets on the tray—first one, then another. She held them close and peered at the casting, the engraving, the chasing, the finishing. She touched two together and listened to the chime they made. She turned them in the light, and checked the colour and luster of the metal. She asked a few questions of the babu, who answered quietly and at some length. At last Sharada was satisfied. "These are very good," she said to Anibaddh. "Now you may be choosing. There is no hurry. Try them."

The bangles were very small in diameter, made to fit over small hands. "Give me your hand," said Sharada, and dipping her fingertips into a small bowl of oil which the servant had brought with the tray of bangles, she massaged Anibaddh's hand firmly, pressing and folding it and making it slippery. "There. Now try."

There was only one bracelet on the whole tray that Anibaddh wanted. Although she examined each of the others, none of them was as beautiful as The Only One. She picked it up—oh, heavy! exquisitely heavy!—and fitted it over her opal-tipped black fingers. It was small. It stuck at the joint of her thumb, stuck fast. It was too small. "Give me your hand," said Sharada again, and even more firmly than before she massaged and pressed the bones of Anibaddh's hand, folding her hand harder, then harder still. Anibaddh winced; suddenly the bangle was on her wrist.

That was the one. So brilliant against her gleaming, oiled black hand!

"I want to give you a present, too," Anibaddh said to Sharada. "Some little thing—a ring, or earrings."

"No," said Sharada, "it is impossible. But you are good and generous, and I am thanking you for your kind desire."

Sharada and the babu discussed the price for some time. Eventually they agreed; Anibaddh gave Sharada her purse, and Sharada completed the transaction. The babu saw them out, with many expressions of his deep respect and esteem and admiration and praise for their discernment and fine taste.

"How come you know so much about gold?" asked Anibaddh as they made their way back through the maze of narrow streets. She could not keep her eyes off her bangle. To think that she herself now owned so beautiful and precious a thing!

"I am of goldsmith caste," said Sharada. "My family name is Swarnokar; it means 'goldsmith.' "

"But you told me your folks are musicians."

"Oh, yes, my father became a musician by accident—because he was blinded and could not do the work of a goldsmith. One day he was playing in a corner of the workshop, as children do, playing with his little flute, and one of his uncles was casting a gold cup, a large piece. The uncle melted the gold and poured it into the mold. Then he must instantly swing it in the sling, around and around, very fast, to make the molten gold fill each edge of the mold. But somehow the molten gold burst through the mold and the sling, and the molten droplets were flung out, and straight into the eyes of the child—my father. And thus he was blinded by gold itself as he played his flute! But it did not kill him, and as it was music he truly loved, not gold, he gladly became instead a musician, very famous and revered."

"Blinded by gold! Mmm. Is that why you don't let me give you some little gold thing?"

"No, Unbound One, not that. It is because I am a widow. And widows wear no ornament, none at all."

"Oh! Never again a pretty thing?"

"I do not miss it. The great weight of gold I have worn! Enough forever. My husband was of course of our caste," said Sharada. "He delighted to adorn me. My arms were covered with bangles. My ankles, too—great massy anklets. Finger rings, earrings, nose rings. Hair ornaments strung with rubies and pearls. A dozen heavy necklaces at a time. It all made a fine display when I went to play my sarode with my father's ensemble at the court at Lucknow. It was bringing a good reputation to my husband's family and attracting the notice of the great courtiers, the great connoisseurs, the great men, the rich collectors. And the orders were coming to his family's workshop because of my fine ornaments. But his brothers were not liking it, nor their wives. And now . . . I wear no ornament ever again."

By the time they made their way back to the attorney's house, the party that had been to the races had already returned, and Mrs Todd had sent for her maid several times. Sharada remained in the kitchen while Anibaddh went immediately to her mistress.

In a few minutes Anibaddh returned. "Don't you go away yet," she whispered to Sharada. "Wait 'til I send up her bathwater. Then I tell you all about it." Sharada waited while Anibaddh had the bearers carry up the big jars of hot and cold water. Then Anibaddh drew Sharada out into the back garden near the poultry house. "She's all fit to burst! She just told me she's fixing to be married!"

"Mrs Todd?"

Anibaddh nodded. "That big red-faced lieutenant who been dangling around all these weeks: Lieutenant Babcock, that's his name. I thought maybe she like that smart little captain best, the one that lended her a horse for her to ride on. But no—she chose the big lieutenant after all."

"Married!"

"That baby's coming in June, ready or not, but look at her now, nobody guess it. She told *him*, I guess? Maybe not. She say he's going up to the east any day now—way up in Assam to fight the king of

Burma. So she's fixing to be married right away and go up there with him, and she want me to go, too."

"Married again! Hindu widows never marry again. It is impossible."

"Oh, it's different for Christian folks. I know of one Christian lady married and buried four husbands, all before she turn thirty-five. And I guess she ain't done yet."

# 17

## *the most fertile Invention & nicest Judgement must be distress'd*

As the two little ships proved themselves capable not only of floating but of swimming; of moving upriver and downriver, with the current or against it; down the wind, across it, or straight up into its teeth, Mr Fleming reverted to his usual mild manner, and there were no more loud disagreements between him and Hector. The little ships turned, they sailed, they steamed—slow or fast. They were named *Castor* and *Pollux*, but Hector always referred to them as *Castor* and *Camber*, a little mechanic's joke of his own. *Castor* had the new rotary oar with one full spiral extending from its stem; *Pollux* had the yet-newer cambered-blade propeller, which resembled windmill vanes, extending from its stern. *Pollux* was Hector's particular pet, though he would have denied having a favorite. He tried to disguise his great relief at their good performance, preferring to let it be supposed that he had felt full confidence in both little ships all along.

The first trials were conducted on the broad expanse of the river in front of the city. It was a convenient but uncomfortably public venue. Many people were interested, particularly the independent merchants and of course the shipbuilders. Observers came up from the shipyards at Kidderpore, where, it was known, a steamship of the conventional paddle type was nearly ready for launch. Lengthier trials saw the little ships steam down past Garden Reach, then back up again, shouldering the powerful tide quite easily both ways. Eventually they ventured out into the choppy shallow waters where the

Hoogly fell into the Bay of Bengal, and there they proved themselves in saltwater, too. Hector reeked of coal smoke and effort every night—clothes, hair, and all.

Finally there came a day when Mr Fleming invited a select party of guests to steam up the river as far as his villa at Serampore, fourteen miles above Calcutta. They would dine at Serampore, then come back down after dark. Catherine and Grace were invited, as were Captain Mainwaring and an old friend of his, another ship captain. The party also included Mr Morris, the factor at the Crawford & Fleming warehouses in Howrah; two independent merchants who traded in indigo and calicoes; the Scottish engineer from the Kidderpore shipyard, a Mr Anderson; and Mr Sinclair, who at the last minute declared himself unengaged by his other work.

At first light the two ships cast off, each with its complement of crew and passengers. Catherine and Grace, and their maid, were aboard *Pollux* with Hector, Mr Anderson, and Mr Sinclair.

Animatedly discussing patent applications, Mr Anderson and Hector made straight for the engine bay, and Mr Sinclair followed them, leaving Catherine and Grace to explore the neat little cabins on their own. These were handsomely fitted out in a miniature version of the best East Indiaman style, smelling still of fresh wood and new varnish, everything convenient, neat, and comfortable. Then they went up onto the deck, where chairs had been set out, and from there they watched the riverbanks slide past.

March had arrived, and the hot season was on its way, but it was still early and cool, with mist rising off the water. The Hindu women were at the river to fetch water and perform their early-morning ablutions. Standing hip deep in the slow-moving green water, they frankly stared at the strange smoking ships passing upward against the current, yet without sails or towlines or oars. Catherine and Grace gazed back just as frankly. The women's brilliant wet clothing clung to their forms as they emerged from the river, looking, thought Catherine, exactly like classical Greek statuary—except for the vivid colours. Catherine felt a great sense of well-being, even delight. There could be no mode of travel more pleasant than this! The scene glided past while she reclined in comfort and ease. The banks of the river were picturesquely clad in exotic, handsome trees, abloom, or heavy with fruit. Here a villa, there a native temple, then a native procession bent on some native business, led by musicians.

And then the river itself, so broad and serene, carried its own interesting sights: a convoy of timber rafts, a native pleasure craft fancifully carved and painted, humble fishing boats, a barge heavily laden with coal. Birds called from the trees on either shore. Catherine was delighted with India. Who could ever tire of this?

Mr Sinclair soon joined her on deck, and talked amusingly about Mrs Todd—now Mrs Babcock—who had just departed for Goalpara with her new husband. "I hope she will be very happy," said Catherine. "But poor Grace does sorely miss her black maid, for no one else will play chess with her at all hours as Annie used to do."

Then Hector and Mr Anderson came up, deep in discussion of various fuels and their virtues; and refreshments were brought. The sun shown down hot, and a canvas awning was rigged. The other ship was close behind them. A faint breeze carried the coal smoke away to starboard.

Before Catherine was ready for the pleasant interlude to end, they approached the Danish settlement of Serampore, a neat and handsome town. Mr Fleming's villa was just above the town itself. Its garden extended down to the river in a grassy green bank. The landing place, however, built of native stone, was not nearly large enough to accommodate the two steamboats. They anchored instead fifty yards off, and the passengers were carried to the landing place in the ships' little launches, called *dinghees* by the native boatmen.

A picturesque stone pavilion stood on a rock overlooking the river. As the passengers came ashore, helped up the flight of steps by Mr Fleming, Catherine saw that there were two people in the shade of the pavilion. One of them—an elderly clergyman, to judge by his collar—rose to his feet as they approached. The other, Catherine saw, was a native lady, dressed according to the Bengal fashion, and seated cross-legged amid a tumult of brilliant silk cushions upon a low carved wooden platform. In her lap was a little dog, scowling and growling at the newcomers.

Then Mr Fleming was at hand to introduce them. This was the Reverend Doctor Carey, the very Dr Carey whose invaluable translation of *Ramayana* had so interested Mrs MacDonald during their passage, and whose Sanskrit *Grammar* had been so useful to Grace in her studies of the Devanagari system of writing. Dr Carey, elderly and churchly as he was, blushed faintly at this reference to his literary achievements.

And then the lady was introduced. Her name was Harini. She placed the palms of her hands together under her chin in the gesture of *namaste*, and smiled warmly. "Welcome, honoured guests," she said in clear good English. "I hope you have made pleasant passage upon the river." Unlike most Hindu ladies whom Catherine had seen, Harini wore no bracelets, no bangles, no hair ornaments, no earrings, no nose ring, and no necklaces except for a small gold cross on a thin gold chain. Was she indeed a Christian? Had she any other name besides Harini? She was not Mrs Fleming, and she certainly looked like no housekeeper. But who was she, and what was she, to welcome guests to this house? And with a respectable clergyman at her side?

Captain Mainwaring now came up the steps and made his bow: "Dear lady!" he cried. "It does my heart good, and my eyes, too, to see you again after so long a time. I have brought him back safely once again, you see, just as I promised. Not that he's been spending much of his time up here at Serampore, eh?"

"Oh, no!" agreed Harini. "Good Mr F has now two new sweethearts, I lament for it. And today for the first time I take sight of my rivals. You bring them indeed before me! Is it for my approval, good captain?"

Captain Mainwaring must have looked daunted, for Harini laughed and explained, "Just there behind you, upon the river—his two beloved steaming ships."

"You must make him bring you aboard for a little cruise," said Captain Mainwaring. "It is the pleasantest thing in the world."

"I should like it so very much," said Harini. Then her attention was claimed by more introductions: to the other ship captain, a Captain Robbins; to the two merchants of indigo and calicoes, Mr Ward and Mr Mitchell; and to Mr Anderson, the engineer.

Catherine could not take her eyes off Harini. She was of a perfect beauty, her features utterly regular and pleasing, her expression animated and cheerful. Her long hair was thick, glossy and as black as the proverbial raven's wing. Her eyes were no less black, but animated and sparkling. Her teeth were straight, white, and regular, and they showed as she smiled, laughed, talked. Catherine realized that her handsome looks were outlined, underlined, highlighted by certain materials and techniques—the artfully applied colours, powders, and tints that British ladies of good reputation did not use, or not to any visible degree. Yet on Harini's smooth dark skin, there was nothing lurid or tawdry—nor even deceptive—about this skillful and frank *afzetting*. In the same way, Harini's clothing—brilliantly coloured and exquisitely draped—flattered her extremely feminine form even though she remained seated on her cushioned platform. Catherine felt for the first time that perhaps her own straight pale muslin dress, of the usual, approved, and unexceptionable European style (though very wrinkled now across the lap), was perhaps not the loveliest shape for a woman's clothing, and wondered how it would feel to wear a costume such as Harini's—if only she had such a graceful form as Harini. Or how it would be to sit cross-legged on a cushioned platform, and laugh and toss her head as she was introduced to strangers.

Mr Fleming's garden was large, well watered, and handsomely furnished with large trees and flowering shrubs and vines. A high wall of stucco or stone enclosed it on three sides; the glistening river made the fourth side. The lawn sloped up to the house, a whitewashed villa with a deep veranda facing the river. There was a general movement among the assembled party; they would go up now to the house, where a festive meal had been arranged for them by Harini. Four wiry native men—bearers—appeared silently; and as the party moved off, they deftly inserted carrying poles into stout brass brackets on each side of Harini's carved platform and, lifting in concert, carried the platform, with the lady on it, amid her guests on the broad swept walk leading up to the house. Harini laughed, and tickled her little dog, and addressed some remark to Captain Mainwaring, who walked at her side, with Mr Sinclair on the other side.

But Catherine had caught a glimpse, as the platform was lifted, and as the little dog scrambled on the lady's lap to keep his balance, of—of something. Or rather, of nothing. Where Harini's right foot should have been, nested in a swath of crimson muslin, there was only a stump, a rough and scarred stump ending at the ankle.

Mr Fleming offered Catherine his arm, but Catherine turned away and startled Hector by taking his arm instead.

Mr Fleming's airy dining room was furnished in the British style, with tables and chairs, plates, forks, and spoons. But the food was Indian; dish after delicious dish cooked in the native manner was brought to the table by servants who bowed to Harini, showing her each dish for approval before carrying it around the table to serve to the guests. Sharada helped with the serving. Eventually, over a richly spiced *biryani*, the subject arose of the unfortunate Dr Macpherson, who had started out aboard *Increase* with them; and of the poor doctor's obsession on the subject of his kinsman James Macpherson.

"Not even you, Dr Carey, with your own impeccable credentials as a translator of ancient literatures, could have made any impression on that unfortunate person, I feel certain," Captain Mainwaring was saying. "He was in the grip of a mania on the subject. Or, I beg your pardon; perhaps you are a believer in Ossian yourself?"

"Oh, no, sir; the poems of Ossian are quite evidently a modern production," said Dr Carey mildly. "And they could have passed current only in our own age. In any other time or place, their singular lack of any reference to the sacred, to divine affairs, would have stamped them immediately as inauthentic. Yet our own age has a blind spot in that regard, or rather cherishes a delusion in that regard. It is only our own age which seeks to explain the inexplicable without recourse to the sacred—anything but a divine presence or force or will! That is why I feel quite certain that the poems of Ossian are a modern production. And that explains also why they had been received with such a fanatical enthusiasm. Every fraud, every deception, every art carries its own betrayal in it." Dr Carey spoke these words with such a gentle expression, such a quiet and mild voice, without force or any intent to convince others, that Catherine was struck by the essential modesty of the man.

Yet another dish was carried in. "Ah, for this I have been awaiting!" said Harini. "But good Mr F says I must give warning before letting you taste, for some persons may have objection to poppy." Catherine looked as Sharada offered the dish: It was a bright green cooked vegetable, glistening with the oil or butter in which it had been cooked, and sprinkled thickly with tiny blue-gray seeds. But it was not beans nor okra nor fenugreek nor anything else that Catherine recognised. "It is the poppy pods, picked green, quartered, cooked in ghee, and sprinkled with poppy seeds," said Harini, "and it is my especial favorite; I eat this every day when the season allows. It has such healthful tonic effect, and then I can reduce my usual opium. May I help you to it, Mrs MacDonald?" But Catherine pleaded that she could not eat anything more.

After their meal, it was proposed to treat Dr Carey and Harini to a little cruise aboard one of the steamships. But when Dr Carey explained that he had to return to his house to meet a printer's apprentice who was coming especially to meet him, it was decided instead to bring Dr Carey to his mission house—on the opposite shore, and a short distance up a quiet tributary. His own little boat, in which he had arrived, could be towed behind.

With all the usual unpleasant fuss and commotion attendant upon such occasions, everyone boarded *Castor* once again. Harini, on her litter, was installed under the awning near Catherine's chair, her little dog still on her lap. But Harini was markedly quieter now; her eyes were heavy-lidded, and her breathing was very slow as she reclined against her bolsters and cushions. After a short time, Catherine saw that Harini was asleep. Dr Carey, who had been pointing out sites of interest on the riverbank, came back to the shade of the awning and, seeing that Harini slept, quietly took the empty chair next to Catherine. "There is no waking ease for her," he said quietly to Catherine, "neither of mind nor of body."

"She seemed so high-spirited when we arrived," said Catherine.

"It is a very great effort which cannot be sustained for long. Yet she always does make the effort."

"Is it the loss of the foot?" asked Catherine.

"Ah, you noticed. Oddly enough, the absent foot still causes excruciating pain—or so she admits when she can be got to admit anything at all. But that pain is somewhat dulled by the opium. No, the greater pain, the pain that cannot be eased even by opium, is the loss of her children."

And still in a low voice, Dr Carey told Catherine the history of Harini: a beautiful girl, cherished by her family, married young and well to a handsome, wealthy, affectionate husband of her own caste. They produced four healthy children in five years—two sons and two daughters—and lived a charmed, happy life. Then one day, when Harini walked into the bathing room among the tall jars of water set to cool, she was struck on her right foot by a poisonous snake, a little black cobra. "It struck just below her ankle bracelet, the thick snug-fitting bangle that all married women wear about their ankles. Pure gold, hers was, for it was a prosperous family," explained Dr Carey. "Her foot swelled immediately. Her people did everything for her, everything that was usual and customary. They said all the prayers, and made all the offerings. Her husband did an extraordinary *puja* at the Kali temple, offering many goats and perhaps his own blood too. No one cut off the gold ankle bracelet, which perhaps prevented the venom from streaming into her whole body, but the skin on her foot dissolved, and the flesh putrefied. The foot resembled a mass of raw meat. Her sufferings must have been beyond imagining. She was not conscious as the poison, whether from the gangrene or from the snake's venom, filled her body. At last her life was despaired of. The last kindness they could do her, the last sacrament they could perform for her, was to bring her to the bank of the holy river—for this Hoogly, you know, is the true Ganges—and let death overcome her there, with the holy mud on her body and in her very nostrils. For this, you see, guarantees *moksha*—release from the eternal cycle of worldly rebirth and suffering. Hindus, you know, believe that to die on the bank of this holy river is salvation itself." Catherine glanced at the river; the water here was gray-green, opaque, smooth-gliding. The muddy red-brown banks were steep and littered with rocks, shards of brown pottery, and discarded rags.

Dr Carey continued: "So they brought her to the river—just a little distance upstream from Mr Fleming's villa, in fact. And there they performed the last rites for her. They chanted their prayers as they laid her half submerged in the lapping water of the river. They smeared her body with the holy mud, and filled her nostrils with it, too. Then they sat by, waiting for her to die.

"But she did not die. Although poisoned with gangrene and venom, her nostrils stopped by mud, still she breathed. Her people waited all night; in the morning still she breathed! Then they left her alone on the riverbank and crept away, back to their houses. To them she was dead; there is no provision for anyone to recover once they have been brought to the riverbank to die. She must die; if she does not, still she is considered dead.

"It was our friend Mr Fleming who found her there in the mud late in the morning. First he supposed it was a corpse, washed up, for sometimes these cremations are rather incomplete if the family cannot afford a sufficient supply of firewood for the bier. But something made him go investigate, he told me later, though he was understandably most unwilling to approach the gruesome, mud-daubed thing. He found that she was quite alive, and actually conscious, though unable to move or speak. He had her carried to his house and had the surgeon over from Barrackpore at gallop. The surgeon amputated what remained of the foot, of course. Interestingly, he said that the mud was probably what had saved her life.

"Mr Fleming sought out her people, expecting them to reclaim her joyfully, but they would have nothing to do with her. They insisted she was dead. Gradually, even against her will, her body healed. But not her spirit. She did not want to be alive. Mr Fleming consulted me; had he done a terrible thing in saving her when she was so unwilling to be saved?

"I came to see her. Of course I am a missionary, Mrs MacDonald, and perhaps you might suppose that it is my calling to baptise as many converts as I can. But I am not eager for ignorant, uninformed converts. I am not among those who hold that every soul who dies unbaptised is condemned to eternal damnation. I am not looking for large numbers, only for genuine conversion, unmotivated by fear or ambition or any other unworthy cause. And this was a genuinely thirsty soul, a soul crying out in the wilderness. Her conversion—and her opium—are what make it possible for her to continue in this life, one day after another. And yet I know, and I am not betraying anything told me in confidence when I tell you, Mrs MacDonald, that the pain which bears the most excruciatingly upon her, body and spirit, is that she never will embrace her children again. It is a deep thirst, she says, a thirst that can never be slaked."

What moved Dr Carey to tell her all this? A small snore escaped the sleeper. Catherine's gaze fell upon Grace, who was leaning over the stern rail to watch the marbled water of their wake. "And so she lives at Mr Fleming's house?" asked Catherine.

"She runs his household. All the servants there now, of course, are Muselmani, for Hindus will have nothing to do with her." Dr Carey looked frankly into Catherine's face. "I daresay that some people may suppose that there is something disreputable in her living there. But I do not believe that is the case, or ever has been, or ever will be. And though Mr Fleming contends that it suits his own convenience to keep this house and all its servants even when he is abroad for months or years, I am certain that he does so only that Harini may have a place to live. It is the pure generosity of his good heart."

Catherine did not choose to argue with him. Yet it was clear that Dr Carey was one of those mild, innocent souls who was unable to conceive of anything discreditable to anyone until it was proved to him beyond all doubt. How pleasant it would be, thought Catherine, to be so naive as that! She looked about; where was he, this pure, generous, good-hearted Mr Fleming? There, at the bow, sharing some joke with Mr Morris. Perhaps he felt Catherine looking at him, for he unexpectedly met her gaze, suddenly quite sober, not laughing now. Catherine looked away, trying not to scowl. The "good Mr F" indeed!

Oh, but she was beautiful, this Harini. Even in her opium sleep.

This Mr Fleming's lady.

Catherine felt very angry, but mostly with herself. Captain Mainwaring had dropped the first hint to her. Men were men everywhere; but she herself had not yet been long enough in the Indies, the land of zenana—of harem—and of opportunity, to contemplate the fact with any equanimity. Why had she expected anything different from Mr Fleming? And what in the world had he expected from her?

When they arrived at the landing place below Dr Carey's villa, it was found that the person whom he had hurried to meet had sent a note to say that he was delayed for several hours.

Mr Fleming said, "Dr Carey, it would be so pleasant to walk 'round your garden before we return, especially if you will accompany us and tell us what we are seeing. Will you be so good as to show us your collection of camellias? I think that Mrs MacDonald and Mr MacDonald might be particularly interested in those. Dr Wallich has told us that a kinsman of theirs—their late brother, in fact, the late Mr Alexander MacDonald—consulted you regarding some specimens of a camellia native to Assam. This would have been perhaps a year and a half or two years ago."

Catherine did not wish to walk around any gardens in Mr Fleming's company. But to hear of Sandy—here, two years ago!—this she could not resist.

Dr Carey said, "Oh, but I remember him very well, and was so sorry when I later heard of his tragic accident. And was he indeed your own brother, Mrs MacDonald? He made a vivid impression. Of course I should be very glad to show you the plants he brought me. Will Mr MacDonald come with us? No; something about the steam engine engages his attention, I see. A marvelous machine. So. Along this path, if you please. Do stay clear of these overenthusiastic creepers, Mr Fleming; they were hacked back only last week, but I think they only redouble their efforts under such treatment, hydra-like. Ah, now here is a novel sight for you! The giant Himalayan lily, in bloom! I had it from Dr Wallich himself."

Catherine's gaze ran up the thick stems, punctuated indeed by giant, lily-like lanceate leaves, alternate; up to the crown of nodding, heavy ivory trumpets well overhead. "They are fragrant, too," said Dr Carey, "and especially free-scented at dusk. I have climbed upon a ladder to smell them. Isn't it an odd sensation, though, to feel so dwarfed by a plant which is otherwise quite familiar?"

"I feel as though I had suddenly shrunk," said Catherine.

"Just so! Now, there are the daturas, their blooms conveniently offered at nose level, and quite as fragrant as the lilies. Angels' trumpets, they are sometimes called, meaning, I suppose, the Last Trumpet, for everything about the plant is exceedingly poisonous. But I have a correspondent in London who advises me that certain experiments are being conducted to establish what the species' medicinal applications may be." Most of the daturas had drooping ghostly white flowers; but some were yellow, and some were rose of differing vividness and fadedness. Their triangular leaves were pale and lax, too. To Catherine, the plants looked menacing, and as deadly as Dr Carey said.

"This way. Here we are. They like this high, light shade, the camellias, under the canopy of these acacias, with their pinnate leaflets. These lovely things are from the mountains of China; those others are from the islands to the east of China, where, I am told, they have been cultivated by the kings and nobles in their gardens since time began. So refined! But look; look. Here are the Assamese plants your kind brother brought me, Mrs MacDonald. It was about the new year of 'twenty-one; I remember perfectly well. We had such an interesting conversation. During the short afternoon and evening which he spent here with me, we discovered a great many interests and tastes in common—rather to our mutual surprise, I think. Not just botanical but literary as well; his feeling for translation and for the classics—the native classics in Sanskrit, I mean—was impressive, and he was most interested in the operations of my printing press too."

Mr Fleming was thoughtfully fingering the long glossy serrated leaves of the Assamese camellias. These, growing in soil that was well-drained, even a little coarse and rocky, looked greener and more vigorous than the specimens they had seen in Dr Wallich's botanical garden below Calcutta, but they appeared to Catherine's eye to be the same plant. "Why did he bring these to you?" asked Mr Fleming.

"He wanted my opinion—my botanical opinion—as to whether they might in fact be tea itself. It is certainly an engaging question." Dr Carey paused and gazed over the glistening river, remembering. "He had found in Calcutta a native of China who had formerly been employed in the manufacture of tea, and he had induced this Chinaman to prepare the leaves from these plants in just the same manner as tea is manufactured in that country. He brought me a small sample of these leaves, so we boiled water and drank some, sitting out above the river in the summer-house. It did taste like tea, certainly; and looked like it, too."

"What was the method of manufacture? How did this Chinaman prepare the leaves?" asked Mr Fleming.

"It is quite simple. The freshly plucked leaves are crushed and rolled in the hand by certain skilled individuals, then left to be exposed to the night air. In the morning the wilted, discoloured leaves are roasted lightly over a fire until they are perfectly dry. And that is all."

" 'Picked, steamed, pounded, shaped, dried, and sealed,' " quoted Mr Fleming, "or so the Chinese ancients assure us. So, sir, what is your botanical opinion?" he asked, fingering the plant once more. He plucked a leaf, crushed it, and rolled it between his palms. "Is this plant camellia, or is it tea?"

"Oh, *my* opinion? I am only an amateur, sir. Who am I to contradict a trained botanist such as Dr Wallich? Who am I to debate whether this is proper *Thea chinensis* or only *Camellia assama*? But names can be exceedingly deceptive. Things may so easily change their names, or they may go by several names. Do I not struggle with language in every translation I undertake? Language is only a human creation, and, like all human creation, it is subject to change and error. But if only this plant were tea! We talked of that until the moon set, Mrs MacDonald—your clever brother and I."

They turned back toward the ghat where *Castor* was tied. "But it is all up to Dr Wallich," said Dr Carey as they made their way. "The directors credit no opinion but his, and he maintains stoutly that tea does not, cannot, thrive here."

Catherine caught the heel of her shoe on a root, and stumbled; instantly Mr Fleming caught her arm to steady her. She recovered herself, and drew her arm quickly away. "Oh, but this path is terribly uneven, I am afraid!" said Dr Carey. "I ought to have the grass more closely mowed."

"It does not matter at all, sir," said Catherine, although she regretted this most unfortunate moment for clumsiness. She was annoyed with herself; and annoyed, as they arrived at the stone landing on the riverbank, that she still felt the place where Mr Fleming had touched her arm.

Aboard *Castor*, Hector was engrossed by some interesting aspect of the packing or the bearing where the shaft passed through the bow, and Grace was leaning over his shoulder and pointing at something. Harini had awakened; she was talking spiritedly with Sharada, who sat coiled at the edge of Harini's litter. Catherine made her way along the bank to Dr Carey's summerhouse perched above the river, and looked out to where the sun, setting now in an orange haze, made a broad swath reflecting in the river. Behind Catherine on the broad grass path under the avenue of blooming mango trees, Dr Carey and Mr Fleming walked together, talking now in low confidential tones.

When it was time to go, Dr Carey himself came to fetch Catherine from the summerhouse. “I am so glad to have met you, Mrs MacDonald,” he said as he escorted her back along the bank toward the landing place. “Although my acquaintance with your brother was unfortunately brief, he left a vivid and memorable impression. He was a person of great talents and, though still young, of considerable accomplishments. There is no telling what he might not have done if an inscrutable Providence had allowed him to remain among us. I know that Mr Fleming thinks so, too. And he has also told me how glad he is to have made your acquaintance—indeed, to have gained your friendship.”

He stopped at the top of the steps leading down to the water. No one stood near them, and he went on in a lower voice: “Now, Mrs MacDonald, do permit an old clergyman one small liberty. I see that you are skeptical and sore, but appearances notwithstanding—and I admit that the situation appears neither regular nor respectable—still, permit me assure you that there is nothing improper in our friend’s relations with that poor lady.”

After a nearly imperceptible pause, Catherine said, “Thank you for your praise of my brother, Dr Carey. It gives me pleasure to hear him spoken of so kindly. But as for what you tell me of—of Mr Fleming, I must know: Is it at Mr Fleming’s request that you make this declaration to me?”

He drew a deep breath, considering, before he replied: “He did ask me to tell you the history of Harini. He is too modest to speak of his own good deeds; and I would be sorry to see him punished for them. But I see your skepticism welling up again, stronger than ever. I am not such an old fool as I appear. I have been married and widowed and have brought up children, and have buried children, and alas, grandchildren. I am no one’s dupe. I cannot force your belief, and I don’t know anyone who can. But if you will not be convinced by any assurance from me, I beg you will consult your own knowledge of the man, your own knowledge of his character.” He nodded toward the boat.

Catherine saw that Mr Fleming was just stepping aboard *Castor* and calling to Hector, “Are we fit to cast off? The mosquitoes are out in force!”

"We are," replied Hector. "We have just been examining that seal, and my niece has suggested an improvement that had never occurred to me."

"Ah, the entire family is so richly talented!" said Dr Carey as they descended the steps to the water and he courteously handed Catherine aboard.

Catherine was in turmoil, deeply agitated. She gazed fixedly at the bank as it slid past in the last light, seeing nothing, but acutely aware that Mr Fleming stood at his ease not far away, hands in his pockets, talking with Mr Anderson, the engineer. She would have so liked to believe Dr Carey's assurances!

She was still trying to calm herself when they arrived at Serampore. Here Mr Fleming and Harini went ashore to remain at his villa.

Once Mr Fleming was not nearby, Catherine became calmer, and the pounding of her heart gradually eased. She consoled herself with her secret—still a secret—her growing assurance that Sandy was alive somewhere in this exquisite, dazzling, frightening country, in this land of gold and beautiful women and tigers and opium poppies and deadly snakes. She was glad that she had never spoken to Mr Fleming of this secret intuition of hers. After all, what was he to her? Nothing, nothing at all.

The river was glassy smooth, inky black. *Castor* and *Pollux* steamed easily downstream, back down toward Calcutta, in the warm, fragrant dusk. Hector was as happy as she had ever seen him. He and the captain of *Castor* indulged themselves at last in a race; and Hector was exultant as his pet *Pollux* gradually drew ahead.

# 18

## *Cut with Strength & prodigious Quickness*

"Oh, ice!" cried Catherine. "Do let us have a wee bit, Hector. We are utterly suffocating, Grace and I. Who could ever have credited such heat? The mercury stands at ninety-three degrees on the veranda, and it is only half past ten. Ah, put this on your neck, Grace. Oh, wherever did you get ice, Hector?"

"Mr Fleming brought it just now. This very ice—oh don't, Catherine, you'll drip all over my charts—this very ice is to be our first cargo. It has been carried from the glaciers of North America by that American brig which came up yesterday. It is Mr Fleming's great coup, you see; we are contracted for its carriage up the river, right up to the Company's station at Patna. There it should fetch a great price, for what little ice they are able to make, up in the country, is poor stuff, soft and quick to rot; nothing at all like these massive clear blocks cut from the ice fields of Juneau. But of course, speed is of the essence. We are to cut up the river in the most dashing style. The record for a passage up to Patna stands at thirty days."

"Something tells me that you expect to do it faster."

"Mr Fleming has engaged to deliver that ice to Patna within twenty-one days."

"Oh, Hector!"

"Oh, Catherine!" he retorted. "And we embark as soon as the ice is transferred aboard *Castor* and *Camber*—within these forty-eight hours if the stevedores can be got to work with a good will."

"Where is Patna? How far is it?"

"Here it is on the chart. It is just about five hundred miles—first up the Hoogly, then on the Ganges."

"In twenty-one days!"

"And the ice melting away every minute in this infernal heat. Pray have the people bring my tiffin down to me at the river, my dear. I certainly shan't have time to come back here for it."

Away he went, but then he came back in to tell her what he had forgotten: "Mr Fleming says that you and Grace are most welcome to remain here, on the premises, in our absence if you would rather not go into lodgings. Mr Morris would look after you."

Catherine did not respond. Rather, when he left again, she turned back to his chart, spread across the table. Tracing her finger up the broad winding Ganges, she saw Ghazipur, not so very far above Patna. Ghazipur, the very heart of the Company's fantastically valuable opium monopoly. Ghazipur, where Sandy was said to have died.

Ever since the pleasure outing to Mr Fleming's villa at Serampore—so unpleasurable!—Catherine had avoided him. Whenever he came to the Crawford & Fleming premises to consult with Hector, she was careful to keep out of his way. Twice, at the shipyard with Hector, she had seen him approaching, and she had abruptly slipped away. He had sent several invitations—to a nautch, to a durbar. She had replied with terse little notes: "Mrs MacDonald regrets that she is unable to accept Mr Fleming's invitation." It was not that she wished to rebuke him, but only that she could not find any way of being in his presence. She tried not to think of him, and during the daylight hours she usually succeeded. As far as she could tell, Hector was oblivious to all of this.

But now, under her finger, lay an opportunity to make her way up to the opium districts where Sandy had, or had not, died. She had to go there if she could. For this she must somehow set aside her unwillingness to encounter Mr Fleming. She must find some way of being indifferent to the nearness of him.

"Let the two of us go up to Patna too, shall we?" she said to Grace. "Pray bring me my lap desk, my dear. I shall have to write to Mr Fleming about it directly."

Her letter was difficult to compose. It required three drafts, over as many hours, with a pause to see that Hector's tiffin was taken down to him. The letter she finally sent was polite and impersonal, but not quite so remote as the notes in which she had referred to herself as "Mrs MacDonald."

When this request had been written and sent at last, Catherine had herself and her maid ferried across the river to Calcutta, as her errands were now suddenly urgent. She bought more floss for her canvaswork: several shades of green, a considerable quantity of blue and russet, and some gray. The ordinary wool worsted that was so common at home was not to be found in the bazaar here; but with Sharada's help she bought silk yarns instead—thick, twisted, lustrous strands of deep-dyed silk. As she recrossed the river to the shipyards of Howrah, she consigned to Captain Robbins, of the homebound ship *Alacrity*, the last of the bagpipe music which she had finally finished copying out, for Mary's safekeeping in Edinburgh.

ꕥ ꕥ ꕥ

ALTHOUGH IT WAS nearly midnight before Hector came back from the shipyard, he found Catherine and his supper waiting for him. She still had not received any reply from Mr Fleming.

"Now, Catherine, what is all this nonsense I hear from Mr Fleming?" he demanded.

"What nonsense, my dear?" she said as she spooned the mutton stew over the fragrant rice on his plate and set it before him.

"And I am vastly annoyed that you have gone around me in this matter, gone and made a nuisance of yourself to him," he said. "Why did you not mention this—this preposterous notion of cruising up to Patna—to me rather than annoying him with it?"

"*Is* he annoyed?"

"*I* am annoyed! It is the most ridiculous thing!" he declared, stabbing fiercely at the mutton. "You and Grace should only be very much in the way. Nothing could be more undesirable than to carry passengers on this first passage. Neither of the ships is fitted out for the comfort of passengers—lady passengers in particular. And I suppose you should require an attendant of some sort as well, your maid, which makes three—"

"Aye, certainly. I have already spoken to her about it. As it happens, she is a native of that region and would be very glad to go up and see her old father there once more if he is still alive."

"But Catherine, it is out of the question. There is no room, and we shall have no time or energy to spare for keeping females comfortable and safe and well fed. Not to mention amused. You would find it not at all amusing, I daresay."

"Amusing! Do you imagine it is amusement that I seek?"

Hector set down his glass firmly. "But what in the world *do* you seek, Catherine? What sort of life do you expect ever to make for yourself and that child in India, of all places?" He gestured about the room in general, at India in general.

Someone was singing, out in the town surrounding the shipyards, the heart raised up on the voice. Drunk, or heartbroken; or both.

"Everyone has to be somewhere," said Catherine at last.

She offered the dish of mutton once more, and Hector heaped a second helping onto his plate next to the spicy potatoes. "It has a very strong taste, this mutton," he observed with his mouth full.

"That's because when it walked into the courtyard at noon, bleating, it was a goat," explained Catherine. "With a Roman nose and long drooping ears."

Hector went on, "If you do not like to remain here in Howrah, nor to take lodgings in Calcutta, Mr Fleming would offer you and Grace the use of his villa up at Serampore. Only he thought you would not take it, that you would not like to go there—though I cannot see why; I thought it exceedingly pleasant."

"Of course I will not go there."

"Aye, Mr Fleming said you would not; but I do not see why."

"Oh, Hector! Surely you cannot have failed to notice the 'housekeeper'?"

"So that is it—the crippled girl. Did you want him to give her up? Throw her out? Would that make you happy?"

"Of course not. It is nothing to do with me. But I certainly will not go there."

"You have been skittish as a ghost lately, Catherine. Flitting away whenever Mr Fleming appears. Of course I have noticed! I am not yet rendered insensible. And now, suddenly, you beg he will carry you and your female train up to Patna. What is in Patna to induce you to overcome your aversion?"

Catherine checked herself, and considered for quite a long moment. A bat squeaked in the eaves. At last she said, "A fine fair question. It is not Patna. It is Ghazipur. I must go up there, Hector. I must see the place for myself."

"The place . . . ?"

"Where, they have told us, Sandy met with his accident."

"Why, my dear? It can do you no good, no good in all the world, to see the place itself. You cannot bring him back to life; it can only cause you more sorrow."

"But I think quite differently, Hector. I do not expect to bring him back to life. You see, I do not feel that he has parted this life. I cannot just believe in this accident."

"Still, Catherine! Still, after nearly two years, are you unable to bear this fact?"

"It is not a fact. His body was never found. And he went to some trouble to send me that parcel, you remember, containing the tea and the shawl—and the bagpipe tunes with the message that he is Not Yet Drown'd." Furthermore, though she did not say this to her skeptical scoffing scientific brother, she could *feel* that Sandy was not dead. If he were dead, she would know it. And she did not know it.

"My dear, you are only grasping at straws in the wind. Surely if Sandy had intended a message, he could have sent us a clearer one than that. Why so obscure? So cryptic? Why no further word since then? And for what purpose behind it all?"

"I do not know yet; I cannot be sure. But it has something to do, I think, with those plants he brought down from Assam, which may possibly be not *Camellia* but genuine *Thea*, after all. I do not understand it yet. But I must look for the people who knew him up in Ghazipur."

Hector shook his head slowly, sadly. "I should very much like to believe that you are right," he said, "but it is impossible. It is only the dear wish of your wounded heart, Catherine," he said gently. "I do not blame you for it. You have had to suffer terrible losses these two years, and I think you have been amazingly brave, my dear—brave and resolute."

His tenderness made tears well up, and Catherine had to look away, blinking, until her vision cleared again. He was so seldom tender.

"But," he continued, "you ought to take this time while I am away to resign yourself, my dear. It will be so much better for you once you have arrived at a state of resignation."

"Hector!"

"No," said Hector. "No. I will not take you there. The decision is mine; Mr Fleming says he leaves it up to me. He has no objection to your coming with us; but I have. No, Catherine. No passengers on this first voyage."

ꙮ ꙮ ꙮ

BUT IN THE morning, everything changed.

Catherine, and breakfast, and her fresh arguments for Hector were all ready by eight o'clock. From the open windows of the breakfast room, she could hear someone being let in at the main door, below. She listened a moment, then, supposing it must be Mr Fleming, hastily beat her retreat. Just then the *khansaman* ushered in the entirely unexpected Mr Sinclair.

He had hoped to find Mr Fleming here, he explained, apologising for the earliness of his call; and it was urgent. "I wish to secure a passage up the river as soon as possible," he said, "and as I knew that Mr Fleming's two new steamships were to attempt a record, I thought that would be just the thing for me. The court at Lucknow is my destination; but I shall easily be able to secure a passage from Patna up to Lucknow."

"But how very sudden!" said Catherine. "What of your commissions here? All your good prospects? What of the portraits of the judge's children?"

"Have you not yet heard over here in Howrah? Oh, Mrs MacDonald, it is a shocking thing; everyone who can will fly from Calcutta. The cholera is here. My three cross little yellow children and their father all perished yesterday, and their mother just before dawn this morning. All dead, all within these twenty-four hours."

Hector walked in carrying a letter just in time to hear this. "Good morning, Mr Sinclair," he said. "A passage out of Calcutta? I have just received word from Mr Fleming about this outbreak of the cholera. Well, we had not intended to take any passengers on this maiden voyage, but under the circumstances you are welcome, sir, to take your chance with us if the risks of an unproven vessel do not deter you. My sister and niece will be aboard, too. We will be crowded, I fear, and there is no foreseeing what difficulties we may encounter. You will not expect comfort and ease, but certainly this is no season to remain here." He shook hands with Mr Sinclair; and then he pressed Catherine's hand too. She met his eyes; was it an apology that she read there?

"Pray come and sit down to your breakfast," she said, and poured coffee for them both, and passed them the eggs, and the griddle cakes made of potatoes. "But how did you hear of this attempt to set a new record, Mr Sinclair?" she asked once their plates were well filled.

"Everyone in Calcutta knows," said Mr Sinclair. "It was the talk of the town yesterday morning, before this other alarming business was known. There is a pool; in fact, I had laid down a small sum myself."

"A pool!" exclaimed Hector. "Is there nothing on which these idle people will not lay wagers?"

"How do the odds stand?" asked Catherine of Mr Sinclair.

"I believe the prevailing view is that the heat of the boilers will melt all the American ice before you ever get so far as Patna. So I got pretty favourable odds, and I stand to make a nice sum," replied Mr Sinclair. "I shall be happy to shovel coal myself if it comes to that!"

***

THUS, ON THE first of April, when *Castor* and *Pollux* set off up the broad river—riding deep in the water, so heavily laden were they with clear cold blocks of ice packed into layers of clean rice straw and mats; and as much coal as they could carry besides—Catherine and Grace and their maid were aboard *Pollux* with Hector. Mr Fleming and Mr Sinclair were aboard *Castor*. It was in fact a setting of sail, not a firing of the steam boilers, for the wind was fresh and favourable. To make the contest more interesting, that portion of the American ice cargo which could not be fitted into the cramped holds of *Castor* and *Pollux* had been loaded onto the river merchant brig *Spur*, which set sail with them. Bettors waved from the ghats. The April Fools' Ice Race was on.

As they passed above Serampore, Catherine could not help scanning the riverbank. There was Mr Fleming's white villa standing in its pretty garden. As they drew abreast of it, she could see Harini in the stone pavilion at the top of the steps; she was waving a scarf like a banner and crying out to the two ships as they passed: Farewell! Farewell! Godspeed! Grace waved back to her.

The little steamships weren't particularly fleet under sail; they laboured along in the wake of the sleek *Spur*, falling behind little by little, until by hot glaring noon *Spur* had gone quite far ahead, beyond the next bend of the broad flat river. Only her topsail could still occasionally be seen gliding eerily above the trees lining the riverbank. "Wouldn't we do better using the rotary oars to augment our sails?" asked Catherine.

"It's a long way to Patna," said Hector, just as though he felt quite calm.

But after a while the breeze faltered. Hector paced up and down, and considered, and consulted with Mr Fleming, who paced alike aboard *Castor* just ahead, both of them shouting into speaking-horns. When at last Hector ordered the boilers fired, the *dandee*s leapt into action. They stuffed the maw of their firebox with as much coal as it could swallow while ministering tenderly to their boiler. Soon they had built up a good head of steam.

Tiffin was brought up to the roof deck where Catherine and Grace sat under a striped awning. At about two o'clock the wind failed entirely, and Hector ordered the sails struck. The underwater rotary oars took over. Imperceptibly, *Castor* and *Pollux* began to gain on *Spur*, whose sails likewise had been furled when they became useless. As *Pollux* came up behind *Spur*, Catherine could see that *Spur*'s towline was out and her *dandee*s were trudging along the worn towpath on the bank, leaning forward heavily against the line. *Castor* and *Pollux* churned slowly past, chuffing and smoking. When *Spur* was well aft at last, Hector came up to the roof deck and picked at the remains of his meal, still too elated and too restless to sit down. "How fortunate," said Catherine, "that you and Sandy mis-spent so much of your youth in tending and mending those stills hidden up the glens. Who could have predicted then that your illicit expertise might produce such a result as this?"

Hector laughed. "Aye, those stills! I daresay that is why so many Scots in particular have contributed so much to the science of steam."

"Just so. Your experience with *uisge baugh*—the water of life—has given you an instinct about the life of water," Catherine said.

"Very poetic, my dear. Actually it is a matter of evaporation, expansion, and condensation, you know. Then metallurgy is an exceedingly important component, not to mention an understanding of the mechanics of impulse transfer and gearing, and the practical difficulties having to do with bearings and packings and lubricants; and the entirely separate and so-intriguing matter of turbulence and flow mechanics—"

"Oh, Hector! Do stop!"

"Oh, Catherine!" said Hector amicably. But he sat down at last and taking another of the little rosy bananas from the bunch on the tiffin table, he peeled it and ate it. "Well, I am glad you are coming with us," he said. "You and Grace."

"No thanks to you."

"Thanks to the cholera, then."

The sun set; the moon rose. As night fell, the steamships continued up the river, throbbing in the moonlit velvety night. Even the pilots kept only a desultory watch, for the river here was deep and wide, smooth and slow, without tricky shoals or sandbars. The crew had been warned when they were engaged that these new ships would not stop and moor along the banks each evening, that anyone who signed onto these ships would not be allowed to go ashore to cook and eat their meals on dry land, as all good Hindus must. These ships had no time for such punctilio; so most of the crew members were Muslim or tribal people or outcastes who would accept this departure from the usual practice.

*Spur* had dropped from view behind them.

Catherine and Grace found their tiny half cabin comfortable

enough except for the insects which had got in between the slats of the blinds and plagued them. Hector in his own half cabin was too anxious and restless to sleep well; he dozed and jolted awake at intervals—twenty minutes? two hours?—to listen to the sound of the engine, to feel the regularity of its vibration. Once, he rose and went to make sure that the pressure regulator for the boiler was still operating as it should and that the engineer had remembered to lubricate the shaft as required. It was, and he had. Hector went back to his bed, but he lay awake wondering whether *Castor*'s engineer had remembered, too. Toward morning he fell heavily asleep at last, and slept until the pilot sent to tell him that a favorable breeze had arisen. Rubbing his eyes, Hector came up and oversaw the hoisting of the sails and the shutting down of the steam engines. Then he checked them over carefully, tenderly, as though he were cooling out and rubbing down and feeding a hot bran mash to a good horse after a hard night's gallop. The boats had never before been operated for so long a period, though far more sustained efforts were to be expected at sea. But like well-conditioned horses, the boats had not suffered from their long run.

They consumed their coal at a great rate, though. About noon, still under sail, they hailed a coal-laden barge coming down from Burdwan and, after brief negotiations, bought the entire vessel, coal and barge and all. The barge was tied to a long line behind *Castor*, and the load of coal started back up the river again, whence it had come.

Late in the afternoon, *Pollux*, ahead of *Castor* now, which was slowed somewhat by towing the coal barge, anchored off a substantial town. Hector and the steward went ashore, and when they came back they brought a small flat country boat well stocked with sheep, goats, fowls, one fine pig, eggs, wine, and firewood for cooking. There were sacks of potatoes and rice, and cabbages and beetroots, too. It fell to *Pollux* to tow this ark; and Hector assigned a boy to make sure that the towline never fell foul of the cambered-vane oar at her stern.

Two days and nights passed; sixty miles of riverbank passed, green and brown, sandbanks and mud, countless villages and villas, temples and steps. The steam engines chuffed steadily, puffing and blowing like carthorses climbing a long hill. The sun blazed astonishingly hot from the instant of its rising, on their right, to its tardy setting, on their left. Brown-skinned natives baked on their boats, and village women came down with their water jars to the river even at full noon. But the chalk-pale, translucent-skinned Scots had to remain under the shade of the awnings, fanning themselves, ears blazing, with angry red spots standing out where mosquitoes had bitten them. The air around the boilers shimmered, and they took care to remain upwind of these whenever any wind could be detected.

The sleeping cabins were above the waterline, for the sake of air and breezes; but even the rare breeze was hot, and the nights were stifling. The cargo hold, however, was mostly below the waterline, and down there it was cool. Catherine and Grace visited the ice several times each day. The hold smelled of rice-straw packing, and of ice melt. Catherine closed her eyes and sniffed, and remembered a brilliant sunny morning crossing a Highland pass after an April snowstorm, ice sparkling and dripping, the running-water sound and the smell of ice melting. She tried to remember how it felt to be cold, but could not.

Hector and Mr Fleming conferred several times daily about their progress, passing between the ships under way on the little rowing tenders, the *dinghee*s. Catherine contrived to be in her cabin whenever Mr Fleming came aboard *Pollux*. They were ahead of schedule thus far. The steam engines worked steadily, never tiring. The crews were made up not only of boatmen and river men but also of ironworkers hired to tend the boilers, men who knew how to keep a coal furnace fired at a steady heat—never overheated and never too cool. There had been no sighting of *Spur* since the first day.

They ate cucumbers in yogurt—very cooling—and fish from the river prepared very spicy; and good butter kept fresh on the ice in the hold. There was tea to drink morning, noon, and night. Catherine dozed, daydreamed, stitched at her canvaswork, and remembered. She imagined Sandy passing up and down this very river, stopping perhaps at this very village to buy fragrant ripe melons. And what would James have made of all this—this other side of the world?

*Pollux* was faster than *Castor*, regularly drawing far ahead of her. Hector knew this was because of the greater efficiency of his cambered-vane rotary oar. So *Pollux* was given the heavier coal barge to tow, and *Castor* the lighter supply boat.

On the morning of the third day, under a bronze sun, the two steamships veered into the westernmost channel of the river, called the Bhagirathi, the shortest route leading up to the main channel of the Ganges. They passed Murshidabad, the still-splendid former capital of Bengal, its gleaming palaces and temples shining in the sun. The Bhagirathi was shallow; its sandbars and shoals and mudbanks shifted constantly. The boats could not proceed at night, for the risk of running aground was too great. At dusk each evening they anchored until first light allowed them to get under way again the next morning. At Jungipur they paid the tax levied for dredging the river to keep a narrow channel open and deep enough for shipping.

Finally, on the morning of the seventh day, they passed out of the shallow languid Bhagirathi and emerged onto the broader expanse of the great Ganges herself. The land flanking the river here was higher and much more interesting. Fields of mulberry were coppiced low for feeding the silkworms cultivated by the villagers, and there were broad fields of indigo. After so long a time in low flat country, as low and flat as Antwerp, Catherine was delighted to discern green hills along both banks of the river and, beyond them, higher bluer hills. In the hazy distance off to the north, she could see tall shadowy shapes that might be mountains.

As they chuffed all afternoon into a lowering sun, Catherine realised that their heading, northerly hitherto, was now much more nearly westerly. She went to Hector's cabin to confirm this on the charts spread out on his table. The Ganges, she saw, came from the northwest, draining all of the northern plains of India, all of the southern side of the high Himalaya. When these waters arrived in the lowlands of northern Bengal, they split into a network of dozens of watercourses, each taking its own route southward into the Bay of Bengal. The Bhagirathi river was the most westerly of these channels, the first to split from the mother Ganges and head southward to the ocean. And this network of Ganges watercourses, she saw, also met and mingled with the waters of the mightiest river of all, the Brahmaputra River, which came down from the Assam valley, far to the east.

Even here in the main channel of the Ganges, the pilots remained vigilant. Twice they changed course abruptly to avoid being drawn into whirlpools, wide and deceptively lazy. Though the water was broad, *Castor* led and *Pollux* followed, and an experienced river wallah was posted at the bow of *Castor* to watch and read the water. They passed well clear of a little sloop aground on an invisible sandbar. Her crew members were waist deep and chest deep in the green water, heaving on stout lines, trying to drag her off into deeper water.

The coal was gone; they sold the empty barge at Rajmahal, on the tenth day, and bought a pair of country boats stacked high with well-dried firewood. Hector spent a long time fussing about the fireboxes as they adjusted to devouring this different fuel.

On the evening of the eleventh day, Mr Fleming invited the *Pollux* party to dine with him and Mr Sinclair aboard *Castor*. Catherine and Grace went over with Hector in the *dinghee* after sundown. Under a canopy, as far as possible from the boilers, a table was set with napery and cutlery, and a pair of pretty little braziers set atop buckets of sand burned pungent herbs to discourage the insects.

"What a charming effect those colours have!" cried Mr Sinclair upon first seeing Catherine, for over her pale muslin dress she wore a thin vivid silk shawl wrapped around her neck and shoulders in the modest native fashion.

Catherine had been putting on flesh, she realised; and although her low bodice above the very high waist of her gown would never attain the ripe fullness sported by the Mrs Todds of the world, she no longer had the bony fragile look of a new-hatched nestling. "Do you think so?" she said. "My ayah induced me to try it. Such a pretty piece of work, too; look at this masterful bit of weaving, this pattern along this end. And then the colours! One does not wear colours like these at home; they would never do there. But somehow, here, they look entirely necessary. Do you remember, Mr Sinclair, months ago—it was in Antwerp, that gray chilly place—do you remember longing, wishing, to discover some new colours in the world? Or to rediscover the old ones? And here they are; and here am I wearing them. Well!" Catherine was surprised to hear herself talking so much. She was apprehensive about being in company with Mr Fleming, she realised (but where was he?); and it made her oddly, nervously talkative. Still, she could not seem to stop herself. She went on, "How have you been entertaining yourself? It seems a long time since we have left Calcutta, but it is only eleven days. Have you been drawing a great deal of scenery?"

"Of course. I am putting together quite a pretty little album of Bengal scenes. I only wish there were time to venture ashore to visit some of the more picturesque sights mentioned by the Daniells and William Hodges."

Mr Fleming's head appeared; he climbed up the ladder from the throbbing engine bay below, and Hector came up behind him. As they found seats, Hector was still explaining, with rotating arms, how something worked or was supposed to work.

"Good evening, Mrs MacDonald," Mr Fleming said as soon as Hector paused in his explanation.

"Good evening, Mr Fleming," she said, and could think of nothing more. But Hector, having still a great deal to say about bearings and lubricants, engrossed Mr. Fleming again, so Catherine turned again to Mr Sinclair. "Perhaps you will have time to make some excursions from Patna," she said. "Or shall you be in a great hurry to get up to Lucknow?"

"I am in no hurry. In fact I have a letter to a gentleman at Patna who has reportedly amassed a pretty substantial collection of drawings and paintings in the native style—said to be well worth seeing," replied Mr Sinclair. "I am told he has a nice taste, and a considerable talent of his own for drawing as well as painting, though he is an amateur. And although he is not in a position to award any substantial commissions on his own account, his recommendation, if I can get it, to carry with me up to the Nawab's court at Lucknow would be worth having."

At a nod from Mr Fleming, the servant brought cool mango sherbets. "What is the name of this artistic gentleman?" inquired Mr Fleming.

"I believe it is a Sir Charles D'Oyly."

"But I could have introduced you to Sir Charles myself," said Mr Fleming. "Certainly I know him. He is the East India Company's opium agent for all of Bihar, and I have known him for some years, even before he was appointed to Patna. It is quite true that he has a reputation as both collector and artist. . . . Ah! Here are the aubergines, and our ducks. Yes, Sir Charles and I are old friends. And then Lady D'Oyly is a charming woman, and she is an artist of some accomplishment herself. I am sure that you, Mrs MacDonald, will like her very much. You do not care for the ducks, Mr MacDonald? They are not barnyard ducks, of course. They are river ducks; that is why they are just a little fishy."

"Oh, it is not that," said Hector, who was neglecting his duck with a look of anxious strain on his face. "Only I am hearing a certain pitch, a certain frequency of vibration which I do not quite like. I beg you will all excuse me for a few moments. I shall rejoin you just as soon as I have set my mind at ease about it." Away he went, carrying one of the lamps, for by now it was growing dark.

"Are we not to drop anchor tonight?" managed Catherine.

"The pilots tell me they know of a quiet stretch of water with a good bottom just a little further ahead where they want to anchor for the night," said Mr Fleming. "Then we shall be in an advantageous position to make our passage up a tricky channel past the Colgong Rocks first thing in the morning. Ah, here is our tea. Will you pour out for us, Miss Grace?"

"I will, surely," said Grace. As she poured, she asked, "Have you looked at the stars? Sharada has been teaching me about the stars. She says all the greatest astronomers have come from India."

"Indeed?" said Mr Sinclair. "What constellations has she been teaching you? Can you show me Gemini?"

"I never have heard of Gemini."

"Never heard of Castor and Pollux, the very twins for whom these ships are named?"

"No, but I can show you the Asvins, and they are twins, too," declared Grace. "Come away from these lamps, and I will show you, if we are not too late." She and Mr Sinclair left to lean against the railing at the stern. The servants cleared away the dishes from the table and went away, leaving only Catherine and Mr Fleming there.

Catherine felt tongue-tied but at last managed to utter, "This Bengal scenery is so well worth—"

At just the same moment, Mr Fleming said, "I hope that you and your little lass—"

"I beg your pardon," she said instantly, and would not be induced to repeat her remark, though he asked her to, and apologised for interrupting. What a silly remark it had been, after all!

Mr Fleming poured tea for her and for himself. Catherine had to look away, for it felt nearly indecent to watch those tapered fingers of his, so assured on the fragile cups. . . .

"What is this tea?" she asked presently.

"This is Qihong, but the water is not excellent. If there is time, I shall send for water at Sitakund. That is Sita's Well, you know, just below Monghyr; it is a bright beautiful water which keeps fresh forever."

A long moment passed while Mr Fleming toyed with a spoon. At last he looked up, drawing breath to speak. Instantly Catherine was pitched violently from her chair and thrown against the table. At the same time, Mr Fleming's chair overturned, dashing him to the deck. There was a gruesome rending crunching noise like the breaking of bones, and a cry from Grace. Then, from below, many men's voices, all at once, all in a babel of languages.

"We've run aground," said Mr Fleming as he gained his feet, and helped Catherine up. "Are you hurt?" Only her shoulder and elbow felt bruised; she had somehow not been cut by the broken glass scattered about. Once he realised that she was all right, he disappeared down the ladder to the engine well. Someone shouted to warn the following *Pollux* to stay well clear.

Grace and Mr Sinclair's pale frightened faces swam into the dim light. "Fire!" cried Grace, for one of the lamps had been toppled, spilling its oil across the dry boards of the deck. Flames rippled outward. Mr Sinclair tore off his coat and threw it over the fire. But the oil instantly saturated the light cloth, and the flames consumed it. Catherine ran to one of the buckets of sand she had seen holding the little herbal braziers. So heavy, too heavy! It nearly wrenched her arm from her shoulder, but she half dragged it across the deck. It was too heavy to lift and throw onto the fire. She plunged her hands into it and threw double handfuls of sand into the blaze; then Mr Sinclair was at her side, doing the same. The fire guttered, leapt up again, then gave up. They smothered it. Mr Sinclair picked up the nearly empty bucket and dumped the rest of the sand over the charred oily stain.

ꕥ ꕥ ꕥ

THE ROTARY OAR at *Castor*'s bow was mangled, and part of the vane broken off entirely. Hector could not be certain that the main shaft was not bent as well. They had stemmed the leak around the gasket through the hull by stuffing it with oakum and tar, and they deployed two pumps, the men on three-hour shifts.

At first light, *Pollux* took *Castor* in tow, making for Monghyr, still thirty miles upriver. The supply boat and firewood boats followed, now under sail. These made slow progress, soon dropping back out of sight, for the wind was scant.

"Why Monghyr?" Catherine asked Hector.

"It is renowned for its foundries," he said. "For its metalworks of all kinds, or so says Mr Fleming. He assures me that the metallurgists there are the best in all of India. I am dubious. Oh, I knew that the rotary oar was vulnerable, too vulnerable at the bow! If only it had been *Pollux* run up onto that shoal, we should just have reversed the engines and drawn her off without the slightest damage."

They limped up to Bhagalpur on the evening of the twelfth day. There they made urgent inquiries of the Company's agents, but the answer was as Mr Fleming had said: They had best go up to the foundries of Monghyr. The supply boat had not caught up with them, nor the firewood boat. They replenished their onboard supplies of mutton, fowls, yams, eggs and pumpkins; loaded *Castor*'s deck with coal for *Pollux*'s boiler; and weighed anchor again at first light on the thirteenth day.

Catherine and Grace took refuge from the heat, insects and glaring sun—and from Hector's palpable agitation—down in the hold with the ice. The rice-straw matting was now very wet, and it no longer smelled fresh or clean. It smelled moldy.

Once, in an effort to distract himself, Hector took out his violin and bowed the first few phrases of a little melody. The instrument was terribly out of tune, and he struggled with it for some time, adjusting first one string, then another. He tried a different phrase—still an unpleasant noise. He put the instrument away and did not get it out again.

On the fourteenth day they made Sitakund. No one sent for any of the brilliant water for which the place was famous. The river was broad and shallow here, and the current strong. *Pollux* had struggled all day to tow heavy *Castor* up against it, straining like a horse dragging logs. It was a relief to anchor at night and rest. Even then, Hector did not allow the workers to let the boiler cool. He said it placed too much stress on the seams and the rivets to alternately fire it, then let it cool. He required the *dandee*s to keep a moderate fire burning even overnight while they lay at anchor. They were in no position to take any chances, he insisted, and fuel was cheap.

Early on the fifteenth day, they anchored off the crowded riverfront of Monghyr at last. Immediately Mr Fleming and Hector climbed into the *dinghee* and went ashore; immediately the beggars and the vendors in their boats came teeming out from the bazaar all along the bank and assailed the newcomers with offers of pistols, guns, necklaces, baskets, toys, forks, knives, kettles, shoes, and birds in cages. Catherine and Grace and Mr Sinclair took refuge in their cabins behind closed blinds, and with stout bamboo staves the guards fended off the boats of the hawkers, who eventually gave up and drifted away.

Hector came back at midnight to change his clothes and sleep for four hours; then he was off again.

Mr Fleming came back in the morning of the sixteenth day to tell the passengers how matters stood. "We have covered almost four hundred miles—three hundred ninety-eight to be exact—from Calcutta. We have yet eighty-six miles to go to Patna, and five days remaining to us. *Castor* is to be towed immediately up to the dock at the shipyard above the town, and her damaged oar removed. The new rotary oar is to be cast tonight, using the metal from the damaged oar as well as such additional metal as we have been able to obtain. The molds are nearly ready, and we hope we have secured an adequate supply of fuel for the furnaces. Then we must allow sufficient time for the tempering, and for the wrought-iron portions of the work. Finally the oar must be carted to the dock and installed. Mr Sinclair and I shall have to sleep ashore while *Castor* is in dock. You, Mrs MacDonald, and Grace are at liberty to remain aboard *Pollux*, or to share our lodgings ashore, just as you wish. We trust our repairs will be finished by the day after tomorrow. That would give us a chance at getting up to Patna within our allotted time. But if *Castor* is not ready, then I will take *Pollux* by herself, and without any passengers. Regrettably, it would be necessary in that case for you to stop here until a later passage, by water or overland, can be arranged."

Catherine and Grace remained aboard *Pollux* on the seventeenth day aching for news, but they received no report from Hector, nor from Mr Fleming. A hazy pall of smoke hung over the town. Only Sharada, who had gone ashore by herself, came back with anything to report: The casting of the enormous rotary oar was the talk of the bazaar. The tricky operation had been completed without mishap, but the smiths of the town were amazed by the astonishing quantities of fuel the *feringee*s had insisted upon using to fire the furnaces. They themselves never found it necessary to fire their furnaces so lavishly as that. They grumbled that there remained neither a lump of coal nor a stick of firewood to be had anywhere in the town, reported Sharada; and it was said that even the fires at the cremation ghat had been temporarily checked. Catherine suggested that perhaps no one had died just then, but Sharada said no, she had seen several muslin-wrapped corpses waiting to be burned.

On the eighteenth day, the merchant brig *Spur* arrived at Monghyr. She remained for only two or three hours, long enough to take on provisions, then set sail again into the lowering sun with an easy breeze behind her. With an impatience that throbbed like an inflamed tooth, Catherine watched the brig disappear up the river.

But at the first light before sunrise on the nineteenth day, *Castor* and *Pollux* steamed out of Monghyr at last. *Pollux* led now. Hector was aboard *Castor*, monitoring how she went with her new-cast rotary oar. She went as well as ever, he said—still not quite able to keep up with her twin. At noon Hector had himself rowed ahead to *Pollux*, and went straight to his bed, remaining there for the next ten hours. He did not awaken even when both ships hove to late in the afternoon to help tow

*Spur* off the sandbank where she had run aground in the fog early that morning. All her people had not been able to drag her off, but *Castor* and *Pollux* together succeeded in pulling her free and into deep water. Then the two steamships proceeded in tandem up the narrow channel, straight into a brisk headwind that had been gradually gaining force since noon. *Spur*, unable to proceed into this wind, could do nothing but drop anchor and lie waiting for the wind to change. Catherine knew just how her people must feel.

The hold where the ice lay was very wet. Cold water sloshed heavily between the ship's frames. Mr Fleming ordered the pumps manned and the ice-melt pumped out. The men pumped in shifts for hours.

On the twentieth day, Catherine, sitting with her canvaswork on her lap as they passed yet another nameless village without stopping, noticed a cluster of low clay mounds along the riverbank. "Sharada," she said to the ayah, who was shelling fenugreek nearby, "what are those curious domed structures with spikes on top, there along the bank under that tree? I have seen so many of them all along the river. Are they wee temples?"

"They are suttee monuments, memsahib. Each one honours a widow who has immolated herself with her deceased husband."

"But there must be at least a dozen at this very spot! And I have seen hundreds more as we have passed up the river!"

"Yes, memsahib. There are very many of them. Very many suttees." And Sharada gathered up her bowl and, tossing the emptied pods into the river, went down to the galley.

Many widows; many suttees. Catherine threaded her needle yet again. She was using the blue and green silks now; and she was working on the little stream which meandered across the bottom of the stitched scene. She was making that stream much larger, much wider than it had been; she was turning it into a broad river. Perhaps, she considered, she would stitch a steamship on the river.

They got under way before dawn on the twenty-first day, having anchored nearly thirty miles below Patna for the night. All day they steamed at full power up against the broad current, the featureless shore sliding past under a blistering bronze sun.

At sunset, Catherine asked, "Where are we, Hector?"

"Eight miles below Patna. More or less."

"And are we to continue in the dark?"

"Aye," he said shortly.

A little later, as the dusk deepened, Grace came with a request: "Catriona, my dear, may I have a sheet of paper? Before it is quite dark, I want to write down the words for a song that Sharada has taught me."

"Yes, certainly. What is the song?"

"Oh, it is an old boat song, I suppose," said Grace, and bent to her task.

After a moment, Catherine looked over Grace's shoulder. She was writing quite easily and deftly in Devanagari script.

"What does it say?" asked Catherine.

Grace sang in her light clear voice, tracing the words with her finger:

नावरिया झांझरी आनपड़ी
मझधार, आनपड़ी मझधार

ना कोऊ पीर मिले
न कोऊ संग साथी
नाम लिये कर पार

"A tasty tune. And what does it mean?"

"Oh, I don't know every word. But it means, roughly, my leaking boat lies in midstream, no saint or friend comes to save me . . . hmm, something something, carry me ashore . . ."

"A fine thing to be singing! Let us try something more auspicious. How about 'Safely Landed'?" suggested Catherine; and the two of them sang the old Gaelic song together: "*Fallain gundith thainig e* . . . Shh, shh; what is that? That boat is hailing us. And music! Who is it?"

Who? It was Sir Charles D'Oyly and Lady D'Oyly in their boat, with his barge following close behind carrying his band of musicians. It was a full escort of honour in fact, all come down to meet them and escort them in their triumph up the last half mile on this evening of the twenty-first day. For ahead in the distance, as they came up at last, rounding one more broad bend in the broad river; there at last! Gleaming in the dusk were the wide well-lit ghats of Patna, and the handsome marble mansions arrayed beyond for miles along the riverbank.

# 19

## *This is one of the True Species*

Something bumped against the *budgerow* belonging to Sir Charles and Lady D'Oyly. With an angry oath, a boatman fended it off with a pole. Catherine looked over the rail, then quickly turned away. But she had seen all too clearly in the noonday light: a corpse, only partially burned, the muslin wrappings merely charred over the rib cage. The skull was horribly grinning, the form horribly buoyant, and stinking. It drifted clear, drifted down the current, spinning lazily in their wake in the opaque gray-green holy river.

Death drifted downstream, surrendered to the current. Live beings had to struggle up against the river. Up, up, always fighting up against the current, thought Catherine. She was very tired. She had not slept well, sharing an airless cabin with Grace. It was late April now, and the nights were nearly as hot as the days. She closed her eyes in the shade of the awning and daydreamed in the heat. She daydreamed of icy Highland streams. She thought of the Spey in spate, the tea-coloured, whisky-coloured water transparent as air magnifying its pebbly bed. She was a salmon, battered and worn, still fighting her way upstream, up against the current, up . . . to what? The spawning grounds, the gravel beds? Up to see for herself a wrecked bungalow near Ghazipur.

"After all there is nothing like being on the spot and seeing for one-self, Sir Charles says," came the voice of Lady D'Oyly.

"Quite," said Mr Sinclair. Catherine opened her eyes to see him dash his brush across the top of his wet paper.

"Sir Charles found the entire business in a shambles," said Lady D'Oyly. She peered narrow-eyed at Catherine, then frowned at the drawing on her lap and applied her pencil. "The most shocking abuses. He has set stringent measures in place for securing the consignments: armed escorts, forms, seals, registers, scales, certificates, assays. When it comes to a thing like opium, one can't be too painstaking. There is nothing like being on the spot and seeing for oneself."

"Just so," said Mr Sinclair, and laid another stroke across the top of his paper.

"I had at first thought it so unlucky that we must run up to Ghazipur just *now*," said Lady D'Oyly, "practically the very minute that your party arrived, for it is not very often that we have such congenial visitors. But *now* is the season when the opium crop comes in; and a business which is to make or break the fortunes of the entire Company cannot very well be left to look after itself. I was so unwilling to go, yet look how fortunately it has all turned out. Ghazipur is quite in your way to Lucknow, Mr Sinclair, and Mrs MacDonald was so obliging as to agree to bear me company. How did you convince your clever brother to manage without you for a few weeks, Mrs MacDonald?"

"Oh, Hector is quite confident of managing everything for himself," said Catherine. "He supposes that food, clothing and sleep require no management at all. When I return, I expect to find him half starved, rumpled beyond disgrace, and exhausted, but he will not have noticed."

"I did not quite understand his explanation of the changes he is making to his steamships," said Lady D'Oyly.

"None of us quite understands, I'm afraid. He has had yet another brainstorm about his rotary oar. It is rather difficult to explain, but he is trying a new placement for it in a slot to be cut in the keel, in the deadwood just before the rudder, you know. Out of harm's way, he says, where he claims that it will have greater propulsive power and improve the steering, too. He is sleepless with excitement about this new idea."

"And Mr Fleming?"

"He would have preferred that this brilliant idea—if it is so very brilliant—had occurred to Hector sooner."

"Oh, but that is the nature of inventions and discoveries, of all philosophical advances," said Mr Sinclair. "It is all so very obvious in retrospect that one mistakenly supposes it should have been obvious in prospect as well. Alas, it never is."

"It is the nature of composition, too," said Lady D'Oyly. "As soon as I have drawn a correct outline, it is perfectly clear that it is correct; how could it be otherwise? But until I have drawn it, I have only a blank sheet of paper. And I have spoiled a great many blank sheets in my time, trying to discover my correct line." She considered her sketch judiciously at arm's length, then added weight to a shadow. "Ah! Pray don't move just yet, Mrs MacDonald. I have very nearly got the folds of your gown."

"Still," said Catherine as she settled back in her chair once more, "as steamships are rather costlier than sheets of paper, Mr Fleming seems to think that Hector should have had his afterthoughts ahead of time, and is hoping that he will not have any more of them in the future. He would like for Hector to stop inventing and discovering, in short. So Mr Fleming remains in Patna to make sure that any more improvements that may occur to my brother will not be tried out on the boats that will be needed to carry down the precious cakes of opium in just a very few weeks."

"Do you know, Mrs MacDonald, I should like to draw your ayah one of these days," said Lady D'Oyly, cocking her head to look critically at her drawing. "She has such an interesting intelligent face and a graceful figure; I should like to add her to our collection. Oh, you have not yet seen our collection; alas, there was not time before we left Patna, but you shall certainly see it when we return. Sir Charles and I have been making such an album of the visages, the costumes, the physiognomies one sees hereabouts, as well as the scenes of native life, and the landscapes, the temples, the ruins. Some of it of course is our own work; but we also have acquired a great many worthy pieces by other artists, even some of the native artists of the district. Some of it is rather primitive, though beautiful in its way; and some of it quite accomplished. Yes, Sir Charles has quite taken some of them under his wing. They are so eager to learn correct modern methods of perspective—and light and shadow, in particular. He talks of forming an art society, open not only to the civilians and the officers but also to the more distinguished natives; but now it will have to wait until after the opium harvest is complete. There! I flatter myself I have got you pretty well, Mrs MacDonald. Ah! And here comes my hardworking husband at last. Have you finished your dispatches and reports, my dear? Come, you are always my severest critic. I cannot get Mr Sinclair to say anything critical at all. Tell me, have I not made a fine job of Mrs MacDonald?"

THE FIRST PIERCING rays of the rising sun raked across the rough land falling away at Catherine's feet, across the ugly slump of steep, broken wasteland running down toward the bed of the slow gray river far below. A vast fan of slumped red earth spread out, away below where she stood—raw, ugly, shattered earth and deep jagged fissures running all down it. It had been mud—the very earth liquefied; now it was cracked and dry and hard. Some trees, the remnants of a garden, remained at the very edge of the massive mudslide halfway down the slope. Catherine looked out over the river. She could just make out—four miles further down, and on the opposite bank—the white villas and pavilions of Ghazipur itself, which they had left behind in the predawn coolness and darkness several hours ago. It was a charming prospect.

Here Sandy had died—crushed, drowned, or smothered by this mudslide on a July night at the height of the monsoon nearly two years ago.

Someone squeezed her elbow: Lady D'Oyly, expressing her sympathy. Lady D'Oyly, speechless at last.

"Here is where the wall of the tank must first have given way," said Major Leslie, pointing with his stick. Only a few muddy stones now remained in the breach of what had once been a broad dam. It had been a large tank—not very deep, but long and wide—impounding the water of a little mossy stream which ran off the farmland behind them, and storing it here for use in the dry season, for use at the villa which had stood on a broad terrace below, to fill its fountains and water its gardens.

"You were among the first on the scene after the disaster, I believe?" said Catherine.

"I was," Major Leslie said, stroking his tremendous mustache. "I immediately organised a rescue team, drafting the villagers who were living up there among those rose fields. We dug while daylight lasted, and again the next day. It was still pouring rain. I am afraid there was nothing more anyone could have done."

Catherine had known that neither her brother's remains nor any of his belongings had ever been recovered. She had thought this was odd and suspicious; but now she was not so sure. This had been a vast mudslide. She did not ask Major Leslie any more questions. Standing here now in the increasing heat, she knew how it had been. A drenching, drowning rain; the liquefied clay soil so heavy that even a shovelful is too heavy, too sucking, to lift; and flowing off the shovel in slow motion like thick heavy slag. It looks solid, but you can plunge your hands into it as though it were water. You can feel something, something—a limb? a shoe? You can close your hand around it and drag it with all your strength up from the sucking mud; it releases with a kissing sound. It is a shoe, a slipper of Nankin silk. Your excavation has filled in already. You are caked in the sticky clay. It is wrinkling, shifting again, slipping; and you must grab the rope and save yourself. There is nothing anyone can do.

Naughty Grace! With no one watching, she had made her way down along the far edge of the slide, down to the grove of trees which were all that remained of the garden once belonging to the villa. Now her pale red head suddenly emerged from their shade into view; and she waved her thin arms, gesturing for Catherine to come down to her. "Come see," she piped. "Do come down, my dear!"

"No, you come up!" called Catherine, but Grace ducked back under the trees and did not come up. "Grace, come up at once!" called Catherine once more, but Grace did not appear.

"Shall I send someone down to fetch her?" offered Major Leslie.

"No, I shall go after her myself," said Catherine. "My ayah—where is she? There you are. My ayah will come down with me." Carefully Catherine made her way down the steep slope, with Sharada following, skirting the deep fissures until she came to easier ground. A little path wound into the dappled shade of a stand of trees. There was an understory of thriving shrubs, knee high, so deeply green, so vivid, so exuberant. The leaves were long pointed ovals, four inches long, with tiny serrations all along their edges. Round plump scaled buds sprouted from the axils and drooped modestly downward. Catherine stopped abruptly, and Sharada nearly bumped into her. Grace popped up from a thicket of the green shrubs. She was chewing a leaf. A hot morning breeze ruffled the peeple leaves overhead, and light skittered over Grace's pale hair.

"He has been carrying water for them," said Grace, and she pointed to a little old white-haired native man who was standing half hidden behind a vine-covered tree. A stout timber yoke—actually the handle of a pickax—lay across his shoulders, with a water jar hanging from each end. "And manure."

"Who planted them? Who planted these bushes here?" said Catherine.

No one answered. Catherine turned to Sharada. "Ask him," she said.

Sharada made a *namaste* to the old man and addressed him in Hindi, *May the blessing of the great god lie upon you, honoured uncle. This foreign lady asks who planted these green bushes.*

The old man came out from behind his tree and replied: *Blessings of the great god upon you likewise, niece. It was my lord Sikander, who lived in the house that was here, and who died in the mudslide.*

*Where did they come from, these bushes?*

He shrugged, saying, *I don't know. Sikander Sahib brought them, seeds and baby plants. From the eastern mountains, he said.*

Sharada translated for Catherine, "He says it was Sikander Sahib who planted them. He was bringing the seeds and plants from the mountains to the east."

"Ask him what the plant is called."

*She asks, what is it called, this beautiful plant*, Sharada said.

*Oh, ah! My niece, what is this beautiful green shrub, greenest of all shrubs? What is it indeed? I, I myself, a lifelong gardener and a pious man, I believe it to be none other than soma itself, divine soma, beloved of the gods. And, indeed, did not the Khasi chieftain from the eastern mountains with his strange-sounding speech, did not even he call it* shama? *Yet Sikander Sahib said it is called tea. Tea*, he said, repeating the explosive little word.

"He says he is believing it to be soma, the celestial herb; and there was at that time a Khasi chieftain here who was calling it *shama*; but Sikander Sahib said it is tea," translated Sharada.

"Khasi chieftain? What is Khasi?"

*Now, oh honoured uncle, she wants to know about this Khasi chieftain.*

*But, niece, I should like to know who is she with all her questions? Who is this foreign female of yours?*

*She is his sister, honoured uncle; Sikander Sahib's twin sister, come all the way from Scotland on a pilgrimage to the place where he died. She has a right to ask her questions.*

*Oh, his twin sister! She does resemble him a little. I make her a* namaste *then, in his honour. Well, what is it? The Khasi chieftain, yes. He journeyed here on the river, from the Abode of Clouds and Mist in the eastern mountains beyond the great Brahmaputra, and he lived in the great house as guest of Sikander Sahib. They plucked the tender baby leaves of my beautiful soma bushes, and crushed them, and dried them.*

To Catherine, Sharada said, "He thinks it was an important man from the hill tribes who dwell in Meghalaya, in the eastern mountains, and he came as a guest of your brother's. They were plucking the leaves of these bushes, and drying them to make—tea."

Catherine plucked a tiny new leaf and chewed it. It tasted juicy and astringent; then sweetness spread across the tongue. "Ask him if he remembers that night of the mudslide. Where was he that night when the dam burst?"

*She wants to know about the night of the mudslide,* said Sharada. *She asks if you remember that night when the wall of the tank burst.*

*Of course I remember it, I remember everything with perfect exactness. That fateful night, that terrible night! And yet I was spared—I, an old man, without wife or children, I was spared. It was the beginning of the monsoon—surely you remember it, respected niece, the monsoon of two years ago. You are from hereabouts, I think. I can tell by your speech and by your looks. It came like the army of the Pandavas meeting the army of the Kurus, did it not? I see you do remember it. I had a dry little shed behind the big house, well thatched and comfortable, where I kept my tools and my bed. I was sound asleep when Sikander Sahib awakened me and told me I must carry a parcel for him across the river to an English lady in Ghazipur that very night! I did not want to go, for it was not my proper duty; I am the gardener, not the* chaprasi. *Also I was afraid, for the lightning was striking all about. And I was afraid, too, of the Thugs, for there had been a great many stranglings of poor travelers in that year, my niece. But Sikander Sahib was strangely fierce. He had already sent out the* chaprasi *earlier on another errand, so I must carry that parcel though it was not my proper duty. He forced me to go out into the terrible night, in pounding rain, and infested by dangerous robbers. And therefore I was not asleep in my bed when the waters and earth came pouring down the hill, and my life was saved.*

Sharada translated the old man's answer. Then Catherine asked, "And the other servants? Were any of them drowned that night?"

Sharada said, *She asks about the other servants, whether any of them were saved by a divine intervention that night, as you were.*

*All! All were spared, my niece! Most had gone already into the village for a wedding, and the others had gone to tend their dying relative. But, oh, the poor ill-fated* chaprasi! *He was not drowned that night, yet he met his fate nevertheless—for was not his body found three days later in a well? Strangled by the Thugs?*

"None of the servants were here that fateful night, memsahib," translated Sharada.

"Ask him if my brother died owing wages to him and the other servants," said Catherine.

Sharada asked, and the old man replied, *But that is another marvelous thing, my niece. For on the very day, the last day of his life, my lord Sikander called every servant into his presence and paid all our wages up to the last* ana, *the last* paisa. *Had he a presentiment? I have wondered.*

*That is marvelous indeed. A presentiment. Or . . . But what happened to the Khasi chieftain? Was he here on that terrible night?* asked Sharada.

*Alas, he was. But of all the people living here, perhaps thirty souls, it was only he and my lord Sikander who met their deaths that night.*

*Why are you still here, honoured uncle? Why do you still bend your old back to tend these beautiful green bushes?*

*Ah, niece, will you ask me that? It is a private vow I have made, a discipline. I have made a vow to Lord Shiva to tend this garden of the divine soma for as long as I shall live. Why else was I spared? And if my lord Sikander ever returns to his garden, he will find it thriving.*

*What do you mean, my uncle? How can he ever return?*

*Oh, in his next incarnation, of course. What else would I mean?*

"What is he saying? Translate, please," said Catherine.

"He is saying . . . he is saying that Sikander Sahib paid all the servants' wages very soon before he died."

"Oh, did he? How interesting . . . Still, he must accept this, from me, for my brother's sake," said Catherine, and she gave the old man ten rupees, two months' wage.

The old man bowed respectfully and said, *Tell the Bibi Sahib I am grateful. I will use the money to buy new tools, for all mine were lost in the mud, and I have no money to buy new ones. Oh, yes, all lost, all except for this heavy pickax. Very curious that it was not lost with the others. Very curious, revered niece. Yes, this one tool is all I have left, and I found it on the morning after the disaster lying—where do you suppose?—just by the fatal breach in the dam. Yes, just thrown to one side, thus. And I had last laid eyes on it the previous night, just when my lord Sikander sent me out of my little dry room into the storm, for I thought then of taking it with me for protection from the Thugs. But I left it behind after all.*

"What does he say?" said Catherine.

"He is thanking you for your generosity, memsahib. He is saying he will use it to buy new tools, so he can be continuing to tend your brother's garden."

Sharada's face was set like stone, and she drew her shawl around her, though the morning had grown hot.

They toiled back up the steep hill with the sun now frankly blazing on their backs. Lady D'Oyly had taken shelter in the buggy, whose awning provided a little shade at least. They settled themselves, and as the buggy lurched forward, she patted Catherine's hand and gave her a look of sympathy. Catherine smiled gently to show that she was not devastated. "It is so very good of you to come here with me," Catherine said, "and so good of Sir Charles to have made all the arrangements." She nodded at Major Leslie, who rode ahead of them on his good bay gelding, and at the detachment of native foot soldiers, who fell in behind the buggy, trotting along in the hot dust. "I am sorry to have given so much trouble, but I am sure you understand how exceedingly important it has been for me to see the place at last for myself."

"Of course, my dear," said Lady D'Oyly, and patted her hand

again. "And Sir Charles did not mind in the least; it has been no trouble at all."

But a considerable deal of trouble had certainly been taken. "Is it really necessary to have an escort whenever one goes about?" asked Catherine. "We are only a few miles from Ghazipur."

"Oh, yes. This region is infested by Thugs who prey upon travelers," said Lady D'Oyly. "It is another of Sir Charles's great headaches." She explained Thuggee in a lurid whisper, which Grace politely pretended not to overhear: "These fellows roam about the country in gangs, strangling travelers for their money and throwing the corpses down the wells or hacking them to pieces and burying them in shallow holes. They do it not only for the sake of the robbery but also as a sort of human sacrifice to their horrid black goddess they call Bhawani. Their weapon is a perfectly innocent cotton kerchief, which they wet and twist to make a thin cord, for strangling their victims. Very seldom are Europeans attacked, but it is wise to appear well guarded and well armed, and to beware any parties of native travelers one may meet along the road. Last year a gang of sixteen Thugs was captured when one who had been caught with his share of the booty was flogged and made to confess. They had been responsible for at least thirty-seven murders during the previous year. Oh, yes, they all were hanged; but still Thuggee continues, and the natives hereabouts dread to make any journey."

Grace interrupted at last. "That smell! Is it roses?"

It was: Atta roses, Lady D'Oyly called them. She made their party halt, and one of the sepoys was sent down to the field below the road to fetch a few blooms for the memsahibs. Native women moved through the field, gathering petals two-handed into baskets slung from their necks, to make the attar of roses, rose oil essence, and rosewater for which the district had always been famous. The rosebushes were small, and they looked baked and exhausted in the heat, as though the small pale blossoms they produced were flags of surrender. But the scent of these small five-petaled flowers! Catherine gingerly held the tender stem, just a little prickly between her fingers, and inhaled deeply of the petals. Rich and complex, powerfully rose. There was another deeper, muskier scent as well, but it was not in the blossom. Catherine sniffed again, trying to find it. Ah! On her fingers, where she had held the rough stem just below the blossom, was a rich musky oily scent, much darker and more erotic than that of the rose petals. Catherine rolled the stem with its oil glands between her fingers to get more of the scent. As they drove along the fine countryside, she surreptitiously passed her fingers under her nose from time to time, to enjoy that musky smell.

They came at last to the tent which had been set up for their breakfast by the servants sent ahead. The tent was pitched in a grove of noble mango trees overlooking a poppy field; and inside were chairs, a table laid with silverware; and plates, cups and saucers of chinaware, on a fresh linen cloth. The cook fires behind were burning well, and in the ten minutes before the breakfast was ready, the travelers walked down to see the poppy field in its stockaded clearing.

Enormous blooms opened just under Catherine's nose, and rather above Grace's red head. The day's poppies, newly struck by daylight, were just casting off their tight green turbans and unfurling their crumpled silk petals, all in shades of purple and mauve, and sparked by the occasional crimson, white, or pink. A broad velvety black cross marked the heart of each blossom. An ardently pitched humming rose from all across the broad field, for each blossom contained a reveling intoxicated court of bees, four or five of them staggering drunkenly around the green baroque galleries at the top of each green ovary, then tumbling incapacitated among the fringe of golden stamens. The bees were ravished, frenzied, dizzy, utterly seduced. Occasionally they would remember their duty, and would dutifully launch themselves—but immediately forgetting it again, they returned over and over to the same flower.

This plantation had none of the sweet seductive scent of the rose fields. The scent of these plants—leaves, flowers and all—was acrid, pungent. The broad leaves were like enormous glaucous lettuces, or like acanthus, more familiar as ancient carved Greek marble than as a living plant. Where a leaf was torn, a thick white sap oozed. Catherine touched it: sticky. She licked it from her finger: horribly bitter!

The workers moving through the field were native men in white muslin and native women in bright saris more brilliant than the flowers. They paid no attention to the newly opened blossoms, the ones full of bees; nor to yesterday's flowers, already dropping their silken petals to shrivel unregarded on the ground. The women sought the flowers of day before yesterday; these were now just plump, flat-topped green pods; inside, the gray-black seeds like ticks were already ripening. The swelling seedpods were shaped like a deep lidded bowl, like a tiny Chinese lidded cup for drinking tea; each with an arcade around its top just under the rim. Catherine watched a woman pinch a pod between thumb and forefinger, and with her sharp little knife deftly cut four vertical slits at the four points of the compass on the swollen seedpod; immediately the bitter sap began to seep from these slashes.

The men had a different job. They had knives too. They sought the seedpods that were older still, the ones the women had cut three days earlier. And from these they carefully scraped off the sap, which had oozed from the vertical cuts and was now congealed—thick and amber-coloured; for this very sap was raw opium, the precious substance itself. The stuff of dreams. The price of all the tea in China.

They went up to the tent for their breakfast. The tea was ready; Sharada waited on them, moving around the table behind their chairs, pouring it steaming from the pot into their cups.

"Ah, tea!" cried Major Leslie. "And the stronger, the better." He drank down his first cup and was poured another. "Well, it is good we made an early start. It will be cooler on the river, and we are only a short distance now from the boats."

"Do you know, Major Leslie, whether my brother had a boat?" asked Catherine. "Or how did he cross back and forth between Ghazipur and his district here?"

"Certainly he had—quite a good little pinnace, and a well-trained crew. I remember my colonel once offered to buy it from him, but it was not for sale. It was lost too, alas, in that monsoon."

"Indeed?"

"Oh, but a great many boats were lost then. You can have no idea, Mrs MacDonald, what a monsoon is like until you have lived through it yourself. There must have been a score of boats broken loose and wrecked on the rocks below the whirlpools that year—not counting the native boats, of course. Some of them were hauled off and repaired, but I daresay some lie there yet, washed up where they cannot be reached, and by now of course not worth the hauling off."

"Was my brother's boat found among them?"

"Not that I ever heard," said Major Leslie after a moment's consideration. "Of course it might have sunk, or been covered by shoaling sands; or it might have been wrecked much further down the river."

"Of course," said Catherine. Her teacup was empty. But Sharada had set down the teapot and was gazing fixedly out the open side of the tent, across the poppy fields. Down the glistening river.

ꕤ ꕤ ꕤ

"SHARADA IS ILL," announced Grace the next morning to Catherine. "She is still lying in her bed."

"Ill! What is the matter?"

"I don't know," said Grace. "She only lies there and does not speak. Will you send for a doctor?"

"I will go and see her myself," said Catherine. Grace followed as Catherine made her way out to the little porch at the back of the house. Several Indian beds like low tables topped by thin mats were lined up there for the maidservants. On one of these lay Sharada, huddled under a light cotton coverlet. Her eyes were open, unblinking, but she only gazed at the wall. Under her bed were two large brass-bound trunks. Catherine placed her palm on Sharada's forehead: cool, dry. Not a fever, then. But her face was swollen, her eyes puffy and red; and her hair tangled. "Shall I send for a doctor?" Catherine asked.

"No," croaked Sharada.

"But what is the matter? Are you in pain?"

Sharada shook her head but did not reply. Did that shake of the head mean yes, or no?

"Is it the belly? Or the headache?" asked Catherine.

"It is my heart, my sorrow," whispered Sharada with a great effort through dry, cracked lips. "I grieve, grieve . . . for my father has died while I was far away over the black water."

"Oh, I am so sorry to hear of it," said Catherine. "But shall I send for a brahmin to say prayers for him? Or a kind old woman to sit with you?"

"No, no, no," said Sharada, and closed her eyes. "Please be leaving me all alone. I will get up later. But I cannot now."

"Well . . . we are going out with Lady D'Oyly to see the palace ruins today, and the pavilion of the fountains. But I will come look in on you again when we return," said Catherine.

They rode elephants for their day's sightseeing, and Major Leslie served once again as their escort. To ride on an elephant was like riding on a mountain, so safe and high and solid. The elephants' leathery feet shuffling on the pavements sounded as though they were wearing slippers.

They were carried first to the Company's stud, and admired there the mares and foals in their paddocks and the virile stallions in their stone stalls. Then, remounting the elephants, they made their way to the ruins of the old palace of the former Nawab of Ghazipur. It was situated high on a bank overlooking the river, behind a sheer rampart with four bastions. There was a wide landing place for boats down below. The centerpiece of the place was a beautiful octagonal pavilion called the Chalis Satoon: the Hall of Forty Pillars. Here, in the central room, the servants laid out the picnic while Lady D'Oyly and Catherine and Grace and Major Leslie explored the delightful place. The graceful carved columns had formerly been plumbed for water, and everywhere were marble channels for water: rills, fountains, sprays, pools, and cascades. These channels were dry now, but Catherine marveled at the engineers who had made this place, at the care and work which had formed this design. Even Hector would have been impressed. There were no walls, but hooks for curtains still remained in the openings of the beautiful shapely arches which formed the many rooms. Exquisitely embroidered silk curtains would have been hung here, rippling in the breezes coming off the river. How delightful this place would have been on a sultry summer evening, with all its rills and fountains tumbling and purling and its silk hangings fluttering, and a band of musicians playing near the balustrade!

They sat down to their lunch in the shade of the central pavilion of the Chalis Satoon. The servants had hung up woven grass mats to windward, and splashed these mats with jars of river water at intervals. The hot wind blowing through the wet mats evaporated the water, and the air was cooled—a little; enough. "Ah!" said Catherine, fanning herself, "pleasant and ingenious, these grass mats! And they smell so sweet."

"What, the tatties?" said Major Leslie. "Have you not yet encountered tatties, Mrs MacDonald?"

"Tatties!" said Catherine, "Are they called tatties? That's what we call potatoes, at home."

"How droll you Scottish ladies are," said Major Leslie, and helped her to the cauliflower curry, the lamb stew, and the peas cooked with cheese. He made the servant bring her a glass of wine and a dish of sherbet. And afterward, when his hookah was prepared for him, he pressed her to try it; and was truly disappointed when she declined.

"I hope Sharada will be better when we return," said Grace to Catherine when they had remounted their elephants after their picnic. "I do not like for her to be unwell."

"You must be patient; she may not be quite like herself for a time," said Catherine. "She must be sadly grieved at her father's death."

The other elephant, carrying Lady D'Oyly and Major Leslie, led the way. It was a relief to escape at last from Major Leslie's effortful gallantry.

"Well, that is rather an odd thing, you know, Catriona," said Grace. "An odd thing because, you see, it was four or five days ago that she learned of her father's death, when we first arrived here in Ghazipur. Why is it only now that she is become so very prostrated? I do not quite understand that."

"Is it so? Four or five days ago?"

"Aye, and it was three days ago that she went and fetched away from her aunt's house the trunks. Did you see the trunks under her bed? She showed me what is inside them—native musical instruments and old books and that sort of thing, left to her by her father. She did not seem so exceeding sad then."

"Hmm. It *is* odd."

"But she was so strange yesterday when we were out along the river at Uncle Sandy's place. Did you notice how scantily she translated for you?"

"What do you mean?"

"Oh, Catriona, can you still not understand any Hindi at all?"

"Alas, I cannot. It is not so easy for everyone as it is for you."

"I thought perhaps you were only pretending not to understand.

But that old gardener had a great deal to say, which Sharada did not translate for you."

"Such as what?"

"Well, he said that Uncle Sandy paid every servant on the very day before the mudslide, paid each of them every last *paisa* of their wages. That is rather uncanny, I think."

"Uncanny? Well, it is certainly very lucky for them."

"And the *chaprasi*, you know, the message carrier, the real message carrier who was strangled by Thugs that very night—she did not translate that."

"Strangled by Thugs!" said Catherine, shuddering. "Was he indeed?"

"Aye, and his body found in a well three days later. She told you none of that."

"But I daresay she did not like to speak of something so terrible," said Catherine.

"And about that pickax, the one the gardener was carrying over his shoulders. He said he found it on the morning after the mudslide. He found it next to the breach in the dam. Perhaps someone caused that mudslide on purpose."

"Oh, Grace! What a thing to imagine!"

"And he said that he had left the pickax in his shed just the night before, when Uncle Sandy himself came in to send him away from there."

"Mmmm," said Catherine. "He said that? Well; I do wonder . . . that Sharada did not consider it worth translating for me."

When they returned to the residency and dismounted their elephants and went inside, they found that Sharada was up and walking about again and attending to her duties, though she was not singing, and her eyes were dull and miserable. When she asked for the night's leave to perform the special *puja* which was due to her father's memory, Catherine granted permission, hoping that the ritual might help to purge Sharada's sorrow.

# 20

## *very obvious to a knowing Ear*

"I am so thirsty to hear anything you can tell me about my brother's time here in Ghazipur," said Catherine to Major Leslie that evening after dinner. Hot summer darkness settled into the corners of the big residency drawing room. Lady D'Oyly sat at the pianoforte, picking out a few chords, while a portly civilian in half mourning searched for a particular song buried in a thick stack of dog-eared music. Sir Charles D'Oyly leaned against the frame of an open window, talking with Mr Wade, another civilian connected with the political administration. A young Mrs Hill, who could neither think nor speak of anything but her new baby, had dined with them, and had sat with them for a few minutes after dinner, but now she went once more to check on the precious infant. "I would take it as a great kindness in you, Major Leslie," said Catherine softly.

"Would you, Mrs MacDonald?" he said. He stroked his mustache and leaned forward so that the springs of the sofa creaked under his weight. "It would be my privilege to oblige you—I would be happy to tell you anything I know—but I was only newly arrived here then, still quite the griffin, and I don't suppose I was ever in company with your brother more than once or twice. Mr Wade, there, is the fellow you might ask. He knows everyone and everything. I believe he was the fellow who actually undertook the investigation, after all that—ah, all that unfortunate business connected with that suttee."

"What business was that?" said Catherine.

"Oh, ah, that—that suttee, you know, which your brother put a stop to, which caused all the fuss . . ." said Major Leslie uncertainly.

"But I have never heard anything about this," said Catherine.

"Indeed! But, oh, but Wade is the fellow who knows all about it. Shall I ask him for you? Mr Wade!" he said, springing up from the sofa and fetching him.

"What is this I hear about my brother's interfering in—in a suttee?" asked Catherine when Mr Wade had settled in Major Leslie's place on the creaky sofa.

So Mr Wade told her. Some two years ago, not long after Alexander MacDonald had been posted to Ghazipur, he had been riding along the bank road above the river one morning and came upon the cremation grounds just as a funeral procession arrived, "with flags aflying and drums abeating. The pyre was ready-built, a goodly stack of dry wood, for these were not poor people but a family of goldsmiths with an enviable appointment to trade not only here in Ghazipur but also in Benares and Patna, and in Lucknow itself," said Mr Wade. "They were come to cremate their brother, quite a young man. The corpse was handsomely decked out in garlands and fine garments. Your brother stopped to watch, of course, as anyone might."

"Of course," said Catherine.

"There was a considerable crowd gathered," continued Mr Wade, "for the family was not only rich and well known, but word had gone about that the widow was to become suttee, so a great many people had come to see the thrilling event. And so after all the chanting and drumming and trumpets and poured offerings and all the rest, the body was laid upon the pyre, the spectators gathering in close all around. The brothers of the deceased then brought forth the widow from her *palki*, all dressed in red, like a bride, you know, for the Hindus do not call a wife a widow until her husband is actually burned. The girl was quite young, apparently—perhaps seventeen or eighteen—for these natives marry when they are mere children. Now, you must understand, Mrs MacDonald, that a widow who is determined to commit suttee is by Hindu law not permitted to take any food or drink after her husband dies; this is to ensure that she does it of her own free will and is not drugged or poisoned by the members of her husband's family, who, of course, if she destroys herself, stand to recover any property that belonged not only to their kinsman but to her as well. And a good suttee will walk on her own two feet to the ghat, and perform her ablutions in the river for all to see, with calm resolution, so that any-one may testify that she has become suttee of her own free will."

"Oh!" said Catherine.

"But in this case, you see, the widow was brought to the pyre in a *palki*. And then her brothers-in-law aided her in getting out of the *palki*, and aided her in walking to the pyre, for it appeared that she could not walk unaided. There was some murmuring about this among the crowd gathered to watch, for this proceeding was not just pukka, you understand. But one might suppose that the widow was overcome by grief and sorrow, or perhaps just by weakness caused by having no food nor drink, and not by dread nor any unwillingness to mount the pyre. So she managed to perform her ablutions—whether of her own accord or not it is not quite clear."

"Just a moment, Mr Wade. How is all this known to you? I do not suppose that you yourself were present at the scene?"

"No, no; my knowledge is derived from taking your brother's dep-osition later, after the event, as well as the depositions of other wit-nesses who were on the scene—though all the others were natives, some of them Hindu and others Muselmani."

The steward carried in a tray with a teapot and cups; and at a nod from Lady D'Oyly—who was still engaged at the piano, Major Leslie now turning the pages of the music for her—the steward poured the tea and carried steaming cups of it to where Catherine sat with Mr Wade.

"I see. I beg you will proceed, Mr Wade," said Catherine when the steward had gone away again.

"The sun was high by this time, for it was about noon. But your brother claimed that the widow seemed blinded, and she held one hand over her eyes. Pretty quickly the eldest brother put in her hand the lighted brand; and with it she ignited the pyre, just as she ought. Then, either with or without some urging or help from her in-laws—for your brother's account differed on this from that of some of the other wit-nesses, who did not all agree—she mounted the pyre, and seated her-self, and settled the corpse's head on her lap while the flames licked up all about. She seemed to faint then, slumping over her husband. But then when a gust of wind made the fire roar up crackling, she came sluggishly to her senses and, struggling to rise, she crawled to the edge of the pyre as if to jump off. But the people roared at her and raised their sticks and would not let her jump off. She staggered to the other side to try that, her clothes and her hair catching fire by this time. . . ."

Catherine sipped her tea; it was too hot still, and seared her tongue.

Mr Wade continued: "So apparently it was at this point that your brother spurred his horse through the crowd, trampling all and sundry, right up to the edge of the crackling pyre itself. It must have been a devilish steady horse. And he reached through the flames and snatched the widow and dragged her out of the fire. Then he galloped straight down the riverbank and into the water, holding the girl draped all but unconscious across his saddle, thus extinguishing the flames in her clothes and hair. The natives of course surged after him in a fury, but he set his horse out into the deep water where the current quickly carried them down and away, out of reach, not daring to come ashore again until he was a good distance down the river."

"My Sandy!" Catherine said.

Mr Wade shook his head and grimaced. "Of course there was a great deal of trouble as a consequence. There was a complaint to the Resident; and an inquiry; and reparations to be paid. A considerable amount of diplomacy and baksheesh were required for smoothing and soothing. Your brother claimed the girl had been drugged; he said her pupils were so vastly dilated that she was blinded for days afterward, and he had acted to prevent a murder taking place under his very nose. The brothers of the deceased claimed he had interfered in a sacred Hindu rite and brought down shame and dishonour upon them all. Eventually your brother was fined and officially reprimanded—not for the first time, if I understand properly—and after a while the fuss died down, as fusses do."

"What happened to the girl?"

Mr Wade frowned. "It's an odd thing. It seems your brother got her as far as her father's house, expecting them to take her in and keep her. But a widow who declares her intention of destroying herself, then fails to do so, is an embarrassment and an abomination. So even her own father was unwilling to have her for long, her presence bringing shame upon the house as well as putting the father's reputation and livelihood at risk. Though your brother did not admit to it, I believe that he paid the father a considerable bribe to keep her there during her convalescence, while her burns healed. And it seems he looked in from time to time to make sure he got his money's worth. But then the old man had to go back up to Lucknow, where he was a favoured musician at the prince's court. And this was just about when the monsoon broke, and—and your brother was lost."

Catherine nodded. After a moment, she said, "Do you know what became of the widow then?"

"There was no reason to keep track of her particularly," said Mr Wade. "But I heard a while later that she had left India soon after, having gone into service as an ayah to a lady who was sailing for home with her infant."

"For home?"

"Yes, a Scottish lady like yourself. I wish I could recall her name. Gordon, or Graham, it might have been," said Mr Wade.

"Guthrie," said Catherine.

ꙮ ꙮ ꙮ

"Yes, it is true," said Sharada, hours later, when Catherine asked her at last. All night, while Grace slept, Catherine had sat up in her nightdress—waiting, thinking, remembering—on the terrace outside her room overlooking the river. It was nearly dawn when Sharada crept in after the special *puja* in her father's honour. The moon was an indistinct oval sinking westward behind the pale buildings of the city.

"It is true," repeated Sharada.

Catherine felt herself trembling, of chill and fatigue and shock. And was there a tremor in Sharada's hands, too, as she let down her shawl from her black hair?

"When I had been married for only seven months," said Sharada, "my husband fell ill and died of—what do you call it?—the rage."

"Died of rage?"

"No, no, *la rage*. He was bitten by a mad dog in the bazaar."

"Oh!"

"The only treatment is excising the flesh in the region of the bite and cauterizing the wound with fire; and this must be done immediately at the time of the bite. But to this he did not consent, because of where the mad dog had bitten him, you see—it was upon the precious organs of generation, and we had yet no children. . . . After he was bitten, he was consulting of course the brahmins, and performing the *puja* they advised; nevertheless he became ill after four weeks. At first there was hope it was only a fever, for there was a fever in the town then. But soon we knew it was the rage. It was during that final illness, I think, that his brothers began to give me poison, but I can remember very little from that time. I am thinking it was the poison from the plant you call thorn apple."

"Datura?"

"Kala datura, yes. I do not remember his death, nor the funeral. Those who nursed me afterward said my eyes were only black, all black. I could neither see nor walk. Nor could I feel the painful burns at first. Later, when the datura left my body, they gave me opium to dull the pain from the burns. It was your brother who brought the opium to my father's house. He brought ice as well, a great kindness, for it eased my agonies.

"At first there was only his voice, speaking Hindi with my father, and with the attendants in my father's house. I liked to hear the sound of his voice, though he did speak so oddly. I could not see then. Later, when my sight returned, I was frightened. So ugly! Excuse me, but so he appeared to me then, at first. So large and pale, like a *rakshasa*! Like a demon. Like a leper. It was the same voice, however. He would try to speak to me, but I was only turning my face to the wall and not answering him.

"He came every day and talked with my father. They talked about music, our music of India. Sometimes my father would play for him—and for me, I think, for my father knew that I was hearing and that the music was medicine to me. Medicine! My father was a master of not one instrument only, but of many, though he was most famous for his playing upon the vina, and he knew many hundreds of ragas. He had taught me also when I was a child to play upon the sarode, and I used to play music and sing for the Nawab of Oudh. But I have told you this already, memsahib.

"I heard them talking about music, talking and playing music. Your brother spoke with respect in his voice to my father, not like other sahibs. I could hear the courtesy in his voice. He addressed my father humbly, as a student addresses his master.

"Then one day my father played upon the *shahnai*, and your brother played the *sur* in accompaniment. The *shahnai*, you know, is a horn, like an oboe, with a powerful voice; and the *sur*, which accompanies it, plays the single tonic note. The next day Sikander brought an instrument of his own. He brought his bagpipe, and he played it for my father. Such a sound—like the *shahnai* and three *surs* together in one instrument! As loud as trumpets, a sound not meant to be played inside a house. Yet I thrilled to that sound. Your brother played for my father a composition not unlike a raga—very beautiful, very moving. It was not like the other *feringee* music I have heard. He was not like other sahibs. I began seeing that his hideous appearance was only an illusion, for no one could have played such music unless he was possessed of a fine soul, a fine courageous spirit.

"I suppose that was when my heart turned, and my spirit was reconciled to dwell in this body. I turned my face away from the wall and opened my eyes to this existence again. I rose from my charpoy. I regained the use of my limbs, and soon I was well enough to serve the refreshments when your brother came to visit my father. One day my father asked me to sing for them, and I did so. I sang a song of Meera's."

Sharada stopped, looking far away. Hearing, surely, that song of Meera's. It was dawn now, the sun a bright disk rising behind the mist which lay on the water. Catherine only watched, waiting—not asking.

After a little while, Sharada said, "I remember one occasion when my father was explaining how ragas live in families, and Sikander said that this was very odd and unfamiliar, that European music was never thought of in this way. And my father argued that your brother was mistaken; and he proved him so by producing a book of *feringee* music ordered in just this way. Your brother became most interested, most excited, for it was a book of bagpipe music, not printed but written by hand. Curiously, the writer of the book was a man of the same name as yours: MacDonald. Joseph MacDonald. Your brother begged permission to copy the book, for he said it was a discovery of great importance. My father would not let the book out of his own possession, but he said that Sikander might come to the house and take a copy of it there.

"So that is what your brother did. Every day he was coming to my father's house and copying the book, one page after another."

"You drew the lines for him," said Catherine.

"Yes, memsahib. And I played my sarode for him if he asked me.

He liked to hear me play and sing. And he liked to talk to me. I liked his voice. He told me a great many things about his travels. Also about his troubles with the *burrah* sahibs. They were angry with him, and he was angry with them also. He laid his plan to prove them wrong."

"Wrong about what?"

"They said no tea could grow in India; but he had seen the very tea bushes themselves growing wild in the misty hills above the Brahmaputra River. They said it was not pukka tea, but he knew that it was. He proposed to go there and make a plantation, but they would not permit it. The stupidity of the *burrah* sahibs was most provoking to him."

"Yes, it would be," murmured Catherine. "And so he planned . . . what? What did he propose to do?"

"Oh, memsahib, he did not like to speak of it; but he promised to tell me all, very soon. I knew only that he was waiting for the monsoon, and then he would put his plan into action."

"Waiting for the monsoon?"

"And . . . and waiting for me. The monsoon came; it came early that year. He could have executed his plan, but he put it off from day to day, even after the rains came."

"Why?" asked Catherine, knowing the answer.

Sharada replied proudly: "For me, memsahib! He wanted me to come with him. No, I said, no no no. Yes yes yes, he said." Sharada gazed out across the river, her fingers twisting the corner of her shawl into a cord. A flight of early swallows emerging from under the terrace swooped low and fast across the gleaming purling river. "But one night, one night in the garden under the full moon, with the heavy rainclouds covering its face—at last, then, I said yes. Yes I will go with you. How could I resist that man? He said he would send for me; and I agreed to be ready to go with him, upon a moment's notice. I waited for his summons. Oh, yes, memsahib! Anywhere in the wide world I would have gone with him or for him. I waited only for his summons. The rains were very terrible that year; terrifying storms came. I waited, and the river rose higher and higher. But instead of his summons, there came out of the storm only the news that his house was destroyed and he was dead." Sharada closed her eyes and drew a deep shuddering sigh, and another, before she spoke again. "I was destroyed also—destroyed. I, too, was drowned and smothered, my own breath stopped by mud. I laid me down once again on my charpoy and hoped to die. I ate nothing for a week, but still I lived. Then, remembering that I had a little store of opium laid by me, I ate it all, but still I could not die. This body would not die; still it breathed. Somehow I lived."

Sharada fell silent. After a while, Catherine prompted her: "And later you became ayah to Mrs Guthrie."

"Yes, memsahib, when her ayah would not go with her over the black water. I have told you this."

"But why did you not resume your profession as a musician?"

"Oh, impossible, memsahib! For who would have me? A widow, an outcaste? I am the most inauspicious of beings. I bring only bad fortune to all those who are near to me. None would have me, excepting only the *feringee*s who do not know. And as for going over the black water, I was bereft of caste already, a failed suttee; so going across the black water could make matters no worse. Or so I hoped at that time."

"I do not believe you are inauspicious to me," said Catherine.

"We are two widows, memsahib. Therefore we are fit company to each other, you and I. But as for Mrs Guthrie, did not she and her infant both die during the long passage? And leave me, the fool of fate, to deliver his parcel to you?"

"Aye, his parcel. Was that the very parcel which he made the old gardener carry through the storm, that last night, to the foreign lady in the town? Was that it, do you think?"

"I do think it now. But I did not know of its existence until I saw it among Mrs Guthrie's belongings after we had sailed. It was a great shock to me, then, to see on it the handwriting of—of him! Of course I asked my lady about it. Oh, it is from that poor Mr MacDonald who was drowned in the floods, she said."

"But Sharada," said Catherine, "I do not believe he is dead."

"Of course he is not dead! I know that *now*, miserable fool that I am! Now, now that I have gone over the black water to Scotland, and lived to return—and now that you, memsahib, have come all the way to India and taken me to see his house and his garden and his gardener in this very district where I began! Now, *now* I know that he did not drown. These two years I have grieved for him, and I did not know. But now I know that he toyed with me, he deceived me, he played his monkey tricks even on me, on me who loved him so wantonly, so well! He promised me, and then he broke his promise and he sneaked away—alive—not wanting me! And still, all unknowing, I was his creature, still delivering his errands for him." Angrily she dashed at her eyes with the corner of her shawl. "And now you will dismiss me, memsahib."

"Will I?" said Catherine. "Because of my brother?"

"Your voice is like his. Your face is like his. When I touch your hair . . ." said Sharada, but she could say no more, and turned away.

"I knew long ago that you had known Sandy," said Catherine.

"How? How could you know this?"

"In Antwerp I heard you singing a tune of his," said Catherine, and she quietly sang the first line of it.

Sharada closed her eyes. "He played it on his bagpipe. It is his own song?" she asked.

"Yes, he made it himself. We always called it 'Port Alasdair,' " said Catherine. " 'Sandy's Tune.' But here is the strange thing, Sharada: he wrote out that tune and sent it along in the package you carried to me. It was tucked into his copy of that important and valuable manuscript of old pipe music which he'd had of your father. But he had put a new name to his own tune: 'Fhathast Gun a Bhith Bàthte'; 'Not Yet Drown'd.' And when I saw that, I knew it was a message for me."

"More bitter it is than the bitter melon, that to *you* he sent a message!" cried Sharada. "To you, so far away in Scotland, and only his sister! But to me, to me, his lover, his beloved, his own heart and breath—for so he called me, that deceiver!—to me, waiting and aching with longing in the town so nearby, he did not send. He sent—nothing, nothing. It was very terrible to me when I believed that he was drowned. But now! Now, memsahib, it is far more terrible."

Scarred, damaged. Two inauspicious widows, fit company for each other.

ഗ ഗ ഗ

UPON RETURNING TO Patna in late May with Lady D'Oyly, Catherine found Hector and Mr Fleming on worse terms than ever; and this despite the fact that *Castor,* formerly the slower and more sluggish twin, was now the distinctly faster ship, a result of Hector's most recent modifications. "He says there is not time now to bring *Pollux* up to the new standard," explained Hector to Catherine, coming in at last after yet another long and useless meeting with Mr Fleming. "If he would permit work to start instantly, there would be time. But we have wasted several days now arguing about it. The first of the opium auctions will be next week, and he wants both ships loaded and started down the river within forty-eight hours afterward. I could still do it; the work required would be easier on *Pollux* than it was on *Castor*. Of course it would, because the engine does not require to be reversed, and she's got her gasket aft already. I know, I know, Catherine, that with these improvements *Pollux* will then perform even better than *Castor* does now. Look," he said, spreading out his tattered drawings and pushing aside the crumbed plates at the table where Catherine had picked at a late supper alone while Hector and Mr Fleming had been arguing downstairs. "Look."

"Oh, Hector," said Catherine, "I am so very tired tonight. Lady D'Oyly has been exceedingly kind, but it is exhausting to have to respond graciously for so extended a period. I cannot look at these drawings just now with any understanding or intelligence. You must excuse me."

He looked at her for the first time. "I am sorry, my dear," he said unexpectedly. "And I have not even asked you about Ghazipur."

"Let me tell you what I learned there," said Catherine.

# 21

## *the whole Scope is perceivd*

"And Mrs MacDonald, do bring your ayah one of these mornings," Lady D'Oyly had said when they had returned to Patna. "I still want to paint her for my collection."

Catherine sat in a low rattan chair in Lady D'Oyly's salon, her perpetual canvaswork draped across her lap. She was engaged in unpicking the yellow hair of the lady in the needlework picture. It was a tiresome chore, but she was determined to give the lady russet-coloured hair instead; she had a skein of bright coppery silk for that. Grace was seated at a central table, occupied in looking through an album of small miscellaneous pictures, the work of various native artists of the district which interested Sir Charles. Just outside, Mrs Hill walked her fretful baby up and down the terrace.

Sharada sat for Lady D'Oyly cross-legged on a carpet, posing with a native stringed instrument held over her left shoulder. The instrument, called a vina, had belonged to Sharada's father. This and a few other native instruments and books set aside in two trunks by an old household servant had made up Sharada's patrimony.

Lady D'Oyly stood before her easel, her palette and brush in hand, with a muslin smock to protect her light gown. She sketched quickly, with the ease of long practice.

The salon was high and airy, with cool pale marble floors. Punkahs hung motionless from the ceiling. One long side of the room, the side that overlooked the river, was open to the outdoors, and tatties hung in all the openings between the columns but one; that mat had been taken down for the sake of the light needed to paint the ayah. Outside on the terrace, the tatty wallahs moved slowly among the strutting posing peafowl, bringing up their jugs of water to be thrown later onto the grass mats, whenever the hot afternoon wind should arise.

The other three walls of the room were hung with pictures, in two or three tiers up to the high ceiling. They were almost all Indian scenes, and many of them were the work of Sir Charles and Lady D'Oyly themselves. Occupying a central position on the long wall was a busy bazaar scene in oils; Catherine had recognised a particular quarter of the Patna bazaar itself. This, she knew, was Sir Charles's work. It was competently done. Other framed sketches had been pointed out by Lady D'Oyly as the productions of her Calcutta friend and teacher George Chinnery. She and Sir Charles had acquired two of Mr Sinclair's admirable river scenes as well; these stood now upon another easel in one corner of the room.

Sharada's face was still. She was facing out toward the river, and the light fell across her face and her long elegant hands, at ease on the strings of the vina. She held the vina against her body as though it were her infant, so nearly her own self. For a moment she closed her eyes; her lips moved, and her fingers moved on the neck of the instrument, and a faint breath of sound came from the resonator gourds. "Do you know how to play it?" asked Lady D'Oyly.

"Oh, yes, memsahib."

"Well, you may play us something, then, if you can do it without losing your pose."

"I must be tuning first."

"Tune it then."

Sharada tuned meticulously, patiently, seeking resonances audible only to her ear. Then, seeming to collect herself, she struck the cascading notes of her scale. Again. Her face changed; her body changed.

Lady D'Oyly, suddenly remembering her brush, began to paint quickly, avidly.

Sharada closed her eyes and sang. Her pure voice was surprisingly low and husky. What did the words mean? Catherine felt certain that Sharada was singing of love, of bereft and hopeless love.

Who was this woman, this widow? This *apsara*, this celestial musician? This lover of Catherine's own beloved brother? This pillar of fire leading onward through a wilderness, through a desert? Of course Sandy had fallen in love with her. Fallen—tumbled, like falling off a cliff—in love with her. Who could not? He had saved her life; then he had heard her sing. She was as exquisite, as rare, as any one of Mr Fleming's *objets de vertu*, only perfect and undamaged. Until then. Until Sandy had abandoned her.

So sad! Why must it always end in sorrow, loss, pain, grief? Catherine felt herself trembling with her own loneliness. Master yourself! she thought grimly. Never let them see it or suspect it. And she heaved a strangled breath, then another, and made the welling tears sink away again, blinking and feeling the flush in her face.

Sharada's music reached its crescendo, its fullest expression, then veered toward resolution—approached and veered again. Again. Is it not to be achieved? Not yet? Yes, now. It is over. The final phrase resonated, then decayed in the marble-floored room.

It is finished.

"Brava!" cried Lady D'Oyly. "Why, she is very accomplished, your ayah, Mrs MacDonald! Has it a name, that song?"

Having no idea herself, Catherine looked to Sharada to answer. "It is 'Kakubha Ragini,' memsahib," said Sharada modestly. "It is for this hour of the day, late in the morning toward midday. The peacocks dancing on the terrace made me think of it."

"Well, it is a charming composition, very pretty. And you have it by memory! I daresay it would be hard to remember it all, so long and complicated. I wonder you do not have it written down."

"Oh, no, memsahib, we do not write down our music in India. Music is to be made fresh, each time, for each occasion, like making delicious food," said Sharada. "Or love," she added very quietly.

"Making up music as one goes along! How peculiar!" said Lady D'Oyly, and she cocked her head and examined her painting. "But I do like what I have got of her expression. This will be a fine addition to my collection of local types. So many of my models, the women in particular, cannot bear to be looked at. But then, if she plays music for an audience, she is accustomed to being looked at."

"She has played at Lucknow for the Nawab of Oudh himself," Catherine said.

"Oh!" said Lady D'Oyly, impressed. "For the nawab!"

"And my portrait has been painted before now, memsahib, on one occasion," said Sharada quietly.

"Ah! Well, I must go and wash my hands. Sir Charles says I am the messiest of painters. Are we ready for our tiffin as soon as I come back? Ayah, on your way out, go and tell the cook that we are ready for our tiffin." And Lady D'Oyly left them to themselves. Sharada uncoiled herself and picked up her vina.

"Wait, Sharada," said Grace, still seated at the round table in the center of the room, where she had been paging through Sir Charles's albums. "Don't go. Come here and look at this."

Sharada came and looked over Grace's shoulder. There was a faint musical crash then as she involuntarily banged the vina against the edge of the table. Shakily she set down the fragile instrument and leaned heavily on the table with both hands. Her breath came coarse and ragged, like an asthmatic's.

"Whatever is the matter?" said Catherine, for she saw that Sharada was struggling not only for breath but for composure.

"Come see this, Catriona," said Grace in an odd voice, in Gaelic.

"Do speak English, Grace, and you mustn't call me Catriona," said Catherine, but she came and looked over Grace's other shoulder. Sir Charles's big album lay open, flat upon the table. Its pages were large, perhaps sixteen by twenty inches, of substantial paper. Mounted onto each right-hand page was a piece of artwork. Facing it on the left-hand page was written in Sir Charles's hand a brief account of the picture's provenance: the circumstances surrounding his acquisition of it, the name of the artist, the date painted and the date acquired, the price he paid for it; the subject of it, the names of the people pictured if it was a portrait; or the location depicted if it was scenery.

The album lay open to a traditional Indian picture of two musicians in a garden—a man and a woman. The painting was skillful; the colours and composition were pleasing. At first glance it was much like a great many Indian pictures Catherine had seen. The two figures sat on a carpet laid out on the terrace before a pavilion, with a tray of refreshments nearby. The garden foliage made a rich dense enclosure about them, a luxuriant textured green wall of tropical foliage starred with flowers. In the foreground were plants in pots, and a small round pond in which ducks sported and lotus flowers bloomed. The sky showed the first bright stars of evening between dark dramatic clouds. The picture itself was bounded by three narrow bands of scarlet, azure, and gold; and above this painted frame was a caption—a few lines of writing in the native script that Catherine now recognised as Devanagari.

But as she looked, Catherine saw that in its details this picture was rather different from others she had seen. Although the female musician, who played a vina, was certainly a traditional type, with Indian features depicted in profile, the male musician was not. He was portrayed full face; he had pale skin and a long nose, and wispy reddish hair escaped from under his turban. His cheeks were puffed out comically and unbecomingly around the mouthpiece of his instrument. Like the female musician, he was sitting cross-legged on the carpet; but what was the instrument he played? Catherine peered closely at it. There could be no doubt that it was meant to represent a Scottish Highland bagpipe, though the artist had got the drones arrayed in the wrong order, with the tall bass drone to the outside. And no piper in Scotland ever could, or ever did, or ever would play sitting down cross-legged on the ground.

Grace pointed to a word written in delicate script on the sash of the vina player. "That says 'Sharada,' " she said. There was a word written likewise on the piper's sash: "And that . . . says 'Sikander.' "

Catherine could not help glancing up into Sharada's face. She was pale; stricken. And her veil betrayed that she was trembling.

"But the most curious thing of all," said Grace, "is this writing above the picture."

"What does it say?" asked Catherine.

"At first I could make nothing of it," said Grace, "for while it is written in the Devanagari script, the words—well, they are just gibberish. They are not Hindi words, nor Urdu, nor anything I could make out. So I tried to whisper them to myself, you know, sounding them out as I used to do—and . . . and Catriona, they are English words but written in Devanagari, not in our English letters. You cannot recognise them as words; you have to read aloud the sounds, then you can hear the English words in them, do you see?"

"No, not exactly . . ."

"If you read the sounds, just the sounds, it says: '*If you love me, beloved, as I love you, then come with me to the abode of clouds and mist, to dwell in a garden of perpetual delight, feasting on music and love and the nectar of the gods. Come tonight, my own heart and breath, at midnight. I await you at—at—'* . . . But this bit I cannot quite make out. It says, *challeesaturn* . . ."

" 'Chalis Satoon,' " corrected Sharada softly. "At the Hall of Forty Pillars. . . ."

"Have they not brought our tiffin yet?" broke in the voice of Lady D'Oyly as she came briskly in again with clean hands.

"We are so very interested in this picture, Lady D'Oyly," said Catherine. "What is it, and where did it come from?"

"Oh, let us see. Yes, that one. What does my husband's catalog entry say? Hmm, hmm, yes: 'Purchased at auction for ten rupees on January 17th, 1822. Musicians in garden. Possibly portraiture but subjects unidentified. Unsigned & artist unknown, but may be Hulas Lal.' Oh, yes, of course! It was the most shocking thing. . . . Do you remember, Mrs MacDonald, my telling you of that band of Thugs which was broken up last year up near Ghazipur? Yes; sixteen of them were hanged—the youngest only fourteen years of age—after confessing to the murders of thirty-seven poor travelers which had taken place in the previous year alone. Dreadful. But this painting, wrapped in a very handsome shawl, was found among the booty of this gang of murderers. They must have taken it from one of their poor victims after strangling him and before throwing the body down a well. After the trial, of course its rightful owner was advertised for, but, as is so often the case, no one stepped forward to claim it, so it was auctioned off with the other unclaimed goods. And that is how Sir Charles acquired it, up at Ghazipur, last year. It is an odd picture, is it not? What is one to make of it? I do not read Indian writing myself, but my *munshi*—my steward, you know—cannot make any sense of it either. But I suppose Sir Charles thought it interesting, and worth setting aside at any rate in this album of miscellany and curiosities. He gave me the shawl that was with it—I have it in my room. I suppose we shall never know."

"Memsahib, it belongs to me," said Sharada, putting her hands together and making a very deep *namaste*. "I am the rightful owner."

ꙮ ꙮ ꙮ

"IT WAS INDEED Lal-ji who made this painting of us: Hulas Lal," said Sharada later, alone with Catherine and Grace in Catherine's little sitting room. "He was a dear friend of my father's, even though my father—who had been blind for many years—could never appreciate any of Lal-ji's beautiful paintings. It was Lal-ji's small joke to show Sikander-ji thus, a joke appreciated even by himself, for your brother understood even our small jokes, memsahib. There was no caption written on it when I saw it last, when my father gave the picture to Sikander-ji."

The picture itself now lay on Sharada's lap, for Lady D'Oyly had been persuaded to part with it to its claimant. Catherine reimbursed her the ten rupees that Sir Charles had spent on it; and Catherine had been reimbursed in turn by Sharada, who insisted. Sharada kept her fingertips on the edge of the paper. She had to touch it, to trail her fingertips over the writing at the top of the picture. "But this is Sikander's own handwriting," she said softly. "I would know it anywhere, to the end of my life."

His own handwriting? How strange, thought Catherine, that although she herself would instantly know Sandy's writing in English or Gaelic, recognise it as easily as recognising his face, his own hand in this unknown script was utterly foreign to her.

"He came in the evenings," said Sharada dreamily. "I waited for him always in my father's garden. I had little sweetmeats awaiting him which I had prepared myself. Nothing was too laborious. He had a liking for our little delicious morsels—even *paan*, which other sahibs refuse. I was teaching him many songs of India. And he was teaching me songs of Scotland. He helped me to speak English. We were talking, singing, playing . . . Oh, those beautiful nights, in my father's fragrant garden! I begged him to stay, stay, and sometimes he stayed even until the sky began to lighten in the east. But he was always afraid of tiring me, of staying too long. I never tired of his company, of his caresses. Of his talk. He spoke of his desire for making tea gardens. He brought me a present, a tea plant in a pot. Look, there it is, in the painting—that one in the corner.

"Only death, I believed, could ever separate us! And after all, it *was* only death that kept us apart! But it was not *his* death; it was the death of the messenger, the poor *chaprasi* by whose hand he sent this. He did send for me! How long did he wait there at the Chalis Satoon in the pounding rain that terrible night? He could not know that his message miscarried. What did he think of me? Why did he not send again? Why did he not come and capture me, taking me from my father's house? Did he suppose I lacked the resolve to go away with him? I would have gone anywhere with him. Anywhere for him. But we went away from each other, each not knowing. I went away supposing him dead. He went away supposing perhaps that I had not devotion enough."

"But where has he gone?" said Catherine. "Where in the world has he gone?"

Sharada came back up from her reverie, her contemplation of the picture on her lap. "But to Meghalaya, of course," she said.

"Meghalaya?"

"To Meghalaya, in Assam, in the rainy hills beyond the Brahmaputra. That is what he says here: 'to the Abode of Clouds and Mist.' In Sanskrit, that is Meghalaya, and it lies in the hills of Assam beyond the great Brahmaputra River."

" 'Abode of Clouds and Mist?' " repeated Catherine. "He would feel at home among clouds and mist. That is what Skye is called at home: the Misty Isle." Sandy! So deceptive, that trickster! How could he have done this? It was like his own handwriting transformed into something unrecognisable, unknown, unsuspected. "But how could he? How could he let us all suffer so!" burst out Catherine.

"But he did send you a message, memsahib, a private message that he was not drowned. He did not wish that you should suffer, that you should grieve. *That* message did not miscarry, for did I not carry it myself! And then you, you and Grace, and Lady D'Oyly, too, were the means of carrying his message to me at last, at last—so very late! He will be amazed when he learns of it. When I find him."

"Do I understand you to mean that you propose to go to Assam to find him?"

"Of course, memsahib. I am going there—with you."

"Hmm! I remember when you said to me, at the inn at Leith, that I would go to India. I knew you were only a charlatan then. Now I am not so sure."

Sharada laughed, a deep, full-throated laugh, her teeth glinting.

"But just how do you expect that we are to get to Assam?" said Catherine. "Perhaps you will arrange a magical bird or a flying chariot to carry us?"

"Those steamships which your brother has made are most wonderful vessels, memsahib. Able to swim against the strong current."

"Unfortunately, the wonderful steamships do not belong to me. Mr Fleming has other plans for them. And in any case there is a war brewing in Assam, or so I have heard. So says Major Leslie. And what will Hector say! I dread to think of it."

"I expect he will roar," said Sharada. "But I myself will walk to Assam if I must. And as you are going there, too, memsahib, and as you will not like walking so very far, therefore I suppose you will be arranging something better."

"BUT IT IS out of the question, Mrs MacDonald," said Mr Fleming. "It would be so unwise for you to go to Assam just now. There, you know, you would be outside even the scant protection which the East India Company affords to Britons within its territories."

He loomed dark and heavy, standing over her in her own little sitting room in Patna, uninvited and unwelcome. For once she had been unable to avoid him.

Who had asked for his advice or his help? No one. Without any reference to him, Catherine had made her own arrangements with Major Leslie for going to Assam. She took a firm hold of her heat-worn temper and answered mildly: "No, Mr Fleming, I daresay you are quite right. I do understand that Assam is not entirely safe. Nor are we entirely safe, I suppose, elsewhere in India. Indeed, Grace and I left Scotland because we were not safe there. It may be that no place in the world is entirely safe. Dreadful things may happen anywhere." Had Hector sent Mr Fleming to try to dissuade her when his own efforts had failed? "I have excellent private reasons of my own for wishing to go to Assam, and the sooner, the better," she said.

"Yes, your brother has told me of your reasons," said Mr Fleming. "I think you might have told me yourself long before this. Why did you never mention to me this belief of yours that Alexander is alive? You knew that he was my dear friend, too."

Why had she not? Why had she held this private intuition back from him, even during their long voyage, when she had still liked and trusted him? She had not wanted, then, to appear silly in his eyes. She had not wanted to forfeit his good opinion then. That was before she had learned that he did not merit her own good opinion. She said, "Oh, being scoffed at by Hector was quite enough for me, thank you."

"I would not have scoffed at you," he said. "I daresay that you are right about this feint of Alexander's. When I knew him, all too briefly, I saw something of his determination, and his cleverness. I did form an impression that he was even then devising some plan, and that no entity so puny, so inconsiderable as the entire East India Company, could thwart his intention once he had made up his mind to it. You warned me once, some time ago, that MacDonalds never do give up."

"And I advised you also, I believe, that we are often proven right in the end."

"So you did. And I told you that we Flemings are just the same way."

Catherine said nothing, only sitting quietly, pretending a calm she did not feel. His presence oppressed her; there was not air enough in the room for them both.

"But there is no compelling reason for you to go there immediately," said Mr Fleming. "Even in peacetime, Assam is infested with tigers, wild elephants, rhinos—not to mention the headhunters in the more distant reaches of the mountains. And it is not even peacetime. The whole of the Brahmaputra Valley has been wracked these last four or five years by the most hideous atrocities. And now the monsoon is due; it may arrive any day. The monsoon comes early and very hard to Assam. Going up that river in June is for fools and madmen. If you will only wait—"

She interrupted him: "Is Major Leslie a fool and a madman, then?"

"Oh, Major Leslie! You may find that he is both those things, and worse. But I did not come to talk about Major Leslie. I was going to say, wait until after the monsoon, and after this voyage to China which your brother and I must make. Wait until October. October or November, if all goes well. The monsoon will be over, the cool weather returned. And then, if go you still must, I will take you up the Brahmaputra in *Castor* or *Pollux*."

That was a generous offer, and unexpected. But unwanted. "Thank you; no," she said. "I have made up my mind to go immediately. And as Major Leslie is already carrying Mrs Hill and her infant up to Goalpara to rejoin her husband, and to take up his new command there, he has invited me to join their party."

He paced to the window and back before saying, "I would advise against it. Certainly not with Major Leslie, of all people."

"And why not with Major Leslie?"

"You would do better to find another escort."

"I do not know what you mean, Mr Fleming. It is a most fortuitous arrangement for all concerned, perfectly suitable in every respect. Major Leslie is a gentleman, an experienced soldier, and well versed in traveling about the country."

After a pause, Mr Fleming said, "One might easily be deceived by appearances. But as I am not in a position to repeat any particulars, I will only say that you would do better to find another escort."

"Such as yourself," she said.

He bowed and said, "At your service, Mrs MacDonald, no later than the twentieth of October, Providence willing. We finish loading our cargo within these two days. Your brother cannot go to the China Sea with an opium cargo alone, without me. He certainly cannot manage the negotiations; it is an excessively delicate business. Nor do I dare venture upon the open ocean without him, this first sea voyage; for he is the only one who thoroughly understands these engines and propelling devices. So you see, Mrs MacDonald, it is entirely impossible that either one of us can afford to take you up to Assam now; nor indeed any sooner than October."

"Alas, Mr Fleming, I seem not to have made myself clear. I do not ask you even to consider making any such sacrifice. I am resolved to go to Assam immediately; and I am entirely resigned to making the journey without you. Indeed, even if you were to offer to throw away all your season's profits and engage to carry me up there this minute—why, sir, even then I should decline!"

"Well, that is magnificent of you, and plain speaking too," he said. "At last. You have kept yourself very much aloof from me, Mrs MacDonald, for a very long time now, for months."

"We have all been very much occupied with our own affairs, I suppose," said Catherine.

"Nonsense. I have seen that you are angry with me; and I can only suppose that it has to do with some misunderstanding regarding that unfortunate woman who lives at my house in Serampore. But you have been avoiding me at every turn."

"Sir, any discussion of your private affairs can only cause pain and embarrassment to us both. Pray do not mention it. It can have nothing to do with me." She rose, looking for the bell to summon her maid; but he picked it up himself and held it muffled.

"I will not be dismissed," he said. "It is high time we had some plain speaking between us. Are friends so plentiful with you that you would send me away, Mrs MacDonald? Is it so very common a thing with you to find so kindred a soul as yours and mine are kindred? Are such friendships so frequent with you that you will refuse to hear me?"

Of course not; such a friendship was the rarest miracle in the world. She never expected it to happen again, not after losing James. She could say nothing to him, for a thick lump rose in her throat, and she set her stony face away from the window so that he should not see, and guess.

He said, "You cannot imagine, Mrs MacDonald, how astonished and overjoyed I was, during the course of our voyage, to discover in you so rare, so valuable a character. I had no expectation of ever meeting with such a woman as yourself, so richly endowed in courage, kindness, dignity, in generosity and magnanimity of spirit. So congenial in wit, in strength and resiliency! In quickness of perception and apprehension! I never imagined that such a woman existed. But before we ever reached Calcutta, I foresaw the difficulty: How was I to communicate to you the existence of my poor ward? Miserable Harini! I could not commit the cruelty of evicting her, shuffling her off to some lodging. I would not condescend to dissemble, nor to conceal her existence. How unfortunate that she is not old and ugly! The only honourable course was frank honesty, and to trust in your discernment."

"Oh, discernment! You pretend to discover in me a bit of discernment! How generous! Perhaps I have a little more of it than you had supposed—enough, indeed, to resent being made a fool of by prearrangement with your missionary friend!"

"Do you resent that I asked Dr Carey to tell you her history? But what more reliable and informed a witness could be found than Dr Carey?"

"Dear old Dr Carey! The most innocent and most biddable of old men, I daresay! What sort of fool do you take me for, sir?"

"Oh, this skepticism is unnatural in you, Mrs MacDonald," he cried. "You are no skeptic by nature, I know. For if you were, you could never have convinced yourself that Alexander is still alive. You, who have ventured all the way to India—you, who intend now to penetrate the jungles of Assam, and all this on the scantiest of evidence—how can you remain so unwilling to believe me, so unable to trust in my good faith?"

"Sir, I have known you for only a matter of months. But I have known my brother Sandy all my life. I know what he is, through and through."

"Yes, you know him to be duplicitous! And therefore you can easily believe that he has deceived us all. But not every man is deceitful. Surely, surely, you cannot think so ill of men in general, and of me in particular, that you are unable to conceive of an innocent relation between a man and a woman."

"Between you and that woman?"

"I give you my solemn word."

"But I do not want any solemn words from you, sir. What can you possibly expect of me? Am I to appreciate some compliment in your declaration, if that is what it is? In your proposal to add me to your collection of damaged beauties? I am afraid, sir, that even damaged as I am, I cannot fall in with your plan for me. Even damaged as I am, I am better than that!"

"I do not understand you! Damaged? What can you mean?"

But that was not a thing Catherine could explain to him. She had not meant to say it. "Pray leave me at once!" she cried. "How fortunate it is that our paths now diverge, and we need never encounter each other again. Sharada! Come in here at once!" she called out, and Sharada came in and stood behind Catherine. Catherine felt herself trembling.

"I hope you will find your brother," Mr Fleming said. He was pale, and his voice nearly choked in his throat. "I hope you will find him, because if he is indeed alive, he can assure you of the truth of what I have told you. Perhaps you will believe him."

The door shut behind him, and Catherine burst into tears. Had she really said all that? Spoken those words? She had, and her whole body ached. A vision of the sea blue cameo glass vase in his cabinet at Antwerp hovered just above the periphery of her mind's eye, especially the shattered stumps where both its arching handles had been broken off. What sort of man could treasure so damaged a thing?

"But what a pity, memsahib!" said Sharada. "That is a good man. Even you must see so much as that. And his steamships are so very much better than that soldier's little boats."

"How dare you?" sobbed Catherine. "Go away!"

# 22

## *the most despicable Idoea*

In her stifling tiny cabin aboard the pinnace which Major Leslie had hired for the passage to Goalpara in Assam, Catherine packed her ears with cotton wool. On the other side of the thin cabin partition, Mrs Hill's six-week-old baby howled. In fact, it howled day and night, despite the full-time attentions of its mother and ayah, and the part-time attentions of Catherine, Grace and Sharada. It was bald and livid, requiring to be held, rocked, nursed or walked constantly. Whenever it did fall asleep in someone's arms at last, and was laid gingerly into its cradle, it writhed itself awake again within ten minutes and resumed screaming. The days were blazing hot now, and the nights hardly cooler. The miserable baby was a hot heavy damp burden, passed around among all the females on board. Catherine envied the servants following on the overloaded baggage boat, laden with provisions and Major Leslie's horses. Surely it was more peaceful there.

The cotton wool muted the baby's howls only a little, but now Catherine could hear her own blood coursing through her veins, pounding disturbingly. It was impossible to read or rest in the suffocating cabin, even with the shutters closed against the brazen afternoon sun, but she did not want to go up into the open air of the shaded roof deck. Major Leslie was probably there.

Sharada let herself into Mrs Hill's little cabin and shut the door gently behind her. On the narrow shelf above the bed she set down a glass filled with a murky fluid. The miserable infant arched backward in its mother's arms; its face was distorted, bright red, swollen by rage, its stretched mouth hoarsely screeching. Its tiny fat fists had escaped from its swaddling and were thrashing the air. Young Mrs Hill was crying, too, tears running down her exhausted wan face. Her dress was in disarray, wet with milk, the bodice open as though her engorged breasts had burst it. Both nipples were raw, inflamed; and an alarming patch of red spread across the top of her right breast.

Sharada took the howling baby from Mrs Hill and tucking it over her left arm, bounced it vigorously. Mrs Hill wiped her nose with the back of her hand and said, "It hurts. He is so rough and angry. He howls until I give him the breast, then as soon as the milk comes he will not suckle. And now there is this painful red place, here. What is wrong?" and her tears began again.

Gently Sharada pressed the swollen red place, and Mrs Hill flinched. "Very sore, just there?"

Mrs Hill nodded and cried, wiping her nose. The baby subsided a little; the rough bouncing surprised him perhaps.

"And hot?"

"Oh, yes; and here and here—so painful and sometimes bleeding, I fear."

"Yes, yes. They will become tougher as you continue. And this hot sore place—well, I have brought you some medicine. You must be letting him suckle no matter how it is hurting. That is the best cure. But this medicine will diminish your pain, and it will calm the baby, too." Sharada took two of Mrs Hill's clean cambric handkerchiefs from her trunk and handed her one. Then she twisted one corner of the other and dipped it into the cloudy-looking liquid she had brought; this she put to the infant's mouth. He started, surprised. Then his tongue came out, and Sharada teased it with the wet cloth. He sucked it. "I have sweetened this with cane juice. Otherwise it is very bitter. Look, he is taking it. A little more I will give him. Then you must drink the rest. I will bring more for you in a few hours. There. There, there . . ."

And within thirty minutes, Mrs Hill and her baby were asleep. It was quiet aboard the pinnace at last.

"Just a water of poppy trash, not very strong at all, with some cane juice to make it sweet," explained Sharada to Catherine. "It is calming the baby's bowel, soothing and settling his intestine, for that is what is hurting him. And it will mute Mrs Hill's pain from her sore nipples and from the infection in her breast until that is drained and cured by nursing. It will let them both rest. I gave the baby just a little poppy water from a cloth to get him started. But now he will receive all he needs through his mother's milk."

"How did you know what to do?" asked Catherine. "Do you know about babies?"

"Oh, everyone knows this. It is the same as we do for a cow with a sore udder."

"But how do you happen to have some of this poppy trash about you?"

"But I always have some; it is so very useful! We often put a small amount of poppy into a dish that is especially hot, especially spicy, so that the stomach will not be disturbed. Just a little—not enough to make you sleepy, only for soothing the digestion. Did you not realise?"

Later in the afternoon, after she had heard the door of Major Leslie's cabin open and close, Catherine went up to the roof deck. As she expected, she found only Grace there. Grace was sitting cross-legged on the smooth wide deckboards whittling at something on her lap; a litter of pale greenish chips and curls lay around her.

"What are you doing?" asked Catherine, sinking into a cane-backed chair and spreading her canvaswork across her lap. It was a stifling thing—too heavy and hot. She rooted in the workbag at her side, looking for her needle.

"I am trying to make a sort of a flute from this length of cane," said Grace. "Sharada made one, this other one—isn't it handsome?—and she showed me how to do it. But it is not so easy. It is not so easy to blow it either. You must blow just so. It is all a matter of controlling the breath, Sharada says."

"Well, don't cut off your finger," said Catherine, threading her needle with with gray silk.

"I'm not a baby, Catriona."

"Thank goodness for that. We've babies enough aboard."

"Aye, poor creature. I don't see why people want them. I wonder if I was so horrid as that."

"Surely not yourself, my dear. Let me see that knife, pray."

Grace held it out to her, and Catherine took it and turned it over, recognising it, knowing it. These uncanny apparitions no longer shocked her. "Where did you get it?"

"Sharada."

"Mmm. It is your uncle Sandy's *sgian dubh*, you know. His knife. Someone has sharpened it, however."

"Can you be sure?"

"Certain sure. I gave it to him on our fifteenth birthday." Catherine closed her eyes and let herself drift. Their fifteenth birthday. It was pleasant to remember that, more pleasant than the other thoughts that intruded when she did not want them . . . Mr Fleming. No, not that again. Think of . . . oh, think of Sandy playing his pipes on the hill when they were fifteen, the year he won the piping prize. Won his copy of Joseph MacDonald's *Compleat Theory*. The letter from Mr Fleming was stowed now deep in her trunk. Oh, don't think about that *again*. The letter he had brought to her on the morning of their departure.

Catherine opened her eyes. Featureless riverbank slid past: trees, and faint blue hills rising beyond in the hazy distance to the north. Another village. A ruined temple on a mound undercut and collapsing into the river. A willowy woman carrying a water jar on her head, walking barefoot up the narrow path from the riverbank.

But she knew that letter by heart. It didn't matter how far away from her she put it, how deep in her trunk she buried it.

"Accursed thing!" said Grace. "I've gone and cut the hole too big. My fingers will never grow fat enough to close that."

"Language, Grace. Don't say that."

"Sharada says it."

"Don't *you* say it. Unbecoming."

Grace snorted.

*Dear Mrs MacDonald,*

*I trust that your natural sense of justice will compel you to read this letter, despite the ill opinion you have formed of me. I perceive that you are determined to proceed to Assam, and will not be deterred by anything I can now say. I beg you will be careful of the dangers to be encountered there; and I hope that your usual prudence will serve you, with regard to the officer under whose protection you travel.*

"Ah! Here you are, you two fair ones," said Major Leslie, coming up onto the deck. "And so diligent, too! Pray excuse me for appearing in my white jacket; you must not think it is carelessness or disrespect, but only a practical accommodation to the heat."

"Certainly," said Catherine. "It is nearly as unbearable for us to see you in your scarlet woolen coat as it must be for you to wear it. I suppose your stock and collar will not admit of any relaxation?" For his stock was tightly wound, and his collar was a little too high; its points extended halfway up his long side-whiskers, producing an effect a little like the blinders on a carriage horse.

"You are all consideration, Mrs MacDonald. But I am quite accustomed to it." He settled himself into the other chair and crossed his legs in their tight white uniform breeches. He tapped his fingernail on the arm of his chair for a moment, then said, "Odd that ladies' dresses are so well suited to this tropical climate but so poorly adapted at home, whereas men's clothing is just the opposite—that is, well suited to our cool, rainy climate at home but ill adapted to these tropical latitudes. Curious, isn't it?"

"I suppose so; as though we had sprung from different climates," agreed Catherine.

"A lady's gown is admirably suited for the . . . one must not say 'display'; one might say rather the 'exquisite unconcealment' perhaps . . . of every feminine charm. Still, in cold weather, it leaves those same rosy charms at the mercy of the unmerciful elements—the lovely neck, the round arms, so very exposed. The fabric of the garment itself so thin and light. And the dainty little red satin ribbons there, about the body—"

Red? "They are green," said Catherine, disliking his close inspection of the ribbons under her bosom, and his references to lovely necks, round arms, and thin fabrics.

"Are they? Well, now you know my secret: all my life I have been colour-blind."

And tone-deaf, too, thought Catherine; for more than once she had heard him tunelessly whistling. She knew also—having by now sat down to several weeks' worth of meals at the same table with him—that he was peculiarly insensitive to his food. He could distinguish sweet from sour (and preferred sweet), salt from bitter (and preferred salt); but any subtler flavors were lost on him. In short he was oddly devoid of taste in all respects. His conversation was similarly awkward and ponderous, and she suspected him of preparing remarks in advance. Catherine had thought at first that a shyness prevented his conversing quite freely and naturally with her, yet he did not avoid her company. Quite the contrary; he seemed to seek her out at every opportunity.

He soon launched, as usual, onto the great subject of his shooting and sporting successes, of which he had an apparently inexhaustible stock of stories. Here he was fluent: "Two buffalo were killed in the water by villagers in boats," he declared happily, "and three more on shore by the men of the detachment . . ."

Catherine's attention drifted again:

*I hope that you will find your brother alive and well. He said little about his travels in Assam, but he did on one occasion tell me that he had formed connections with an important family of chieftains in, I believe, the Khasiya Hills, or perhaps in Jyntea or Cachar; and he referred to them as The Princes of Tea Root. Possibly this was only his joke, but I mention it here because even so insignificant a hint as this may be useful to you in your quest.*

*Every word spoken at our last meeting remains seared in my memory; I have been able to think of little else since then.*

Major Leslie was saying, "blood was flowing from the shoulder of the leading one, and I myself fired without any effect. . . ."

Catherine stitched doggedly at her canvaswork—finishing off a length of thread, tying it, then threading her needle again with the gray silk. Under her fingers, a new shape grew. The grayish lump of rock on which the now-russet-haired lady sat was becoming something else entirely. It was no longer a rock. It was becoming a large gray-brown elephant.

"But when I looked along the road in the line of the charge, I perceived it was completely cleared," Major Leslie continued.

Thinking of Mr Fleming's letter made a great heat rush through her, but a heat of what? Anger? Shame? Fear? Remorse, regret.

> *We have terribly misunderstood each other, it seems; and it would be folly to hope that any letter can bridge the gulf which now lies between us. One misconception, however, must be corrected before we part: namely, your supposition that my admiration of you stems from nothing more than a depraved taste for "damaged beauties." Nothing could be further from the truth.*

Oh, do stop thinking of it! Over and over again! she chastised herself. So tired of remembering this.

"The men on foot began beating the bushes under direction of the shikari," Major Leslie said, stroking his mustache.

> *I do recognise, certainly, that you have been hurt, that your spirit has suffered a grievous injury. But just as the iron ore is alloyed in the fiery furnace, then hammered, wrought, quenched, and cooled, to emerge at last as tempered steel, so too may an injured spirit emerge finer than ever from the forge of its ordeals—not only undamaged but tempered, annealed, stronger than before. Certainly it has been thus with you. I do perceive that you are made of a finer, purer metal than any woman I ever knew; and that you are fitted now for any test you may encounter, in this world or the next.*

A heat seemed to radiate off Major Leslie, even warmer than the hot air coming over the water from the hot land. Two red spots flushed his cheeks. His clothes fit him very snugly. He stood—perhaps excited by reciting his own exploits—and strode back and forth as he spoke. Or perhaps he was proud of his height, for tall he certainly was, well above the common height. Yet his shoulders were rather sloping, and not as broad as they looked in his better-tailored and better-padded wool uniform jacket. And then his hips looked curiously wide, rather womanish, in the white uniform breeches.

Such an immodest dress, a man's! A kilt so much handsomer and more modest. And surely more comfortable, more airy. Oh, do think of something else . . .

What if Sandy cannot be found? What if she is too late? Why had she not understood immediately, after meeting Dr Wallich and Dr Carey, that Sandy had gone to Assam? She should have gone directly to Assam, not wasted time making long detours to Patna and Ghazipur. So many regrettable errors, so many wrong turns.

> *And now—now that I have discovered, at last, the finest woman in the world, am I likely, do you think, to plunge her into the ignominy of a degrading connection? Do you indeed consider me capable of this? How have I deserved that you should think so ill of me?*
>
> *If, during the course of your travels, you will do me the justice to reflect upon what you know of me, and upon what you may yet learn of me from others; then, when we meet again (as I trust we shall), it will be upon a better understanding. And you must forgive me if I assert the right, even now, to subscribe myself, dear Mrs MacDonald, your most devoted friend in this world,*
>
> *Pieter Fleming*

It was like pressing a bruise frequently, too frequently, to see if it still hurt. It always still did. And she was troubled to find how little command she had over her own mind.

❧❧❧

MAJOR LESLIE'S PINNACE and baggage boat anchored each evening close to land, either at a safe distance from the eroding undercut bank of a sand island, or along the river shore itself. All the Hindu crew and servants—men, women, and children—would go ashore each evening and bathe, and prepare their evening meal over their cook fires. The Europeans seldom ventured ashore after dark, but as they lay hour after hour in their hot stuffy cabins aboard the pinnace, seeking elusive sleep, they could not help but hear the voices ashore: the laughter, jokes, stories, talk talk talk and often music—singing, drumming, and strange Indian instruments—for hours and hours. There was not much sleeping on those short, hot, dark nights.

Grace wheedled permission from Catherine to go ashore one evening with Sharada; and after that she made it her invariable habit. Soon the people got accustomed to her presence and paid her little attention. This was the way she liked it; she was there amid the talk and the music—listening but invisible. And by now she could understand almost all the talk that ran around her, even some of the jokes and the slang and the country accents and the words of the songs.

The pinnace had made her way down past the familiar place where the Bhagirathi ran off southward toward the sea, and had now achieved at last the great confluence where the waters of the Ganges and of the Brahmaputra met and mingled. Gradually the riverbanks had receded and the boat emerged onto a broad inland sea of murky water, the green forests and the fields hazy or invisible in the distance on either side. In this broad muddy complicated lowlands, many waters met, mingled, then divided again into their various changing shallow channels, to run spreading over the lowlands down to the Bay of Bengal. In this place where waters joined and separated, the essential distinctions between upriver and downriver, between running against the current or with it became indistinct. The current itself was muddled; there were strange, powerful eddies; and mile-long sand islands would pile up overnight in the wide channels, then erode away for no reason.

This night, they had moored alongside a vast high dry sand island planted with ripening watermelons and vigorous sapling trees. Here the crew and servants had eaten their usual fare: tiny fishes netted from the river; eggplants in a spicy sauce; potatoes in another spicy sauce; red lentils, cucumbers and onions in yogurt; a relish of pickled okra; and plenty of sweet watermelon. The cook fires had burned down, and the stars were a dazzling splash across the velvety black sky. The soft sand where Grace lay had cooled at last, and it stuck to her arms in streaks where watermelon juice had run down. Sharada had her musical instruments. A few of the boat wallahs had their instruments, too: a double-ended horizontal drum, and a native fiddle held upright in the lap. Grace liked to lie with the other children just outside the light from the dying fires and hear the singing—sometimes boisterous, sometimes plaintive. Sometimes everyone sang together, a song that everyone knew. Sometimes one person sang alone.

"Come, Miss Grace, I need you to play this," said Sharada, appearing in the warm darkness. She put a tall four-stringed instrument into Grace's lap.

"But I don't know how."

"I will show you. It is not difficult. This is called *tanpura*. Look, you hold it thus, upright against your shoulder. And you pluck the strings thus: slowly, evenly, each in turn, with your other hand. The *tanpura* provides the drone to accompany the melody. I will tune it for you. These two middle strings are my *sa*. Close. Close. Ahh! There. *Saaaaaaaa*. Do you hear? They are perfectly in tune. Now the bass string, this fourth one: *kharaj*. It is an octave lower. Almost . . . there. That is good. Thus far, the same as your three drones on your bagpipes, nay? But here on the first string we add another tone: we want *pa*, between the two. Wait; that is not quite right. Pluck it again; let me hear. Again . . . there! *Paaaa*. That is all. You touch each string in turn, gently, steadily. You make a veil of sound for the background—not a plonking plucking but a steady shimmering veil of sound. Yes, just so. That is good. Play. This man Rajesh will drum. I will sing."

Grace felt nervous and self-conscious at first, but then she stopped thinking about the people looking at her and started listening to the sound of the *tanpura* and the way Sharada's voice sounded, so lithe, in front of the background of sound she was making. She tried to make the sound like a shimmering veil, and after a while it did seem like that, with colours blending like the colours in a rainbow, or like moonlight glowing behind a scrim of mist . . .

The people liked it. They praised Grace, too, after the song ended. More, they clamoured. Sing us another. Sing one of Meerabai's. Do!

Sharada's eyes met Grace's. She leaned over and tuned one of the middle strings just a little. Then she nodded, and Grace began again.

Sharada sang. As she sang her first phrase, there was a sigh of recognition, of appreciation from the people. Ah, yes; this one!

Grace understood the words. This was the meaning of Sharada's song:

*What is my native shore but him?*
*What swims in my heart but his name?*
*My boat, when it breaks*
*Where call I*
*But to him?*

*Time after time,*
*Then again.*

*Let me hide,*
*Meera says,*
*in these folds.*

*The tide of the world*
*comes close.*

Then Sharada borrowed the two-ended drum and launched into another song, accompanying herself as she sang.

*He has left his stain upon me*
*The colour of moonlight he has stained me. . . .*

Singing these words, she lifted her arms and turned them toward the people, showing the pale burn scars. There was a collective intake of breath caused by the sight of the gleaming white scars, and by the sudden silence of the drum. Her voice sang unaccompanied. Then at the last possible moment, the drum spoke again, and the audience sighed its relief as she continued:

*Beating both ends of the earthen drum*
*I sing, sing before the boat people*
*Respectable city dwellers think me mad*
*Mad for the Wily One*
*Raw for my dear bright one*

*Stained the colour of my lord*
*Birth after birth,*
*In country after country, Sharada says,*
*Still I seek him.*

Afterward, the man Rajesh leaned over and whispered into Grace's ear, "Do you understand? Yes? It is another *bhajana* of Meerabai's, a very famous one, but she has changed it. She has inverted it and made it her own song. So clever! So deft! So gracefully done! She is a superb musician, this one."

ꙮ ꙮ ꙮ

ON THE ROOF deck of the pinnace, Catherine heard this distant singing and the cries and applause that followed. Mrs Hill had just gone below to feed her baby again, and only Major Leslie remained on the roof deck with her. "Such a caterwauling they make every night!" said Major Leslie. "And then they do go on so, for hours and hours."

"I like to hear them," said Catherine.

"Do they not disturb your rest, Mrs MacDonald? You have only to say the word, and I shall forbid it."

"No, they do not disturb me in the least," she said. "I quite like to hear their music." She would in fact have liked to go ashore among them, as Grace did; but she knew that this was not possible. Her presence there would change everything.

"Music! You are generous enough to grace that discord with the very word? Most charitable of you, Mrs MacDonald, I declare. But then, you always are so exceedingly gentle, so very mild. It does not surprise me that you are willing to forgive even this primitive wailing, this savage howling at the moon."

"Oh, Major Leslie, do not forget that I am a Scot. This music is no more primitive nor more savage than the old songs that I have heard all my life. We have not all had our tastes formed by listening only to the exquisite strains of a Mozart or the poignant expressions of a Rossini."

And in fact Catherine liked very much to hear this nighttime singing. As she drifted in and out of sleep during these brief stifling nights, it reminded her sometimes of the midnight wakings of her early childhood, all alone in her not-quite-warm bed, and the comfort she derived from hearing distant sounds of singing, talking, peals of laughter, drifting up the lower regions of the big chilly stone house that had been home. Night was the fit and meet time for people to amuse themselves with music, talk, and laughter.

But he said, "I would not have you disturbed for the world, Mrs MacDonald. You cannot conceive, dear Mrs MacDonald, how much your comfort and well-being are of concern to me."

"But I am always quite well and comfortable; and so I daresay is Mrs Hill. Pray do not be concerned with us. It is entirely unwarranted and unnecessary." She said this in the most repressive tone she could muster, and referred to Mrs Hill quite deliberately, for she began now to feel uneasy about the tendency of his tone and meaning.

But he would not be repressed. "Oh, Mrs MacDonald!" he cried. "Dear Mrs MacDonald. So very modest and self-effacing! How shall I express myself? Do I dare? But dare I must. How shall I tell you how I long for the right, the inestimable privilege, of making your comfort and well-being my own legitimate care, my foremost concern, a right with which I may concern myself always? Oh, do not shake your head! Do not turn away from me, dearest Mrs MacDonald! Catherine! Dear Catherine!"

"Major Leslie—"

"Say Henry. Oh, do let me hear it pronounced by those dear lips!"

"Major Leslie! Sir!" said Catherine quite energetically. She succeeded in extricating her hand, which he had seized; and rising from her chair, she put several yards between herself and him—the width of the deck. Here is an unpleasant turn! She uttered the necessary words and phrases: impossible, never, out of the question; and the like. Also such words as liking, esteem, compliment, and gratitude; then repeated impossible and never. She did her best without actually insulting him.

But he was not easily made to understand her meaning. He referred to his prospects, his family, his connections. He gave her to understand the magnanimity of his heart, that he forgave her for her widowhood and her stepdaughter, and that he considered her the sweetest, the gentlest, the mildest, the most deserving of his protection and guidance of all womankind.

If only she could escape without laughing aloud! Herself: sweet, gentle, and mild! If only Hector—or Mr Fleming—could have heard this! Major Leslie had not the slightest understanding of her essential character despite the weeks he had passed in her company. But then, she reminded herself, this was a man who was tone-deaf, colour-blind, and barely able to taste his food. He perceived only that she was female, unmarried, not ugly, and not poor. And British women with such excellent matrimonial qualifications were exceedingly scarce in India. Once more she expressed her meaning, more definitely, and made to leave; but he threw himself onto one knee before her, blocking the little passageway; and seized again her hand.

She struggled to free herself, but then she was grappling against both his hands at her waist.

"Is it the girl?" he was saying hoarsely. "Is it the girl? But she means nothing to me, nothing. She shall be put ashore at the next village! She and the little half-castes!"

"It is dark as a cave; I cannot see a thing!" cried out another voice—Grace's clear high voice.

"Well, wait a moment, then, for me and the lantern. You need not go skipping ahead so very hasty," said Sharada, and the dark shape of her head appeared above the rail.

Major Leslie released Catherine and, rising quickly to his feet, sullenly withdrew. Catherine fled to her cabin, with Sharada and Grace close behind. Without a word Sharada dug into Catherine's trunk and found the full bottle of whisky which had been Captain Mainwaring's gift. She poured a good inch of it into a cup and gave it to Catherine, who was still panting.

"Well?" said Sharada after a few moments.

"Well, what?" said Catherine, and coughed, for it was a very strong whisky.

"That," said Sharada, and gestured with her chin toward the deck they had just fled.

Catherine wiped her eyes, but Sharada was not softened. " 'Would you dismount an elephant to ride on the haunch of an ass?' " she demanded, quoting a line of song.

"What on earth are you talking about?" said Catherine.

"Is it to be him, then?" said Sharada, gesturing again with her chin.

"Him! He is an ass!"

"Ah! We are agreeing, then. I feared perhaps you are not knowing an ass when you are seeing him."

"How dare you!"

"Oh, but I dare a great deal, memsahib. I dare anything. Everything! Just as you do."

Catherine wiped her nose, and sniffed. "For the same undeserving person too."

"Mad for the Wily One," agreed Sharada, and, setting aside Catherine's empty cup, began to help her undress.

"What did you say about dismounting an elephant? I wish I had an elephant," said Catherine.

"But you had, memsahib. Mr Fleming offered to take you up to Assam in his steamship. But no, you are preferring to ride upon the haunch of an ass."

"Impertinent!"

"No, memsahib, most pertinent. In any case I am not talking about boats or asses. I am talking about men."

"Do not talk to me about Mr Fleming."

"As you wish, memsahib," said Sharada, and held up Catherine's nightdress to slip it over her head.

"What did he mean? Did you hear him? What did he mean about a girl and putting her ashore at the next village?" asked Catherine as her head emerged from the garment.

"His *bibi*, of course. And the two little babies. Are you not knowing? All this time you are not knowing? But of course. She is aboard the luggage boat, she and the two little children of which he is the father. She comes of good family, too, but very poor. Oh, the things the memsahibs are choosing not to know!"

"Beastly! Why must they be so beastly, these men?"

"Some are not. My Sikander is not. Your Mr Fleming is not."

"He is not *my* Mr Fleming. And how can you say such a thing? He lives with that woman, that Harini, in his house."

"Surely he has explained to you, memsahib, that there is no sexual congress."

"Am I a fool?" demanded Catherine. But she was shocked at Sharada's frank declaration.

"But it is quite true, you know, memsahib."

"Sharada, how can you possibly assert such a thing?"

"She told me so herself. But she did, memsahib! So she told me that day when we all were going up there in the steamships for the little feast at Mr Fleming's house, and then to the garden of Dr Carey. She lamented to me then that he never would touch her, not though she was bringing to bear upon him all the high arts of seduction, not even though she was begging this favor of him in frank words."

Catherine bridled, scoffing: "I cannot believe she said anything to you of the sort!"

"But so she did nevertheless," insisted Sharada. "Hindu ladies who have rejoiced in ardent husbands are not like the memsahibs, such frightened virgins forever! No indeed! She so bitterly laments her four little children, and she is wanting nothing else in the world but a baby in her arms, to fill their so-painful emptiness. Nothing but that can be giving her solace, and this he knows very well, your Mr Fleming. But he does not and will not, she told me, because she has a husband living still. It is a misconduct, he says, and so he never is gratifying her in this matter."

Could this be true? Certainly there was no baby. Catherine thought about this: A woman who had produced four babies in five years of marriage could very likely produce another with only the slightest . . . encouragement. Presently she said, "I still do not see how this subject could possibly have arisen between you."

"Oh, yes, why speak to me? The poor creature; she is so very lonely, for no one will speak with her. Good Hindus have nothing to do with her; to them she is dead. As for me, I am outcaste, so she and I can be consorting. And she was asking if you are in love with her good Mr F."

"She asked you that!? What did you say to her?"

"I said yes certainly."

"What made you say that?"

"Anyone can see it is true. And as for fearing in Harini a rival, why, there you have no cause. But surely he has told you this himself! Are you not choosing to believe him? Oh, so clever, and still so foolish!"

ꙮ ꙮ ꙮ

THE NIGHT WAS hot, and Catherine lay awake for hours counting over her errors. So many wrong turns! At last she attained a restless, shallow, sweaty sleep. But thunder awakened her before dawn, great claps of it rumbling through her body. Quickly she put on a wrap and went up to the roof deck of the pinnace. They were still anchored next to the big dusty island. Flashes lit up the strange green sky where curtains and veils of rain moved over the distant blue hills to the north, blown like curtains at a window. Then big heavy droplets dimpled the surface of the river—here is one, there is another, here, and here.

The breeze comes, sudden gusts of cool air. Flashes, great thick bolts of lightning, straight down. Ashore, cattle bawl and dogs bark. The sound of heavy droplets slapping leaves. The smell of dust, which has been dry as ashes for six long months. The green light! More rain; the ground wetted, moistened. The teak deck wetted. The surface of the green opaque water dimpling, wrinkling, dappling. Rocks gleaming, dull jasper suddenly glistening bloodred. The dust laid at last.

Then real rain, steady rain.

A chill runs across the skin. Eyes can open wide now to the strange dim yellow sky. A cool wind redoubles the sound of rain, making droplets pelt down from wet leaves as well as from the dark sky.

Wet earth, wet leaves, wet rock—these new smells.

A tiny rivulet appears in a rut, finding its way. The rain softens, lightens. Is it over so soon? No, merely gathering its force; now it is a strong heavy steady downpour. Catherine is drenched, dripping, sodden, and still thunder rolls down the sky, and flashes light it up.

It is here, it is here, it is here, it is here—at last! The long parching is over.

Everything is moving.

Is that steam, rising, blowing?

Smells lying dormant in the dust now rise steaming to the nose.

Her mistakes, her missteps, her detours, her wrong turns, her failures to see and to understand—suddenly Catherine comprehends: These are just what have brought her *here*. These are not errors; these are the route. These are not errors any more than the bends in the river are errors.

She is not damaged; she is whole.

Sharada is singing a monsoon song:

*My lover has gone away*
*to some distant country.*
*Dripping wet in our doorway I stand*
*to see the clouds burst asunder.*
*Sharada says, nothing can harm him;*
*this passion has yet to be quenched.*

# 23

## a Sett of Men approaching an Enemy

"I get to this point," said Grace, "and then I don't know what to do. How to go from here." She was bent over her chessboard, studying and reenacting a game she had recently played with Sharada. Fewer than a dozen pieces remained on the board, and both queens had been captured. "It's the most interesting, and the most difficult. I know what I need to do, but I just cannot see how to do it."

"I know the feeling," said Catherine, looking out the window over the wet roofs of Goalpara. The everlasting canvaswork lay across her lap, but Catherine had no heart for it.

"When I played this game with Sharada, I wanted to resign at this point—my position appeared so hopeless. But she wouldn't let me. She made me play it out to the end."

"And how did it turn out?"

"I forced a draw. But she says I could have won. She says I missed something important, but she will not tell me what it is. I am trying to see it for myself."

They had arrived at last at Goalpara, in Assam. The last four weeks of struggling up the broad swollen Brahmaputra in monsoon rains had been nightmarish. It was without doubt an undertaking for fools and madmen. After Catherine had refused Major Leslie, he had taken to having his *bibi* brought to his cabin quite openly every evening. Catherine had not noticed her before, but she could not help noticing her now, and feeling sorry for her: a pretty girl, though tired looking, for she had an infant and a two year old to look after all day. And she was certainly young—very young! Sharada said that Major Leslie had bought her, at the age of twelve, from her impoverished parents.

It had been a vast relief, when at last the little boats had reached Goalpara, to part with Major Leslie and his little family.

Here in Goalpara, at the lower end of the Assam valley, an hour seldom passed without rain. Mrs Hill's husband, Colonel Hill, was the commanding officer of the station. He had evicted a couple of his subalterns from lodgings to make room for Catherine and Grace, for the town was very full. Many of the soldiers, with only canvas tents for shelter, were extremely wet and uncomfortable, though the camp was on high ground. The forces posted here presently consisted of one regiment of Europeans; four battalions of native soldiers, called sepoys ("two-legs"); a company of native artillery; and a company of native cavalry. Each battalion of five hundred sepoys had its complement of native officers in the dozens, and its European officers, too: a captain, two lieutenants, three ensigns, and one sergeant major. The town, and the high ground surrounding it, was a morass of soldiers and officers, cattle and horses, wagons and cannons, elephants and bullocks, camp followers and hangers-on, merchants, moneylenders, and prostitutes.

There were political deputations in the town, too, coming and going; the deputations were from the various tribal chieftains in the hills of Jyntea and Cachar, Meghalaya and Manipur, and from further afield as well.

One evening, Colonel Hill had explained to Catherine in confusing detail the history of the conflict, but she remained baffled by the convolutions. Apparently a succession dispute had sparked the present hostilities some three or four years ago, and two rival claimants to the ancient Ahom kingdom of Assam, in the heart of the rich Brahmaputra valley, had enlisted support in various quarters. The claimant who had actually succeeded in taking possession of the throne was Chunder Kaunt, who was backed by the king of Burma and supported by Burmese generals and advisors. The immensely rich kingdom of Burma lay beyond the great mountains to the south, and this king of Burma had lately been issuing outrageous demands, threats, and insults to the East India Company. He was also picking off Englishmen—elephant hunters and that ilk—all along their contested border down near the coast, around Chittagong and Arakan. It was perhaps not surprising then that the East India Company took the view that Chunder Kaunt was only a pretender, a puppet of the Burmese king, and that the rightful successor (who had applied to the English for help) was in fact Poorunder Singh. And so the East India Company had succored Poorunder Singh, and allowed firearms and unofficial advisors to go to his aid. Alas, these firearms and advisors had not been sufficient to secure him a victory, and this rightful claimant was routed and the borders between the two forces had become scenes of unspeakable atrocities.

Once seated on the Ahom throne, however, the pretender Chunder Kaunt promptly tired of his high-handed Burmese ministers. So he dismissed them, and assassinated the ones who would not be dismissed. Thereupon, the East India Company revised its view that Rajah Chunder Kaunt was merely a puppet and pretender, and allowed firearms and advisors (the very same advisor, in fact—a Mr Bruce) to go to *his* aid now that *he* attempted to expel the hostile Burmese. For a year or so, the fighting had gone this way and that, with no clear or decisive victory for Rajah Chunder Kaunt; nor for Poorunder Singh (who was indeed still in the running); nor for the Burmese forces from the south.

But then last year the king of Burma had sent to Assam his mightiest general, leading an army of 18,000, who had finally routed Rajah Chunder Kaunt—and took up the cause of Poorunder Singh! Alas, consensus remained elusive, for the East India Company had discerned by this time that its original candidate, Poorunder Singh, had in fact no legitimate claim and was merely a puppet of the Burmese.

The mighty Burmese general and his army soon discovered they could do without Poorunder Singh, too, and installed instead a governor to rule Assam as a province of Burma. Then the general and his army had gone home, leaving some two hundred men to support this new governor; for it was becoming clear that the mighty general and his army would be needed soon along the disputed coastal territories of Arakan and Chittagong.

Thus Assam had been left relatively quiet for the last eight or ten months. Or so it seemed. All the tribal princes in the hills took the opportunity to rearm and negotiate alliances as fast as they could; and certain supply masters in the Honourable Company's forces along the Assam frontier had gotten quite opulent while the supplies, ammunition, and arms for which they were responsible had seemingly evaporated or been lost or spoiled or stolen or simply disappeared.

A very bad business, it seemed to Catherine, when all was explained to her. Despite Mr Fleming's warning, she had somehow failed to fully understand the ugliness of the situation here. But here she was. And now that she had succeeded in getting here, what did she propose to do next? Where was Sandy? How was she to find out? And how was she to get to him, wherever he was? The rain outside was sluicing down, and someone had burned some food nearby; it smelled terrible.

"Aha," said Grace to herself, and moved a pawn.

Sharada scratched at the door and came in. She did not look discouraged at all. She looked pleased, her black eyes glittering. "A letter for you, memsahib," she said, and handed Catherine the letter, dry, from under her shawl.

A letter—here, in this remote fold of the world! It was a handwriting that Catherine did not recognise, but certainly a woman's hand. She opened the letter, and glanced first at the signature; but it was an unfamiliar name. As she read, however, she realised who it was:

*Weiking House*
*The Gold smiths bazaar*
*28th June 1823*

*My dear Mrs MacDonald,*

*I cannot express my delight in learning that you are actually here, in Goalpara! I would call upon you instantly, only that my confinement has been so recent, that I am not yet permitted to go out, and therefore I beg you will do me the favour of calling, just as soon as you are able,*

*upon your most devoted friend,*
*Mrs Maria Babcock*

*ps: It is a daughter, and I have named her Constantia, just as I said I would. Surely you remember.*

*pps: My lodgings are behind the bazaar. Your servant knows the place.*

Sharada watched Catherine's face as she read, watched as the understanding dawned there. "But it's Mrs Todd! How astonishing!" cried Catherine at last. "Wherever did you come across her?"

"I was as astonished as yourself, memsahib, when I chanced to be catching the sight of a perfectly black and shining face at the market this morning. It was of course our friend Anibaddh, who took me back to her mistress and the baby. It is a fat pink strong girl, the poor creature, born only a few weeks ago. But no father, alas, for the poor little infant! For Lieutenant Babcock took fever and died a month before the birth, and Mrs Babcock is left a widow yet again, and the poor infant born an orphan."

ꕥ ꕥ ꕥ

"So very good of you to come to me!" cried Mrs Babcock and wiped away her tears. "But you were ever kind. Oh, dear, I seem to have been crying a great deal lately. You must forgive me. But I have had such sorrows . . . not that there have not been joys as well. Oh, dear! It is only that I am so happy, and—and—astonished to see the face of a friend once again, and in such a place as this, and after all I have been through."

Anibaddh brought in the infant to be admired: a bald waxy grub with a face like a pink potato. "Oh, she will be a beauty," said Catherine. "One can see it already. Constantia, a lovely name." Anibaddh seemed even more statuesque than when Catherine had seen her last in Calcutta, and in response to Catherine's inquiry she flashed her bright smile and declared herself very well.

"I think *she* is very well and happy," said Mrs Babcock when Anibaddh had taken the baby away again. "I know it is selfish of me, but I cannot help feeling a little angry with her. I fear she is about to leave me, to be married."

"Married! Here! To whom?"

"It is the son—no, no, the nephew, I believe, so very difficult to understand the families of these people—the nephew of one of the important native chieftains, who has been here in the town on political business these last two months. He *is* very handsome! And he declares that she is a goddess, Kali herself, the finest woman he has ever seen. Imagine that! My black maid! They would make a handsome couple, it cannot be denied, and I suppose it would be a very good match for her, for he is of an eminent family, as these things go among the natives. How they manage to talk to each other I do not know. But I suppose it must be settled soon one way or another, for his people are soon to leave the town and go back to their hills. I have begged her not to leave me alone here. But—love! Who can defy it? He was so very good to me, my dear Babcock! And this time, you know," she added in a whisper, "I am a genuine widow, an actual respectable widow. Ah, me! Are hearts made for this, to be so twisted and wracked? But you, Mrs MacDonald . . . well. I shall have them bring us some tea. No, no, you must stay and talk to me. Do not dream of running away so soon. We have been through too much together for a mere formal visit of a quarter of an hour. Now, tell me, how in the world have you washed up on this particular shore?"

And so Catherine told Mrs Babcock a version of her story, omitting the most personal aspects.

But Mrs Babcock immediately inquired, "But what of Mr Fleming? I cannot understand how he has let you make your way up into this wilderness to seek your brother all alone when he has those marvelous steamships at his disposal. Oh, do not tell me, Mrs MacDonald, that you have quarreled with him!"

"Oh, no, not to say, exactly, *quarreled*. . . ." said Catherine. But she corrected herself: "Oh, aye, I suppose we have quarreled, in honest truth. It was about—oh, it was quite foolish. I cannot explain it."

"That is a great pity," said Mrs Babcock decidedly. "He is a good man, and he held you in the highest regard—anyone of judgment would, of course—but it was always your company in particular he sought out. Your tastes and interests were so very compatible—oh, music and books and those clever bluestocking sorts of things. I would have been terrified, myself, to try to say anything intelligent to him, but your conversation suited him very well. And not just your conversation. Anyone could see, it was just your own self entirely which he admired so."

"Oh, no, I daresay not—I never noticed anything particular in his conduct," protested Catherine.

"Do you mean that you two quarreled, and parted, without his even declaring himself?"

"Oh, Mrs Babcock, you must excuse me if I cannot discuss any private communications I have had with Mr Fleming."

"I beg your pardon! One must not pry. I suppose he did declare himself then. But there I go again! A thousand pardons! Here, let me refill your cup. It is dreadful tea, but a great luxury nevertheless here in this remote wilderness. My dear Babcock went to I don't know what lengths to get it for me. Now I promise to say nothing more of Mr Fleming. The important thing is that here you sit before me, in the very flesh, and your poor dear lost brother is actually alive after all!"

"Or so I am determined to believe," said Catherine, draining her cup—it *was* poor, stemmy stuff. "And here I am, undoubtedly, but I have no idea what to do next or where I am to look for my brother. I cannot get even so much as a map of the district. I have only the faintest idea where we are, or where anything else is. Apparently all the maps and surveys are closely guarded secrets during so dangerous a time as this."

"Oh, but I can give you maps and surveys," said Mrs Babcock. "Indeed, there is a chest full of them which I have not had the heart to go through. Oh, yes, for my dear, dear Babcock was a surveyor. No one has come for them yet. Let us have them brought."

Anibaddh and Sharada carried in the heavy wooden chest between them. But what of its stout padlock? A search through Lieutenant Babcock's effects turned up no keys, although carefully wrapped in silk and put away with his uniform saber was a handsome watch, the sight of which reduced poor Mrs Babcock to tears once again, for it had been her wedding present to him. But she bravely composed herself after a few minutes and returned to the matter at hand. "There is nothing for it then but to smash the lock," she said, still blotting her nose with her wet handkerchief.

"Oh, no, we mustn't," said Catherine.

"We must, and we shall," said Mrs Babcock.

But the padlock proved very robust. Even Anibaddh's vigorously bashing it with the poker had no effect. "I send for the blacksmith?" Anibaddh said at last, breathless. "Maybe he can cut it off."

"I can be removing it, I think," said Sharada. And turning away modestly for a moment to reach under her petticoat, she brought out an ugly thing: a large pistol, of dull steel.

"Where in the world did you get that?" demanded Catherine. "Do you mean to say that you carry such a thing about you, upon your person?"

"I purchased it at Monghyr when we were stopping and waiting for the forging and repairing of the steamship," said Sharada calmly. "Very good firearms are made at Monghyr. It is the place of all places for buying steels and arms of every kind. A lady is perhaps needing such a thing at some time. But I am not quite knowing how to use it." She peered doubtfully up its long barrel.

"Don't!" cried Catherine, and snatched it away from her.

"I think you just point it, like that, and then you pull that trigger underneath," suggested Anibaddh. "It's loaded?"

"Yes, I was watching the merchant inserting the powder and the ball," said Sharada. "He was demonstrating to me just how that is done. But it may have fallen out perhaps?"

Gingerly, Catherine examined the hammer and the copper percussion cap. "It appears to be loaded, and there is the cap to make it fire," she said. "But I cannot be certain whether it is properly charged. It may indeed fire, if it has not got too damp in all this time."

"But how do *you* know about guns, Mrs MacDonald?" asked Mrs Babcock.

"Was it all for nothing, the rising from my warm bed all those frosty autumn mornings to go with my brothers after the red deer and the grouse, and reloading for them, my fingers stiff with cold? But never to this day have I shot anything myself. Stand well back, and put your fingers in your ears. The ball may go through the floor. There is no one downstairs, I trust?"

"Only a basement, and no one is there," said Mrs Babcock. "But I do hope it will not wake the baby."

Holding the pistol in both hands at arm's length, Catherine took aim, and wished her arms were longer. The others put their fingers in their ears, and shut their eyes for good measure.

Slowly, slowly, Catherine squeezed the trigger, more than half expecting that nothing would happen. And then the pistol fired. The detonation was a shock, and Catherine's hands and arms and chest and eardrums felt the impact.

Anibaddh was the first to come forward; she fingered the lock on the chest. Alas, the lock itself still hung intact, but then she saw that the plate to which the hasp was fastened was loose, and the wood to which it had been solidly bolted was now shattered. She wrenched it free, and Mrs Babcock came forward and opened the chest.

They all peered in, and a swarm of white ants came teeming, boiling up from inside. "Oh! Oh!" cried Mrs Babcock. "The horrid, disgusting creatures! What is to be done?" The ants poured over the side like infantry at the charge.

"The window!" said Catherine, and threw it open. Sharada and Anibaddh lifted the chest by its handles and tumbled it out onto the wet stone pavement below. It spilled its contents across the narrow street and into the running gutter in the middle of the passage: a shredded mass of dirty frass and litter, for the ants during four or five undisturbed weeks had consumed much of the paper, and built a Rome amid the rest.

Sharada and Anibaddh went down to save what might be saved, and Mrs Babcock went to her baby, who had indeed been wakened by the commotion. Catherine was left alone in Mrs Babcock's little sitting room overlooking the street.

The street was only just wide enough to permit the passage of a moderate-size elephant. Catherine was able to determine this because a moderate-size elephant came along and, obedient to the orders of its mahout, came to a stop just outside the window, its pink and gray spotted ears slowly flapping. The man mounted on the elephant's back—not the barefoot mahout astride its neck but the great man riding in dignity upon the elaborate howdah strapped to the elephant's back—was higher than the window itself. There were half a dozen attendants, too, following behind on foot.

Catherine had never looked an elephant in the face before. Its eye looked at her, and blinked. The elephant had long curved eyelashes.

"What are you doing, you beautiful Unbound One?" said the great man on the howdah, in English.

Anibaddh drew herself up—very straight, very supple—and said, "Good day, Prince Teerut. I'm looking for maps of those hills of yours. A lady upstairs, she want to go there."

"My men shall search, Unbound One," he said, and his attendants came forward at his gesture.

"Never mind; ain't a thing worth saving," said Anibaddh. "It's all just dirt. Where are you going on your elephant?"

"I am going here, to seek you. My uncle's business in this city is finished. He prepares to return to our braw high lands in the Abode of Clouds and Mist. But my own business, it is not finished. I cannot go with him. I cannot go away from you. I am coming here to beseech you, that you will return with me. That great noble family which has no daughter—which yearns for a daughter—they will adopt you, Unbound One, as their own daughter, and then we can be married, you and I."

Anibaddh looked at him for a long time, her hands on her hips. "Well, Prince," she said at last, "I don't care to talk about it in a loud voice, out in the street. Please get on down and come out of the rain."

Catherine watched as an attendant carrying an ornate ladder hurried forward and planted it against the elephant's side, and the great man climbed down. Another attendant held a marigold-coloured silk umbrella over the great man's head. It was hard to judge his age; he might be in his twenties. He was of Anibaddh's height, with fine skin the colour of milky tea. His features were regular and handsome, though foreign, resembling slightly the Chinese men whom Catherine had seen in Calcutta, and his hair and mustache were of the glossiest black. His body was well formed, with flat belly and broad chest, and his tunic and loose trousers were made of a shimmering pale golden silk. He wore several gold rings set with large gems. Could they really be rubies, diamonds, and emeralds, of such a size?

There was nothing bashful in Anibaddh. She drew herself up and returned his gaze. She, too, Catherine realised, was beautifully formed, fully as feminine as the indecent stone carvings of goddesses which adorned the native temples in this city. Her only ornament was a thick gold bracelet on her left wrist. They did not touch each other, nor speak. They only looked at each other.

Finally Anibaddh said, "My lady with the baby, she beg me not to leave her here all alone."

"You shall bring them with you. You shall bring as many attendants as you please. You and all your ladies shall ride on elephants."

Anibaddh laughed; and the elephant flapped its pink-spotted ears again at the sound.

❧❧❧

"I AM GOING with Anibaddh," said Sharada later to Catherine when they were back in their own gloomy damp rooms again. Sharada smoothed the cloth over the table and laid out the cutlery for Catherine's dinner. "First we are traveling upon boats up to Gowahati. That is ninety miles from here, up the Brahmaputra River. Thence we are going overland, on elephants and oxen, southward, up into the Khasiya Hills, into the high lands, up to the lakes and waterfalls and the piney forests of Meghalaya."

Catherine maintained her stony silence.

"You come too, memsahib, you and Miss Grace," said Sharada, and uncovered a dish of stewed fish cooked with eggplant and some kind of succulent greens. "We all can go. He is of important family, this Prince Teerut, and he offers to be carrying us all."

"But how utterly absurd!" Catherine burst out. "It is out of the question that we should do so preposterous a thing as that. Only imagine explaining such a plan to Colonel Hill! It is so foolish, so reckless, so—so exceedingly imprudent. And as for you, have you the slightest reason to expect you will find Sandy there rather than anywhere else in this wilderness, this trackless jungle?"

"Yes, memsahib, I have reason. I am feeling his presence there."

"Oh, *feeling* his *presence*!"

"Certainly, memsahib. When Mr Fleming comes into the same room with you, do you not feel in your flesh that he is there? You feel, I am sure of it. So you know in your own body what I am telling. I can feel Sikander's nearness in my flesh. I can feel where he is. There is a heat in my flesh on that side of me where he is, like feeling the heat of the sun falling on that side of my body which is turned toward the sun. It is the same thing."

Catherine snorted, and Sharada went out of the room, closing the door rather more decidedly than was necessary.

The dish of fish and eggplant was spicy, but Catherine was becoming accustomed to spiciness. Was there poppy in it? Possibly; but it was delicious, and she was hungry. And what was this strange vegetable? Not so different from sea-tangle.

Heat in her flesh! What unseemly language! And from a widow! Let glowing coals cool, banked in their own ash.

If only they would cool.

Could she indeed feel Mr Fleming's presence in a room? she asked herself. Aye, in truth she had felt it. She had always been uncomfortably aware of it, like a pressure of air, making it a little more difficult to breathe, to draw a deep and easy breath. She could feel him even now, perhaps, behind her. Far away, back down the river, behind her, between her shoulder blades. She looked up at the window to orient herself: yes, she was indeed facing more or less eastward. And she had left him more or less behind her, to the west. But by now, must he not have passed back down the river again, and have passed already through Calcutta? By now, surely, he and Hector had set out in the twin steamships across the Bay of Bengal, making for Canton with their cargo of opium. Her shoulder blades might be mistaken, must be mistaken. And so Sharada might easily be mistaken, too.

But Anibaddh's Khasi prince—speaking remarkably good English, and where had he learned that, pray? and with a dash of Scots in it, for surely he had said "braw highlands"—this Prince Teerut had offered to bring them all, as the attendants of his bride, as her maids and matrons of honour. As Anibaddh's servants, in fact. To bring them all into Meghalaya, to the Abode of Clouds and Mist.

Had she any other way to go there? Any prospect but this?

Was she still utterly determined to go there? Still certain of finding Sandy?

Catherine wiped up the sauce from her plate with a morsel of flat soft bread dotted with white seeds. There was another thing to be considered, a curious and troubling thing which Sharada did not know. The curious thing was this: Mr Fleming had referred in his letter—*that* letter, engraved in her memory—to Sandy's associates in Assam, The Princes of Tea Root. Was that a joke of Sandy's? Was it only a misunderstanding, a mishearing, on Mr Fleming's part? Was it merely a coincidence, only another trick of the gods, that this sounded so like Prince Teerut?

Grace's chessboard stood at the far end of the table, the pieces left as the battle had ended. The white king stood checkmated by the black queen. That is odd, thought Catherine; both queens had been captured already when she had seen the board earlier. How had this happened? When Grace came in, she asked her.

"Aye, and so blind of me not to have seen it sooner!" said Grace, helping herself to the last piece of flatbread. "But now I will never forget. I had only to get my pawn to the far edge of the board—a matter of only a few moves, and no way for white to stop me. Once queened, then, my new black queen had the white king in checkmate in a matter of one more move."

From black pawn to black queen. Now she is puissant; she can go everywhere. She carries everything before her.

WELL, HERE AM I, arrived at the far edge of the board, at the very edge of the world, thought Catherine later as she lay in bed beside Grace. And now who will queen me? The rain had stopped, the clouds had blown away; and now moonlight poured across the roofs of the city, quite as heavy and liquid as the rain. Sharada had packed up her own belongings—her two chests of musical instruments, books, and papers—and carried them away to the house behind the Goldsmiths Bazaar, to be ready for the morning departure, and to help Mrs Babcock pack what she and the infant Constantia would need on the journey into Meghalaya.

"We must go, too, Catriona, you and I," said Grace's voice.

"I didn't know you were awake," said Catherine.

"The moonlight wakened me, glaring in my eyes. But we ought to go. I feel certain of it."

"I don't feel certain of anything. I have never felt so uncertain in my life. The heart has gone out of me. I feel all adrift, in a small boat, in a blind mist."

"How else are we to make our way? In any case, I should like so much to ride again upon an elephant. I do like elephants. In *chaturanga*, you know, Indian chess, the bishops are elephants. Otherwise, what? Shall we just wait here until Mr Fleming comes to fetch us away again?"

"Certainly not; what are you talking about? Why should Mr Fleming come here?"

"Sharada says he will come. When I have to choose between two moves at chess—and I cannot see very far ahead, you know, in the game—I have made a compact with myself always to choose the boldest move, or the one I have not tried before. Before, when I was timid, afraid to move, I used to lose."

"Chess is only a game. Even if you make a foolish move, you lose only a game."

"But Mrs Babcock is going."

"Oh, Mrs Babcock, the paragon of good judgment!"

"What do you suppose we may lose if we go with them?"

Catherine did not answer, but she thought, we may lose everything. All. Ourselves. Our lives. We may be lost forever.

"Well?" insisted Grace.

"Be quiet, you. I am trying to think."

Grace turned over again with a deep exasperated sigh, and pulled the sheet over her face to keep the moonlight out of her eyes. Soon she slept.

But Catherine could not sleep. She was thinking about Mr Fleming. About that feeling in her body about where he was. He was coming here. Sharada said he would come. Perhaps in several months, in October or November, after his voyage to China, he would come.

What would he find when he arrived here? Would he find herself, timid, paralyzed, unnerved; sitting, waiting, too frightened at last to proceed any further on her quest? And would she then allow herself to be rescued by him from this place, rescued from her dead-end failed search, taken back down to the well-traveled river routes, back down into the populated cities?

But if he did not find her here? If he arrived here and found only that she eluded him still, retreated before him still, disappeared into the unmapped highlands, the *terra incognita* of Meghalaya, what then?

How far would he follow? How long would he seek her? How far would he pursue her beyond this edge of the world?

What becomes of those who flee their own happiness?

It was a long time before Catherine slept. But she did at last; and when she awoke again before dawn, it was with music streaming through her head. The music was "Sandy's Tune," "Not Yet Drown'd." She rose from her bed and packed her scant belongings into her trunk once again, for another journey.

# 24

## *To play amidst Rocks, Hills, Valleys, & Coves where Ecchoes rebounded*

Prince Teerut had procured a couple of European-style officers' tents for his bride and her attendants so they would feel comfortable on the journey up into his highlands. He and his important uncle, the Hima Syiem, had obtained a great many other European-style things, too, in Goalpara—things whose long, awkward shapes were well wrapped in canvas and oilcloth, to keep them dry despite the frequent downpours. These precious swaddled objects were unloaded first from the boats after each day's passage upriver toward Gowahati, and a special guard was set over them each night.

The infant Constantia was kept well swaddled, too. She seldom cried during the daylight hours; she usually slept while they were traveling. Sharada said it was because she was so constantly rocked by the motion of the boat, bucking upriver against the heavy monsoon current. But Constantia wailed at night, when all was still, until Sharada rigged up a sort of hammock which could be slung from the tent poles and swung by a cord, like a punkah. Vigorous rocking soothed her. "She will be wandering, all her life, this one," predicted Sharada. "She must always be moving."

"Like yourself," said Catherine.

"And yourself," replied Sharada.

"Alas! Not by choice," said Catherine.

"Fate or choice—who can be telling any difference?" said Sharada. She opened the brass-bound chest that contained her belongings and unwrapped a gorgeous native violin—shaped and painted like a peacock—and its stout bow, resembling a shallow hunting bow, strung with a broad band of horsehair. "Music this evening, because it is for once not raining. Mrs Babcock will bring a mat to be spreading on the ground. You, memsahib and Grace, please are bringing cushions for Anibaddh and yourselves? The cushions from the tents."

The cushions from the tents were stuffed with sweet dry grass. Catherine and Grace arranged them on a bamboo mat which Mrs Babcock had rolled out like a carpet under a canopy set up for them by Teerut's servants. They set the best cushion, the one with the silk cover and the silver and gold embroidery, upon a little platform in the middle, for Anibaddh, and they arranged the others around it, lower, for themselves.

The fire was burning well, considering how wet everything was. This camp was in a sandy clearing not far from the vast Brahmaputra, on a spit of land at a confluence where a smaller tributary tumbled down from the hills. Tall thickets of elephant grass and bamboos, twice as high as a man, stood like walls around the clearing. There were no villages of any size nearby. The footprints of a large tiger had been seen in the mud at the river's edge, and the uneasy guards drew in a little closer to the fire as evening fell, for tigers were sometimes amazingly bold.

Teerut's servants had set up another canopy for him and his uncle on the opposite side of the fire, and a comfortable place had been made for the musicians as well; so there were three little pavilions arranged around the fire.

"I'd rather midges any day," said Grace to Catherine, slapping at a mosquito.

"They mean no harm—only kissing you," said Sharada. "Come, Miss Grace, will you play *tanpura* for us? Go fetch it, pray; it is in my big brass-bound chest in the tent." Grace did as she was bidden.

Someone had set out several bowls of betel nuts to make *paan* later, when the time should arrive for refreshments; and had strewn flowers all over the mats in each of the pavilions. The flowers were orchids, Catherine noticed, the exquisite spotted orchids which trailed in extravagant cascades all through the towering trees gracing the banks of this vast river. There was a generous scattering of the crimson flowers which littered the ground under every tall silk-cotton tree, too. On impulse

Catherine tucked a cluster of small pale violet orchids into the ribbon at her bodice. Incense burned in brass braziers set all about, sending up thin scented plumes of smoke to discourage the mosquitoes. The smoke mingled with the thick-bodied mist, which lifted and drifted and descended at random.

The musicians settled themselves. Prince Teerut sat opposite, with his venerable uncle, the Syiem. Mrs Babcock settled onto her cushion on the other side of Anibaddh with baby Constantia in her arms. The musicians tuned their instruments painstakingly, taking their time. They had all the time in the world.

Grace seemed perfectly at home among them as Sharada helped her tune the *tanpura*. Then they began to play. Sharada's *taus* had a most beautiful voice, its tone celestial, thought Catherine. Not woody or reedy like an Italian violin, but more like an exquisite ringing human voice, thanks perhaps to its metal strings. How would a harp sound if its strings were bowed, not plucked? What would Hector have made of this sound? She let herself be carried upon this music, letting it hold her up—as the broad river carried their boats each day. Watching Sharada's hands at play, she let herself think of Mr Fleming. His hands. The square, broad nails of his fingers. The shape of his knuckles. His hands, that first time he had given her tea aboard *Increase* so long ago, holding the kettle, tipping it, pouring steaming water into the little Chinese teacups and the teapot, overflowing them. Water, overflowing. Music, overflowing. Rivers, boats, cups, petals, water, hands. . . .

Prince Teerut sent a servant with a tray of refreshments to the ladies' pavilion: a little flask of rice wine and several onyx cups. The servant, a handsome boy, bowed low, then knelt before Anibaddh to serve her. He poured wine into one small cup and offered it to her. Anibaddh took it and drank the wine, slowly, with her eyes closed. Then she looked across the smoky fire and, meeting her prince's eyes, she smiled bashfully. She put her hands together over her heart in the Indian gesture of *namaste*, as Sharada had taught her, and bowed to him. He returned the *namaste*, and Catherine thought (though it was hard to tell, for the heat of the fire between them distorted him, made waves of him) that he, too, smiled. The handsome boy then filled the other two cups for Catherine and Mrs Babcock, and went away again. The rice wine tasted of yeast. The onyx cup was polished smooth, pleasant against the lip, and a delightful shape and weight in the hand.

"I wish I had something tasty to send back across to him," whispered Anibaddh to Catherine. "Don't we have any little thing at all from us womenfolk?"

Catherine thought. Then she whispered, "I have in my trunk some whisky given me by Captain Mainwaring. Would that do?"

"Oh, yes, ma'am. Do you mind?"

"Not in the least. Shall I bring it on a tray?"

"That's so kind of you, Mrs MacDonald, ma'am. And you take it across to him? Here, you can use this tray."

This Catherine did. To be a lady-in-waiting to the Black Queen was an honour, she reminded herself as she washed the little wine flask and the cups at the river. Then she dried them carefully with a clean towel. She opened her trunk, in the dark corner of the ladies' tent. Here was her canvaswork, beginning to smell rather damp, too. There was the male figure, the man with his spaniel, smiling upon the russet-haired lady who was mounted now upon an elephant. It struck her sharply that the man resembled Mr Fleming. Had he always?

She could hear the music still: Sharada's lovely open-hearted singing voice. She pushed aside the canvaswork and dug deeper. Here was the bottle of whisky. She held it up, letting the day's last light from the doorway of the tent shine through it—the colour of amber, the colour of tea. A bottle of home, she thought: home water, home peat, home barley, all distilled down to this concentrate and carried all this long way in this thick glass bottle. She opened it, smelled it. It smelled of Scotland. It smelled of men. The true contraband *goût*! She filled the little ceramic flask, then put her bottle away. She arranged the flask and cups on the tray, and added the spray of pale orchids from her dress as a grace note.

Sharada's trunk stood open, too. Grace perhaps had forgotten to close it when she had come for the *tanpura*. Everything inside was wrapped in lengths of cotton or silk cloth, a jumble of colourful, strangely shaped bundles, alluring in their mystery. Catherine knew that Sharada had musical instruments, and probably some books. And surely, somewhere amidst it all, was that precious portrait of herself and Sandy.

The venerable old Syiem had retired to his tent by the time Catherine returned. Only Teerut and his people remained in his pavilion. Catherine bowed to Prince Teerut, and knelt down (as gracefully as Sharada would have done, she hoped) to set down the tray and pour a dram of whisky into one of the onyx cups. Then she held up the tray, offering it to him. He took the cup, and drained it. She could see that it astonished him and made his eyes water. He cracked a grin in spite of himself, and she smiled back. Here was a man whose sense of dignity did not prevent his laughing, even at himself! This was an excellent quality in a man.

"What is called, memsahib, please?" he asked.

"Whisky," she told him. "Or rather, *uisge baugh*. It means the water of life."

"No, no, memsahib. Yourself the name, please?"

"Oh! I am Catherine MacDonald," she said. "Sir," she added, wondering what the proper form of address might be for a Khasi prince. Ought she to say, Your Highness?

"Please you will fill cup again," he said. "And fill two; you drink with me." Catherine filled two cups. "Water of Life, memsahib Ka taryng!" he said, and drank it; and Catherine did the same. Mild as mothers' milk; but it caught at her throat and made her cough just a little.

But suddenly Teerut's face changed, his dark eyes focusing on something behind Catherine. Catherine turned and saw behind the musicians' pavilion a rhinoceros not fifty feet off, far too close, an enormous male. It had emerged from the wall of tall grass surrounding their camp. The musicians stilled their instruments, hands laid across strings and resonators. The drifting mist made a pale scrim between them and the sullen, suspicious animal. Its funnel-like ears swiveled, and its heavy head swung ponderously from side to side as if mounted on a hinge. It peered about with small rheumy eyes as it snuffed the air. The guard posted nearest to it silently fitted an arrow to his bow. But an arrow against so armoured a beast would be no more than a mosquito; nor would a well-aimed ball from a rifle have much more effect. The rhino looked nearsighted and foul tempered.

There was only the sound of the river chuckling over its rocks; and the labored breathing of the rhino. Then it exhaled—a sound like a steam engine venting pressure—suddenly turned on its haunches, and as quick and nimble as a warhorse at the *volte* it galloped a few steps forward toward the ladies' tents, their canvas forms looming in the mist. No one breathed. The rhino stopped again, uncertain, and peered about once more, ears swiveling.

Constantia wailed.

The beast's heavy head swung toward the sound, and again it changed direction and ran a few steps toward them . . . and stopped. Catherine felt frozen in horror and impotence; mired in nightmarish helplessness.

Then Sharada moved, a fluid movement both quick and slow. In one smooth sweep she laid down her *taus* and raised the bow before her while fitting something small and dark—a betel nut from the bowl beside her—against its band of horsehair, as though it were a bow for archery, not music. She drew back the string near her eye, and let fly her missile into the tall grass not a dozen feet beyond the rhino. The betel nut whispered into the dense clump, and the sullen brute spun about once more to glare suspiciously at the sound. Quickly Sharada let fly a second nut at the same spot. Then the guards, understanding the tactic, let fly their arrows, too—not at the beast but rustling into the grass behind it—a tempting diversion. The rhino looked about one last time, then, irritably switching its thin whip tail, trotted lightly back into the wall of grass, as it had come. The grasses closed like a curtain behind it, as though it had never been there at all.

ꕥ ꕥ ꕥ

THEY REACHED THE city of Gowahati on the thirteenth day, and left it behind on the fourteenth. The women and their trunks and chests, as well as the precious canvas-wrapped long objects and a great quantity of other goods and supplies, were all loaded upon carts and wagons to make their way up to the place where the elephants awaited them, in the hills outside the city. There were eight wagons altogether, and seven of them were drawn by bullocks. But the eighth one, the one which carried the women, was drawn by a horse, an ugly hammer-headed spavined gelding with a clouded blue eye. The driver was a very thin man with a frequent cough, and arms hardly thicker than the frayed reins of the horse's bridle. Neither man nor horse looked fit for work.

Catherine offered the driver an orange from the supplies which had been loaded onto this wagon with her and the other women, but he frowned and shook his head at her. Catherine took this for a refusal, and wondered whether he considered the orange sullied, polluted by her outcaste touch. She peeled it herself, and shared it with Sharada, who sat beside her. Catherine relished each segment, bursting with sweet delicious juice. She marveled at the towering leafy forest through which the narrow rough track wound, up the flank of a long, steep hillside outside of the city. The vast trees were teak, Sharada told her. A ship's worth of timber in each tree, or so it appeared to Catherine. A great fleet of ships grew upon this hill.

The horse was not fast, but he was not so slow as the plodding bullocks hitched to the other wagons, and gradually they drew ahead of the others. Catherine could hear Sharada singing quietly to herself, under her breath. Sharada sang all the time, these days. She seemed untroubled by any doubts about anything.

Catherine heard a faint humming, too, a little like the buzzing sympathetic strings of a sitar, a buzzing drone from some unseen source. Then the horse kicked, and the wagon lurched. Grace cried out; and the faint humming erupted into a buzzing swarm of angry hornets—for the horse had stepped squarely upon the opening of their nest in the ground.

The horse kicked several times, shattering the dashboard at the front of the wagon, then burst into a ponderous gallop, urged on by the driver's whip and shouts, for the man's bare arms were suddenly studded with angry stinging hornets. The women on the wagon hung on and batted at the insects, but their best defense was to wrap themselves in their shawls.

The hornets did not pursue them very far. The wagon crested a small rise at a tremendous pace, and gradually the hornets fell away behind them. But the horse was at full gallop now, and did not slow even for a bend in the road. The wagon swung perilously to the left, where the ground dropped away steeply into the forest below.

"Stop! Stop!" cried Catherine, and Sharada was shouting something, too, at the driver, who was hauling on the reins, the inadequate sinews of his thin arms standing out. "Tell him to stop the horse!" Catherine cried to Sharada.

"The horse does not stop; the hornets have stung it!" said Sharada. In fact Catherine could see a few hornets still clinging to the horse's haunches just above and below the breeching; if the horse would sit back against it, the breeching would function as a brake.

"Is there no drag?" cried Catherine. There was a hand lever for the drag brake, but the driver had no hand to spare for it. Anibaddh climbed forward and seized the handle, throwing all her weight onto it, but the wooden brake shoe was worn to nothing and only clattered uselessly against the rim of the wheel.

The track steepened here, still downhill, then disappeared ahead, around another right turn. The ground fell away steeply to the left; to the right it rose in a solid rock wall. The driver was now sawing at the reins with all his strength, but the horse threw up his head and showed no inclination to slow. Then the frayed right rein snapped. The horse's head bent hard around to the left, unbalanced by the remaining left rein, and he lurched perilously. Which was the horse's blind eye? Catherine could not to remember. Ahead, the right turn was much closer now. At this speed, could they make that turn? Could the horse see it? What lay beyond?

The horse stumbled, and for a moment Catherine was sure he would fall. But somehow he recovered himself, getting his legs under him again, staggering. Certainly he lacked the strength now to stop the heavy wagon.

Catherine saw Grace's pale, horrified face. Grace had suffered this before. This could not be permitted to happen again. Not this.

"Your pistol!" Catherine shouted, seizing Sharada by the arm.

"What? What?"

"Your pistol! Give it to me!" cried Catherine, shaking her, and Sharada hiked up her skirt to her thighs, modesty forgotten. There was the ugly heavy gun, snugged safe in a cloth pocket gartered against her leg. "It is loaded, with proper powder and ball," Sharada said, tearing it free and handing it to Catherine, "I think."

"I pray that it is," whispered Catherine to herself. With the heavy pistol in her left hand, she scrambled forward, up onto the driver's seat, then forward more, till she was lying against the shattered dashboard. Sharada clung to her legs to keep her from pitching out. The horse's tail lashed her face, and its sweating straining hindquarters and hind legs flashed before her, below her.

"No! no!" cried the driver, seeing what she held, and she felt him plucking at her shoulder, or perhaps weakly kicking at her. Where should she aim? The brute's head? Too far away, and moving too rapidly; what if she should miss her one shot? She leaned to the left—oh, the open air there, open space, and a deep fall!—as far as she dared. Holding the pistol in both hands at arm's length, she aimed behind the horse's shoulder, forward into the meager heaving ribs just behind the left foreleg, six feet away. She squeezed the trigger.

A red hole erupted in the horse's sweat-streaked hide, and the blast of the pistol knocked her braced arms awry. The poor beast went crashing down, heavy and helpless as a felled tree: knees, head, neck, chest all entangled in reins and harness, collar and traces. The wagon shafts fractured like bones. The wagon slid, skidded, spun around to the right, around the sudden dragging weight of the shattered horse—the right rear wheel collapsed but the others held—and came to a hard stop not an arm's span from the lip of the dropoff.

Oh, triumph! Oh, exultation!

Oh, most exquisite revenge! For an instant—as Catherine lay against the dashboard of the wagon still holding the pistol—the broken brute dying in the red dirt was instead that wicked beautiful chestnut mare, the one with the gait of the doe on the hill, the one to blame for all her griefs. Then Grace leapt upon Catherine and embraced her, sobbing. Catherine burst into tears, too, while the driver burst into laments and curses.

Prince Teerut paid the driver a considerable indemnity for his horse, far more than it had ever been worth. He also tried to make Catherine accept a reward for her heroism in saving his bride, but this she refused. From then on, instead of calling her memsahib Ka taryng, he called her memsahib Ka ryngkap, meaning Lady of the Silver Quiver of Silver Arrows.

Prince Teerut seemed to enjoy Catherine's company, and he liked to practice speaking English with her. He also enjoyed *uisge baugh*. One evening in camp along their route through the high hills, Prince Teerut and Anibaddh and Catherine sat together talking and sipping a little of Catherine's remaining whisky. Grace sat nearby, too. On the evenings when she wasn't needed to play *tanpura* with the other musicians, she often whittled. She carved little figures, human and animal, from the curiously gnarled sticks that she picked up.

"It is from your land faraway, this water of life, memsahib Ka ryngkap?" asked Prince Teerut.

"Yes, sir, from Scotland," said Catherine.

"Scot-land, Scot-land. A man from Scot-land is in our hills, in our Hima. He has taught me to speak the excellent English. I speak the excellent English, aye?"

"Oh, aye, sir, excellent, indeed. Pray, who is this man from Scotland?"

"Friend to my uncle is the Scot-land man."

"Your uncle, the Hima Syiem?" asked Catherine, nodding toward the old man's tent.

"No, my other uncle; my mother's younger brother brought the Scot-land man here," said Teerut.

"What is his name, this Scot? Is he here still?"

"Is he here still? I do not know. We shall find him perhaps after crossing the river. Soon we will come to the Bor Soree River, and crossing it we come into our Hima, our own district."

"But what is his name, sir, this man from Scotland?"

"It is a strange name; I cannot say it. But we call him *Sur Bylla*."

"Sur Bylla?"

"Aye, it means . . . a borrowed tune from another district, a borrowed tune which we adopt and then we sing it or play it, too, because we like it. The Scot-land man, he is like that—a borrowed tune."

After this, Catherine felt no doubts about finding Sandy. But each day as they proceeded—mounted upon elephants, ascending into these beautiful misty highlands graced with pine forests and waterfalls, orchids and butterflies—she felt that the ordinary world of mortals was falling away behind her; that she was passing into another distinct world; and who could ever follow her here? Who would?

Catherine felt perfectly safe on an elephant, so much more reliable than a horse. She and Grace and Sharada rode on one; another carried Anibaddh and Mrs Babcock and the infant Constantia.

The mists came and went around them as their party made their way—on elephants, on bullocks, on foot—up the sloping, grassy tablelands toward the high wooded escarpments rising to the south, visible now and then between curtains of mist.

"What are those stones?" Catherine asked Sharada, "those great stones standing up on end? We have passed several groups of them now."

"Oh, in honour of the ancestors perhaps," said Sharada. "I don't know—they are very old. Some of them are altars, for offerings. I am thinking they are everywhere in these hills."

"In Scotland there are great circles of stones like that from the ancient times," said Catherine. "No one knows who put them there, or why."

"It is just a thing that men are liking to do everywhere in the world—setting stones up on end. Oh, men!"

The sun was low, and a brilliant rainbow filled the east, at their left, by the time they arrived at last at the fording place on the bank of the Bor Soree River. Across the river stood a considerable town of thatched houses and stone terraces set well back from the river's edge and comfortably settled in a wide lap of open grassland below the forested hills. The water was running high, but not too high for crossing. One by one, the bullocks and the elephants and the men on foot made their way across the slippery stones.

The elephant carrying Catherine, Grace, and Sharada had tender feet, and she picked her way unwillingly across the sharp rocks at the water's edge, her mahout prodding her behind her ears with his toes and with reproachful words: *ah geet! ah geet!* The elephant proceeded through water that came up above her knees at the middle of the river, but suddenly she missed her footing and pitched hard to her left, nearly unseating Catherine, who grabbed thin air—and then the howdah and Grace—and just managed to save herself.

*My lay!* cried the mahout. But a brass-bound chest containing Sharada's belongings came loose and tumbled down the elephant's side into the streaming water. It was still attached by a loose binding, but it was pulling the howdah sideways. The chest was made of wood, and it floated for a moment. But it was not made to be watertight, and in any case the current caught it and pulled hard.

The mahout turned the elephant downriver and told her *eh dur! oota!* in no uncertain terms, prodding now with his *ankush*. Chastened, the elephant reached with her trunk for the chest, but as she moved forward the current carried the chest forward, too, to the end of its tether. *Oopa dur!* cried the mahout, and this time the elephant managed to reach the chest, and with a groan she lowered herself a little, just enough to wrap her trunk around it and drag it from the water. Then, forgetting her tender feet, she made quickly for the shallows and burst up onto the far bank as water streamed off her gray flanks. She gently set down the chest, upside down, on a tussock of grass upon command. Water drained from its brass-bound corners.

"Oh, Sharada! All your things! Your musical instruments!" cried Grace.

"The instruments will take no harm. But there are other things. I must dry them if I can." They dismounted, and Sharada went to attend to her precious things while the rest of the party spread out to dry themselves upon the riverbank.

Another fainter rainbow had appeared above, outside the first one, its colours reversed. Catherine walked up a little rise to see it better. She wanted to be alone for a few minutes, before the party pulled itself together again and proceeded to the night's camping place just below the town. Voices floated up to her, voices speaking languages she did not understand. Would she ever understand them? Had she been in these misty hills forever? Would she remain in these misty hills forever? Among strangers?

The mist blew down again and blotted out the rainbows. Even the voices below her suddenly became muted.

For no more reason than that, Catherine wept. Such an indulgence, such a relief, these tears in private. She recalled a tune, a *ceol mhor* tune that Sandy used to play for her on the pipes sometimes called "Cumha

Catriona," "Catherine's Lament." It always filled her with so sublime a sorrow, so fierce and acute a sorrow that it resembled joy. It felt like this.

The hot tears cooled on her face.

Off to the east, where the wet hills rose up, there was something to hear.

She listened.

How could it be a piper? How could it be the sound of bagpipes?

There was no path, no trail across the open grassland, the rolling rising ground, dotted by trees looming here and there out of the mist. Catherine's shoes and stockings were soon drenched—heavy and squishing; she was hurrying, breaking into a run where she could, panting, climbing.

The music stopped, and so did she. Waiting.

It began again. The piper tuned, adjusting the drones. He played a particular little spring, a phrase to tune against. Surely not everyone tuned in just that way, using just that phrase?

She breasted a knoll and suddenly found herself in a garden, a plantation of knee-high shrubs set in an orderly grid across the gently sloping red clay hill. She knew very well what they were, these glossy, compact dark green plants. She waded between two rows of them, still making her way upward. Their stiff branches grabbed at the fragile fabric of her wet skirt.

Very near now.

She left the tea plantation behind and ascended into a misty woodland. Then the trees fell behind her as she crested the slope, emerging onto a grassy place dotted with rocks and walled in by mist. She could see only a blank whiteness on all sides.

But he was here. She stood still, and the sound of the pipes rang all about her. And he was playing his own tune, "Not Yet Drown'd."

He finished the *urlar* and began the first variation, the thumb variation with the highest notes. As she stood, the tricky breeze came up again and the mist thinned, then blew away.

There he was, with his back to her, facing an enormous upright gray stone, standing up close to it and playing his pipes to its rough glistening surface—just as he used to do at home. It was so he could really hear the pipes, he used to say, really hear the sound breaking back onto him, off the stone surface three feet away.

The mist had settled in droplets in his raging hair like a faint halo. She reached up and felt her own—just the same. He played the *taorluath* singling, then surged ahead into the doubling, forward, moving strongly now. Then settled back again for the *crunluath*, so abstractly, baroquely ornamented that the original tune was almost submerged. Yet a purer, more essential version of the underlying notes still shone, like the largest rocks in the river still above water—wet and glistening—when the river runs high. Then the little rocks are submerged and only the big important ones remain, standing up in their swirling liquid collet settings, big cabochon gemstones set in smooth gold; never mind now the little ones set in busy figured enamels. Then the plunging urgency of the *crunluath* doubling, like a river approaching a fall. Over the edge, then, into the air: the *crunluath a mach*. Catherine lost her place in it, the phrases closing over her head. Which way is up?

Then, at last, the still, deep black pool at the bottom once more: the majestic return to the opening phrase of all, the first line of the *urlar*.

It was ended. He stopped. Silence came rushing back in to fill the tear that the sound of the pipes had made. Removing the mouthpiece, he stepped forward and licked the wet stone in front of him.

"Thirsty work, my darling," said Catherine. "I have a wee bit of whisky still, but not with me just at the moment."

He turned.

Like looking into a mirror.

# 25

## *a gracefull Conclusion to the whole*

"Disgraceful, I call it," said Grace.

"What is disgraceful, my dear?" asked Catherine, distracted, for she was searching through her workbag, a messy tangle by now of various vivid silks and worsteds.

"Sharada's songs, of course! Can you not understand them? Still, after all this time? Indeed, you have no taste for language, Catriona. And she goes about all the day long singing under one's very ear. All about preparing beds and strewing them with flowers for lovers to disport themselves upon; and limbs aching with longing, heavy and dark as monsoon clouds. And so on. I don't think I ought to be permitted to hear this sort of thing."

"Oh, dear! I daresay it is exceedingly indecent. So many of these Hindu songs are. It is a thousand pities that you pick up these languages so quickly. Pray, try not to listen, or at least not to understand."

It was true that Sharada sang all day; and to judge from her languor, her heavy-lidded eyes, she did not sleep much at night. Grace continued, "And while of course I *am* very glad that Uncle Sandy is not dead after all, still I don't quite *see*—"

"That is a relief. You are much too young yet to 'quite see,' " said Catherine briskly. It was quite obvious that Sandy did not spend his nights in sleep either. Catherine could not fail to notice the blue shadows under his eyes, like bruises against his pale skin. She changed the subject: "Where do you suppose all my copper-coloured silk floss has got to?"

"Well, do *you*?" said Grace.

"Do I what?"

"See—understand—what all the fuss is about," said Grace. "It's only Uncle Sandy; he's not the king of Burma. He's given us all a great deal of trouble as a matter of fact, slipping off like that. Tricky, I call it, at the very least. But to hear Sharada carry on, you'd think he was the young Lord Krishna himself. I am losing respect for her, and after all this time, too. She's changed."

"You have a point," admitted Catherine.

Here at Sandy's airy house, days and nights were joyous—to a greater or lesser degree depending on the individual. Catherine was ashamed to acknowledge that she felt disappointed and sore at heart. Surely she ought to take delight from the success of her long hard quest? From the fact that Sandy was not dead? And from his joy and Sharada's?

But joy was not what she felt.

And as to the disappearance of the copper-coloured silk floss, she felt inexplicably annoyed. Surely she had not used all of it on the lady's hair in her canvaswork.

Sandy's house stood on the breast of a slope overlooking the tea gardens, outside the town above the Bor Soree River. The house was of the local type, set on a raised platform of packed earth. Walls of woven bamboo screens were affixed to a stout frame of bamboo timbers, then plastered thickly with smoothed mud inside and out, and generously whitewashed with lime. There were several large rooms, and screens and curtains were moved about for privacy where needed. The roof was grass thatch, and the eaves were deep, making a wide veranda all the way around. An airy room at one end had a platform for the cooking fire. The hole in the thatch overhead for a chimney was just like that of a Highland croft.

Catherine rose early these mornings; she was too troubled to sleep well. And Sandy, who had always been an early riser, generally joined her on the veranda with steaming tea in the misty half-light before the dawn, before the rest of the household was stirring. They would drink tea and quietly talk over all the many astonishing things that had happened to them since they had parted five years before.

He was now half a head taller than Catherine, taller and sturdier than when he had left Scotland. They had been only eighteen years old the last time they had seen each other. Catherine often caught herself gazing at him, drinking up the sight of him, so thirsty was she for the sight of his face, his limbs—so familiar, yet rather different now, too, after all this time. There was a great deal of catching up to be done.

But she was surprised, after the first joyful transports of their reunion had receded, at how furiously angry she felt toward him. And one morning, without quite intending it, she burst out bitterly: "Did you never give a thought for us? How could you have done this to us? How could you have let us all grieve so for you?"

He was taken aback: "But I sent you those messages!"

"That parcel? Do you call that a message?"

"But you did understand what it meant—my little tune retitled just for you. You have said so! And I knew, Catriona, that you—you!—would understand it."

"Well, and so I did," she admitted grudgingly, "obscure though it was. But Hector always refused to believe in it, and he persecuted me about it most unjustly."

"Hector! So deficient in imagination! He lacks the conspirator's temperament. But it did occur to me that my parcel might not reach you, or you might not study it closely, or you might not succeed in convincing Hector of its meaning. So then I sent him that other message, which even he could not fail to understand. It had to be nonsense, of course, or anyone who knew Gaelic could have deciphered it. But I knew he would recognise my handwriting—right across the front sheet of the *Calcutta Gazette*, printed just exactly a month after my 'drowning.' Ha ha! Whatever did he make of that, our Hector? I have often amused myself in thinking of his puzzling over it! But I knew that you would be able to tell him what it meant."

"Whatever do you mean? We never received anything of that kind."

"But I saw it sent off to Calcutta by *dak*, by the mail carrier, you know, from Dacca, with my own eyes. I had a native scribe in the bazaar there send it under cover to the captain of the *Regent*, down at Calcutta."

"Ah! The *Regent*, the East Indiaman *Regent*?"

"Aye; in Dacca I had a glimpse of the shipping digest and saw that she was due shortly to embark for home. That must have been, oh, late August, I daresay, of 'twenty-one."

"But the *Regent* was lost off the coast of Mauritius that October, my dear."

"Lost?"

"Foundered, sunk. Only six survivors were picked up afterward by a French ship. Without their mail pouch, of course. The ship's master had disembarked at Ceylon, refusing to go any further, for he declared that the ship was not seaworthy. But the captain would not hear of it. Then so soon, so tragically, the master was proven right. It was a great scandal; people were talking of it, and Parliament took up the matter of fraudulent surveys and repairs."

"Is it so? My message for Hector was lost then at sea . . . I did not know that. Somehow that news did not penetrate here, to these misty mountains. But I did my best, Catriona. I did not wish you to grieve for me. I wanted you to know that I was alive, though I could not yet tell you plainly where I was and what I was doing."

"Were we ever to hear of you again?"

"Certainly, my dear. It is not so easy to send letters from here, you will understand; there is no post. But now that the secret of my great enterprise must come out within a very short time, I had been preparing to send word again to Scotland, to you and Hector there. Aye, we are just about to burst upon the world in a blaze of glory with our first chests of tea. What a sensation we will make! With this first tea in the world that is *not* from China!"

Someone stirred inside; then Grace wandered out and joined them on the veranda. She was rubbing her eyes, and the hair on one side of her head was squashed flat. "I had such an odd dream," she said, "about butterflies and elephants, I think."

"Catriona, my dear, will you care to walk out with me?" said Sandy, coming onto the wide veranda one day after their midday meal. "I must go up to the firing sheds to see about a new batch of coal. Do come with me. You can give me your opinion of it."

"Coal is the one subject on which I have no opinions, but I will walk out with you," said Catherine. She put away her canvaswork and rose to join him. "Where is Sharada? Won't she come with us?" she asked.

"Oh, no," said Sandy. "She is . . . oh, I don't know, asleep, perhaps." Catherine knew very well that his offhand tone was assumed. He always knew just where Sharada was.

They walked out to the rows of dark green plants that covered some eight or ten terraced acres of gently sloping hillside. The soil was a rough red clay, with ditches dug through it here and there for drainage. Most of the plants were scarcely knee-high. But in two of the terraces, the plants were noticeably larger and older. Although pruned severely, they were pushing out copious new growth of the tenderest green from every scape. Half a dozen Khasi girls—up from the town, Catherine supposed—were wading among the plants with baskets slung from their necks. Into these, they were tossing the tiny shoots of green which they pinched off the burgeoning plants.

"These larger plants were found growing wild in the hills, and we dug them up and moved them here—filthy, heavy work!—to be the parents," explained Sandy. "From these we are plucking already, once every fortnight or three weeks. The others, the wee plants, are mostly seedlings, and too young yet for plucking—not until next year. We are trying to root some cuttings, too, with encouraging results—cuttings from exceptionally good wild plants which were unfortunately too large or too distant to be dug up and moved. They do strike roots amazingly, in this climate, if set out in a bed of river sand and manure for a season."

"How astonishing, Sandy, to see you turned farmer!"

"I doubt I should break my back for turnips and barley, but I am exceedingly fond of my tea bushes, my darlings! But come along; there is the manufactory. No need for walls—only a good roof and an oven for the firing. Getting enough dry fuel has been a difficulty in this season. There's endless wood, but it's wet. Of course there is cow dung, but we seem to require more of it than the cows can produce; and if we use it all here, the townspeople complain of none left for their kitchen fires. No peat, of course; but there is coal to be had, and plenty of it. It will be a matter of organizing the carrying."

There was bright-haired Grace, sitting among the women in the factory shed. Three dogs napped under the bench where she sat. She had a big round rattan tray of leaves on her lap, and one of the women was showing her how to bruise them and roll them, working them over and over with long slender fingers. Other women were tending the oven; and sorting, spreading, raking, and tossing the leaves. "This has been our first real plucking season, and our first full-scale season of manufacture," said Sandy. "Look." He opened a brass canister and plunged his fingers into the black curled leaves.

Tea.

"Smell," he said, and held it under her nose. Obediently she sniffed.

"We manufactured *lu cha* and *qing cha* at first," he said. "Green tea and oolong tea, you know. It was quite acceptable—as good as what comes out of Fu-jian. But when we tried manufacturing some in the *hong cha* style, black tea, the fully fermented tea—ah! Well, let me brew some for you. You shall taste it, and judge for yourself." He dipped some water out of the brimming rain barrel at the corner of the shed into a blackened tin pot, and set it on the hottest part of the stove, saying something in another language to the Khasi girl, who tossed a couple of patties of dried cow dung onto the fire. His remark made her laugh, quite at her ease. The dung patties quickly caught fire, and the smoke that wafted up smelled like incense.

"How do you pay them?" asked Catherine, nodding toward the women.

"I do not pay them. They do not work for me. They are their own masters, and their husbands' masters, too. That is how these Khasi women arrange matters. It was the most baffling thing in the world to me when first I came into these hills, Catriona. The women own everything. Houses, lands, goods, livestock—all property, in short—passes from mother to daughter. And not to the eldest daughter but to the youngest! I felt as though I had stumbled into some Amazonia."

"How very wise of Anibaddh to marry among the Amazons," said Catherine.

"And into so highly placed a family. Teerut is a nephew of my partner here, you know, who is the brother of the Hima Syiem, the great man of the entire district. She will enjoy great privileges here. Perhaps she will wish to plant some tea gardens of her own. These women are planting dozens of them all through the hills. Tea doesn't require prime rice land, you see; it does very well in the wasteland—the poor, lean red hill soils.

"Now it is only a question of finding the best market for our tea. It is a pity that Mr Fleming did not come up here with you. I should have so liked to show all this to him, and to offer him the privilege of carrying this first lot to Europe. What a coup that would be for Crawford and Fleming, in the mercantile world! How gratifying to poke the eye of the Honourable Company! And some small amends, too, for my having so abruptly cut off all contact with him when I made up my mind to be 'drowned.' He was a kind friend to me."

"So he has been to us all," said Catherine, aching to speak of him, yet unable to bear it.

"There—the water is boiling," said Sandy. "Here is a teapot—no lid, alas. I wonder where it's got to? But here are two cups, and quite clean enough for MacDonalds from Skye." He threw a generous pinch of tea leaves into the teapot, and poured the boiling water over them. "Ah! Do smell that, Catriona. Isn't it lovely?"

It smelled sweet and rich. "Like malt," said Catherine.

"Like the malt sheds at home, eh? It is most unusual, most distinctive—and yet, not a fault. And the colour as it pours! So rich a red, so coppery. Taste it."

She did. The hot, malty, full-bodied liquor spread across her tongue. Then the sweetness after the swallow. "It reminds me of the tea you sent me, in that little ivory coffer," she said. "Very like it, only somehow more so. Maltier."

"Just so. That tea I had sent you was made from my plants at Ghazipur. I had collected those plants up here in Assam, of course. But growing down there, in that rich lowland soil, that easy lowland climate, they were not so entirely, so distinctively, themselves."

"Like Scots who go to London, and dwindle by degrees into Englishmen," said Catherine.

Sandy agreed, laughing. He looked very pleased with himself.

Catherine set down her cup, suddenly angry with him again. "Sandy, why could you not have sent in your resignation to the Company, then gone about your honest business in open daylight, like other people? Why all this subterfuge, this duplicity?"

"Because, my dear, the Honourable Company would have prevented this with all its might, and its might is very mighty. Do you not see? Their sole remaining trade monopoly is tea. They have it all their own way; no one may carry tea to Britain or its possessions but themselves. The trade is profitable only because they may set the price to suit themselves. And if they were to lose their monopoly? It would be the end of the Company. It will be fatal to them to lose control of the commodity. And now—thanks to me—they *will* lose it."

"But could you not have set up plantations and manufactories as you have done here on their behalf? Surely they would lose no control thus. It would be like their opium productions."

"So I proposed, in a lengthy letter to the Company's Court of Directors. Their reply, when it came, was to reprimand me, and to bid me submit to the superior judgment of my betters, who assert doggedly—and quite wrongly—that this plant is not the true tea."

She scowled, still.

"Come, my dear, if you have done," said Sandy. She put her shawl over her head and went out with him into the drizzle. They made their way up to the forested slope at the top of the far terraces.

Suddenly he spoke again: "And then a little later, Catriona, after I had spent some time in Ghazipur superintending the Company's opium business, I was glad that they had not taken up my proposal. I saw in Ghazipur a great deal to disgust me. The Company have persecuted the small farmers, pressed them far harder than the mogul's greediest zamindars ever did, harder than the cruelest Highland tacksman at home. The Company would never have allowed any independent production of the sort we are doing here—never. The Company insist upon vast plantations, and all under their own control. No one is allowed to produce any commodity of value—opium or tea—for any independent trade on their own account. The landlords get rich while everyone else starves. I do not like it. It reminds me unpleasantly of—of Scotland."

They came up to the open ground above the highest terrace; it was the place where she had found him. Across the grassy clearing stood the tall stones, towering twice as high as a man except for one, which lay flat on the ground. It was a very convenient height—like a gigantic garden seat. It was wet, however; and as it had probably been an altar, she did not quite like to sit upon it.

"Well," she said, frowning, "I still do not see why you must forge your own death."

"My position as a dead man is so much more secure than if I were alive! It was Mr Fleming who led me to see this. If, after the—ah—the controversies I have had with the Company, if I had then politely resigned their service in order to pursue my own enterprises, sapping their bulwarks, it is exceedingly unlikely that they would have granted me a license of residence or left me in peace. The Company has a history of taking a very high hand with anyone whose activities they dislike. They have issued peremptory summonses to indigo planters to appear here or there to stand trial on the evidence of bought witnesses. They have forbidden planters to return to their estates. And they have not hesitated to deport—in chains, when it suits them—anyone whose conduct or activities they do not approve. And that is only for indigo. There is a great deal more at stake for tea, my dear. You will certainly understand that this has been a job for a dead man, being so much less likely to attract the notice of the authorities—until now, when it is too late for them to stop me."

Catherine made no reply, only picked at a brilliant chartreuse-coloured lichen growing on the stone nearest at hand.

"It was not a gratuitous deception, Catriona."

❧ ❧ ❧

STILL CATHERINE FELT angry and sore at heart. One evening, just before nightfall, when she and Sandy were walking above the river-bank, along the path leading between his house and the town, she said to him, "Sandy, there is a certain matter—and I cannot let it pass, though it is no affair of mine. But how could you have dropped Sharada as you did? How could you have given up and gone away from her so easily?"

He stopped in the path and turned to her. "You mean, how has she brought herself to forgive me for that?"

How indeed? thought Catherine. How at all? But certainly not so promptly, not so freely, not so as to sing improper songs all day while her eyes and limbs drooped heavy from lack of sleep.

"There I did err most grievously," said Sandy. "Of course I know *now* that I ought never to have doubted her heart, her resolve, her courage. But give me credit at least, Catriona, for diffidence, for humility. When she did not come that terrible night at the Chalis Satoon, I sorrowed, grieved, raged like a child denied a favorite plaything. But then, unwillingly, miserably, I concluded—reasonably enough, I am sure you will agree—that she did not choose to make a ruin of her life just for love of magnificent me. And if she did not choose of her own free will to come to me, after all we had said and done, I resolved I must learn to live, or die, without her."

"But Sandy, you ought certainly to have considered that your message might have miscarried, or that she might have been prevented somehow from responding to your summons on such short notice."

"So I did, Catriona, and that is why I went back for her. Has she not yet mentioned this to you? She did not know it herself, of course, until now. I did go back again, to beg her once more to come away with me. I had proceeded downriver at great speed on the floodwaters of the monsoon, feeling very sorry for myself, and very bitter toward her for her inconstancy. I got so far as a village just below Monghyr, and there I found I could go no further. A fever of the brain came upon me and I was unable to leave my cot. I lay there plagued by dreads and feverish horrors, assaulted by wishes, doubts, imaginings: what if somehow she had not received my message after all? Oh, that is only my pride and wishful thinking, I rebuked myself. Only my weakness. But I could not overcome this weakness. I could not make myself proceed any further without her. My fever abated after ten or twelve days; then, still weak and shaky, I reversed course and made my way back up to Ghazipur again, with great difficulty against the flood current. All in deepest secrecy, of course, for I had taken such vast trouble to be drown'd that it was of utmost importance that I not be seen by anyone who might recognise me, nor even my ghost—and I was a mere ghost of myself just then.

"I had to travel incognito, in mufti, at night whenever possible," he continued, "not to be seen or guessed at by any European. I arrived in Ghazipur, just five weeks after that terrible night. But her father's house was shut up and she was gone, gone! I had much ado to find anyone who would speak of her at all, for the Hindus regard such deeds as hers with deepest horror: a failed suttee; and now she had gone away, over the black water, or so it was rumoured: outcaste, anathema, lost forever. No one knew where she had gone—only that she was utterly lost, cast into the abyss, as though she had fallen off the ends of the earth.

"And still, you must remember, I had every reason to suppose that she had spurned me. In deepest despondency I reversed my course yet again, passing down the river once more. On two occasions I came very near to drowning myself, so despondent was I, so sunk by melancholia. Oddly, Catriona, it was the thought that I had assured you that I was not drown'd which prevented me. I felt some obligation to remain alive, because I had assured you that I was! Still, if I had fallen by chance into the river, I would certainly have taken no stroke to save myself. But I did not fall into the river. Eventually I told myself to be a man, to resolve to live without her if she would not have me. And I have had no solace here in these misty mountains but my bagpipe ever since. It is undoubtedly the case, however, that my piping has improved. I am now able to play all those old laments with a far more expressive pathos than formerly. Ha ha!"

His laughter only made Catherine angrier, and lonelier. She said, "How can you laugh?"

"Catriona, may I not laugh now, after our suffering is ended? Have I not been punished? She has suffered for my error, but have I not suffered, too? Perhaps if you have any imagination, you can find some compassion for me as well as for her. But if she can forgive me, Catriona—if *she* can forgive me—must you bear me a grudge on her behalf?"

"And still, after all that, after all the trials Sharada has undergone, after she has demonstrated her faith and courage and valour as never any woman has been called upon to do, what return is made her? Why, Sandy, only this: You prostitute her; you make her your concubine! She is too good for that, and too good for you. Why do you not marry her in all honour and good faith?"

"Because, Catriona, because—as you, even you, must have learned by now—we cannot always have everything we want."

"Cannot have everything we want! Is she to be your concubine because you do not want her for a wife?"

"No, Catriona, you have got it backward. It is I who cannot have what I want. She will not marry me because she is a widow. She says she cannot. A Hindu widow does not ever remarry. It is impossible; it cannot be done."

"Could she not become a Christian, and thus be permitted to remarry?"

"A convert, like Mr Fleming's Harini?"

Catherine nodded, forbidding herself to wince at the sound of these names conjoined in his mouth. It was getting dark now, and she hoped he could not read her face.

"Alas, it will not do," said Sandy. "She will not renounce Hinduism and become a Christian, and she will not marry me. Nevertheless I do consider that she is my wife. Upon my honour, I consider that I am married to her and that she is married to me, and any children who may be born to us will be the honest fruits of our true marriage."

Catherine shook her head, still resisting him.

But Sandy had not finished. "Have you never made any such mistake yourself, my dear?" he continued gently. "Have you never, by error or pride or obstinacy or fear or diffidence—have you never fled from the thing that is best and dearest to you? Your own heart's true desire? Supposing perhaps that you cannot possibly deserve to have such happiness as that? That you cannot have what you want?"

Catherine scowled at him, her scalp prickling; how could he know? "Sharada has told me all about it," he said.

Of course she had.

But Catherine could not bring herself to speak of it. She stood quite silent in the dark, thinking. Sandy had suffered bitterest disappointment and had accepted it, and proceeded on his course despite it. But now, unexpectedly, and against all odds, he had his rich reward. His rich reward had sought him across half the globe, increased now in value a hundredfold.

Still, even Sandy could not have everything he wanted.

But she, Catherine, had all these painful lessons before her still, and no prospect of relief or reward. She, too, had thrown away her happiness, had heedlessly gone away from the good man who might not choose to make a ruin of his life just for the love of her. What becomes of those who flee their own happiness? Have they any right then to sorrow, to grieve, to rage? Here was the lesson in which she had now to school herself: We cannot always have everything we want. Sometimes we must learn to live, or die, without.

Or reverse course, go back, seek again?

Sandy said, "There is no irregular connection between him and Harini."

"So Sharada has assured us both, apparently," said Catherine.

"No, I speak from my own knowledge, my dear. But I do not know quite how I am to speak of this to you. It is so very difficult." He shuffled one foot on the sandy path before going on: "It must have been a year or so after Harini's terrible misadventure that I made Mr Fleming's acquaintance, and went to spend a fortnight at his house as his guest. By then, Harini had recovered her health; she was out of any danger with regard to the snakebite and the gangrene and the loss of the foot. However, it was plain to see that all was not well between her and my host. And one very hot night, as I lay tossing and turning in my bed in the darkness . . . well, she came in to my bedchamber, creeping along somehow. Ah, Catriona! I do not know how I can tell you this! Well, I—ah—but not quite. I did not quite, because she was . . . and I had assumed, just as you had, that she was . . . you understand. And I his guest, and I could not just . . . and so I told her. And then she told me that I need feel no disloyalty to my friend Mr Fleming, that he never touched her. Indeed he had repeatedly rebuffed her, though he knew very well that nothing in the world but a baby could ever console her for the loss of her own children. But he would not, she said, for the reason that she had still a living husband. And a baby was just what she wanted of me. The only consolation she could hope for in all the world would be another baby to hold in her arms."

Catherine knew this had to be true. "So," she said cruelly, "did you oblige her?" She regretted her words, even as she spoke them.

"What do you think?" he retorted. He turned down the path and strode away, leaving her alone in the dark.

ରେ ରେ ରେ

ON THAT NIGHT, great festivities were to take place in the town on the bank of the Bor Soree. The Hima Syiem and Prince Teerut, with their entourage, had been staying as the honoured guests of the great man who lived in the best house. But this was the last night of their stay. Tomorrow, they—and Anibaddh, with her lady, Mrs Babcock—were to pack up and proceed higher up into the hills. Tonight was the celebration of the agreements and goodwill that had been reached. There would be gift-giving and speeches as well as food and drink, music, dancing, and farewells.

Everyone was invited. Anibaddh, Catherine, Sharada, Grace, and Mrs Babcock with her infant were received among the women along one side of the big dance hall, and given a good place to sit, and served delicious food brought to them on enormous leaves used as platters; sweetmeats of rice and honey, tiny smoked fishes, roasted meats. They could see Sandy across the hall among the men.

In the middle of the room were the dancers. The girls of the town were dressed in their best silken sarongs, and were weighed down by massy necklaces of gold beads and red coral. They danced sedately, demurely, in an inward-facing circle while the young men, in their exquisitely pleated gold turbans, danced exuberantly, showing off behind the backs of the girls, dancing a larger circle outside of them. The musicians, in one corner, played tirelessly: a hornpipe, several double-ended drums, a tambourine, and an instrument like a bamboo mouth harp that sounded like a nest of bees. Sometimes they sang.

Eventually, when the music stopped, it was time for the presentation of gifts. The Hima Syiem presented the great man of the town with a long canvas-wrapped object. This, when unwrapped, proved to be a British percussion-cap rifle, and it caused a sensation. The great man's speech upon accepting this gift was energetically delivered, and it went on for some time, warmly acclaimed by all those who could understand it.

Then the great man of the town presented the Hima Syiem with a splendid tiger-skin shield decorated with tassels of red-dyed goat hair. Catherine noted that the tiger must have been immense, for the shield was nearly six feet high, without head and tail. This present was also much admired, and Prince Teerut delivered the speech of thanks, which, though briefer than their host's, was certainly as well received. At last the alliance was ratified by the consumption all around of a quantity of rice liquor. This was not the mild, yeasty rice beer that Catherine had tasted before; this was unmistakably a distilled spirit. As the piper took up his hornpipe once again, Catherine could feel her head swimming.

As the ceremonies concluded, and the music and the dancing resumed, there were still more presents to be exchanged—private exchanges, unofficial presents. Prince Teerut now made his way across the hall to Anibaddh and offered her a small silk-wrapped parcel on a polished tray. She unwrapped it: a tiny box upholstered in silk, exquisitely embroidered and decorated with appliquéd iridescent butterfly wings. "It is a betel nut box, of course," Sharada whispered in Catherine's ear. "That is a traditional betrothal present here." It was a lovely thing, a promise of all the blissful pleasures and treasures to be laid up during a long, fruitful lifetime of marriage.

What gift could Anibaddh offer in return? Catherine wondered.

But Anibaddh was prepared for this. From her sash she drew out a little silk-wrapped object. She placed her gift onto the same tray and presented it to Prince Teerut with a graceful bow. Teerut received it and unwrapped it. Catherine saw the gleam of gold, then recognised it: a gold watch, and ticking blithely, it seemed, for Teerut held it to the ear of first one person, then another, causing amazed delight to bloom upon each face in turn. It was the very gold watch which had formerly been Mrs Babcock's wedding gift to her dear Babcock. Catherine looked across at Mrs Babcock, whose eyes were brimming. But she was smiling through her tears; and on the arm that held the sleeping infant Constantia, she now wore the gold bracelet that had formerly been Anibaddh's.

Now, another gift passes from hand to hand.

A cloth-wrapped packet tied with black silk cord passes from Sharada's slim brown hand to Sandy's freckled broad hand. He cuts the cord—using his own *sgian dubh*, which Catherine gave him on their fifteenth birthday and he has recovered at last from Grace—and proceeds to unwrap it.

The outer wrapping is of waxed khaki-coloured canvas, quite stiff. Inside is another wrapping of pale silk. It goes around and around, at least a yard of it. Removing it is like unwinding a silkworm's cocoon. But now, here is the thing itself, the kernel of the nut: a book—a neat, thick volume no more than six inches across and eight inches high. It fits easily in the hand, a pleasure to hold, to turn over and over. It is handsomely bound in the Lucknow taste: in tooled azure leather stamped with lotus blossoms around the border in gold leaf. But the front cover is on the back, for it is bound for reading from right to left—in the Mughal style—not left to right in the European style.

In Sikander's freckled hand, the book falls open to a page somewhere in the middle. It is not a printed book; these pages have never been through a printing press. They are the product of some human hand. It is a manuscript of music.

The paper is foxed and spotted with molds. The ink is faded to brown. One edge of the volume has been wet—quite recently perhaps—and the paper there is buckled and wavy; and some of the ink has run. Is there a great deal of damage? Is the manuscript all run away, dissolved and drown'd?

No. There is the familiar stave—fourteen rows of five lines filling each small page from top to bottom, left edge to right, front and verso; each with its sketchy treble clef, its two sharps, on C and F, and the nine notes. Who needs more than nine notes? Bagpipe music.

" 'Rory MacLeod's Lament,' " Sandy reads out quietly, for that is the title of the venerable old tune written out by hand on this page. "My darling, my beloved, it is a great treasure. An inestimable treasure."

Sharada smiled, her face ducked down modestly, pleased by his pleasure. "I knew you were desiring it, from the very moment of first casting your eyes upon it."

"What is it?" said Grace, craning her neck to see.

"A very curious and valuable manuscript," said Sandy, "formerly belonging to Sharada's father." His voice sounded strangely choked as he continued. "He had kept it all his life, saved it as a memento of the *feringee* friend of his youth, who wrote it out so long ago—back in the 'sixties—before dying of fever, twenty-three years old and far from home."

"But what is in it?" said Grace again.

"Look," said Sandy, showing it to her. "It is a collection of old Scottish bagpipe tunes—the *ceol mhor*, the old traditional *piobaireachd*—written out by the very hand of Joseph MacDonald. It is a vastly valuable thing in itself. And it is doubly valuable to me, for—for—it was over these pages that I fell in love. Each tune I have copied out while my darling sat nearby and talked sweetly to me, or sang beautifully to me, or drew the lines on the page for me. Each tune is in itself a precious artifact, and each tune is also for me a memorial of an evening spent in a garden paradise in the company of my beloved. I remember the evening of this one, Sharada, dearest: 'The Pride of Barra'—do you remember?" He sang the first phrase of it, and Sharada laughed.

"I remember most assuredly," she said.

"Alas, I had not nearly so much pleasure myself from copying your copies all over again during that long voyage," said Catherine drily.

"Copying them all over again!" said Sandy. "How tedious! Each and every one?"

"Aye. It was a four-month voyage, you know."

"My own little tune among them?"

"Aye, even your tune, with your secret message for me in its title. And sent them back to Mary, in Edinburgh."

"But why?"

"Because Sharada told me I must. She hinted, in the most mysterious way, that they were very important and must not run the risk of loss at sea. I sent some home by Captain Appleton's *Minerva* from the Cape Verdes, and some from Cape Town; and the last of them from Calcutta by Captain Robbins's *Alacrity*. And I asked Mary to take them all along to Mr Clerk."

"That depraved old Edinburgh lawyer?"

"Aye, the same; he collects these things. He owns Joseph MacDonald's other manuscript, you see—the manuscript of *A Compleat Theory*. Oh, aye! He showed it to Hector and me—nearly a year ago, I suppose, having then just acquired it. It looked very much like this. Except for the binding, of course."

"Ha ha! But I am utterly charmed, my dear! I wonder if all your copies came safely to Mary. And if she has taken them to Mr Clerk. How astonishing if my tiresome wee tune should be received among the canon of the authentic old great music by such a chance as that! Even I could not have created such a delightful forgery, such a charming fraud, as that! And to think that you, Catriona, have done it for me!"

Even Catherine could not help laughing at this. "But do you consider it tiresome—your wee tune?" she asked then.

"Oh, aye. I never liked it much, or perhaps I have not yet done it justice. But it is the tune that I am charged with, I'm afraid—the little tune that chose to come through me, my own droplet running its course into the Ocean of Music. One would of course prefer to let loose a truly great tune upon the world, but we cannot all produce great tunes. And I daresay the small tunes are of some use, too."

"Certainly yours has been of considerable use, to us. And in any case, it is fairly launched in the world now," said Catherine.

Sharada shook her head and said, "I do not understand why the *feringee*s so value the writing down of music. Could anyone forget important music? Can memory become so decayed as that? Surely, the greater the treasures entrusted to the memory, the more trustworthy it is becoming. And any music that could be forgotten, and by everyone at once, cannot have been worth the keeping. Paper is not music. It is only paper."

In reply, Sandy only sang another little phrase, a piquant little phrase, which Catherine did not recognise. But Sharada flushed; clearly she knew it and was moved by it. And when Sandy reached out, she let him take her hand, though she could not look in his face. Her slim brown hand rested in his broad freckled hand like a bird come to her nest.

Catherine had to turn away, turn to the dancers and musicians across the room. Her vision blurred; the torches in their sconces on the wall seemed to swim and waver, and the bitterness in her heart rose up to her throat.

Then there was some disturbance across the hall near the door. The Khasi men rose and crowded toward the door. Then they fell back again. The musicians faltered and stopped. The dancers came to a standstill. Everyone turned to look as half a dozen newcomers entered the hall.

*Feringee*s.

How? How? How could he be *here*?

Pieter Fleming.

He looked about the hall in the flickering torchlight.

Catherine rose, knowing that her face was flaming. She was hardly able to draw breath. He came across the hall, between the dancers in disarray, and stopped before her. He held out his hands. In them was a tangle of little figures. She reached out for one. It was a small carved effigy, a carefully whittled female figure—with a tuft of copper-coloured silk floss for hair. She took another—much the same. He held a dozen of them cradled in his two hands.

"One left at each camp along your route," he said hoarsely, "set upon a tall stone next to the ashes of the fire."

"Sharada!" cried Catherine, looking about.

"Not I," said Sharada at her shoulder. "But I am wishing to have been so clever."

There was Grace, blazing Grace. "Of course I did," she said. "How else was he to find us?"

Catherine reached forward; and he let all the little carved figures into her hands, cupped beneath his.

Thathast Gun a Bhith Bàthte Not Yet Drown'd

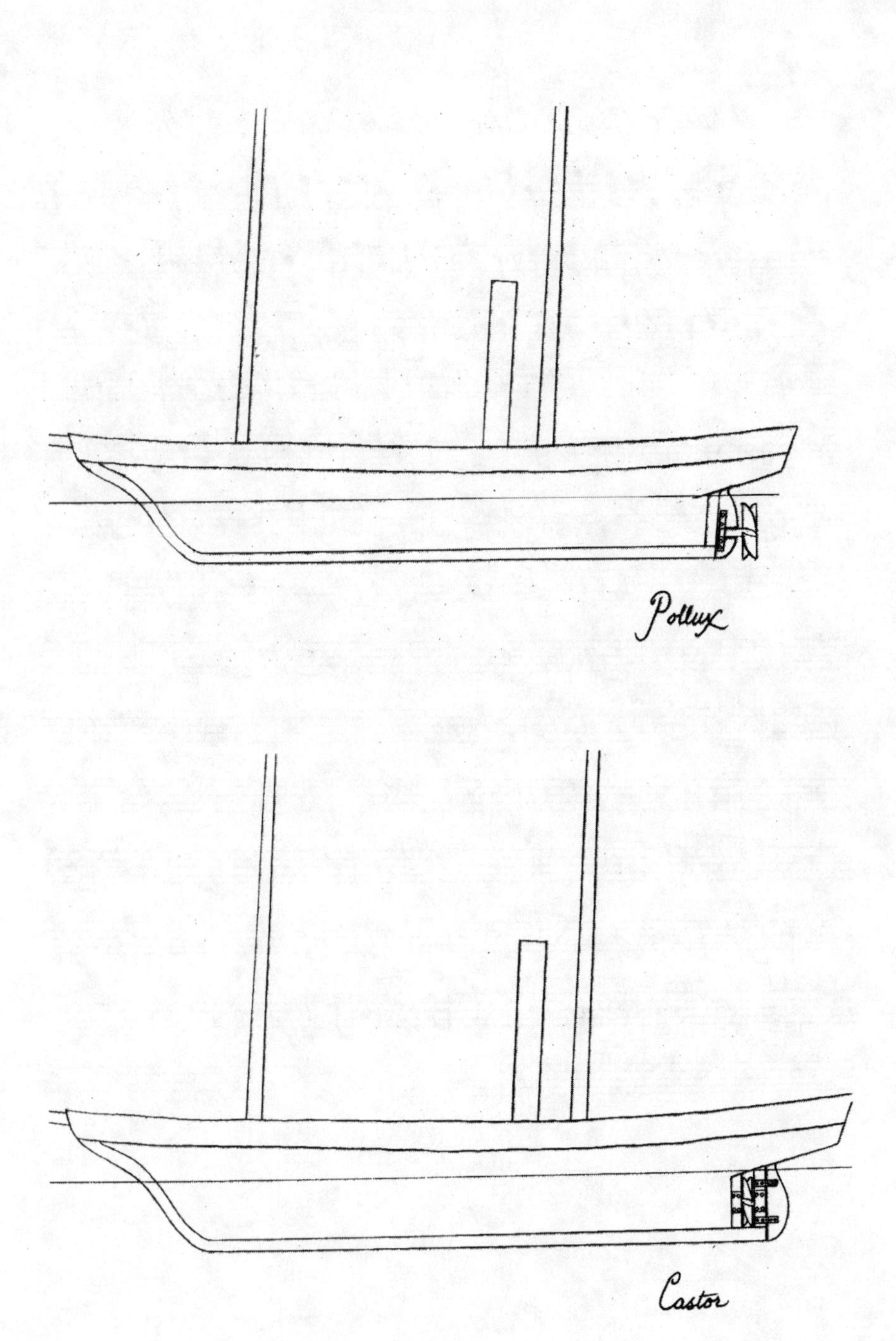
Pollux
Castor

# *Author's Afterword*

Some of the characters, events and artifacts in this work of fiction are not fictional. King George IV did indeed visit Edinburgh in August 1822, setting the city awhirl. John Clerk did own the original manuscript of Joseph MacDonald's *A Compleat Theory of the Scots Highland Bagpipe*; after Clerk's death it was sold at auction in 1833 to David Laing. The manuscript now resides at the Edinburgh University Library. All the chapter titles in this novel are derived from that text. Lord Charles Somerset was governor at the Cape of Good Hope from 1814 to 1826; slavery remained legal there until 1834. Dr Nathaniel Wallich, superintendent of the Asiatick Society's Museum and Botanical Garden at Calcutta, maintained until after 1830 that the plant samples brought down to him out of Assam by various collectors were not true tea. Dr William Carey—missionary, translator, publisher, and horticulturalist—did cultivate a notable garden at Serampore; it was largely destroyed by monsoon floods late in 1823. Sir Charles D'Oyly was appointed the East India Company's opium agent for Bihar in 1821; he and his second wife, Eliza, residing at Patna, were energetic amateur artists and collectors. And by 1829, Teerut Sing, Rajah of Nungklow, was taking up arms against British adventurers building roads through his realm.

Rotary marine propellers were first proposed in the second half of the eighteenth century, but practical progress was slow—due largely to misconceptions about flow dynamics—despite the publication (in Latin) of Daniel Bernoulli's insightful *Hydrodynamica* in 1738. Even sail theory remained primitive at this time, though sails had been in practical use for millenia.

The East India Company's last remaining monopoly—"the exclusive right of trading with the Dominions of the Emperor of China, and of trading in Tea"—was terminated by an 1833 Act of Parliament, and the Company was directed "with all convenient speed, [to] close their Commercial Business." From 1839 onward, British planters cleared vast tracts of Indian forest and established huge tea plantations in India and Ceylon using Chinese and Assamese plants. In 1839 and again in 1856, Britain waged war upon the emperor of China, asserting the right of British merchants to sell opium in China. By 1900, Indian tea production had surpassed that of China, and India has remained the largest tea producer in the world ever since.

In 1762, James Macpherson's *Works of Ossian* were all the rage. That was also the year of Joseph MacDonald's death in India, where, he wrote to his father in Scotland, he had been engaged in making a "collection of Highland music and poetry, which I have formed a system of, in my voyage to India, and propose to send soon home . . . in order that those sweet, noble, and expressive sentiments of nature, may not be allowed to sink and die away; and to shew, that our poor remote corner, even without the advantages of learning and cultivation, abounded in works of taste and genius." The collection he made never arrived in Scotland. Perhaps it may still exist somewhere in India. If so, it is Not Yet Found.

P. Kingman
Potter Valley, California, 2006